THE VANISHING PLACE

THE VANISHING PLACE

ZOË RANKIN

Berkley
New York

BERKLEY
An imprint of Penguin Random House LLC
1745 Broadway, New York, NY 10019
penguinrandomhouse.com

Copyright © 2025 by Zoë Rankin

Penguin Random House values and supports copyright. Copyright fuels creativity, encourages diverse voices, promotes free speech, and creates a vibrant culture. Thank you for buying an authorized edition of this book and for complying with copyright laws by not reproducing, scanning, or distributing any part of it in any form without permission. You are supporting writers and allowing Penguin Random House to continue to publish books for every reader. Please note that no part of this book may be used or reproduced in any manner for the purpose of training artificial intelligence technologies or systems.

BERKLEY and the BERKLEY & B colophon are registered trademarks of
Penguin Random House LLC.

Chapter images courtesy of Shutterstock (house), Vecteezy (fern), and AdobeStock (key)

ISBN: 9798217188093

An application to register this book for cataloging has been submitted to the Library of Congress.

First published in New Zealand and Australia, in 2025, by Moa Press,
an imprint of Hachette Aotearoa New Zealand Limited.

Berkley hardcover edition: September 2025

Printed in the United States of America
1st Printing

The authorized representative in the EU for product safety and compliance is
Penguin Random House Ireland, Morrison Chambers, 32 Nassau Street,
Dublin D02 YH68, Ireland, https://eu-contact.penguin.ie.

For Robear

PROLOGUE

THE CHILD DIDN'T know it then. Her mind was too muddied by hunger and fear to think beyond her next steps, but she was about to become the second most interesting thing to have ever happened in Koraha.

Her arms, more bone than flesh, trembled as she pushed against the heavy door and collapsed into the cool air of the grocery store. The floor, smoother and shinier than she thought possible, caught her hands as she stumbled and fell forward, leaving two dirty smears. Her body slumped as though there were stones in it, but then she spotted them, a glimpse of red, and she pulled a forgotten strength from her bones.

Later that day, as news of her arrival ate through the remote town, its ninety-two inhabitants would offer different accounts of what the child did next, their stories spanning the aisles of their only shop.

The lights on the fridge flickered and the girl dragged herself toward it, half-walking, half-stumbling. There was only one witness, a pimpled cashier, but the boy didn't move. A few minutes later, when he eventually reached for the landline, he'd stutter as he tried to communicate the scene to the town's lone police officer.

The girl, her throat and mouth parched and raw, lunged at the display of cold fruit and ripped a plastic box of strawberries from the shelf. She tore off the lid and hooked her fingers into the juicy red flesh, stuffing the berries into her mouth two at a time. The juice dripped down her sunburned face and stained her handmade dress. With the rush of sweet liquid, she felt her body coming back to her. Throat first. Then lips. Then cheeks. Like when they scoffed spoonfuls of honey straight from the hive.

Her favorite dress, an eighth-birthday present, was muddy, and the neckline was stained with something sour. She wiped her hands down the rough cotton and stared past the lanky cashier, spying the milk fridge. Rallying her legs, she shuffled over to it and wrenched the door open, her tongue pulsing. Real milk wasn't allowed where she came from—just lumpy white powder water. But there, in front of her, sat liter after liter. She reached out and unscrewed one of the blue caps, then she lifted the bottle to her lips. The milk spilled out in a torrent, soaking her face and clothes. When she couldn't drink any more, she slid to the floor and rested her head against the fridge door, her little body spent.

As her thumping heart settled, she stared down at her grubby arms and legs, looking for some sign that she wasn't the girl she was a few days ago. That since she'd started walking—running—she'd changed. As her brain adjusted to the surge of sugar and calories, her mind stirred up images of what she'd fled from. As the memories took shape, she contemplated sticking her fingers down her throat and spewing them all up.

She cocooned her face in her hands, trying to shut the memories out. But the horror had settled in her. She couldn't unsee it. Couldn't blink it away. Her eyelashes brushed her palms, where dirt had congealed with blood, and she started to shake. Later that evening, as a silver-haired woman wiped her down with a cloth, the girl would wonder whose blood it was. She'd wonder if it was the blood of one person, or two, or three.

When she glanced up, a pair of hands reached for her, forearms veined and strong, and she lashed out. She swiped at the air and kicked with her legs, but the man held her still.

"You're okay, kid," he said, his voice soft. "You're safe. I've got you."

The girl stopped fighting and let him hold her—why, she didn't know. It was bad to let him, against the rules. But she sank into him, into the smell and warmth and safety of the strange man, too tired to unjumble her thoughts. As the policeman's heart thrummed in her ear, she knew it was bad—that she would be one of those children now. One of the children whose faces filled the front pages of those dangerous newspaper things.

"I'm Constable Lewis Weston," he said. "What's your name?"

"Anya."

She slapped a hand to her mouth, wanting to put the word back. It was then that the policeman flinched, the muscles in his arm tensing slightly. But it wasn't the blood, or the mess, or the state of her clothes that had startled him. *Nope.* It was her face.

Something flared in her chest and she gathered herself, remembering the rules. She didn't belong in this village. She didn't belong with these people. Outside people wouldn't understand. And if she told him the truth, if she answered any more of his questions, she would be punished. The past few days would grow teeth and horns, and the truth would consume her; it would swallow her whole and she'd burn forever.

"Where did you come from, Anya?" His voice was kind. A trick. "Are you with your family?"

The large volume of cold milk churned in her stomach and she closed her eyes. She buried herself away, safe in the quiet. It wasn't hard. She'd gone days without speaking before.

"Is there anyone we can contact?"

She scrunched her eyes and lips tight, not letting anything slip out.

"Anya?"

She would go with the officer, first to the small police station and then to a stranger's house. She would let them bathe her and feed her and dress her in new clothes. But she wouldn't speak. Not when they asked about her home. Or her parents. Not when they asked her why she was in Koraha.

And that night, when she overheard them whispering, she would lock their words away. She was a ghost, they said, something unnerving and impossible. Anya, they murmured, looked just like the girl who had gone missing nearly twenty years ago.

The exact same face.
The same green eyes.

NOVEMBER 2001

THE WEST COAST BUSH, NEW ZEALAND

THE FOURTH OF them burst into the world like a storm. Loud and messy and out of the blue.

Mum's newest bush child.

He slipped into the small hut screaming. Into their middle-of-nowhere home. Just trees and ferns and his big voice.

The baby was impossibly tiny, all smooshed and scrunched up, and his skin was pale purple. It was impossible that he was even there—his miniature body wrapped up in Effie's wool jumper—because Mum hadn't been pregnant. There had been no bulge under her T-shirt. No swelling in her bra. With Aiden, Mum's belly had swollen and grown white lines, but this time, her stomach had stayed its normal shape.

Effie held her new brother in her arms and tried to push the tip of her finger into his tiny mouth.

"Shh, baby."

When Aiden was tiny, Mum had spilled over with milk. Sometimes it had dripped through her shirt and Effie had looked away, embarrassed, the damp circles reminding her of a leaking cow.

"Sorry, little boy. I don't have anything for you."

The baby opened and closed his wrinkly purple fists and tried to push his face into Effie's jumper. At almost nine, her chest was still flat, but the baby didn't seem to notice.

"Stop it."

The boy's searching lips creeped her out, and Effie wanted Mum to take him away. Mum needed to feed him and bathe him like she did with Aiden. Babies needed to be fed all the time, but Mum hadn't moved since the baby had slipped from between her legs an hour ago. Dad had thrust him at Effie, his newborn body sticky with white slime, and slammed their bedroom door in her face. Dad's face had been strange, his familiar eyes dark in a way that Effie didn't recognize.

She stared at the closed door. Other than the main living area, where they cooked and slept and did schoolwork, it was the only room in their back-of-beyond hut. Effie adjusted her position on the sofa, careful to hold the boy's head. The younger kids had been sent outside to pick mouku and pikopiko to steam for dinner. There was no noise apart from the baby's cries and the tōtara trees knocking on the corrugated metal walls. Mum's screams had stopped ages ago, when the little hand on the clock was pointed at three. Effie held the boy tight, afraid she might drop him. She'd seen Mum hold Aiden a thousand times, but the baby was so floppy and fragile, and he didn't seem to do anything but cry.

"It's okay, little boy. Mum will be out soon."

Effie tried not to look at the bedroom door, or to imagine what was happening on the other side of it. Feeling bad things made them real, that was how the game worked—Mum's inside-out feelings game. Sometimes in the winter, the hut got so cold that Effie's toes went blue. Then Mum would knit them all bright-colored hut socks and odd-shaped quilts. But Effie hated the hut on those freezing days. It was too cold. Too small. Too ugly. It wasn't like the proper houses she saw in town. But Mum said it was. Mum said that it was a proper home. She decorated their hut with pots of ferns and hung homemade art from the walls. Mum said that home was a feeling, a warm yellow tingle. So, they'd practice. They'd picture lots of yellow things. The sun. Kōwhai trees. Bumblebees. Hurukōwhai. Buttercups. Until the warm outside feeling became real and her toes didn't feel so blue.

But it wasn't working now. Effie needed Mum to make the game work. She needed Mum to come out of her bedroom and make everything normal again.

"Shh. Please." Effie shook the baby gently. "I don't know what to do."

Before Aiden came out, Mum had walked the six hours through the bush to the Roaring Billy Falls. Then she'd taken the tinnie across the river and hitched to Koraha to find a midwife. Mum had lined up small bottles by the sink—important baby vitamins—and she'd stopped hunting with Dad. But Mum hadn't done any of those things with number four. He'd just arrived, screaming like thunder.

Effie reached across the sofa for one of Aiden's old wooden toys. She shook the homemade rattle above the baby's head, but it was no use.

"Please, please stop crying."

Then, over the noise of his wails, she heard a crash from the bedroom—something breaking—and a pained angry yell. Effie wanted to run at the bedroom door, to batter at it with all her might. But Dad had been clear. No kids.

She held the baby tight, as if squeezing him might spare his tiny ears the sounds of anger. Then she closed her eyes. After the second crash, Effie slumped to the floor and pulled her knees in, supporting the baby. She needed to run, to get help. But there was nowhere to go. Just trees. No one to help them.

Effie rocked the baby and whispered words she'd only read in books, about a man in the sky who could save them. She was still rocking and muttering when the bedroom door creaked open and Dad appeared.

He was crying. Full, ugly tears. Effie froze, not wanting to be noticed. He would be embarrassed; Dad hated the weak bits in people. She'd never seen him cry, not even when the skinny hunting dog died. But now his face was a blotchy angry mess and his shirt was stained dark red.

"Get up," he muttered.

But she couldn't. He didn't look like Dad.

"Dad?" she whimpered.

But he didn't hug her. He stepped past them and yanked his jacket from the hook. Then, without looking at her or the baby, he stormed out.

The boy stirred in Effie's arms and she crawled forward, the wooden floor bashing against her knees. It was too quiet, too still—the hut limp like a gutted pig. Like there was no heart in it.

"Mum?"

Effie peered into the wrecked room. Mum's chair was broken in two, and her mirror lay in splinters across her favorite braided rug. The sheets and the floor were damp, stained with blood and another clear liquid. Effie stumbled to her feet, fighting pins and needles, then inched toward the bed. Toward Mum.

"Mum?"

Effie shook her arm.

"Mum!"

But Mum was already gone.

2025

ISLE OF SKYE, SCOTLAND

"THIS IS BEYOND humiliating," Effie shouted as she struggled to stand in the gale-force winds. She pulled at the hood of her jacket, trying to shield her face, but the rain stung her cheeks.

"No," Blair shouted back, their bodies huddled together. "What would be humiliating would be dying on the side of this bloody mountain because you're too stubborn to ask for help."

"We can get down ourselves. You can lean on me."

"No! We absolutely cannot." Blair dug her fingers into Effie's arm, clinging to her, as a gust of wind threatened to topple them. "There's no way I'm walking out on this ankle. The rocks are like ice, and it's going to start getting bloody cold and dark."

"I can get—"

"We need to call mountain rescue."

"I *am* mountain rescue," yelled Effie, her words diluted to a whisper by the elements.

"Right now . . ." Blair said as she lowered them to a crouched position on the wet ground, "what you are is a stubborn idiot who's about to watch her best friend freeze to death with a sprained ankle. Or, quite possibly, get blown down the Dubh Slabs to end up as a puddle of flesh and bones at the bottom."

"I would never let that—"

"Then *phone* them."

Blair gestured with her gloved hand, and the small plastic buckle caught the side of Effie's eye. The tender area of cold skin screamed on impact, but she blinked it away.

"I can't." She glanced down as water dripped from her hair. "I'd never live it down. Keith would rib me about it forever and—"

"For Christ's sake, Effie. Listen to yourself." Blair rubbed furiously at her arms. "We could die. This isn't some game. This is our fucking lives."

"Greg will be on call," Effie murmured, without meeting her friend's eyes.

"So?" Blair's mascara had started to leak down her face. "That's great."

"We broke up last night."

Blair shuffled across the wet rocky ground, guarding her left foot, until they were snuggled together. Then she put a drenched arm around Effie.

"You need to phone them," she said again, but her voice was softer.

Effie looked out at where the Cuillin Ridge should have been. But there was nothing to see but gray and cloud and lashing rain. On a good day, she could have named every point from Loch Coruisk to the end of the curved mountain range—a route she'd completed a number of times. She'd once run the Black Cuillin stretch—all twenty-two summits and eleven Munros of it—in just four hours and three minutes, barely an hour off the world record.

"I know," said Effie.

"Oh, thank god." Blair exhaled. Then she buried her face into Effie's chest. "Cos there's no way I'd have the energy to fight you on it."

"Well . . ." Effie managed a smile. "I'm fully intending to tell Keith that you did—that you resorted to blackmail and forced my hand."

"Whatever gets me into a helicopter and off this fucking mountain with my fingers and toes still attached."

Effie sat for a moment, feeling the weight of her friend against her, then she pulled her phone from her pocket and cocooned it between her ear and hood.

"It was just bad luck, you know." Blair reached out and took Effie's hand. "Bad luck and shitty Scottish weather."

"Thanks, Bee."

Effie closed her eyes and held 2 for the mountain rescue team, a team she'd been a part of for eight years. As it rang, she prayed it wouldn't be Greg who picked up. The last thing he'd said to her, as she'd stormed from his flat, was that she'd end up dying alone on the side of some mountain. And as she'd slammed the door, she hadn't hated the idea.

"I know this shouldn't be in the least bit funny," said Blair, unable to keep the amusement from her quivering lips as Effie got off the phone with Keith. He'd promised to have a team deployed as soon as possible.

"It's not." Effie groaned and reached into her rucksack.

"But . . ." Blair smiled. "Come on, it's going to make for a great story."

"It's not."

It would take a while for the helicopter to fly in, and the wait would be more pleasant without the elements trying to drown them. Effie pulled out the storm shelter, wrestling against the wind, then she and Blair stood nose to nose, chest to chest, torso to torso, under the fluorescent-orange sheet. The waterproof fabric came down to just below their bottoms, leaving their legs exposed to the downpour.

"Right," said Effie, their faces just inches apart, "on three, we sit."

"Got it." Blair giggled.

"And," Effie continued, "remember to pull the seating panel underneath you so the water stays out."

"Loud and clear." Blair suppressed a laugh as a gust of wind thrust her forward and their cheeks smooshed together.

"One . . ." Effie started, ignoring Blair's snorts. "Two. Three."

As they lowered to the ground, the material formed a protective tent around them, their world reduced to a billowing orange bubble.

"This isn't so bad," Blair shouted over the flapping fabric. "Romantic, even."

Effie rolled her eyes. "Christ." She rubbed a hand across her face. "Seriously, even now?"

"Now what?"

"I don't know." Effie couldn't help but smile. "I thought that maybe, just maybe, the threat of death might have dampened your . . . your . . ."

"My what?"

"Your infuriatingly persistent enthusiasm."

"Aw, come on." Blair nudged Effie's leg with her foot. "You love it."

"I tolerate it."

"And I tolerate you nearly letting us die on our girls' day out." Blair smirked. "So we're even."

Effie smiled back, and for the next few minutes, they sat in a comfortable silence as the orange nylon flapped around them and the rain pummeled the two circular windows.

The natural light had all but vanished from the evening sky, swallowed up by October's bleakness, and they were relying on two head-torches. One remained off, safe in Effie's pocket, while the other was around her hat. Half an hour later, when the phone buzzed twice in her pocket—two texts coming through at once—Effie knew something was wrong. Removing her gloves, she opened the messages. The first from Keith. Then Greg.

"What is it?" asked Blair.

Effie looked at her phone, then back at her friend. "The chopper from Stornoway had to turn around . . . because of the severe winds."

"So"—Blair took a breath—"no helicopter?"

Effie shook her head.

"No cozy airlift out?"

"I'm afraid not," said Effie.

"What happens now?"

"Keith said they've already prepped a team to head out on foot."

Blair's eyes widened. "In this?"

"Yeah." The muscles in Effie's stomach tightened. "They know what they're doing, Bee."

"Fuck." She glanced down at the flooded ground. "So did we."

The shelter muted the outside storm, creating an eerie quiet. But after a minute's silence, Blair looked up. "How long will it take them?"

"Five to six hours," said Effie. "Maybe longer. The conditions are—"

"Less than ideal," finished Blair.

Effie actually laughed. "Yes. They are definitely less than ideal."

"And this plastic bag of yours," said Blair, gesturing at the emergency shelter. "It can hold its own?"

"You, my friend," said Effie, "are sitting within 275 grams of mountaineering gold. I can personally guarantee you an almost warm, almost dry, mostly bearable night."

"Excellent. It already sounds better than night shift at the hospital."

"Fewer intoxicated patients. Less assistance with toileting."

"God, I hope so." Blair grimaced. "Neither of us is peeing until I can urinate without fear of it blowing in my face."

"I'm sorry," Effie muttered. "Again. For getting us into this situation."

"We just got caught out, Effie. The weather turned and conditions changed." Blair sighed. "Then I did my bloody ankle. Shit happens, and sometimes there's nothing we can do about it."

Effie squeezed Blair's hand.

"So," said Blair, "what happened with Greg?"

"I'm not sure this—"

"This is *exactly* the time." She grinned. "It's not like I'm going anywhere. So spill. You owe me some gossip at least."

"You're awful. You know that, right?"

"Yes, I do."

"It was nothing. Nothing new, anyway." Effie fiddled with her zip. "The same hashed-out argument."

"You being an irrational commitment-phobe?"

"Yeah."

"Couldn't you just get a set of keys cut for the poor man? He's at your place half the time anyway. Then maybe, down the line, you might feel differently."

"No." The word came out harsher than Effie intended. "Sorry. It's just . . . it all feels too hard. Greg, he's . . ."

He's not him.

"I'm not ready," said Effie. "Besides, the whole commitment thing looks better on you."

"I do make it look exceptionally good." Blair placed a hand on Effie's leg. "Bloody hard work though. Ewan required some serious pre-wedding training."

Effie looked at her friend. "I said things, Bee. It wasn't good. I think it might really be over this time."

"Why didn't you call me?"

"I almost did." Effie offered a half smile, knowing she didn't need to say anything else.

"So . . ." said Blair, "just so I know where we're at—tomorrow, once we're off this sodding mountain, will I be taking you for a massage and a sauna, or for beer and chicken wings?"

"Beer." Effie forced a smile. "A lot of beer."

"Well, that I can—" Blair swore suddenly as a rock thumped into the tent a few centimeters from her head, and she lurched to the side.

"You okay?" Effie leaned forward.

"Yeah. Shit." Blair patted her chest. "Just caught me by surprise. Jeez, that wind's strong."

Effie peered through the small plastic window, but visibility was down to a few meters and the sheets of rain blurred even the closest patches of heather and rock.

"It's going to be a long night," said Blair.

"Perhaps not long enough." Effie buried her face in her palms. "I can already imagine the headlines." She peered through her fingers. "'Local police officer saved by her own rescue team. Cold and wet cop grateful to be alive.'"

"'Incompetent police officer endangered beloved best friend.'"

Effie raised an eyebrow as a puddle of water leaked in around her right foot.

"Come on," said Blair. "No one reads the paper anymore."

"Keith does."

"Yeah, Keith definitely does," said Blair, feigning concern. "He'll probably frame them and mount them somewhere prominent in the station."

"You're awful."

Effie shivered, the waterproofing on her jacket long since defeated, then blew warm air down her collar. Her fleece was sodden too. The color had drained from Blair's face, her eyes darkened by smeared makeup and exhaustion, and each time she coughed, the guilt twisted Effie's insides. People were stupid to trust her, to think she would do anything other than fail them.

Effie tucked her knees into her chest as the shame pulled her mind back. No matter what she did, the past was always there, lapping at her shins. It was like standing at the edge of a vast ocean, the water sucking at her feet as she tried to wade back to the shallows. He was always there, floating just beneath the surface, his fingers clawing at her ankles and pulling her farther out to sea. One day he would eventually drown her. And as the water poured down her throat and her arms and legs gave up, Effie would apologize to him over and over.

I'm sorry.

The howl of the wind pierced through her, louder than her thoughts, and Effie bolted upright, her body disorientated and cold.

Blair was staring at her, her skin white and her eyes wide—her expression one of terror. Effie's chest tightened as her brain fired and realization poured through her. It wasn't the wind; it was Blair who had screamed. Effie followed the direction of Blair's eyes, and she froze, her blood running cold.

There, in the small circular window, was a face.

A stranger. His left eye filled with blood.

NOVEMBER 2001

EFFIE STUMBLED BACK to the bedroom door with the baby hugged into her chest, unable to look away from the strange figure that lay in Mum's bed. It had Mum's clothes on, and Mum's face, but the important bits were all wrong.

"Mum?"

Effie gripped the baby, her voice shaking as tears dripped down her face and her tummy threatened to spill out.

"Mum?" she said again, louder.

Mum needed to wake up. She needed to stop playing. The baby wasn't meant to be here. Mum hadn't mentioned having another one—three was plenty, she said. There was no cot set up in the corner. No nappies on the line. Mum had sewn for weeks before Aiden came, but there were no lengths of fabric on the table. No reels of thread.

Effie jiggled the baby a bit until his little eyes closed fully. Then she took a step toward the bed—toward the thing that was both Mum and not Mum. Like, from a distance, Effie couldn't be sure. The thought tingled in her skin as she inched closer. Securing the baby—his sleepy body like water—Effie reached out a shaking hand and touched her mum's forearm. It was warm. Effie inhaled. Mum's skin was still warm.

"Dad!" Effie screamed as she clutched the baby and rushed from the room. "Dad!"

Dad had got it wrong. He'd made a mistake. Dad always said that it was impossible to skin possums when they were still warm—that you had to wait until they were cold and proper dead. But Mum was warm. She wasn't proper dead. Effie hurried from the door and out onto the porch.

"Dad!" She shouted his name at the dense bush. "Dad! Come back."

Then she hurried across the deck and down the steps, the baby screaming, and aimed her scrawny frame at the wall of ferns and rimu and rātā trees. Dad would have headed for the river. It was the only way out. There were no paths or tracks other than the occasional deer trail. Every few months when they went to town, it was the water that guided them out. Other than the Roaring Billy River, it was just bush—thick green forest for kilometer after kilometer, farther than Effie's legs could take her.

"Shh, baby." She kissed his head. "You need to come with me."

Effie turned, her mind in a whirl, as she scanned the outside of their small hut. There was no Aiden. No Tia. The only sign of her siblings was an upturned basket, the fresh pikopiko ferns spilled out on the ground. And next to it was Aiden's wooden rainmaker.

"I can't leave you here, baby. You have to come too."

The baby's face crumpled as he screamed. His eyes wrinkled into two slits, the thin lines lost in puffy flesh, and his mouth formed a dark hole. The noise hurt both her ears and her heart, like how she loved and disliked him all at once. The confusing little thing made of the same stuff as her, the same blood and other ingredients, flailed his tiny arms and legs, and she tried to soothe him.

"Don't cry, baby." She didn't want him to be sad. She didn't want him to hurt or cry. "Shh. Shh."

But she didn't want him there. She wanted Mum. It wasn't a fair trade. No one had asked her. Having both of them might be okay—the baby and Mum—but not just him.

"Come on. Let's get Dad." Effie bounced him in her arms. "He can help Mum."

Spying a length of rag on the deck, she picked it up and wrapped the baby to her chest, just like she used to do with Aiden. It helped a bit, having him all squished in; it quietened him a little. Then she headed into the forest. The river wasn't far—fifteen minutes if she didn't miss the marked trees. As Effie slipped into the bush, the kahikatea and tōtara towering above her like green giants, she felt the first drops of rain falling from the high branches. Her feet stumbled with the extra weight as she navigated the carpet of ferns and moss, but she bashed through the thick vegetation without pause, digging her feet in as it got steeper.

Effie was Dad's favorite. He never said it, never did anything to make the young ones suspicious. But Effie knew. Dad always kissed her last before bed, and he let her do things that the others couldn't. Like cleaning out the trout and going bush with him to check traps. Mum said that Dad loved them all the same. But he didn't. Dad had given Effie his red hair and his green eyes—made her just like him. And when Dad had been out all night, tracking deer or chamois, he'd always leave a handful of supplejack tips on the table for her, and Mum would fry them up in oil. Even when Dad was tired and grumpy, maybe a little scary sometimes, he aways had a smile for Effie. But not that afternoon. He'd left without even looking at her.

Like he wasn't Dad at all.

Effie pushed the ferns aside, using her other hand to shield the baby's head from the spits of rain as the first rumble of thunder rolled through the green valley. She paused and looked up through the thick trees, the blue sky almost gone as the storm clouds moved in. On any other day, she would have turned around, respecting the black sky, and curled up in the safety of Mum's bed. But on no other day had her mum been almost dead.

"We'll be okay, baby." Effie reached out, touching the pink strip of plastic that Dad had tied around a tree. "Not too far now."

The bush thinned as she neared the river, and the ground became less steep. But the rain had turned from spits to heavy drops, and the baby was too quiet. Holding the back of his head, Effie sped up.

"Dad!" she tried screaming, but the wind gobbled her words.

She kept running another fifty meters or so, until she caught sight of the Roaring Billy River—a thread of dark silver that cut through the trees. Then she saw him. *Dad.* He was wearing his waterproof poncho and he was waist-deep in water, already a third of the way across the river. Effie blinked against the rain as she stepped from the cover of the trees. Her heart raced and she tried to shout, but the sky was too heavy; it squashed her voice. She stumbled across the small white rocks, getting closer to the river. Dad was in the wrong place. He wasn't at the shallow bit. He was too deep. Too far down. They always crossed farther up where the river got thinner over the gravel bar, where Dad had shown them, again and again, that it was easier to wade across. There the water was only thigh-deep and the current was slow enough that Effie could catch herself. On their last trip to town, Dad had encouraged Effie to cross the river by herself, rather than on his back. She'd waded out slowly, positioned between Mum and Dad, fighting as the water tugged at her feet and cringing as the icy liquid neared her waist. Twice she'd felt the river snatch her. Twice her dad had saved her.

"Effie?"

She turned at the whisper of her name. "Tia?" Effie stumbled across the stony ground, the baby silent now, and knelt down. "What are you doing here?"

Her little sister, tiny for six, sat on the rocks with her knees tucked under her chin, swatting away sandflies. Her wet top clung to her shoulders, soaked by rain and a mass of sopping black hair.

"You'll freeze out here," said Effie. "Or get eaten. Where's Aiden?"

"Dad said that . . ." Tia's face streamed with tears. "That if he gets swept away . . . that you'll watch me. But I don't want him to get swept away."

Effie pulled at her sister's arm as thunder tore through the sky and she tried to shield the baby from the rain.

"Where's Aiden?" she shouted.

"He wouldn't stop crying," Tia sobbed. "He was screaming and screaming."

"Where is he?"

Tia raised an arm, her body shaking violently, and pointed at the river. "He's . . ."

Fear seized Effie's chest as she turned and squinted through the rain. Dad wasn't alone. He was hunched under the weight of his big rucksack, and Aiden was in it. His little head popped out of the top, lolling from side to side. The river was too high. It was too fast.

Effie lurched forward and screamed into the air. *"Dad!"*

The rain lashed down in sheets, heavy and threatening. Crossing in the rain wasn't allowed. Dad and Aiden were going to die. They wouldn't make it to the other side. Then Mum would die too. The baby stirred against her chest, the wild beat of her heart forcing him alive, and five little fingers clutched her thumb.

"I want Mummy," Tia sobbed.

Effie stared at the river. Meter by meter, Dad moved farther away, pushing his way through the water, the bottom of the backpack dipping into the waves. Dad never left Tia on her own. And never by the water. During the summer, when the sun turned the river bright turquoise, Tia spent hours bobbing and splashing in the shallows, but Dad was always close by. Laughing. Skimming stones. Fishing for eels. Dad never left her. He never left any of them.

Effie wiped a hand across her eyes. Dad was wearing his travel rucksack, the big one with extra pockets that he used for long hunting trips. Effie wanted to scream, to shout for him to come back, but the fight in her had thinned, diluted by the rain.

"Effie." Tia tugged at her sleeve. "I'm cold now."

She reached for Effie's hand, her fingers like ice, and Effie wanted to cry. The cold of her sister, and the tiny warmth of her brother . . . it was too much. It was too wet and too cold. They needed to be inside. The baby needed milk and warmth and dry clothes. She needed to get him back to Mum.

Mum.

"Come on." Effie squeezed Tia's hand. "Let's go home."

"But we need Dad."

"Dad will come soon," she lied.

Effie took a final look at the river. They were past the halfway point—only one way to go now. Dad always had a smile for Effie. Even if he was busy or tired. Whenever he headed into the bush, he always stopped at the last visible point and looked back, one arm raised, and smiled at her as she sat on the hut steps. But Dad didn't stop. He kept striding through the water, his body lurching with the current, and a black ache closed around Effie's heart. His head didn't turn. He didn't look back.

"Come on." Effie guided the three of them back to the cover of the trees.

The crowded ceiling of branches sheltered them, easing the rain as Effie's insides drowned.

2025

EFFIE STARED AT the young man, their faces separated by millimeters of transparent plastic.

Blair dug her fingers into Effie's arm. "Holy shit, I think he's hurt."

But Effie didn't move. The young man's panicked expression rooted her to the spot, his blood-filled eyes wild with fear. It was the same expression that haunted her at night, that woke her up in a cold sweat. The boy, the one from all those years ago, had looked at her with that same frightened expression.

Effie's every instinct told her to get up. To help him. But the hammering in her heart drowned it all out, and she was a child again. A child, hiding in the bush, her hands pressed to her ears, listening to his screams.

"Effie." Blair shook her arm. "Effie, we need to help him."

Her friend's voice broke through something in her, and Effie turned her head slowly, not quite understanding. Not quite there. Slowly Blair leaned in, closing the gap between them, and touched her forehead to Effie's.

"You're not there," Blair whispered. "You're safe."

Effie closed her eyes, letting her friend's words bring her back to the howling wind and the torrent of rain. When she opened them again, the boy and the bush had gone.

"Well," said Blair, a smile lifting the corners of her mouth. "Safe might be a bit of a stretch. We're still stranded on the side of a mountain with a potential psycho outside our tent—again, a stretch. It's more of a plastic bag, really."

Effie squeezed her friend's hand, the moment acknowledged, then set aside. Blair wouldn't mention it again, and for that, Effie loved her.

"I'm going to go out and talk to him," said Effie. "I need you to stay here and stop the shelter from blowing away."

Blair frowned.

"I'll be fine," said Effie.

"I know that. It's the kid I'm worried about." Blair gave a small smile. "Just . . . be nice."

"I'm always nice."

"You know what I mean. Be gentle."

Effie rolled her eyes as she lifted the side of the tent. The rain was relentless. It lashed across the mountain in sheets, the ground wet and treacherous, and the fall of darkness wasn't far off. She wiped her eyes, her legs not yet steady, then the blow came. Sudden and unexpected. The young man's arm collided with the side of her head, all the sensations in her body rushing to that single spot, and a ringing shot through her skull. The force knocked her sideways, her feet stumbling on the wet rocks, and she fell onto her knee. Effie winced at the pain of bone hitting rock and tried to regain her balance, staggering as the storm hammered at her back.

"Jesus Christ," she swore into the wind.

Her mind blanked for a second, disorientated, then she turned to look at him. He was a complete mess, crouched on the ground, knees tucked to his chest, swaying and muttering, and not in nearly enough clothes.

"I'm sorry. I'm sorry." He looked up at her, his young face swollen and bleeding. "I panicked. I'm sorry. I wanted your tent. I didn't mean . . ."

Effie touched a hand to her eye. The boy's watch must have caught her cheekbone.

"You could have just asked," she said as she crouched down next to him. "I mean, bloody hell, who punches someone before trying a simple 'please'?"

Battling against the wind, Effie pulled a foil survival blanket out of her rucksack and wrapped the flapping sheet around his trembling shoulders.

"I'm sorry." He sniffed, his jaw quivering. "I'm sorry. I'm just so cold. And I hit my head."

"You're an idiot. That's what you are."

Her tone, less than caring, got a look from him, meaning that he was lucid at least. And thankfully, the rain had been making his eye look worse than it was. The kid had given the blood vessels in his eye a decent rupturing, but it wasn't actively bleeding. Just a nasty bruise really.

"What the hell are you doing up here dressed like that?" She handed him a Turkish Delight chocolate bar from her pocket. "Who's with you?"

"No one. I was just . . ."

Effie had to stop herself from clipping the back of his foolish head.

Tears streamed down his face as he fumbled with the pink wrapping. "I thought it would be cool to run the Slabs. There was this guy on TikTok who did it in—"

"Jesus." Effie rubbed her face. "What's your name?"

"Craig."

"And," she said, trying to be gentle, "how old are you exactly?"

"Eighteen."

"Well, Craig, despite you being a complete imbecile, there's a chance you're not going to die up here tonight."

His eyes flashed with fear. Another encouraging, coherent sign. The kid was mainly just cold and wet. And stupid.

"You're going to get into my shelter," said Effie, "with my friend Blair. Who, lucky for you, is a nurse, and much more tolerant than me. Then you're going to wait for the rescue team to arrive."

"What about you?"

"I'm going to hang out here and enjoy the view."

"You can't come in too?"

"There's not enough space."

"But—"

"Just get in." She took his arm and guided him toward the shelter. "Before I change my mind."

Effie forced her saturated body into her survival bag and sat on the ground, then she tightened the cord so that only her face poked out in the rain. The small vacuum-packed item had lived at the bottom of her rucksack for over five years—an emergency backup. Maybe she was overprepared, and maybe her bag was always the heaviest, but Effie had grown up with a fierce respect for nature. She'd grown up learning how to survive it. Learning how to survive him.

Effie knew what it felt like to die. She knew what it felt like to shiver so violently that her teeth ached and her vision filled with white dots.

Darkness had settled over the mountain. The watery light from her head-torch illuminated the red bag around her legs, and drops of rain lit up like white streaks in the blackness. Keith and the team would be struggling to find a route through the swollen streams, and the slippery rocks would slow them down significantly. It was going to be a long night. Effie glanced at the shelter, at the glowing dome of orange, and hugged her knees, the orb of light sending a forgotten chill down her spine. For a moment she felt the wet ropes digging into her wrists and ankles, pinning her child-sized body to the ground. Fear pulsed in her stomach. She was going to die. She was going to die in the darkness, a child abandoned in the dirt and the trees.

Then, for a second, there was an orange flicker of light.

Of hope.

Gone. Vanished, before little Effie had had time to scream.

Her head lolled forward, the tendons in her neck straining, and the pain jerked her back to the present. She blinked and rubbed at her face. She had to stay awake. She had to stay alert, and she had to keep herself visible for the rescue team. Her body started to shiver. Shivering was good. She just had to keep shivering, to keep generating heat, for another few hours.

Effie put the time at around 9 p.m.—almost four hours since she'd made the call. With any luck, Keith and the team would be with them around 11 p.m., maybe later, given the worsening conditions and the initial delay with the helicopter. She closed her eyes, the darkness absolute, and practiced walking the trail in her mind, crossing every burst stream and navigating each slab of rock. Blair would need to be stretchered down, and the kid would require babysitting. It was going to be a long walk out in the dark.

She rubbed at her wrists inside the survival bag, her mind never fully free of the bush, and waited.

―

The first flicker of light came at midnight—a line of small white dots on the horizon. Effie blinked once. Then again. Then she ripped the whistle from inside her sack and blew it until her cheeks hurt.

Forcing her legs to move, she stumbled to a stand and turned her head-torch up to full beam.

"Here!" She slipped the survival bag down to her waist and waved her arms. "We're over here."

She watched, her heart racing, as the line of dots increased in size and started winding slowly toward her.

"Over here!"

Water dripped down her sleeves and the wind stung her cheeks, but she didn't stop waving. She would get Blair off this mountain, and the kid too. She refused to watch anyone else die. Effie kept shouting until she could make out the familiar wide grin on Keith's face. As he neared, the bush memory stung her again—his boots caked in mud as he approached and lifted her small body from the dirt.

"Gosh, is it good to see you." Keith's smile spread from ear to ear as he reached over and hugged her.

"Thanks," Effie managed. "For this."

"Well, I couldn't go leaving a damsel in distress, now could I?"

"Don't." Effie hit his arm. "Don't you even dare."

He held his arms up in mock surrender. "I joke. I joke."

Effie frowned.

"Seriously, kid." His expression softened. "You did the right thing. I'm proud of you."

"So, no ribbing?"

"No ribbing." Keith winked. "For a solid week at least."

Effie went to say something when she caught sight of Greg through the rain. And despite trying so hard not to feel anything, heat swelled in her chest and she had to look away.

"The two of them are in the shelter," she said. "Blair's ankle will need strapping."

"Two?" asked Keith.

"Blair will explain." She blew out a lungful of air. "You'll see. Just make sure you give the good energy bars to Blair."

Keith patted his pocket. "I'm one step ahead of you."

"Thanks." Effie smiled.

"Make sure you eat something too," said Keith as he stepped away, the folded rescue stretcher hanging from his back.

"Here."

Effie turned at the sound of Greg's voice. He held out a pile of waterproof clothing with a chocolate Bounty bar on top: Effie's favorite.

"You okay?" he asked.

"Yeah." She took the pile of clothes without meeting his eye. "You didn't need to come out in this."

"Keith needed a twelfth person. For lifting."

"Oh."

They stood in silence for a moment, barely a meter apart, as the rain battered the mountain. A gust of wind caught the emergency bag that was still wrapped around Effie's legs, and she staggered forward. Greg caught her in his arms and held her for a moment, her face pressed into the familiar warmth of his chest. Then, unable to look at him, she pulled back.

"I should get changed," she said. "And check on Blair."

"Thank you," said Greg. "For asking for help." His eyes filled with genuine relief. "I know that can't have been easy."

Effie managed a small smile, the ache pulsing beneath her ribs, then she turned away.

"Wait." He reached for her arm.

"Don't." Effie blinked her eyes free of water, the dampness no longer just rain. "Please, not here."

"It's not . . ." He glanced at his shoes. "It's something else."

She frowned.

"Some guy's been trying to contact you." There was a trace of hurt in his voice. "He's called the base station like five times. Left multiple messages."

"What did he want?"

"I'm not sure exactly." A formality had returned to Greg's tone. "He said his name was Lewis."

Effie's heart missed a beat.

"And he mentioned something about a girl." He turned his head away from the wind. "I don't know, he sounded pretty desperate."

Lewis. Her Lewis. Effie pressed a hand to her stomach.

"Effie," said Greg. "Are you okay?"

"I . . ." She let out a breath. "I don't know."

NOVEMBER 2001

"WHY WON'T IT DRINK?"

"Tia, stop." Effie slapped her sister's hand away. "You're dirty."

"It's not opening its eyes."

"He's tired." Effie touched the end of Aiden's milk bottle to the baby's lips, but he didn't do anything. She frowned. "Maybe the bottle's too big."

Aiden always clutched at the bottle with his chubby hands and the milk sloshed into him.

"Why doesn't Mum feed it?" asked Tia. "Aiden can share. He only has a little bit of milk from Mum now."

"Mum's resting," Effie snapped, her throat tight.

Just that morning, before the screaming and the bleeding had started, Mum had stoked the fire and baked raisin cookies in the big metal pot. Then, smiling her big sunshine smile, Mum had lifted Tia onto her hip and they'd twirled around, laughing and singing, as the room filled with the warm smell of cookie dough. But that mum was gone. She was still in her bed—Effie had checked when they got back from the river—but her smile and laugh weren't there. Effie had covered her with a clean blanket and left a cookie by her bed before tiptoeing out—letting her rest.

"Maybe it doesn't like milk."

"He," said Effie. "It's a boy."

"How do you know?"

Effie tried to tease the teat into his tiny mouth. "I just do."

His little body wasn't doing the right things. Babies were meant to cry and flap their tiny arms. Aiden had cried for hours, his body almost red with it, and his screams had filled the hut. Effie had tried to lock him outside once. And when Aiden was real small, still new, he used to kick his legs and arch his little body into a bridge. But the new baby had stopped crying, like two hours ago. Even when Effie prodded his tummy, he stayed quiet. The baby wasn't doing any of the right baby things.

"Please eat." She poked his lips with the soft teat.

Effie had made up the milk just like she did at breakfast—one small cup of powder and one big cup of water.

"Where did he come from?" asked Tia.

Effie frowned. "From inside Mum."

"Did Dad put him there?"

"Yes."

"When?"

Effie touched a finger to his motionless little face. It was all squashed and yellow—just two lines for his eyes and one for his mouth. "I don't know."

She didn't even know what color his eyes were. She stroked his cheek and stared at him. Maybe he needed the sleep. Aiden had slept loads when he was tiny. Mum used to carry him when she dug in the vegetable garden and when she foraged for kōtukutuku berries and pikopiko. But when Effie prodded at the baby, he didn't move. Babies were meant to move. And babies were meant to drink milk.

"Tia," she said. "Go get a teaspoon."

Tia jumped up from the rug, naked but for her undies, and scurried over to the kitchen corner, her gangly legs tripping over the pile of their wet clothes. Tia's skin barely covered her skeleton, like the bones were trying to pop out at her hips and elbows.

"Here," said Tia, holding out a teaspoon.

Effie set the baby on the sofa, the old couch made nice by one of Mum's knitted blankets, and dripped a few drops of milk onto the spoon. Then she held his head gently, like a bundle of fragile moss, and parted his lips with the spoon. Tia sat close, her dark hair dripping onto the sofa, and Effie could feel the racing of her sister's heart.

"Here, baby," said Effie, "open up."

His tiny yellow face stirred, and his mouth opened.

"He's drinking," squealed Tia. "Look, he's drinking."

"Shh. You'll scare him."

Warmth leaked through Effie's chest as the liquid dripped into him. It didn't make sense how something so small and breakable could be real. The spoon emptied, and Effie's throat got all filled up. Fragile, breakable things didn't survive in the bush.

"Give him more," said Tia as she bounced on the sofa. "Look . . . look . . ."

The baby's lips puffed at the air like a fish.

"He wants more." Tia pointed and beamed. "He's hungry."

For the next half hour, they dripped milk into their tiny brother. Effie couldn't stop looking at him. Then, as best as they could, they cleaned him up and wrapped him in one of Aiden's cloth nappies. They didn't speak about the bigger stuff. Not about Mum. Not about Dad or Aiden. Not about the too-deep river and the too-fast current.

As darkness crept in, Effie piled up a stack of twigs and lit the wood fire. The heart of the hut, Mum called it. Dad had built the firebox using an old fuel drum. He'd tipped the barrel sideways and made a door and a chimney. Mum used the top for cooking—a heavy iron square that popped in and out. When Mum took it off, flames snuck out and the kettle boiled real fast.

Using a glove, Effie opened the door and threw a piece of wood in. Even in summer, babies needed extra heat. Mum said baby skin was so thin that all the warmth leaked out. Once the fire was going, Effie pushed the table and the four homemade stools aside, then made a bed of blankets in front of the sofa. She didn't know how to build the cot, and their sleeping corner was too far from the heat, but the blankets were clean and soft.

After wrapping the baby up, Effie placed him on the little floor bed and sat back on the sofa, watching him.

"What do we do now?" asked Tia.

Her little sister hopped up next to her and snuggled in.

"We wait for him to cry, then we give him more milk."

They sat side by side, their feet dirty and their bodies bare, and watched as his chest filled and deflated. The kitchen bench flickered and shone in the firelight, and the floor around the firebox gleamed. At the opposite end of the room, a curtain hung on a wooden rod where Dad had built a sleeping nook for them, with a double bed on the bottom and a single on top. None of them used the top bunk though.

Effie and Tia curled up as the summer sky darkened and the heat from the fire slunk up the walls. A gnawing hunger twisted in Effie's stomach, and she wrapped her arms around her middle. Tia did the same thing. But neither of them moved. Mum was the one who usually cooked, Dad and Effie sometimes too. But Mum's cooking was the best, especially her bread. She'd bake it for hours in the heavy black pan, and the smell of bread would make Effie's tongue sweat. On weekends they even got Vegemite. Hunters left it in the Thomas River Hut, and Dad would bring it back from his hunting trips. Effie pulled her knees up, squishing the twisted knot away with her thighs. The idea of food felt strange without Mum. The hut felt empty without her.

"I need to check on Mum," said Effie eventually. "You watch the baby."

Tia nodded.

Effie lit a candle and tiptoed over to her parents' door, careful to avoid the squeaky floorboards. Holding her breath, she stopped in front of it. Mum said it was polite to knock, in case her and Dad were busy. But Dad was gone. Deep in the bush gone, or washed down the river, proper gone. Effie touched the door with her fingertips. Mum would be fully rested soon. Before long, she'd be ready to get up—to feed the baby and make bread. Mum would know how to get Dad back too. Mum and Dad were two parts of one thing, Mum said, and parts couldn't exist separately. Dad would come back for her.

"Mum . . ." Effie eased the door open and slipped inside. "I gave the baby milk."

She walked over to the bed, not looking at the mess or the broken chair or the blood on the sheets.

"He's sleeping now," she said. "Tia's watching him."

Effie set the candle on the small bedside table next to the untouched cookie, and pulled back Mum's blanket. Then, just like she did when there was a storm, she nestled in next to her. As their arms touched, skin brushing skin, Effie bit deep into her lips and scrunched her eyes closed, refusing to feel it. Never. Ever. If she didn't feel it, then it wasn't real. If she didn't feel the cold, then it wasn't there.

"We changed his nappy too."

Effie adjusted her position so that they lay side by side with their heads level. She closed her eyes and added in the missing bits—the smell of her mum's soap and the warmth of her breath. She ignored the stiffness of her body, the way her arms rooted to the bed like trees and how her fingers fixed in a tight curl. Then, gently, Mum reached for Effie's hand, their fingers entwining, and whispered a story into the candlelit room.

After a while, Effie turned and peered at the door, listening for the sound of footsteps. "He'll be back soon, Mum."

She touched her mum's arm. The cold—that wasn't there—clothed her mum's skin like one of her knitted shawls.

I know, darling.

Mum kissed her forehead and Effie snuggled in. But she didn't cry. If she cried, if she felt anything at all, then her mum wouldn't come back either.

Good night, sweetheart.

"Good night, Mum."

2025

EFFIE SAT IN the car outside her house—her own little piece of Skye—and gripped her phone. She hadn't seen Lewis in seventeen years.

She pressed the phone to her chest, her body shaking from fatigue and the lack of a proper meal. Maybe it was nothing. Maybe Lewis had a kid—a girl. Maybe they were planning on visiting Scotland. Lewis would be thirty-five now, a grown man just three years older than her. She closed her eyes and tilted her head back. What if there wasn't any of her Lewis left in him? Life changed people; it shaped them and turned them into something different. Effie barely recognized herself some days. What if she made the call, and the boy who'd saved her—whom she'd held in her heart for nearly two decades—had vanished?

A dog's bark startled her and Effie opened her eyes, her pulse softening as she glanced out the window toward Loch Harport. A blanket of shadow hung in the sky, the clouds heavy and low, as the yellow glow of the rising sun emerged from the water. Lewis reckoned that sunrise was just God messing about—showing off. Not that either of them had believed in God, but there was something about throwing his name around that had made them feel powerful—just two scrawny kids at the end of the earth.

The dog barked again and Effie reached for the door handle. "I'm coming. I'm coming."

She stepped out into the morning air, dressed in a selection of the mountain rescue's spares, and walked over to her front fence. Keith had made her shower at the station and eat two Clif Bars, but the cold had taken something from her. It had hollowed her out, leaving a tiredness in her bones. She'd had to beg Keith to let her drive the seven miles home. He'd made her list all twelve Munros on the island, from lowest to highest, to prove she was lucid. It had taken her less than twenty seconds.

"Hey, boy." Effie reached over the fence and rubbed the dog's ears. "Sorry I'm a bit late."

Rimu jumped up, his body shaking with excitement. He bounced beside the gate, panting and spinning until Effie opened it.

"I missed you too." She knelt down and scratched his head, the thick Icelandic sheepdog fur falling out in her hands. "You really need a brush, buddy."

Rimu circled her legs as she walked to the red door. Hers was the last house in the row, semi-detached with white walls and a fully enclosed garden. Effie had bought it seven years ago, for two main reasons—the village of Carbost had a total population of 164 people, and from her garden, she could see over Loch Harport and out toward the Cuillins.

"Come on. Let's get inside."

Effie opened the door, kicked her shoes off in the hall and walked through to the living room. There was little in the way of decor other than a well-stocked bookshelf, two braided rugs (both handmade), and a large coffee table that she'd built out of driftwood. The walls were bare but for one print of the Cuillin Ridge Traverse (from Blair) and a small framed drawing of a silver fern (also from Blair).

"You hungry?" Effie smiled at Rimu. "Stupid question."

With the dog at her ankles, she walked through to the kitchen and poured dry food into his bowl. As the kettle boiled, she stared out the window at the water, her mind miles away. Why was Lewis calling her?

Why now?

Effie had finally managed to mold a life for herself—a life where she didn't think about them every day. But from the moment Greg had mentioned Lewis's name, Effie had felt herself being dragged back.

She looked at the dog. "We'd better give him a call, then."

Rimu's tail wagged and he followed her through to the living room. Then he jumped up onto the sofa and rested his head on her lap.

"You know this is absolutely not allowed, right?"

Rimu stared up at her with wide pleading eyes.

"Just this once." She ruffled the back of his neck. "But if you tell anyone, you're straight outside. No sympathy."

The dog settled in and Effie checked her watch. It would be early evening in New Zealand, on the opposite side of the world. She typed in the number Greg had given her, then held the phone so tight her cheek started to sweat on the screen.

He answered on the second ring. "Effie?"

Her stomach stirred from fear and excitement and everything in between. He sounded just the same, and yet totally different.

"Effie? Is that you?"

"Yeah." She closed her eyes and took a breath. "It's me."

There was a long pause. But not awkward. Nothing had ever been awkward between them. Even when she was nine and he was twelve—their ages and genders theoretically incompatible—they had just worked. Everything about Lewis had been safe and light—his smile, his personality, his voice. Effie had always felt sort of gray and grumpy around him, and yet at the same time, he was the only person who made her feel the exact opposite. He was the only person who didn't treat her like "the wild girl" from the bush.

"So," he said. "How are you?"

The absurdness of it—after nearly two decades—made her laugh. She actually fucking laughed.

She held a hand to her face, to her smile. "I'm alive."

"Excellent." Effie could hear the emotion in his voice. "I could really do with you being alive right now."

"What's happened, Lewis?" She bit into her lip. "Did something happen to . . ." She couldn't bring herself to say their names; she hadn't said her family's names out loud in years.

He hesitated. "There's been a situation in Koraha, and . . . I think I need your help."

"My help?" Effie frowned. "I don't understand."

Lewis let out a long breath. "A kid turned up a couple of days ago. A girl."

Images rushed through Effie's head—*click, click, click*—like the snapping of a camera, and the past flashed in front of her. One sibling after another. *Tia. Aiden. The baby.* Effie held the phone as her spine tingled. Something was about to happen, something bad. Unless, of course, she hung up. And kept running.

"She came out of the bush," Lewis continued. "I found her raiding the fridge at On the Spot."

On the Spot. A lump clogged Effie's throat, regurgitating forgotten things. On the Spot had been the only store in Koraha. It was where she'd had her first ice cream—an Eskimo Pie. And where she'd split a kid's lip open. Some boy, a few years older than her, had thumped into her, his elbow out, and murmured that she smelled like possum feces. Effie had been holding a Granny Smith apple, and she'd hurled it straight at his head.

"I think," said Lewis, "that she's probably about eight years old. But it's hard to tell. She's so small and thin and—"

"Malnourished?" The question slipped out before Effie realized she'd spoken.

"No. I don't think so. Just scrawny. But . . ." Lewis was stalling; Effie could feel him protecting her from something. "She was starving and disorientated, like she'd been walking for a couple of days. And she was covered in blood."

"Hers?" Effie leaned forward on the sofa, the police officer in her sparking to life, a shield masking something far darker.

"I don't think so. Her legs and hands were fairly beaten up, probably from the bushwalk, and she had the odd scar, but she wasn't bleeding. Apart from a few scratches and bruises, she was relatively unharmed."

"What happened?"

"I don't know."

Effie frowned. "What did she say?"

"Anya."

"Sorry?"

"Anya." Lewis sighed. "That's her name. It's all she'll tell me. I've tried everything, but she won't talk to me. To anyone."

"But *can* she speak?" asked Effie. "Does she know how to talk?"

"I think so. I mean, I'm guessing she can talk. She did say her name, and she seems to understand everything that I tell her, and I caught her flicking through a book," he said. "I think she's *choosing* not to speak."

There was a silence, heavier and louder than before. Effie closed her eyes. She should hang up.

"Effie," Lewis said eventually, "she looks just like you."

His words stopped her—her heart, her lungs, her voice.

"She has your green eyes," he said. "And your red hair."

Effie clutched the phone, tethering herself to the conversation. "What are you saying, Lewis?"

"Something's happened to that child," he said. "Something bad.

I don't know what. But she won't talk, and she barely eats. The poor girl has witnessed something horrible and . . ." He hesitated. "I think, given the strong resemblance, that she's come from your family's place."

The hut.

"No one knows how to get there, Effie." He paused. "No one except you."

Rimu raised his head, and Effie touched a hand to his pricked ears.

"No one except me," she said, barely audible.

The route was ingrained in her. Every land marker. Every bend in the river. As the oldest child, she had the bush etched into her skin—Dad had made sure of that.

NOVEMBER 2001

MORNING CAME. BUT no Dad.

Tia didn't say anything, and neither did Effie, and a big quiet hung in the air, filling the hut.

Tia sat on the floor with the baby as Effie mixed up powdered milk and poured oats into three bowls. Mum would need to eat something to give her energy. The hut felt smaller without Dad and Aiden in it. And with Mum resting, things were a mess. The kitchen was cluttered, and there was nowhere to put the bowls. Effie placed two on the floor, making it hard to angle the large bag of oats. She cursed as oats spilled out and scattered under the sink. Mum hated mess. Mess meant rats, and Mum hated rats even more.

The baby had moaned on and off all night, only sipping tiny amounts from the spoon. Effie felt ill from the mixed-up sleep, like there was vomit behind her eyes and in her brain, and she wanted to shout at something. Not sleeping good was like being shat on by a possum.

"Shouldn't it be hot?" asked Tia as she took her bowl.

"Oh." Effie stared at the cold soggy oats. "I forgot."

Tia shrugged and started eating. Her eyes were puffy and black. The possum must have shat on her too.

After taking a bowl through to Mum and stacking it on the messy bedside table, Effie returned and sat next to her sister. She couldn't eat. She just stirred it, then set the bowl aside.

Together, she and Tia spent the morning trying to work out what the baby wanted. It was exhausting, worse than grinding a million sedge seeds into flour. They didn't know how to wrap a baby, or how to tie a nappy properly, and neither of them had dared touch the dirty cloths. But the baby was mostly clean. And he slept and he drank, a bit anyway, and pooed, which seemed to be it with babies.

Effie stood at the sink, the ache in her eyeballs impossible to blink away, and tried to wash the pile of dishes, not wanting the mess to make Mum angry. But her head kept dropping forward and her eyelids wouldn't stay open. Tia was snoring on the sofa, her mouth wide, and the baby was sleeping beside her in his floor bed. Effie splashed water over her face to try to shock the tiredness from her eyes. The first palmful did nothing. So she did it twice more, spilling water down her top and over the floor. Her lips quivered as she dipped her hand back into the bucket, and she wanted to cry. There was barely any water left.

"Stupid shitty water." Effie kicked the bucket. "Stupid shitty bucket."

It was Dad's job to check the water. But her stupid shitty dad wasn't there. Effie kicked the bucket again. Maybe he'd drowned or fallen or been shot by a hunter. Not that she cared. She dug the heels of her hands into her eyes, refusing to cry.

All her life, they'd worked as a team—Mum and Dad and the kids. Growing vegetables, collecting and boiling water, baking bread, hunting deer, fixing the hut. The bush was too big for just her and Tia, and now the new one. The bush was an unforgiving thing that would eat them up. Effie bit into her lip until the pain shrunk all the other thoughts away, then she reached for the bucket and headed to the stream.

For hours, she sloshed back and forth from the stream. She relit the fire and boiled liter after liter of water. Not boiling it meant a gutted-out stomach, like Dad's stag knife rummaging through her insides, and three days spent on the compost toilet. Twice Effie stopped to help Tia with the baby. They gave him more sips of milk and piled up more soiled nappies, but his body had gone a weird gold color, and the white bits in his eyes looked like yellow butter.

"Shouldn't he cry more?" asked Tia.

Effie didn't know. She didn't know anything about babies.

"Aiden cried loads when he was tiny."

Effie stroked two fingers over his little head. His hair was light red—not like the young ones. Tia and Aiden were all Mum—thick black hair and dark eyes. But not Effie. Effie was a double of Dad.

"He's probably just tired," said Effie. "Babies need lots of sleep."

She set him on the floor and tucked the blanket over him. Then she squished onto the sofa with her sister.

"When will Mum be up?" asked Tia.

"Soon."

"I don't like looking after a baby," she said. "It's hard."

Effie stared at the small creature on the floor, muted by it. By everything. She didn't know how to be a mum, and definitely not to something so new, but she couldn't tell Tia that. Tia was only six, and six was a lot less than almost nine. Almost nine was a big age, Dad said, filled with big responsibilities.

"I think we forgot to eat lunch," said Tia.

"I'll make us something soon." Effie's eyes wouldn't stay open. "We can have dinner early."

Her stomach growled and her body ached and drooped. Her bones felt heavy and empty at the same time, and her arms and legs had glued themselves to the sofa. There was nothing she could do but lie there and close her eyes.

It wasn't until later, when a scream pierced through the fog, that she willed her eyes open. But it wasn't a baby's scream. Effie rubbed her face, trying to bring her mind back to her body. The scream vibrated through her again, the fear and desperation in it flooding her chest.

"Effie!" Tia burst from their parents' room, her face a mess of tears. She fell to the floor, the crack of her knees making Effie wince.

"Tia." Effie rushed over and huddled next to her. "I told you not to go in there."

"Mum's bleeding." Tears choked Tia's words. "There's blood everywhere."

"I know." She pulled her sister into her. "I know. That's just baby stuff. That's just . . ."

Tia's head shook violently against Effie's chest. "No," she cried. "Something's wrong. She wouldn't wake up."

"I told you not to go in there."

"I had to." Snot and tears drowned her sister's words. "I had to go in."

"Why?"

Tia sniffed and wiped at her eyes. "I thought Mum might have taken it."

"Taken what?"

"The baby."

Effie spun around, her brain dizzy. His floor bed was empty. He was gone. There was just a pile of blankets and a single teaspoon. There was no baby. No brother.

"Where is he?" She pushed herself up, finding energy in some angry buried place, and ran for the door. She thrust it open and rushed outside.

"Baby!" she screamed.

She glanced at the empty deck, then yelled at the wall of trees, her fingers balling into fists.

"Baby!"

Her throat burned and her eyes stung. But there was nothing. No one. Just kahikatea and miro and solid forest.

2025

"THIS IS MAD." Blair hobbled across Effie's small kitchen. "You get that, right? That this is totally mad?"

Effie lifted the kettle and poured two cups of tea. "Milk?"

"You can't just get on a plane to New Zealand. It's like . . ." Blair shook her head at the milk bottle. "Like a really fucking long way."

Effie carried the mugs through to the living room, and Blair limped after her.

"And this Lewis guy. I mean, what do you even know about him?"

"We grew up together." She smiled. "You'd like him."

"Oh, I'd like him." Blair rolled her eyes. "Well then, that's just peachy. You just jump on a plane to the other side of the planet and go meet some guy you haven't seen in fifteen years."

"Seventeen." Effie sipped her tea. "Seventeen years."

"And what?" Blair's eyes widened. "Just cos some random kid appears from the trees, you're off to help? Don't they have other police officers in New Zealand? Or other people who can talk to trees?"

Effie raised an eyebrow. "I don't talk to trees."

Blair sat on the other sofa, ignoring her, and Rimu nuzzled into Blair's legs.

"Traitor," said Effie.

"Is this about Greg?" Blair asked. "Is that what you're running from?"

"No. It's got nothing to do with Greg," said Effie. "And I'm not running. In fact, for the first time in my life, I think I might actually be doing the exact opposite."

"You've got nothing to prove by going back there. You know that, right?"

"Bee..."

"You survived the bush, and then you escaped. You moved on. What good is there in going back?"

"It might help a little girl."

"That's bullshit. You can help little girls here." Blair leaned in. "Either you've gone mad or you're hiding something."

Effie stared into her mug, then looked out the window at the sea loch and the heavy sky. She had only ever shared parts of her past with Blair. More than she'd told anyone else, but still, just parts. Blair knew the bush-girl story, the neglected kid who'd grown up in the wild. But the worst bits—the darkness that had slithered into their lives after her mum died—those Effie had locked away.

She focused on the salt loch. There was barely any difference between the water and the sky, like a bleak watercolor of gray and charcoal.

"It's not some random case," said Effie as she turned back to look at Blair. "Not some random child."

Her friend frowned.

"Lewis said that the kid looks just like me."

Confusion, then shock, spread through Blair's features. "Wait, how old did you say she was?"

"Around eight," said Effie, smiling slightly. "Don't worry, she's not mine."

"Right." Blair let out a breath. "Okay."

"Although I think we might be related somehow. And Lewis thinks that she's come from the hut."

"Shit." Blair looked suddenly serious. "And she was covered in blood?"

Effie nodded. Then she squeezed her mug, needing something to occupy her fingers. "Blair, there's something that I—"

"You and Lewis," interrupted Blair, "why didn't you keep in contact?"

Effie glanced back at the window. "We couldn't."

She didn't say anything else, and Blair didn't push it. She simply reached forward and lifted her mug from the table. And for a few quiet seconds, they just sat like that.

"Shit," said Blair eventually.

"Yes." Effie managed a small smile. "Shit, indeed." She took a breath before continuing. "And Lewis thinks my dad might be involved with whatever horrible thing happened to her."

"Jesus." Blair puffed out her cheeks, her eyes wide, then she exhaled loudly. "Right."

"I need to go back," said Effie. "I need to find out what happened to my family."

There was a beat of silence.

"And you'll need someone to watch Rimu."

"And I'll need someone to watch Rimu."

NOVEMBER 2001

THE SOUND THAT stopped her was impossible.

Effie spun on the deck, Tia already at her side, and grabbed her sister's hand.

"Listen," she demanded.

Tia's face was a wet snotty mess, her eyes red and puffy, and strands of dark hair caught in the corners of her mouth. She wiped her face and put on her bravest voice. "The cicadas?"

"No. No." Effie closed her eyes, making her ears work better. The bush bugs ticked and thrummed, shrieking between her ears. "The other sound. Listen."

A tiny noise poked through the loud buzz of cicadas, like acorns shaken in a tin can. Effie stared at the ground, at the upturned basket of pikopiko ferns.

"Where is it?"

"What?" Tia sniffed.

The noise stopped, leaving nothing but the loud cicada hum. Then it started again, the rattle of acorns.

"Aiden's rainmaker," said Effie. "It's not there."

"I can hear it." Tia's arm started to shake. "I can hear it."

"Come on."

Effie pulled at her sister, following the faint wooden raindrops, and they ran around the back of the hut to the vegetable garden.

They stopped dead at the same time, hands entwined, and Effie felt the pulse of her sister's heart. There had never been anyone else at the hut. No one was allowed, Dad said. The hut was a special place just for them. *A secret*. But she was there, sitting next to Mum's mint plants. Her head and body were turned, but her familiar white hair hung down her back, a waterfall of silver. Like she could be a witch.

Effie bit into her cheeks, not knowing what to do, not knowing how to fix this wrong, forbidden thing. Then, out of the corner of her eye, she saw him.

Aiden.

Her little brother, only two and a half, was kneeling among the lettuces and the zucchini leaves. His face was screwed up in a look of concentration as his little fingers dug in the dirt.

"What's June doing here?" Tia whispered.

Then the woman turned, her long wavy hair almost reaching her waist—the roots bright white but the ends dark silver—and she smiled at them. But it was like her eyes and mouth didn't match. Her smile was warm (like when she snuck them Pineapple Lumps from her pockets), but her eyes were sad. And there, bundled up in a shawl and held to June's chest, was the baby. On the ground was an empty milk bottle.

"Give him back," Effie demanded. She took a few steps toward June and made her face serious, like Mum did when they were in trouble. "He's ours."

"I know, sweetheart." June lifted the baby and set him in Effie's arms. "I was just letting you girls sleep."

Tia inched out from behind Effie's legs, her voice small and timid. "Did you bring us candy?" she asked.

"I did." June smiled, but it made her eyes look sadder. "Would you like one?"

Tia nodded and scurried over to her. They knew her, the woman with the long witch hair; they saw her every time they went to Koraha. Mum and Dad always visited her house. Dad did loads of jobs when they went on their trips to town—building and fixing things—and people shoved money into his rough hands. There was always something broken at June's house, so Dad would sort it and Mum would drink tea on June's deck. Then Dad would take her money, and June would sneak Tangy Fruits and Snifters from her pockets.

Effie patted the baby and jiggled him. It was strange seeing June in the bush. She looked too old to be there.

"How old are you?" asked Effie.

June looked up, with Tia sat on one of her knees and Aiden on the other. They were both sucking on lollipops. Sugary yuck, Mum said, full of rubbish.

"You look old," said Effie.

The woman smiled at that. "I'll be fifty come winter."

"Why are you here? No one's meant to be here. It's private."

"Your dad just needed a bit of help after everything that happened."

Dad.

"Where is he?" Effie held the baby tight, her voice getting louder. "Where's my dad?"

"He'll be here soon. He's just busy. He's sorting something." June's voice sounded odd, like when Dad lied to Tia about killing possums.

"Busy doing what?" Effie shouted. "What's he doing? Tell me!"

"Effie, maybe you should—"

"Where's my dad?" Her body shook, her insides hot and jittery, and the young ones inched back from her, moving farther into the curve of June's lap.

"Sweetheart, why don't you give the baby to me and we can—"

"No." Effie jerked back.

The baby cried then, his face bright red, and his trembling body scared her. Effie pressed a hand against his back, their hearts racing together. She was afraid that she might break him, the ugly little thing, more yellow than white, that was part made of her. His slimy red hair was hers, and his angry little frown. Effie swallowed down a salty sob.

"How did you make it stop?" she asked, her voice wobbly. "How did you get him to drink that?" She nodded at the bottle.

"Maybe try holding him a little less tight." June looked almost nervous—a strange expression on a grown-up's face. "And try to keep your voice a bit quieter. He's sad that you're sad."

"Oh."

Heat spread through Effie's chest. *Love.* Love for the little stranger who didn't want her to be sad.

"It's okay, baby," she whispered. "I'm okay."

The baby's crumpled face smoothed out, like ripples disappearing from a puddle, and the redness in his cheeks faded.

"See. You're a natural."

June beamed, and Effie hated how much she liked the compliment.

"Does he have a name?" June asked.

It hadn't occurred to Effie to name him. He wasn't even meant to be there.

"He's number four," said Tia. "One, two, three, four."

Four.

"Little Four." June smiled. "Come." She lifted her arm, meaning for Effie to sit. "I also brought some lolly cake from the shop."

Effie's tummy ached and rumbled, the hunger making her brain spin, and she sat next to them. She perched by the mint plants—surrounded by the smell of Mum in the morning—and rested Four against her shoulder.

"Would you let me hold him?" asked June. "Just while you eat."

Slowly, Effie handed him over, then she unwrapped two slices of lolly cake. Her throat was like dry grass, the lack of saliva making it hard to swallow. As she chewed, the bush breathed softly, pulsing like a live thing, calming her.

Once she'd licked the last crumbs from the aluminum foil, Effie reached back for the baby, but the stillness of him stopped her. He was too cozy—too asleep—to move. Giggles of laughter came from the mud kitchen where Aiden and Tia were playing, their little bodies caught in the changing light. The sun had lowered in the sky, its long golden fingers stroking down the trees to the earth, and the air had turned a perfect yellow.

"How long were Tia and I sleeping?"

"Most of the afternoon," said June. "It will be sunset soon."

She looked up suddenly, a barely there glance. But her face did that lying thing again.

"When did you get here?" asked Effie.

"Midafternoon."

"How did—"

A voice stopped her, and Effie jerked her head around. *Dad.* It was unmistakably Dad. She jumped to her feet, her skin tingling, but as she went to move, a hand gripped her ankle.

"Effie, wait." June's face was scared and sad and pale. "Just—"

"I heard Dad." She pulled her leg free. "Where is he?"

"Please just—"

But Effie was gone. She heard it again. His voice—a grunting. Effie ran after it, sprinting to the front of the house as fast as her legs would take her, and she burst through the front door.

It was empty. No Dad.

But his rucksack sat on the table surrounded by a number of items—tubes of cream and tins of powdered milk. One of the tins had been opened, and the yellow powder dusted the floor. Barely stopping to think, Effie ran from the hut and into the bush. She sped up at the sound of rustling and groaning. She pushed her way through the ferns, the rimu branches scratching at her arms, until she reached their clearing.

Dad was there.

Digging.

His body was hunched over, his huge hands gripped around a spade. He thrust the metal blade into the earth—in and out, in and out—as dirt sprayed into the air.

"No!" Effie screamed. *"No!"*

She hurled herself forward, tripping and stumbling onto the ground, but Dad didn't look up. His mind was lost to a faraway place. She picked herself up and flung herself at him. She clawed at his arms and chest, but he didn't stop.

"No!" Effie shrieked. "Stop. Stop!"

Dad dug into the earth, spadeful after spadeful, as shafts of light filtered through the trees, and tears streaked his cheeks.

"Please!" Effie's throat burned. "Please! She's not dead. You have to help her. Stop!"

She balled her fingers and pounded at his back, punching and begging with tiny fists, but the dad mountain didn't budge. He couldn't put Mum in that hole. Effie wouldn't let him. Mum would suffocate in the dirt.

Sweating and panting, she staggered back. She needed to get back to Mum. But as she turned, a twig snapped under her foot—a tiny insignificant sound—and Dad stopped, and the spade fell limp in his hands. For a moment, he stood frozen, silhouetted in the fine golden mist. Then the spade thumped to the forest floor. Dad turned and stared at her, his eyes wild and unblinking.

"Dad?"

"Effie." He frowned, his lips barely moving.

"Please, Dad. You have to stop."

A bolt of fear flashed through his eyes, as if he'd only just noticed her, and he looked at her, panicked. Then his eyes darted back to the pit in the ground, and her eyes followed his. Effie's legs collapsed beneath her, her knees sinking into the mud, and she closed her eyes, willing it away.

No. No. No.

But the image congealed and flashed behind her eyelids—the small patch of material poking out of the dirt.

"I'm so sorry. I'm so sorry."

The words floated in water around her.

"I'm so sorry," Dad muttered.

An intense pressure crushed Effie's arms and chest, but she didn't fight it. The big black pain inside her was too huge. Dad lifted her and held her tight, his strong arms holding the broken bits of her together.

"I'm so sorry, sweetheart." His breath was stale, and his body smelled of dirt and salt. "I didn't want you to see any of that. I thought that . . ." His voice broke, and his tears dripped onto Effie's face.

She kept her eyes closed as Dad carried her back to the hut, her body limp and baby-like, and he placed her on the sofa. Then he sat next to her and clung to her like he needed her for breathing.

"I had to, sweetheart. I had to bury her." He pressed his lips to Effie's forehead. "Mum was dead, sweetheart. You know that."

The pressure increased around her ribs, his arms squishing her tighter, and Effie curled her fingers around his muddy hand.

"Don't cry," she whispered and squeezed his hand. "Don't cry, Daddy."

Effie leaned into him, Dad's favorite little girl, and patted his arm, helping him to breathe.

"You're okay, Daddy."

2025

EFFIE STARED THROUGH the plane window.

With the time difference, she'd lost most of a day—as well as the motivation to watch another second of in-flight entertainment. She was also pretty sure that she smelled. Thirty-seven hours, and three flights, was too long to exist in recirculated air.

She barely remembered the long journey to Scotland nearly two decades ago, but there was a lot about that week that she'd blocked out.

Rubbing her eyes, her body clock somewhere in the middle of the night, she peered out the glass at the bright afternoon sky. As the sun caught on the snow-capped peaks, a rush of heat spread through her chest, and she swallowed the lump in her throat. It was truly beautiful. Breathtaking.

Home.

For more than half her life she'd lived on the other side of the earth. But home—the sense of belonging that hung heavy in her bones—was down there, beneath the clouds. The bush had never left her—it had lain dormant in her core, no matter how deep she'd buried it.

The Southern Alps spread out below her, infinite and spectacular, as the plane dipped toward Queenstown Airport. The peaks of the Remarkables poked out through a basin of thick white clouds like a snapshot from a *National Geographic* magazine. Effie kept her fingers to the window as the plane sank into the clouds and the world disappeared. Nothing. Just a wall of white mist. Then, miraculously, the clouds parted and a long strip of water appeared between the mountains—the lake leading all the way to the airport. It wasn't until the wheels thudded on the runway that Effie realized she'd been holding her breath. Up there, looking down, she'd kept picturing them. Somewhere in the vast expanse of bush, hidden in the trees.

What happened to you, Tia?

Where are you?

Effie closed her eyes as she stepped off the plane and inhaled the warm spring air, letting it soothe her. By the time she'd made it through customs and ordered a coffee, she was fine. She found a seat at the Patagonia café, sat down with her long black and a sandwich, and logged on to the Wi-Fi. Within seconds, her WhatsApp started beeping, making Effie smile. She took a sip from her cup and started scrolling through the messages—all from Blair.

> *Are you there? Message me as soon as you land. x*

> *And when you get to Koraha. x*

> *Is the coffee good? I've heard that Kiwis make a good coffee. They invented the flat white apparently. Who knew? x*

> *Google says that you can bring your OWN WINE to restaurants. I knew I should have gone with you. x*

Miss you. Love you. x Ewan (big soppy weirdo) says he loves you too. x

Ewan says no great loss with Greg. Apparently he always thought Greg was too short for you. x

Ewan says you should find a hot Kiwi barista. x

Ewan is now trying to make me a flat white. x

According to Qantas, you should be in Queenstown. Message me. x (Ewan's flat white was bloody good—don't tell him though, I've told him he needs to keep practicing.)

Rimu is doing great. Doesn't miss you at all. Think we'll keep him. x

Effie rolled her eyes. Blair would be spoiling Rimu rotten. Ewan probably even more so; he was a giant softy. Effie liked Ewan. He and Blair had tied the knot just over a year ago at a small ceremony at Fairy Glen. There had been a lot of umbrellas and a lot of whisky. Effie smiled as she typed a reply.

I'm officially in New Zealand and I can confirm that the coffee is fantastic. Unfortunately, the barista is wearing a wedding ring. I'm just grabbing a quick bite then I'll drive to Koraha. About 3 hours.

Blair replied immediately.

Are you sure you should be driving?

Slept surprisingly well. Had 3 seats to myself from Dubai. Isn't it like 3 a.m. in Scotland? GO TO BED!

Will you see Lewis today?

Go to sleep. Love you. Say hi to Ewan and Rimu. x

Don't let Rimu sleep in your bed. x

Too late 😊 x

Effie slipped the phone back into her pocket and sipped her coffee, which she had to admit was extremely good. There was probably even a coffee shop in Koraha now. But other than that, she doubted Koraha would have changed much—that was how the West Coast worked. The same small town. The same people. People who believed that Effie was still missing—the bush girl who'd vanished into the trees.

She chewed on the end of her thumb. Returning to Koraha was risky. Effie knew that, and so did Lewis. Going back meant exposing what Lewis had done all those years ago.

"Lewis." Her voice had broken on the phone. "What if the police . . . If they find out what you did for me, they'll . . ."

"I have to help her, Effie. And I can't do it without you."

"But—"

"Please, Effie." He'd paused. "I know what I did. And I'd do it again. Gladly."

It was because of that final word that Effie was sitting in Queenstown Airport. Because she owed Lewis her life.

Effie glanced down at her hands and stroked a thumb across the inside of her wrist—brushing over the small letter tattooed there.

A

She traced his initial with her finger, the shaded font making it look like two *A*s, one on top of the other. The stab of pain felt as real and frightening as it had all those years ago. Then she blinked and pulled her sleeve down. Some truths were best left buried.

It was after seven o'clock when she drove her rental car into Koraha. A rental car implied a short stay. A quick visit, then back to her real life.

For the last hour, she'd driven through the wildness of the Haast Pass, the remote roads bending through mountains and bush. The beauty of the country was mesmerizing—even after everything. It was like breathing fresh air, like her untamed blood had been craving it.

But Effie had to stop as she neared the Roaring Billy Falls, afraid that the shake in her arms might make her veer off the road. She'd pulled onto the verge, her heart racing as she glanced over at the bush. There was nothing to see from the road, just trees and a jagged skyline, but she knew the trail to the falls by heart. She knew the sweet smell of the podocarp forest and the feel of tawhai bark. A world of a thousand greens, where trees rose to the sky like gods.

As she'd sat in the car with her fingers gripping the steering wheel, she'd pictured the moss-cloaked matai and the towering miro trees. Just a ten-minute walk would have taken her to the Haast River. Then a boat across the water and a six-hour tramp through dense bush would have taken her to the Roaring Billy River crossing and the hut. The barbed silence moved through her, as if the blades of silver fern traced her skin, then she started up the engine and drove off.

Now Effie sat in her rental in the driveway, unsure if she could get out. Eventually, a figure appeared a few meters in front of the car, walking straight at her. Effie stared through the windscreen. Her hair was still long, the silver falling to her waist, but the once voluminous strands had thinned and dried out.

Effie stepped from the car and walked straight into the woman's arms.

"I've missed you, baby girl."

"I've missed you too, June." Effie clung to her, just like she'd done as a child. "I'm sorry that I—"

"Hush, now." June gave her a final squeeze, then pulled away. "We'll have none of that. Grab your bags," she said. "Kettle's on, and I've made Afghan biscuits."

"You baked?"

June smiled, her weathered skin crinkling around her eyes. "I've learned a few things in seventeen years."

Seventeen years.

"Come on. There's real food too."

Effie grabbed her one rucksack from the car—just a quick visit—and followed June inside. The small house had barely changed; it was like stepping back in time. The same floral sofa, complete with arm protectors, and the same red countertops in the kitchen.

"So, is there any more news on the girl?" asked Effie as she took a seat at the cluttered kitchen bench.

"Let me see you eat something first," said June, dishing up two plates. "Dinner and an Afghan. Then I'll answer your questions."

Effie couldn't help but smile as she dug into her lamb and three veg. She hadn't realized how hungry she was. She lifted her head and glanced past June toward the back screen door. June must have replaced the mesh. *Obviously.* Effie had ripped it to shreds.

"So," said June. "Ask away."

"Where is she?" asked Effie. "The girl."

"At the clinic. I'll take you there tomorrow."

"And Lewis?"

June smiled. "He's there too."

"What exactly do we know about her?"

"Not much. She turned up at the supermarket on Friday morning searching for something to eat. Poor child was famished."

"Where did she come from?"

June glanced down at her plate, then her eyes flickered toward the window. "From the bush."

"Are you sure? I mean, Lewis said she won't talk."

"I'm sure."

"How?"

June reached a hand across the table. "Because she looked just like you when you turned up. Scared. Dirty. And with those same green eyes."

Two girls. With eyes the color of the forest and blood on their clothes.

DECEMBER 2001

DAD WAS GONE again when Effie woke up.

There was a big cold space on the sofa, the warmth of him gone too. But Effie didn't run from the hut. She didn't scream at the bush. Dad was real gone this time. She could feel it in her chest, like a hole had opened up. And no amount of screaming would bring him back.

Effie pulled herself up from the sofa and walked around to the kitchen. Dad was gone and now June was there—like a gift he'd left for them. A stupid early Christmas present.

Effie didn't speak, and June didn't try to make her. They stood side by side, washing dishes and putting them away. June didn't know the right places for the bowls or the cutting boards, and she used the wrong towel.

But then, Mum was dead, so what did it matter?

The baby was asleep in the corner (June had assembled Aiden's old cot), and the young ones were sleeping in the nook. Effie didn't know where June had slept; she didn't want to think about it.

Once Effie had dried Four's bottle, she walked outside and sat on the deck. After a few minutes, June followed her.

"This is for you," she said, handing Effie a small package. "Lewis left it at my house."

June smiled and walked back inside, leaving a cup of mint tea for Effie. It was annoying that June was being so nice. Effie didn't want nice. She wanted something to scream at.

She opened the gift—a single shell threaded onto a black waxed string—and placed it over her head. Staring at the trees, she held the shell between her fingers and moved it along the string.

"Mum and Dad are gone, Lewis."

She rubbed her forearm across her face, as close to crying as she'd been. But she blinked the tears away. She wouldn't cry. She wasn't some stupid blubbering little girl.

Four days passed before Effie spoke to June. She mumbled answers to all her stupid questions—about the greenhouse and what the young ones ate and how to get water—but she never proper spoke to her. Aiden, however, clung to June's legs like a mussel, and Tia talked at her continuously.

"How did you get here?" Effie asked eventually.

June sat on the sofa after putting the baby down, then she looked at Effie as if they chatted all the time.

"Well," she said, thinking. "Your dad appeared at my house that night, around nine or ten. It was just getting dark. He must have practically run down that valley with Aiden. I doubt he even stopped to take a breath. Your dad said he managed to catch a ride at the falls and made the whole trip in five hours." She shook her head in disbelief. "Just the walk alone took us nearly double that on the way back. I have a bit of trouble with my right knee, you see."

"Dad stayed at your house?"

"Well, not really. He left Aiden so the boy could sleep for a few hours, then . . ." She hesitated. "Then he went to the shop for supplies and a couple of—"

"On the Spot?"

"Yes. It was late, and I tried to get Jonathon on the phone, but he wasn't answering so—"

"Dad broke in." Effie frowned.

"Well, yes." June looked almost guilty. "But he needed stuff for the baby. And I'm sure he left money."

"Then what?"

"Then we headed back here. Your dad can't have slept for more than a couple of hours. We set off at 6 a.m., and I drove us out to the falls. Then we took your family's tinnie across the river and walked in."

"And Dad dug a hole for Mum."

"Yes," she said softly. She moved her hand across the sofa toward Effie's leg. "Then he buried your mum."

For a long moment, it was quiet.

"Thanks," said Effie eventually. "For the lolly cake."

Then she got up and walked toward the bedroom nook.

Two more days passed before Effie asked June another question, when they were hanging nappies to dry outside.

"Why did Dad leave us?"

June paused, her arms reaching up to the line, then she turned. "Oh, baby girl."

She dropped the linen back into the basket and took a step toward Effie. Then June hugged her. Effie froze, keeping her arms glued to her sides as the warmth and the pressure and the smell of perfume wrapped her up.

"Your dad has his own secrets, sweetie." June swallowed, like she was trying not to cry, then she pulled away. "Things that make this even harder for him. Things that make everything harder for him."

Effie snorted and scuffed at the ground with her foot. "Dad said it was his dream," she muttered, "to live in the bush, away from everything. Just him and Mum and his stupid vegetable garden."

"You don't like it here?"

Effie shrugged. "Mum said the world was changing too much, with phones and TV and the internet, and all that other modern crap. Mum wanted to live like Heidi, you know, the weird girl who liked goats."

June smiled. "I loved that story."

"It's a stupid story. No kid can be that good all the time."

"True."

"And I like TV." Effie picked at her sleeves. "Do you think Dad's a good man?"

"Yes." June stepped closer and held Effie's shoulders, their faces level. "Yes. Your dad is a good man, and don't you believe anyone who says otherwise."

Effie looked at her, at her wrinkled eyes and her white hair, and wanted to believe her. But Lewis was her best friend—her only friend—and Effie couldn't un-remember what he'd told her.

She couldn't forget the otherwise thing that Lewis had said.

2025

EFFIE ROLLED OVER in the single bed and checked her phone. It was almost 6 a.m. She'd slept right through. There was just one new message from Blair.

Be safe. Rimu sends kisses. x

Effie lay on her back and stared up at the ceiling, not sure what she was meant to be feeling. If Lewis was right, she was about to meet a member of her family that she hadn't known existed until a few days ago. What feeling was meant to go with that? Excitement? Fear? Should she have brought her a gift?

Shit. Effie rubbed at her face. She wasn't good with children.

She got up, showered and dressed, and headed through to the kitchen to find June waiting for her with a coffee.

"Morning, sunshine." June smiled. "I thought I heard the shower."

"You're up early," said Effie, taking the warm mug.

"Plenty of time to sleep when we're dead."

Effie breathed the coffee in before taking a sip. "What time does the clinic open?"

"Nine." June nodded toward the selection of fresh bread, Marmite and fruit on the table. "But we'll head over as soon as we've eaten."

Effie frowned. "Does Lewis know we're coming in early?"

June sliced into the loaf. "He doesn't want the locals seeing you just yet. Most folks think you're still missing." She raised an eyebrow. "Or dead."

After a quick breakfast, they drove June's ute the five hundred meters to the clinic—to avoid prying eyes. Effie smiled as June grunted the vehicle into third, the seventy-something-year-old woman with tasseled floral sofas and a Ford Ranger with bull bars and a snorkel.

As they turned the corner, the blue roof of the small community health center came into view, and two decades unraveled in an instant. Effie gripped the door handle, her body shaken with the memory.

"You okay?" asked June.

"Yeah." Effie let out a breath. "I'm just glad Anya has you and Lewis."

June turned off the engine. "You know, we're not even sure it's her real name."

Effie frowned. "How come?"

"Lewis will explain."

They walked across the gravel carpark toward the back door. Effie slipped her hands into her pockets, then took them out again. She'd never been so aware of her hands, of her arms, just hanging there with nothing to do.

Before they reached the door, it swung open with a clang, and Lewis filled the frame. He waited, one hand on the door, his eyes fixed on Effie. The gravel crunched beneath her feet, matching the thud in her chest, as she returned his gaze. His clothes were creased, likely from pulling a back-to-back shift, and his hair was shaggy. His hair was brown the last time she'd seen him, a boy of eighteen, but it had grayed at the sides. Despite the exhaustion and stress that hung from him, it still caught her off guard—the pull she felt toward him, as though the last seventeen years had never happened.

Her Lewis.

His face had thinned out, making his cheekbones more pronounced, and he had a short beard—stubble, really. But his eyes, a deep black-brown, were the same. He managed a soft grin as his gaze roved over her.

"You're here?" he said, as if he hadn't been the one to book her ticket.

"Yes." Effie forced an awkward smile. "I'm here."

For a moment, they stood a meter apart, neither of them saying anything. Then Lewis stepped forward and pulled her into a hug. He'd always been lean, but there was an unfamiliar strength to him now. He held on to her so tightly that Effie found it hard to breathe, but she didn't say anything. She would have struggled to breathe even if he hadn't touched her.

"Thank you," he said, pulling away. "I really . . ." He ran his hands through his disheveled hair.

Effie, her chest threatening to burst open, was unable to look at him. Unable to look away. Then June cleared her throat.

"Right, you two." She stepped past them, and Effie finally took a breath. "As fun as this is, we're on a time frame. So let's save the emotional reunion for later."

Lewis moved aside and they walked into the cool building, with the same pale yellow walls and shiny floors, and Effie tried not to think about the last time she'd been there.

"A time frame?" she asked.

"How about we all take a seat?" June moved over to the small waiting room, just five plastic chairs. "This might be worth sitting for."

"Where's the kid?" Effie glanced around the room.

"She's sleeping," said Lewis, his voice changed. "We set up a bed for her in the empty consultation room. With only one nurse practitioner, it's rarely used."

"One nurse?"

"Yeah," he said. "Kyle, he's great. We also get a visiting GP a couple of times a week. She was here yesterday."

"Did she do an examination of the kid?"

"Yes." Lewis wouldn't meet Effie's eye, as though looking at her made him uncomfortable. Like there was something he wasn't telling her. "She said that Anya was still suffering from mild dehydration, and also diarrhea. She has a number of minor cuts and bruises. Again, nothing serious, probably just from the bush. Although there is one reasonably bad scar down her right thigh. Old. Most likely a burn. Fire perhaps, or a hot object."

Lewis hesitated, his eyes flicking even farther away.

"What?" asked Effie.

"We found marks on the girl's ankles," said June.

"Ligature marks?" Effie asked, even though she didn't need to. She knew, every part of her knew.

"Yes," said June. "It looks like the girl was tied up, at least for periods."

"Has she spoken again?"

"No, not since she told me her name."

"Which might not be real?"

He sighed. "Apparently, between 2015 and 2018, there were only forty-six babies named Anya in the entire country. But not one of them was in the West Coast."

"Not one that was registered anyway," said Effie. She rubbed her forehead. "And what about missing children, runaways, kids that might have—"

"Nothing." Lewis shook his head, his eyes dark and his skin pale, the kind of grayish tinge that Blair got after a week on night shift. "I spent Saturday canvassing the village. June helped."

"Not exactly a big job," said June, "with a total of ninety-two residents and only the kid from the shop having a clue what we were talking about."

"And tourists?"

"I visited the motel and the backpackers," said Lewis. "Then I drove around the freedom camping spots. But nothing."

"Just rubbish and human filth." June tutted. "It's disgusting what these young backpackers think they . . ."

Lewis glanced up and June stopped.

"And the locals?" asked Effie.

"They've agreed to keep it quiet," said Lewis. "The locals here tend to keep things private—Koraha's business being Koraha's business."

"There's already been a heap of stuff dropped off." June nodded toward the reception desk. "Clothes, toys, books, food. People are like that here. Good, solid folks."

"So you found the girl on Friday afternoon, and it's now Wednesday."

"Yes." Lewis nodded once. "Monday was a public holiday, Labor Day, so we couldn't get the GP in until yesterday."

"Things don't exactly move fast around here," said June. "Next police station is an hour and a half away, in Franz. Just another sole-charge officer there, too. Greymouth and Christchurch are the nearest cities for anything important."

"What about child welfare services?" asked Effie.

June and Lewis glanced at each other.

"That's the time frame issue," said Lewis.

"Are they sending someone down?"

"Not exactly." Lewis chewed on his lip. "I haven't contacted Oranga Tamariki yet."

"I don't understand." Effie looked from Lewis to June.

"I'm not obligated to inform them"—Lewis shifted in his chair—"if I can place the child with a family member."

"With you," said June.

"What?" Effie stood and took a step back. "You can't be serious.

I don't even know her." She pressed her palms to her forehead. "She's never even met me."

"Well, let's just ship her off to the authorities, then." June raised an eyebrow. "From the West Coast bush to Christchurch. You're right. She'll fit right in."

"June, that's not what I—"

Lewis held his hands out, more diplomatic than Effie remembered. "I think we should all take a moment."

"We don't even know if we're actually related."

"Please." June rolled her eyes.

"And wouldn't this O-Otanga something—"

"Oranga Tamariki," offered Lewis.

"Wouldn't they want proof of a family relationship?"

"Ha." June laughed.

"I'm just asking you to think about it," said Lewis. "Please, Effie."

"Just think quickly," added June.

"This is insane." Effie's thoughts spun.

There was a soft thud, then another, and she turned around.

Effie gasped.

The kid was there. Her arms hung at her sides, red hair falling to her waist, and she stared at them. *Shit.* Her feet were bare and she was wearing a *Frozen* nightdress that came halfway down her shins. A small green pendant hung around her neck, the jade stone clear against the light blue cotton, and she had a silver scalpel clasped in one hand.

"Didn't you clear out the consultation room?" Effie hissed.

"Of course I did," whispered Lewis. "She must have taken it from Kyle's room."

Shit. Effie blinked twice. The kid looked just like her.

Lewis took a step forward, his movements slow and unthreatening, but it was too late. The girl lunged forward, a blur of limbs and matted hair, and threw herself at Effie. She collided with Effie like a bullet, her scrawny frame more bone than flesh. Effie reacted on instinct, ready to protect herself, to pull the child into her and hold her tight.

But Effie stopped. Stunned.

The child was hugging her. The girl's thin arms were wrapped around her body, clinging to her, and she was crying.

"Please," she whispered.

Effie lowered her head so she could hear.

"Please," she whispered again. "These people are bad. We can't trust them."

DECEMBER 2001

EFFIE SCRIBBLED ON a piece of paper as June and Tia played cards at the table.

June had brought three packs with her, and Tia played Uno about fifty times a day. There was some wild card that seemed to let you do whatever you wanted. And it was obvious that June was letting her sister win. Which, Effie reckoned, made the point of playing pretty stupid.

"You can't do that." Tia giggled. "It has to be green. Not blue!"

"Silly me. What about this?"

"No." Tia snorted. "That's red."

"I don't think I have any green," said June, putting on a ridiculous fake frown.

Tia reached over the table and peeked at June's cards. "You do," she squealed. "You do. Look." She pulled at June's cards. "It's hiding."

Effie rolled her eyes. They should have been out fishing or foraging for berries, not playing card games. They hadn't had eel or trout in weeks. June was rubbish at bush stuff. Useless as, Dad would say. But then, Dad was gone, so he was useless as too.

June wouldn't let Effie go spin fishing by herself, or even set up the net—she didn't want a kid whacking a fish's brains and insides out. But it wasn't exactly hard; Effie had watched her mum and dad do it hundreds of times. Dad took Effie fishing all the time—even let her do the gutting—and Effie always helped Mum with the smoker. Smoked trout was the best. Much better than June's hard bread and lentils. June was obsessed with lentils.

"Do you want to join in?" asked June.

"Nah. I'm good," Effie mumbled.

June had nearly choked on a mouthful of lentil slop when Effie suggested hunting, the conversation over before it had even started.

June had been there for about four weeks and she'd almost killed them twice. She'd tried to feed them tutu, thinking it was asparagus or supplejack or something. She'd boiled it up and chucked it in with the vegetables from the garden. Just a couple of bites and that would have been all of them dead. Gone. Dad said that just one tutu shoot had once killed two circus elephants.

Two.

Then, the other day, June had taken all of them for a walk to get some fresh air and exercise. Which was mental. They lived in the bush—fresh air was literally everywhere. Effie hadn't been paying attention to the markers—she'd been too grumpy—and they'd got lost. The dense bush had become tricky and unrecognizable, and they hadn't found their way back until sunset, starving, thirsty and covered in sandfly bites. Aiden had itched until he bled. He was still covered in angry red bumps.

Effie tiptoed over to the sleeping nook. She pulled back the curtain and peered in. Aiden was spread out on his mattress with his arms above his head, and Four was sleeping next to him. June was good with baby stuff though. She was good with Four.

"Right, you two." June stood up. "Let's see how our feast is coming along."

"Yay." Tia bounced up. "Then presents!"

"After lunch." June smiled.

The smells in the hut were incredible, so good that it was making Effie's stomach hurt. It was Christmas Day, Mum's favorite day, and June had been cooking since the morning. Effie had helped her bring in the last deer leg from the outside meat safe, the remains of Dad's final spring kill. Effie had chopped and trimmed the meat for a stew. She'd held the foot between her legs, just like Dad did, and tried to remember everything he'd taught her. Large chunks first, then trim. June had watched in silence, none of her mutterings or gasps, then she'd placed a hand on Effie's shoulder.

"Your mum would be proud."

It was the best thing that had happened in a month.

Two hours later, after Four had been fed and changed and put back down—babies slept a crazy amount—the rest of them sat around the table. They'd set out two wooden stools and a thin bench. In the center was a pot of venison stew, a large bowl of rice, and a plate of steamed chard and broad beans from the garden. June had also made them each a small flower crown; she was better with flowers than fish. Mum would have loved all of it.

"Right," said June, holding her hands out. "Shall we say grace?"

Tia frowned, already reaching across the table for the rice, then slunk back. "What's grace?"

"It's where we thank God for our meal."

"But"—Tia's frown deepened—"you made it. Why would we thank him?"

"It's just a nice way of—"

"Dad says God's not real," said Tia. "But Mum growls at him when he says that. She says it's disgraceful to God people."

"Disrespectful," offered Effie.

"Well," said June, "people can believe in different things."

"What do you believe in?" asked Tia.

Effie turned to look at June. Mum and Dad didn't talk about God stuff. It made Dad angry.

"Well . . ." June paused, thinking. "I'm not sure I know exactly."

"Then why were you going to thank him?"

She laughed. "How about we just thank the bush instead?"

"Thank you bush for beans and stew," Tia said. Then she reached for the spoon and started serving herself.

Effie smiled. She couldn't help it. Maybe it was Christmas, or the meat, or the fact that June had a tin of peaches and creamed rice for dessert. But she felt a tiny bit less dark. The feeling continued through lunch—well, more like dinner by the time the stew had finally cooked—and when they sat down for presents, it was more than just her stomach that felt warm and full.

June had made Effie and Tia a small journal each, using scraps of paper sewn together with string. She'd decorated the covers with pressed ferns. She'd also sewn them each a summer dress from a floral sheet she'd found in Mum's room. As Tia twirled in her new dress, and Aiden spun and giggled with her, Effie slipped a small flat package across the table toward June. Inside, wrapped up in a dried leaf, was a pair of Mum's earrings—two silver ramarama leaves.

"Don't open it now," said Effie, without looking at her.

Mum said ramarama were beautiful but hardy shrubs, just like her kids. But Mum was gone, and her siblings needed June now.

"Thank you." June pressed the small gift to her chest. Then she reached into her pocket. "I've got one last thing for you and Tia. But perhaps you might keep them for now, until your sister's a little older."

June placed a small box in the center of the table, the cardboard so worn that it had lost its shape.

"One belonged to your mother, and the other . . ." June paused, her eyes stuck on the little box. "The other used to belong to your grandmother."

"The one who died?"

"Yes." June blinked and cleared her throat. "Yes, baby girl."

"Can I open it?"

June nodded and Effie picked it up. She undid the single piece of ribbon and removed the lid. Her heart pumped as she lifted out the two pounamu stones, both on strings of silver. Effie held the jade swirls in her palm. The stones were perfect, no darks spots or flaws, and their color was as green and vibrant as the trees.

"Kahurangi greenstone," Effie whispered, hearing her dad's words. "It means 'precious treasure.'" She looked up. "The West Coast is the only place in the world that you can find it."

"Yes." June reached over and moved the two pendants. "And when you put the two swirls together like this, they form a heart."

Effie stared at the green heart, her own heart still pounding, like something in the stone was calling to her.

"Thank you," she said, the words little more than a whisper.

June squeezed Effie's wrist. "They belong to you."

That night, Effie helped June bathe the boys in the big bucket on the floor. Aiden took up the whole thing; just his nose and forehead popped out of the top when he sat down. But Four was like a little fish in a pond, a chubby white blob, apart from the purple birthmark on his neck. It was strange how tiny and huge a four-week-old human could be. He was so small in his cot and in the bath, but when he screamed and demanded to be held, the sound filled the whole hut.

Tia wiped her arms and face with a cloth, still in her dress and still chatting. Effie and Tia had been excused from baths that night, it being Christmas. And girls, Effie was utterly certain, smelled a lot less. They also hadn't made a trip to the river that day, so the water was running low. Effie hated sloshing buckets up from the river; it rubbed her hands raw and wet her clothes. Hopefully it would rain overnight and the roof drums would fill up again. It had been odd, a week of no rain. It always rained in the bush.

As soon as the three young ones were in bed, Effie helped with the last few dishes, then she hurried into her parents' room. She'd started going in there now to feel close to Mum, to lie on the bed and tell her all sorts of things. June didn't mind, as long as Effie didn't make a mess of things and didn't get dirt on the sheets. June didn't go to bed till dark, so Effie could also use the room for reading and drawing in her notebook.

Effie crouched down and lay on the floor, then she squeezed under the bed. She knew exactly where she was going to keep Mum's necklaces—a secret spot that only she and Tia knew about now. Right at the back, she dug her fingers under the loose floorboard and lifted it up. Then she placed the small box inside.

For the next hour or so, Effie stretched out on the bed and read and talked to Mum, telling her about Christmas, which wasn't actually the worst. And about how she'd trimmed the deer leg. Which June hadn't even gagged at. Eventually, when Effie slipped from the bed, it was later than she'd realized, and the glow from the kerosene lamp was the only light in the dark. She inched the door open, clutching the lamp in one hand, and peered into the living area, but there was no sign of June. Effie frowned as she stepped into the room, empty apart from Four asleep in his cot. The curtained nook was quiet and still.

"June?" Effie whispered.

A pressure built in her chest as she crept over to the front door and stepped outside.

"June," she whispered again.

She walked across the deck and held the lamp up against the night, the sky so dark it was hard to imagine the bush was even there. She moved around the side of the hut, stepping over a collection of discarded toys and gardening tools.

"June," she called, though not loud enough to anger the night things. The first prickles of fear tingled her skin. Unknown things lived in the dark.

"June?" she said, barely a whisper. "Are you there?"

Effie continued around to the vegetable garden. The large cages—set over the chard to keep out possums—loomed like dark figures. They were horrid things, built from driftwood and sheets of old wire that had torn the skin from her fingers more than once. As she moved closer, the light from her lantern spilled over the broad beans, and a pair of white eyes glared at her. Effie gasped and stumbled back as the creature scurried off through the leafy rows.

Stupid ugly possum.

Effie swore at herself, then kicked the dirt. She went to turn back—June was probably just peeing—when she heard it.

A cry.

A soft, sad cry, diluted by the hugeness of the sky and the trees.

Holding out the lamp, Effie continued around the back of the hut. As she turned the final corner, she saw a dome of light. And there, crouched on the ground with her back to Effie, was June. A liquid cold trickled down Effie's back, a not-right feeling, and she quickly turned her lamp off. There was something about the moment, something wrong, something Effie wasn't meant to be seeing. As soon as Effie's flame went out, June turned her head toward her, just like the possum. Her eyes were wide and shocked, and her face was pale. With her long silver hair and wild eyes, she looked like a witch.

Effie didn't move. She froze to the spot, barely breathing, and willed the night to hide her away. Eventually, June turned back to a metal box on the ground. Effie watched as she sifted through the contents. After a moment, June held up a single piece of paper and ran her fingers across it, reading something, then she folded it carefully and tucked it into her pocket. After placing the other items back, June locked the box. Then, using a long stick, she pushed it as far under the hut as she could.

Effie closed her eyes, like she did when she was small, to try to make herself invisible. She prayed that June would walk the other way around the hut.

Please. Please.

The haunting call of a morepork echoed through the bush—*quork-quork quork-quork*—and when she opened her eyes again, June and the dome of light had gone.

Without a match to light it, Effie left the lamp and inched along the side of the hut to where June had been. She hugged the wall as she moved through the dark, using her feet and hands to guide her. She crouched down on all fours, feeling along the ground under the hut with her fingers.

She lay flat, squeezing her body into the cramped space, and shuffled forward on her thighs and forearms, the soil gathering under her fingernails. The dirt and a thousand unseen bugs itched at her skin, but she wriggled farther in. Her muscles burned as she stretched her arm out, straining and searching with her fingers, the weight of the hut making it hard to fill her lungs. She scrambled forward, the gap shrinking, and something sharp dug into her stomach. Effie winced, coughing in dust and cobwebs.

Yuck.

Then she felt it. The side of the box. Her fingers grazed the hard surface, but she couldn't quite grip it. She was jammed, sprawled in cobwebs and possum shit, and the smallness of the space was making her feel sick.

Stupid box.

Effie started to wriggle backward when her fingers grazed over something else. Something smooth. Grunting, Effie pinched the piece of paper between her fingers and slithered out from beneath the hut. She dusted herself off and slipped it down the back of her shorts, then skulked around the dark deck. Once she was sure that June had gone to her bedroom, Effie crept in the front door and scurried across the room to the nook.

Neither Tia or Aiden stirred as Effie lit a candle and held the black-and-white photo to the light. She didn't know who she was looking at. Two children, a boy and a girl, sat next to each other on a stone step. Effie frowned. The boy in the photograph looked older than the girl, Effie's age maybe, and the girl was about Tia's size. The boy was laughing and the girl was holding his face. She was kissing his cheek.

Effie turned the photo over and whispered out the words that were written on the back.

"To the boy who tried to save my life."

Her stomach fluttered, and she thought suddenly of Lewis.

2025

THIS WAS MAD. Totally and utterly mad.

Effie and the girl sat in the back seat of the ute, both silent, as June drove. The girl, still in the *Frozen* nightdress, hadn't spoken to her again. If anything, she seemed more withdrawn, as though she regretted speaking to Effie at all.

Christ. Effie closed her eyes and bit into her cheeks. *Jesus effing Christ.* She had a kid now—a living breathing human that she was apparently responsible for. And what the hell she was meant to do with it—with *her*—she had no idea. *Bloody Lewis.* Effie rubbed at her forehead, trying to alleviate the tension that had settled behind her eyes.

Eventually, Effie looked over at the kid. Anya was hunched forward, her legs tucked to her torso, tugging at the hem of her nightdress, trying to stretch it down like it was the most important thing in the world. The pounamu pendant tapped against the girl's chest as she rocked. And, as the ute turned a corner, Effie touched a hand to her own neck, to the other half of the greenstone heart.

"Where did you get that necklace?" she asked.

The girl turned and glared at her before pressing a finger to her lips. "Shh," she hissed. "No talking."

Effie forced a polite smile. "It's not nice to talk to people like that."

"Then stop talking to me."

Effie flinched. "You can't just tell—"

"Quiet," she whispered. "You're breaking the rules."

"What rules?"

The child's frown deepened and her green eyes narrowed. "You're not very clever, are you?"

Effie glanced up at the rearview mirror, catching the hint of a smile on June's face.

"Mum lied about you," Anya said. Then she turned back to the window.

"What did you just say?" Effie grabbed the girl's arm. "Who's your mum? What did she lie about?"

The kid stared at Effie's hand, and Effie jerked it back.

"Sorry. I shouldn't have touched you. I just . . . your mum . . . what's her name?"

Anya turned and started banging at the window, pounding her tiny fists into the glass. She pulled at the handle, scratching at it, and the door opened a fraction.

"Jesus." Effie lurched over and pulled it closed. "What are you doing?"

"If you keep talking to me, I'll jump out." Her voice was cold.

Effie gawked, speechless.

It was June who spoke then. "It's okay, kid. No more talking."

The girl sat on the floor in June's living room, rifling through the pile of clothes that the locals had dropped off. She'd refused breakfast initially, standing in the kitchen doorway shaking her head until June suggested she might like to eat by herself in the living room, where no one would talk to her.

The porridge bowl, licked clean, sat upturned on the floor next to her as she divided the clothes into two piles.

"She only picks out the dresses," said Effie.

June leaned on the doorway next to Effie, nursing a cup of tea in one hand.

"Strange," said June, taking a sip from her mug. "You'd think that pants would have been more practical in the bush."

Effie stared at the girl, not knowing what to do or say, her thoughts thick and heavy.

"I'm sorry," said June, "that you and Lewis didn't get a chance to talk properly. That can't have been easy after—"

"It's fine." Effie cleared her throat. "I'm good. I'm fine."

June grinned. "Well, that's a lie, dear."

"I'm not—"

June held her hands up. "No judgment here. Nothing wrong with a wee lie to get us through the tough stuff."

June nodded as Anya lifted up a dark blue dress.

"How is he?" said Effie eventually. "Lewis, I mean. How's he been?"

"You know what men are like. Never give much away."

"But . . ." Effie picked at her fingers. "He's happy? Settled?"

June's expression was hard to place.

"You'd have to ask his wife that, love."

Wife.

"Lewis is married?"

June's eyes remained focused on the girl. "Charlotte. A nice girl. A primary teacher from Christchurch. They met when Lewis was working there."

"Lewis lived in Christchurch?"

"Seventeen years is a long time, dear. Things change."

Effie swallowed the shake in her voice. "He doesn't wear a ring."

"It's complicated," June said. "And long distance is hard."

"She still lives in Christchurch?"

June nodded. "Koraha isn't for everyone."

"Why didn't Lewis stay in Christchurch?"

June turned and looked at her. "You'd have to ask Lewis that." She took another sip of her tea, then turned back to watch the girl. "Oh, I like that one. The green will go nicely with her hair."

Anya placed the dress on top of the pile, and a quiet settled in the air.

"I think I might go for a run," said Effie. "Fight off the jet lag. Would you mind . . ."

June squeezed Effie's arm. "Off you go. We'll be just grand." She nodded at the keys on the kitchen bench. "Take the ute and head up to Monro Beach. It's a nice path through the bush, and you'll have the place to yourself."

"Thanks."

"Take a couple of hours," said June. "I can call Lewis if I need anything. Then when you get back, we're going to have to face this thing head-on."

—

As the light splintered through the bush, Effie was a kid of seven years old again, encased in a sphere of green. In a world of matai and kahikatea trees. Huge ferns poured down from the skies, the dead fronds forming skirts around the thin trunks, the bark turned olive by a covering of moss and leaves.

Effie's feet pounded into the ground as she sped up, trying not to put a face to Charlotte's name, but her throat and lungs stung with the effort. *Lewis has a wife.* Effie kept pushing until her head throbbed and her breath exploded in jagged gasps, and she spat into the dirt. But she couldn't outrun it—the thought of Lewis, and the images of what the girl might have witnessed.

The track started to climb slightly, the fire building in Effie's calves. But she kept running, one foot in front of the other, her mind filled with Tia and the young ones as the path descended into a shallow gully. Tia was there, in her every breath.

What happened to you?

A threadlike stream trickled through the trees, following the path to the edge of the bush, then out into the vast swaths of sea.

Effie stopped when her feet reached the white sand, and held her arms out. There was nothing. Just air and water and sand. Empty enough that she could almost breathe. The gray ocean mirrored the overcast sky, and rocky stacks rose from the stirring waves. The water called to her, her heart drawn to the untamed beauty of the dark sea and the ashen sky.

Effie pulled off her shorts and T-shirt, swatting at the sandflies, then ran straight for the waves and the swirl of whitewash. The force of the cold water slammed against her chest like a brick, shrinking her lungs, and she gasped at the air, but the oxygen couldn't fill her body fast enough. The swell pulled at her legs and Effie dove in, her body returning to the womb. Submerged. Enclosed. She shut her eyes, the darkness absolute, and the waves calmed. Beneath the surface, her body moved with the gentle swell, suspended, and her pulse slowed. Not shivering. Not wet. Just boundless in her floating. Numb to the blade of fear that had slipped between her ribs.

It wasn't until she burst through the surface, craving air, that the fear rushed through her. A dread that came from a place far deeper than the ocean—that what the bush had left of her might not be enough. Effie could barely tolerate herself, let alone a child.

Effie stuck out her tongue, catching the specks of rain, then yelled at the sky. The breeze blew through her, chilling her skin, and she shouted again. Like if she screamed hard enough, all the hurt and darkness that she'd inherited from him might ebb away.

Finally, her throat prickling, she turned back to the beach. A tawaki penguin shuffled along the rocky headland, the distinctive yellow crest running above its eyes. Suddenly, the bird stopped, its white stomach puffed out, and stared at her.

"Hello," Effie whispered.

Then it turned and slipped beneath the water.

Once she'd wiped herself down with her T-shirt, slapping the sandflies from her skin, Effie dressed and ran back to the ute.

Her heart was still thumping when she walked up the drive and unlocked June's front door. She had barely stepped inside when twenty kilos of child hurled into her stomach, punching the air from her lungs.

"Lock the door," shouted June.

The child was breathing fast, the panic and anger in her too much for her small frame. Her forehead was shiny with sweat, and her long red hair stuck to her cheeks and neck. Anya pushed at Effie with both hands and slapped at her chest, the door handle stabbing into Effie's back. Grimacing, Effie tried to focus on the girl, to melt the world away until it was just the two of them. Just a scared adult and a scared kid.

"Anya," said Effie, her voice calm. "You're okay. You're safe."

The girl pulled at Effie's T-shirt, not hearing her, not really there at all.

"You're safe here."

Effie wrapped her arms around the child and held her still until only her head continued to move, shaking from side to side.

"You're safe," Effie said again. "Take a breath. Just breathe."

Effie glanced up, catching a glimpse of June and Lewis in the hall. Lewis took a step forward, but Effie shook her head.

These people are bad. We can't trust them.

Holding Anya, Effie lowered them both to the floor. The child's body had drained of fight, her limbs left defeated and motionless.

Effie rested her chin on Anya's head and pulled her in, and gradually Anya's eyelids fluttered shut. The poor kid was exhausted.

Without moving, Effie looked up at June. "What happened?" she mouthed.

"I don't know." June shook her head.

Effie frowned. "Something must have upset her."

June let out a breath. "Everything was fine. She was sitting in the living room doing a jigsaw. It was incredible, she picked up this five-hundred-piece bird one, and she just started doing it. Then . . ." She hesitated, her eyes widening. "That's when I turned the TV on and . . ." June touched her fingers to her mouth. "She just . . . she went berserk."

Effie looked down at the girl. "What was it?"

"Just the news," said Lewis.

JANUARY 2002

IT WAS REAL hot. The type of hot that peeled the skin from the tip of Effie's nose and left wet patches under her arms. June said they should wear hats, that the sun was a nasty bugger, but Effie never remembered.

She sat on the deck peeling beetroot, the juice staining her fingers purple. The knife snagged on a lumpy bit and slipped from her hands, landing on the deck with a clunk. She bent forward to grab it, and when she looked up, her dad was there, stepping out from the bush. He was smaller than she remembered.

Less giant.

Effie worked the knife around the beetroot skin. Not moving. She pressed her feet into the wood, anchoring herself to the earth like a pāua. Her heart and chest thumped, ready to erupt, but she wasn't about to run and flail at him like some kid. Dad had been a right shit walking out on them, and stillness was the only way she could think to punish him.

She threw the peel on the ground. She'd be like a stone. She wouldn't move or feel anything, not till her dad proved that he was real.

He walked across the grass to the hut, but he didn't call Effie's name or raise his arm. Dad knew he'd done bad. He looked at her, both of them staring, the way Mum said was rude. Too long. Too forceful. *Christ, Effie, you'll scare the locals doing that.* And as her dad got closer, Effie wanted to punch him in the stomach. His red hair was a mess, and one of his eyes was black and shiny. A black purple. Not too different from a beetroot.

Dad set his rucksack on the ground and sat next to Effie. Then he pulled a pocketknife from his bag, picked up a beetroot and started peeling. There was no way they'd be eating it; his hands were filthy. One hand was burned too. The skin was red, and his thumb was covered with gross blisters.

They sat like that for a bit, silent as their fingers turned purple. It made Dad's blisters look worse, like angry taniwha skin. Eventually, to stop her head from bursting, Effie spoke. Not the big stuff though. Just words to fill the quiet.

"June says you're only twenty-seven."

"Yep."

"She says that's pretty young to be my dad." Effie scuffed the deck with her feet. "Like a kid having a kid."

Dad smiled at that, his hard face cracking a bit.

"But," Effie shrugged, "I think you look old."

"I feel old."

She pushed her cup of water toward him, and something quietened in her stomach as he took a sip.

"June taught me about decimals," said Effie.

"Maths?"

She nodded. "And how to multiply fractions. June makes us do school stuff every day."

"Even Saturdays?"

"Yep." A smile escaped her. "Tia hates it."

The warm expression leaked onto Dad's face. Then he lifted his arm, and Effie moved into him. He was dirty, and his clothes smelled like old water. But she didn't pull back.

"You've grown," he said.

"I turned nine three days ago."

Dad's arm tightened around her, and his eyes did a weird blinking thing. "Effie, I'm so sorry."

She shrugged. "You're back now."

Then she leaned in. Dad wasn't much good at sorries, at all the mushy stuff. The Mum stuff. But Effie reckoned it wasn't his worst.

Throughout dinner—trout, finally—no one spoke.

Except Tia. Tia didn't know how not to speak.

No one mentioned the state of Dad—the skin melted off his hand and the light gone from behind his eyes.

June looked proper mad though.

Effie's neck tingled as the minutes crawled past, like sandfly bites wanting to be scratched. As Tia chatted, the storm bubbled in June, her face getting darker. Dad hunched over his fish, not looking up. Effie didn't blame him—June looked scary as.

All the way through dinner, Dad's and June's eyes never met. Then June declared it a no-bath night. She and Effie got the young ones ready for bed, then June read stories in the sleeping nook before kissing them all good night. Dad didn't touch Four even once. After tucking Aiden in, Effie hurried off to the bedroom, forgetting to brush her teeth, and closed the door. Then she sat on the floor, running her tongue over her furry teeth, and waited with one ear to the door.

"Five days," said June in a shouted whisper. "Five days, you said. It's been over a month. A month since you walked out on your kids. I didn't know if you were coming back. I wasn't sure if . . ."

June's voice trailed off and the front door slammed.

After a few minutes of silence, Effie eased the bedroom door open and slipped out. She crawled over to the window and peered through the glass, the summer evening still light. As she spotted them, her heart beat against her ribs and she had to stuff her fingers into her mouth to stop from yelling out.

Dad lunged forward and grabbed June's arm. He tugged at her, dragging her away, and June stumbled behind him. She swatted at him with her free hand. A fly swatting a mountain.

Oh god. Oh god.

Effie stared at the scene, at the fear etched into June's face and the man wearing Dad's clothes—the man who'd put Mum in the ground.

"Stop," June yelled. "Stop."

Panic flooded Effie's brain and she slid to the floor. The dad outside wasn't hers. He'd come back different. Effie pushed a palm into her chest, trying to slow the pounding. Then a sharp noise split the air, and she turned and pulled herself back up to the window. The air ripped again. The crack of splintering wood, followed by the screech of June's voice.

"Stop!"

Effie pressed her face to the glass. But June was alone. Unhurt. Dad stood a few meters away, punching one of the vegetable cages. He hit it so hard that the frame cracked and a piece of wood flew across the grass. He kept punching and kicking at it until the heavy wooden frame lay in sticks on the ground. Even from the window, Effie could see the blood dripping down his knuckles. When the final piece fell, Dad collapsed to his knees, and a noise like nothing she'd ever heard burst from him. It scared Effie more than the smashed wood.

June walked over and knelt next to him. She put an arm around his shoulders, and Dad, Effie's mountain, buried his face into June's body and wept.

Without making a sound, Effie inched the door open, just enough to let the sounds and the whispers of the bush leak in. The song of a bellbird carried through the air as Dad lifted his head and stared at June. His voice, small and broken, caught in the breeze.

"I can't find her."

Effie frowned. Dad was confused. Of course he knew. It was Dad who'd put Mum in the dirt. He knew exactly where she was.

"I'm so sorry." He lowered his head again. "I've lost her."

Then June started to cry too.

Effie wanted to run out, to sprint across the grass and grab Dad's hand. She wanted to take him into the bush, to the mound of earth with Mum sleeping underneath.

Look, look. She's here. Mum's here.

But Effie didn't move.

2025

EFFIE STOOD IN the doorway and watched the child sleep.

It hurt to watch her, like looking back in time.

Anya had pulled the covers from the single bed and arranged them on the floor. She was coiled up in the corner with a wall of pillows around her, safe in her alcove. Next to the bedding, the child had set out two pots of herbs taken from June's kitchen. *Mint.* It was a smell that lived inside Effie, the cool fresh scent blended with memories of Mum and the Before years.

"Come on." June motioned to Effie. "Let's have some tea."

Effie followed her through to the living room, where Lewis was waiting, and she sat in the chair farthest from him. If she got too close, she couldn't think.

"She's still sleeping?" he asked.

"Yeah." Effie gave a half smile. "She's exhausted."

After the incident with the TV, Effie had carried Anya through to her bed. But when Effie had gone to check on her half an hour later, she'd been on the floor.

"Sorry," said Lewis, looking at June. "About the TV."

He nodded at the monitor, which lay on the carpet with a cracked screen. The offending plant pot, also smashed, had been tidied up and binned.

"I can get you another one."

"Don't be daft," said June. "I never really liked it anyway."

Effie dug her fingers into the chair. "What do you think happened to her?" She glanced at Lewis. "Out there."

He sighed. "We just don't know. No one's seen anything suspicious, and there's been nothing to—"

"No." Effie stopped him. "What do *you* think happened?"

"I don't—"

"Please." She didn't look away.

They stared at each other, neither conceding, and Lewis ran a hand through his hair. *No ring*. Then he lowered his arm, his eyes boring into her.

"There have been a couple of reports from climbers," he said, "out in Moeraki Valley."

Effie frowned. Moeraki Valley was north of the hut, over the Thomas Range and another ten kilometers through tough terrain. Very few people made it out that way, just the occasional keen climber or backcountry tramper.

"Apparently food and some bits of equipment have been going missing from Horseshoe Flat and Middle Head Hut."

"When?"

"The last couple of months," said Lewis. "Since the summer season opened up."

"So no one's out there over winter and spring?"

"It would be very unlikely." Lewis frowned. "The creeks get too flooded to cross."

He rubbed his face, his fingers catching on his lips, and Effie gripped the chair.

"Apparently," he continued, "there have been sightings of a man. Nothing up close. Nothing definite."

Lewis looked at her—seeing too much—and Effie's chest ached.

"One climber mentioned red hair," he said.

"Dad?" she whispered.

"It's just speculation," said Lewis.

"But you think he's still alive?" She glanced back toward the bedroom. "And that Anya . . . that she could be his?" She struggled to swallow. "That Dad could have—"

"No." Lewis shook his head. "I imagine Anya's dad is some tramper who stumbled across the hut over the years. A hunter heading into the backcountry, perhaps."

"But she's got Dad's red hair," said Effie, "and his eyes. My eyes."

"Tia could have passed on your dad's genes too."

"So you think Tia's her mum?"

"It would make sense," said Lewis. "But in all honesty, we can't be certain."

"Just certain enough to lie to Oranga Tamariki?"

"Come on, Effie. You know it was the right thing to do."

She didn't answer.

"Have you heard anything from Tia?" she asked.

Lewis shook his head. "Not since you left."

"And Four?"

He shook his head again. "I'm sorry, Effie. Since your dad last took you and the kids bush, no one's heard anything. No one outside of this room knows what happened that day."

Effie closed her eyes and she was right back there—to that day—and she was running at him. *Dad.* Effie hurled herself into his body, pulling at his arms and thumping at his torso, but it was too late. Dad's mind was already lost to that dark faraway place.

Run, please. Run.

Effie was always too late.

"No one else knows that you escaped," said Lewis. "That you left New Zealand."

"I need to go back," she said. "I need to know what happened to them."

Lewis leaned forward, closing the gap. Doing exactly what Effie knew he would. From the day that she met him on the beach, her five-year-old legs jelly as the sea tried to suck her backward, Lewis had been trying to save her.

"I can put in a call to Franz tomorrow," he said. "There's another sole-charge officer up there who can—"

"No," Effie interrupted. "I need to go alone."

"What?" Lewis looked at her. "You can't be serious."

"Isn't that why I'm here?" She held his gaze. "Cos I'm the only one who knows how to get there?"

"Yes. But *with* me." Lewis stood up. "So you can go there with me."

"No."

"No?" He moved toward her, both of them standing now, his face close enough to touch. "You do realize that I'm in charge of this investigation. That this is my case."

Effie took a breath. "But there isn't a case anymore."

His brows raised. "Excuse me?"

"This morning you had a missing girl." She forced herself to stand still, to quiet the swell in her stomach. "But she's not missing anymore, is she? She's with family." Heat pulsed through her chest. "She's with me."

Lewis gawked at her. "You've got to be kidding. God." He ran his hands through his hair. "You haven't changed. You're just as stubborn as—"

"You said it yourself." Effie put her arm out, stopping June from intervening. "So long as the girl's with family, there's nothing for Oranga Tamariki to—"

"She was covered in blood, Effie. Jesus. And she has marks on her ankles. There's no way that kid hasn't been—"

"But there's no proof. No proof of an actual crime." She swallowed. "Not yet."

"So take me with you. Let's find proof. Let me help you."

Lewis was close enough that she could feel the heat from him. Standing there, his gaze set on her, Effie was suddenly that five-year-old again—a scrawny redheaded girl being rescued from the waves by an eight-year-old boy.

"I can't," she said. "You know I can't."

"That's bullshit." Anger spiked Lewis's voice. "That's childish bullshit. This isn't some bush game, Effie. God knows what happened out there. I can't let you just march off without any—"

"I know how to take care of myself."

A fire rose in her, her body hurting in a way that it shouldn't.

You'd have to ask his wife.

"And I don't need your permission," she snapped.

He walked across the room, then turned back. "It's my job to go out there. It's not up to you this time, Effie. This is not your decision." Something flashed across his face—hurt, regret—then it vanished. "What you're doing is impeding an—"

"Then cuff me." Effie held her hands out. "Arrest me, or let me go alone."

The look that Lewis gave her cut her in two, and Effie bit into her tongue to stop herself from flinching, from reaching for him.

Lewis didn't say anything, which hurt more somehow. He simply walked out, closing the door behind him, and Effie watched through the window as he got into his ute. It took her a moment to realize that her arms were still hung there, suspended in front of her.

"Well now," said June, "the two of you handled that very well."

Effie turned, disorientated, as June collected plates and mugs from the coffee table.

"Do you think I'm wrong?" she asked.

"I think," replied June, balancing a tower of china, "that it's possible to be both wrong and right at the same time."

"I can't take him out there." Effie scratched at her wrists. "I've never taken anyone out there."

The hut was a special place just for them, Dad said. A secret.

"What I do know," said June, "is that boy cares for you very much."

Effie shook her head. "It's been seventeen years, June." She paused. "He doesn't even know me."

June just smiled. "If you say so, dear." Then she walked out.

Lewis's ute turned the corner and drove out of sight. When Effie turned back, June was standing in the doorway with a radio tucked under her arm.

"I'm off to bed," she said.

Effie frowned. "With the radio?"

"The TV I can live without. But not my morning dose of Corin and Ingrid."

"Do you think she'll be okay?" asked Effie. "The kid."

"One day at a time." June smiled. "That's all we can do."

Effie rolled over in bed and checked the time on her phone.

Five. Almost.

The blue hour. She turned to the window, the curtain left open, and stared out at the inky sky. Coming back had changed something in her. It had blotted and smudged her memories; things that she once thought to be true—to be unquestionable—had blurred. The smell of bush air and the warm salt breeze had made her memories harder to trust.

Effie unlocked her phone and swiped down to Blair's name, then pressed the phone to her ear.

"You're up early," answered Blair.

"Jet lag."

"Sure." A kettle whistled somewhere behind Blair. "Absolutely nothing to do with the kid."

Effie sat up. "Lewis thinks she's Tia's daughter."

Effie could almost hear Blair frowning, adding it up. "But the girl's dad . . . who would—"

"We don't know." Effie moved her tongue around her dry mouth. "It was only ever my family in the hut. But that might have changed."

"So a niece," said Blair.

"A niece." Effie swallowed. "Maybe."

She looked at the window, silent for a moment.

"How's Rimu?" she asked eventually.

"Good." Blair hesitated. "Good." Hiding something.

"But?"

The kettle clicked off. "Greg came over to visit him yesterday. He brought some of those dentist chew things."

Effie always forgot about the dog's teeth.

"And Greg?"

"He's okay. Sad in that quiet-man way."

The line went silent for a few seconds.

"It's just," began Blair, "I was thinking about you and Greg, and maybe now with . . ." She trailed off. "He's a good guy, Effie. Maybe it wouldn't be the worst thing for you to have some support."

"I'm fine."

Effie stared at the latch on the window. Her issues with commitment had never just been about Greg. Of course they hadn't. Her stomach tensed and swirled despite herself, despite how ridiculous and childish it was. She and Lewis had just been kids. It had been a lifetime ago.

"How's Anya?" asked Blair. Not pushing. Not prying.

Effie blinked Lewis's face from behind her eyes. "I should probably go check on her."

She threw back the covers, slipped on a pair of jeans and pulled on a jumper.

"Has she been sleeping?"

"Erratically," said Effie. "Odd hours. And she's made a bed on the floor." She stepped into the hall. "Anyway, I should go. She's not wild on people talking. I'll call you later."

"Love you."

Effie walked to Anya's door, slowly and quietly, not wanting to frighten her. As she inched the door open, she caught a flicker of movement in the corner of the room.

There was a faint tapping sound. *Tap, tap, tap.* But nothing else. Half of the room came into view, everything still in its place.

Effie pushed the door wide, and the light from the hall spilled across the carpet, a ribbon of white reaching from Effie to the bundle of covers. She turned to the source of the tapping, where the wooden rod at the bottom of the blind rapped against the wall. Effie stepped inside, slow and careful, and knelt by the girl's sleeping area. The bump of her beneath the duvet was impossibly small, a little living thing curled up into almost nothing.

Effie reached out, her heart racing as she touched her hand to the tiny mound of human. But her hand sunk to the floor.

The girl was gone.

FEBRUARY 2002

TWO PĪWAKAWAKA, THEIR tails spread out like fans, darted between the trees. The birds had been following them for twenty minutes, flitting from branch to branch.

Effie hunched low in the ferns like Dad, quiet and still, with the gun on the grass beside her.

"There," whispered Dad. "You can just make out her ears."

Effie stared through the hanging fronds, in the direction that he was pointing. There was no clearing or cut-out trail—the bush ate them up, their bodies gobbled by a vast magical greenness.

"There," he breathed again. "Can you see her?"

Dad had been back for two weeks, not long enough for her to fully trust him, but the harder-to-control parts of her—the bits that were made of Dad—wanted to impress him.

Effie peered into the silver beech leaves. Every bit of her hurt; her legs and arms and feet. There was a space between her shoulders that had started to throb, bruised from where the gun had been slung over her shoulder. They'd walked all day—Dad teaching Effie to navigate—trudging through thick bush for so long that her legs had gone from tired to sore to numb. Then back to sore again.

She squinted. "I see her," she squeaked. "I see her."

"Shh." Dad touched a finger to his lips. "You'll spook her."

The chamois looked up, turning her head in their direction. A brown band looped from either side of her nose, up and around the back of her horns.

"Right, Effie." Dad's breath was warm on her face. He smelled bad, like sweat and wet earth. "You've got this."

"But . . ." The chamois was so alive. The blood beat through its body, pulsing just like Effie's. "What if—"

"You'll be fine."

Dad lifted the gun, and Effie held it the way he'd taught her. Then she breathed. In and out. Not trapping the air in. Not letting it burst her open.

The small antelope was beautiful. Its summer coat was light, honey colored, and its curved black horns rose up like a crown.

"Now," Dad said.

"But—"

"Now."

Effie's lip trembled, and she was suddenly more scared of Dad than the animal or the loaded gun. Dad's voice had changed, just like that. Warm one moment, cold the next, like when the wind changed direction. Effie didn't want this Dad.

She focused on the animal. Dad would come back if she just shot it. She squeezed the trigger, forcing her eyes to stay open, and when the chamois dropped to the ground, Dad let out a proud yelp. Effie beamed as he hugged her, but there was a strange metallic taste in her mouth. She ran her tongue across the front of her teeth, licking away a thin coating of blood. She must have bitten through her lip without realizing it.

Dad's arms wrapped around her. "Well done." His smile took up his whole face. "Your first chamois."

"June won't be happy." She'd gone nuts when she found them practice-shooting behind the hut.

"Ha." Dad laughed then. A proper belly laugh. "No, she won't. But she'll eat bloody good this week. Don't think I can stomach any more lentils."

His face lightened. Effie had done that. And she could see, hiding behind his eyes, the Before Dad. The Dad before Mum died.

"Come on, little Rimu."

Rimu. Effie's throat got smaller. Or something in it got larger. Dad hadn't called her that in months.

Dad did the next bit himself, and Effie stood a few meters away, watching through her fingers. He boned the body out, keeping the cape and skin, and made a backpack out of the body. Effie felt queasy as he hauled the dead carcass onto his shoulders. From behind there was no Dad, just a lolling chamois head. He'd half-hacked its legs off too, and the stumps flopped about as he walked. It made Effie want to hurl onto the grass. Thankfully, Dad let her walk in front after a bit.

A couple of hours later, after multiple navigating fails by Effie, they made it to the unfamiliar hut. Dad had marked the secluded hut on the map with a black dot, and told Effie to lead the way. It was only three grid squares north from their hut—three squares and a trillion identical trees. Exhausted, they sat at the wooden bench and Dad made them dinner. It was strange, staying somewhere else in the bush. When Effie was Aiden's age, she'd thought that their hut was the only one in the world. But this hut was bigger than theirs. It had two bedrooms with bunks, as well as a living area. But it was grotty. Mum would've hated it.

Effie had needed to cover her mouth when they'd walked in, to stop from breathing in the stench of death. *Possum.* Dad had found it in one of the bedrooms and chucked it outside. The hut was filled with cobwebs and dead flies. Effie had wiped down the table with a scrap of cloth and found a brush to clear the floor a bit. She'd also found a charm bracelet when she was brushing under the sofa and slipped it onto her wrist. She didn't wear jewelry other than the pieces Lewis made for her, and her arm looked quite pretty.

"Where are we?" asked Effie.

"We're just at the end of the valley. The Thomas Range is on that side"—Dad nodded to the right—"and Cuttance is on the other. Moeraki is straight over that ridge there." He nodded north.

Effie groaned. "But we walked for *ages*." Learning to navigate was the worst. It all looked the same. Just green, green, green. "Sorry," she mumbled.

"You're doing great." Dad smiled. "Tracking's bloody hard, and that chamois didn't know where it was going. It wasn't just you taking us in circles." He winked. "But heading straight down the valley, without getting lost, probably would have taken about forty minutes." His smile widened. "Maybe more with all of them bloody pee stops."

Effie glared at him, then she turned away, hiding her smile. "You're a dope," she muttered.

She glanced around the hut, confused by it. The kitchen was way fancier than theirs, with big metal surfaces and taps and stuff, and there was expensive furniture, like a store-bought chair and a steel bed in one of the rooms. There was even a gate around the fire and matching cutlery in the drawers. But the place was yuck. Even with the possum gone, it still smelled of animal droppings and must.

"What's this hut called?"

"I don't actually know." Dad shrugged. "Don't reckon it has a name. Some rich guy owns it."

Effie grimaced. "Well, he's not very tidy."

Dad chuckled. "I doubt he's stepped foot in here in years. There are loads of private huts dotted around the country, buried away in the bush. Some just get forgotten about, I guess. Rich punters with too much money."

"How'd you find it?"

"Oh . . ." A shadow passed across his face. "Just some hunting trip a couple of years ago."

"Well, you could have cleaned up a bit. It's gross."

Dad grinned. "It's grand. Just a bit of dust." He tossed Effie a couple of carrots from his rucksack. "Bit of an airing and she'll come right."

Over the next hour, they chopped and ate and chatted, then headed to bed. Dad took the dead-possum room with two bunks, and Effie took the room with the bunks and the fancy bed in the corner. There was no chance she was sleeping with the possum ghost, and Dad snored like a deer in rut so she wasn't about to share. Dad had laughed at that, spitting out his coffee, and it made Effie laugh too.

She lay her sleeping bag out on the steel bed and turned on her head-torch. She'd never had a room to herself, or even a whole blanket, and the space felt endless without Tia and Aiden. No noise. No warmth. Effie picked up her sleeping bag and slipped into one of the bottom bunks. It was better being squished into the small space, easier to get comfy without all that extra room. Effie lay flat on her back, staring at the bunk above, but she didn't turn her head-torch off. The dark didn't scare her—it was no different from closing her eyes. But there was something odd about the hut. Effie turned her head, sending brightness into the faraway corners, then she snuggled into her sleeping bag and inched away from the wall, leaving the light on.

It was a moment before her pulse settled enough to focus. And then she saw it. Squinting, Effie reached up, her fingertips brushing the slats of wood in the base of the bunk above her. Carved into the wood was a name—sort of strange and flowery. Probably for a girl. Effie whispered it out loud as she touched the letters. Then her eyes caught on a fleck of white, where a piece of paper was poking out, jammed between the mattress and the slats. Sitting up, she pulled the paper free and opened it. As she read, the words slipped under her skin.

He has me shut up. Help me.

It was signed off with a single letter.

D.

Effie shuddered, her body both sweaty and cold, and shoved the note back between the slats. Then, tumbling from her sleeping bag, she hurried from the room and into her dad's bunk.

"Effie? Are you okay?" Tiredness made his words long and heavy.

"I don't like it here," she whispered.

He curled his arms around her, constricting the punch of her heart. "Sleep, little one."

Effie felt for the bracelet on her wrist and twirled one of the charms in her fingers—the one shaped like the letter *D*. Over and over. Until at some point she fell asleep, and the silver *D* fell limp on the mattress.

It wasn't until the next morning, when the chamois was strapped to Dad's back and they'd walked for long enough that the blisters on Effie's heels throbbed, that she noticed the bracelet was gone, probably slipped off when they were tidying up. Effie was about to ask Dad about it, and the note too, when he turned and looked at her. His face was all serious, and the expression emptied her mind out.

Don't leave again. Please don't leave.

"I made a deal with June," he said.

She nodded. Maybe she nodded. None of her was working right.

"June's agreed to stay on another month with us. To help with the baby."

Us. Us was good.

"Under one condition," he said. Then he smiled. "Afterward, I'm to take you kids to live in Koraha for six weeks."

Six weeks.

"With you?"

"With me. At June's house."

Warmth flushed through Effie's face. "And I'll see Lewis?"

Dad laughed. "Yes. You'll see Lewis."

Effie adjusted the gun on her back and marched on.

Six whole weeks.

By the time she made it to bed, her head was spinning with thoughts of town and ice cream and Lewis, leaving no space for anything else.

2025

EFFIE SPED INTO Lewis's driveway and jumped from the ute without bothering to take the keys from the ignition. She pounded on the door, picturing Anya hurt somewhere, bleeding and crying, and she started to shake.

"Jesus, Effie."

The door opened and Lewis stood there, bare-chested, in a pair of tartan pajama pants. "It's not even six."

Then he paused, seeing her. Not the police officer. Not the stubborn woman he'd argued with the evening before. Just the little bush girl shaking on his front step.

"Jesus," he said again, softer.

Then he opened his arms and she walked into them, pressing her head against his bare chest. For a moment, she considered never moving again, but it was Lewis who pulled away, Lewis who belonged to someone else now.

"What happened?"

Effie took a step back, righting herself. "She's gone. I've driven twice around the village, but she's gone."

"When did—"

"Half an hour ago. I went into her room to check on her but she wasn't there."

Lewis stepped aside. "Come in."

"No." Effie shook her head. "We need to go now. We need to find her."

Lewis reached out, his fingers brushing her shoulder. "Let me send a WhatsApp message to the village, get the locals looking, then I'll chuck on some proper clothes. Five minutes and we'll be back out there. I promise."

Effie stepped past him into the house. She could still smell him on her, the warm earthy scent of his skin. "There's a WhatsApp group for the entire village?"

"You know, for barbecues and village gripes mainly. The usual stuff." Lewis shrugged. "Lecturing freedom campers on how to use a toilet and getting Instagrammers to piss off."

A soft laugh escaped her and Lewis squeezed her hand—the gesture too fleeting—then he reached for his phone.

―

In less than ten minutes, they were side by side in Lewis's police vehicle. Half the village was already out. Early risers, Lewis said, overly enthusiastic.

They drove the narrow Haast-Jackson Bay Road first, thinking Anya would have headed away from the town and off the main highway. For twelve kilometers, the view barely changed. Bush and shrubs lined the road, obscuring the Tasman Sea to their right, and thin transmission towers rose up every hundred meters. Effie wound down the window and breathed in the salt air, letting the West Coast breeze wash over her. Eventually, she turned back to Lewis.

"She's not here," she said quietly.

"We'll turn around at Okuru River." Lewis nodded at the endless ribbon of tarmac. "It's just up ahead."

Effie looked out the passenger window, her mind clicking over the same two words, as her eyes scanned the verge. *No body. No body. No body.*

Lewis's phone rang as they were headed back, and he pulled over.

"Okay," he said at last. "I'll be there in ten minutes. Don't try to touch her."

He exhaled as he hung up, then he turned to Effie. But she'd heard enough of the call to make sense of it.

"Apparently, one of the locals—"

She closed her eyes. "Just drive."

Neither of them spoke as they drove back to the village, the clouds gathering and darkening overhead. By the time they reached the Koraha junction, the rain was battering so hard on the windscreen the wipers could barely keep up. The start of the long one-lane bridge came into view, and Effie stiffened in her seat.

She watched as the blur of bodies emerged, the collection of spectators gathered halfway across the vast bridge. Effie took a breath, trying not to hate them for it. After the car had eased to a stop, she climbed out, pulled a jacket on over her shoulders and forced herself toward the circus. She was a police officer. This was not new. This was not shocking. People were the same everywhere.

"Where is she?" Lewis asked, shaking the hand of a man with a wavy mullet.

"About two hundred meters farther along." The man nodded in the direction of the bridge.

The Haast River Bridge, 20 meters high and 750 meters long, was striking. The vast strip of steel hung in the mist—grand and foreboding—before disappearing into the murky abyss. Effie wiped the rain from her face, her heart pulsing in her fingertips as she followed the exposed length of road with her eyes, ready to jump into the gray void without hesitation.

"We all backed off to this passing bay," the man continued, "after what the kid did to Mim."

Lewis frowned. "How is Mim?"

"Pretty shook up. The kid proper went for her." The man shook his head. "Like a wild thing set loose."

Wild.

The word, the weight and sharpness of it, stabbed between Effie's ribs and she turned away. She looked out at the bridge, the horizon drowned in fog, searching for a sign of life in the watery distance. A blot of color. A flash of movement. But there was nothing. Just a wall of gray.

"Don't you listen to him." An older woman stepped from the crowd. "I'm just grand. Barely a graze." Her face was scratched and bloodied, her cheeks torn by tiny fingers.

"Mim." Lewis touched her arm. "What happened exactly?"

"Poor child's terrified, that's what. One of the boys spotted her, loitering way out on the bridge, and I volunteered to walk across. There was no sense us all trekking out and frightening the poor mite. But the child didn't want me talking to her, I'll tell you that much. The moment I opened my mouth, she ran for the barrier." An expression, too soft for the woman's weathered face, settled in her eyes. "A jump that high could break a thing like her. She's nowt but skin and bone—"

"She was going to jump?" Effie stepped forward.

"She was definitely thinking on it. I tried to grab her"—Mim paused, touching a hand to her scratched cheek, and sighed—"but she darted farther along the bridge. Ran straight back to the railing. After that, I thought it was more dangerous for her if I stayed." Mim looked right at Effie. "It was like I was the thing she wanted to jump from."

Effie peered back at the bridge. "I need to get to her. She's my responsibility."

Lewis nodded. "I'll keep everyone back."

"Their homes would be a good distance," she replied.

"I'll try."

As Effie went to walk away, Lewis grabbed her hand. Like they weren't strangers. Like they hadn't been living separate lives for seventeen years.

"You got this, bush girl."

Lewis smiled and Effie turned away, momentarily glad of the rain on her cheeks. Of the water that masked her tears. It was pouring now. Not a meek sort of drizzle, but the type of wet that sliced through your bones. She ran a hand along the white railing and peered over the side. The river surged below, swollen by months of rain.

Please be alive.

Thick sheets of sleet and mist blurred the road, making it impossible to see more than twenty meters ahead. Twenty meters of hope at a time, that was all she had. For twenty meters at a time, the kid was still alive.

Please be alive.

As Effie moved forward, her eyes were drawn to a smudge of color, a ball of limbs curled on the ground.

Oh god.

The *Frozen* nightdress. The child was there. Huddled on the ground. Effie cleared her eyes. Anya's head was buried between her knees, the bones of her shoulders poking through the drenched cotton. She would be freezing—probably hypothermic. She needed warmth, dry clothing, a doctor and a kind voice. *Now*.

Except not this kid. *Fuck*. Mim's scratches were proof of that. Effie closed her eyes, swearing and grinding her teeth, and when she opened them again, Anya was staring straight at her. *Wild*.

An animal backed into a cage. Effie exhaled and stepped forward, making the girl flinch.

Small steps. No words. No talking.

Effie covered her mouth with her hand and shook her head.

No talking.

Anya stared back, unmoving. The moment stretched into eternity, then she nodded once, and Effie took another step forward. Then another. Inching closer. The bridge hummed, the wind passing through the railings in a high-pitched whistle. Effie stopped when she was a few meters away. Close enough to see the hollow expression on Anya's face.

Effie reached an arm out slowly, and the words slipped from her. "Anya, I just want to . . ."

Fuck.

Before Effie could stop her, Anya lunged at the railing and climbed over. Onto the wrong side.

No.

Effie threw a hand to her mouth, not letting any sound leak out, and peered over the side. The fall probably wouldn't kill her; the child wouldn't reach enough speed to break bone. But twenty meters was a solid jump, and there was no guarantee that Anya could swim. Effie flicked her eyes back in the direction of the girl, and Anya thrust a hand out, fingers splayed. *Don't come any closer.* Effie held her hands up in surrender. Anya was faced inward, with nothing but air beneath her heels. She was trembling, but she was holding on, her knuckles and fingers white from the effort. A good sign. A will to live. Effie reached out and held the barrier next to her.

Don't jump. Don't jump.

There was a calm area of water beneath the girl—the spot where she would likely land—an eddy where nothing moved, dead and black, waiting for her. It was low enough that it would hurt. *A lot.* Ten meters higher and she would die on impact. But this height, if she got it wrong, would feel like hitting concrete. She would feel everything.

The elements whipped around them, but the girl stayed perfectly still, her eyes fixed on the river. Suddenly, the distant blast of a car horn tore through the mist and they both turned. Then Effie saw him—materializing through a gap in the clearing sky.

No.

Lewis stood next to his car. He was already out of his shoes and jacket. Ready to run. Ready to jump.

Effie gave a desperate shake of her head. Immediately, Lewis stopped and retreated.

She turned back to Anya, pleading with her eyes, gluing her to the railing.

He's not coming. I promise. He's not coming.

Anya seemed to consider her, to wait, and Effie used the moment to slip her hands behind her neck and unclip her pounamu necklace. Anya watched as Effie held her arm over the railing, letting the dark green stone dangle above the river. The silver chain slipped through her fingers toward the water, and Effie caught it at the last moment.

Anya gasped. "No."

Effie looked across at her. "I won't drop it," she said. "But I need you to come back over the barrier."

The girl nodded, as if the greenstone heart had some power over her. Then she started to shake violently as the cold cut into her nervous system and her arms trembled with the effort of holding on. Effie pocketed the necklace quickly and extended her arm.

A vacant expression washed across Anya's face as she swayed on the edge, her heels bobbing in nothingness, and her left hand came away from the railing.

No!

Her exhausted body lurched backward, her free arm flailing in the gray void, then she collapsed. Forward, not downward—not tumbling into air. The child fell against the barrier and slipped into Effie's grasp. As Effie pulled her over the railing, the air stilled. No rain. No noise. It was as if the world had skipped a beat, before reality seeped in and the two of them spilled onto the ground, their bodies tangled in a heap.

"Are you . . ." Effie began.

But at the sound of her voice, the girl stiffened and a fury glazed her eyes.

No talking. Got it.

Effie covered her mouth and started to push herself up. But Anya was already wriggling and kicking, tearing herself free. Then she was on her feet, running across the bridge. Across the river. Toward the line of bush and trees.

The bush.

Blood pounded in Effie's head.

The bush. Of course.

She scrambled to stand. Anya wanted to go back to the bush. She wasn't running away; she was running back. But she was going the wrong way; she needed to cross the river much farther up.

"The hut," Effie screamed. Louder than the river. Louder than the wind.

Anya turned and stared, her long auburn hair whipping around her face.

"I can take you there," Effie shouted. She pointed across the bridge toward Koraha. "But we have to go that way."

Time slowed. Second after second, pulse after pulse, and neither of them moved.

Then the girl held out her arm.

Come.

MARCH 2002

EFFIE LAY IN the double bed with Aiden clinging to her like a leech.

They'd been in June's house in Koraha for five days. The walk out with the baby had taken forever. And Aiden had gone mental whenever Effie tried to carry him. He'd collapse to the ground howling, and start to eat the grass. Which was gross—animals peed in the grass. But June said it was normal, just big emotions in a small body.

It had been stupid going such a long mixed-up way, but Dad didn't want June knowing the route back. Which made no sense. Unless maybe Dad didn't want June coming back by herself, in case she got her foot stuck in a hole and the sandflies ate her alive.

Aiden kicked out, still asleep, and Effie groaned. His top half was sticky with sweat, but his feet were like ice blocks. In the hut, Effie liked sharing with Aiden and Tia, but in Koraha, they wriggled too much and took up too much space. Effie lifted Aiden's limp arm from her chest and plonked it back next to him. Maybe it was because there was more of her now that she was nine. None of her shoes fit. Shoes were a thing in Koraha. June had bought them all a new pair. Even Four. And Four couldn't even roll over.

Effie slipped out of the bed and threw on shorts and a cozy jumper. A few streets over in his nan's caravan, Lewis would be doing the same thing, waiting for the sun to finally appear. Effie gathered her red hair into a ponytail, not bothering with a brush. Then she unlatched the window—just like she'd done the last four mornings—and started to clamber out.

"I want to come."

Effie stopped and turned back. "Go back to bed, Tia."

Tia frowned, her eyes still sleepy, and crossed her arms. "Where are you going?"

"None of your business." Effie hauled herself over the windowsill. "Go back to bed."

"I'll tell Dad."

"Fine."

Effie slipped down and started to run across the garden, the early morning grass damp beneath her feet. *Shit*. She'd forgotten her shoes. She looked back at the house. Tia was pressed up against the window with her nose flat to the glass. Effie gave a small wave. She would sneak one of the candies from the jar in June's kitchen and give it to Tia later. Unless, of course, Tia told Dad about her running off. Then Effie would rub dirt in her sister's hair.

Effie ran along the grass next to the pavement, avoiding the pointy stones that jabbed her toes. She swore as the dog at number 22 went berserk. It jumped at the fence like a deranged wallaby, and Effie's heart pumped so fast that it threatened to pop out of her. She sped up. But no matter how fast she ran, Lewis was always there first. His nan didn't seem to care where he was. Lewis didn't have parents. He'd had them once, obviously, before the "nasty business" with the log lorry when he was seven. But he didn't talk about his mum and stepdad.

By the time she made it to the end of the road, her ponytail had come out and she had to wipe the hair from her face. She spotted Lewis from across the road. It was hard to miss him with his ridiculous red Crusaders cap. The best super rugby team ever, Lewis said. Effie had no idea what super rugby was, or what made it so super, but Lewis never shut up about it. Crusaders this, Crusaders that. *Yawn.* It was more like stupid rugby. She might have told him how boring it was, but then Lewis always smiled when he talked about it. And Effie had never had a boy smile like that around her.

Lewis was lying on his back on the slide, throwing a rugby ball into the air. When Effie got closer, he turned and grinned.

"Cripes. Did you run through a bush or something?"

She rolled her eyes. "It was that crazy dog."

"Rex." Lewis nodded as he sat up. "Last month he climbed the tree in Mrs. Bennett's garden. Stayed up there the whole day, thinking he was a bird or something."

Effie's eyes widened.

"Honest to god." Lewis touched a hand to his chest. "You can't make this crap up."

She frowned.

"Come on, bush girl." Lewis jumped up and took her hand. "I'll teach you to throw proper."

Heat rushed through Effie's face. Friendship rules were strange and tricky. Lewis was sort of like Tia and Aiden, just older—like a bigger brother. He said silly things that made her laugh and he made her mad sometimes too, like when Tia took her stuff. Except Effie wanted Lewis just for her, and she didn't mind sharing things with him.

"Dad says I'm going to school tomorrow," she said as they walked toward the grass pitch. "Will you be there?"

"Yeah. But you'll probably be in the younger class. There's only two teachers."

"Is school good?"

"I like it." Lewis shrugged. "Although it's very uncool to say that."

"Are you cool?"

He laughed. "I live in a caravan with my nan. And my best friend's a nine-year-old girl who plays with possums."

Best friend.

"I don't play with possums." Effie stuck her tongue out.

"Who skins them, then?" Lewis's smile grew, filling his face.

"Have you ever killed a possum?"

"Nah. Killing things makes me want to vomit."

"You're weird."

He shrugged again. "I guess so."

"I thought all boys liked hunting."

"I thought all girls wore dresses." Lewis grinned. "And shoes."

Effie punched his arm, and he laughed.

"I've had sandfly bites that hurt more than that."

She frowned. "You're an idiot."

"Tell you what, you learn to throw this ball straight, then I'll go hunting with you."

"That's a stupid deal." She scowled. "That ball isn't even round."

Lewis laughed, and a tingling sensation spread through Effie's stomach as they walked toward the field. The tall rugby posts appeared up ahead and she started to run toward them—determined to be first—but her body was jolted to a violent stop. A sharp pain shot through her shoulder as she was tugged backward, her arm almost wrenched from its socket.

"Ow."

For a moment she thought it was Lewis mucking about. But as Effie turned, fear kicked in and she tried to wriggle free. It was a man, a stranger. His fingers dug into her wrist as he pulled her toward him.

"Hey." It was Lewis shouting. "Let her go."

The man, with hair to his shoulders and arms covered in puffy veins, smelled of sweat and cigarettes. Effie squirmed in his grip, his breath hot and moist on her face, but he was too strong.

"I see you, girl," he spat, the words spraying on Effie's cheek.

Lewis lunged at him, trying to pry the man's arms from Effie's body, but his stringy muscles were useless. Kids, even twelve-year-olds, were nothing compared to adults. The man kicked, slamming his foot into Lewis's stomach, and Lewis fell back, landing on a rock with a sickening thud.

"Leave him alone," shouted Effie.

The man strengthened his grip, and a new fear, colder than the first, flushed through her skin. He was trying to drag her with him, to take her away. She thrashed and scraped with her teeth, but it didn't help. A horrible sound crawled out of the man's mouth and he pushed his lips to her ear.

"I know," he sneered, panting, and warm saliva trickled down Effie's face. "I know what he did to that nice girl. He needs to be punished."

Effie tried kicking, but the man lifted her up so that her legs flailed in the air. She screamed and he thumped the side of her head with his own. The pain was instant, like every feeling she had was suddenly in her head, and she blinked white spots.

"Let go of her, you ugly shithead."

A blur of red—Lewis's cap—flashed through the white spots, followed by a yell and a sudden release. Dazed and on the ground, Effie looked up. Lewis and the man were mushed together somehow, and one of them was bleeding. There was a rock the size of Four's head discarded a few meters away, and one edge was splotched with blood.

"Run!" Lewis yelled.

But Effie's legs wouldn't move. Her muscles had frozen, hard and weighty, like maybe they weren't even hers.

"Effie, *run*!"

Adrenaline pushed through the cloud, her head impossibly heavy, and she stumbled to stand. Lewis needed her. The man was on top of him, forcing his head into the ground, and Lewis was too scrawny to fight back. Too scared to even hurt a possum. But as Effie stumbled forward, his eyes met hers. Pleading.

"Please," he mumbled. "Go."

She turned, her heart pumping, then she ran.

"I know what he did to her," the man shouted after her. "I know."

Effie sprinted from the park, her lungs screaming as her legs carried her up the road. Then arms wrapped around her, scooping her up, and she was no longer running.

Dad.

"Lewis . . ." Tears dripped into Effie's mouth. "Lewis is—"

"Come on."

Dad lifted her onto his back, her body draped like the dead chamois, and he ran back in the direction that Effie had just come from.

―

That evening, Lewis sat on the sofa bed in June's living room with Tia on one side and Aiden on the other. Aiden kept gawking at him like he was a superhero, and making him play silly kid games.

After they'd been to the clinic and the nurse had given Lewis loads of pills and two ice packs, June hadn't let him go back to the caravan. *Not a hope in hell,* she'd said. His nan hadn't even come to see him, which Effie thought was pretty shitty, but Lewis hadn't mentioned it. Maybe it was because they were already in huge trouble. After hugging Effie so tight that she might pop, June had gone proper mad. Like ballistic. Aiden had even burst into tears, and he wasn't the one in trouble.

"Will the broken rib pop out of your skin?" asked Tia.

"Nah." Lewis smiled.

"Did the nurse sew your ribs back together, then?"

"That's not quite how—"

Tia's eyes widened. "Do you think she forgot?"

"I don't think—"

Tia frowned. "Do they just float around in there forever?"

Lewis laughed—a half laugh that made him grimace. "They just sort of fix themselves, I guess."

"Do all bones fix themselves?"

"I—"

"My arm has bones," said Aiden. "Look. They're hard."

"Yes, they are," Lewis said. "You've got very strong bones."

"That's cos I eat spinach."

"No." Tia rolled her eyes. "Spinach is for muscles."

"Okay, okay." June walked in carrying towels. "I think that's enough questions for one day. Bath time."

"Can I go after?" asked Effie.

"Yes." June looked at her. "But it's still an early bed for you."

Effie sat on the sofa next to Lewis as the young ones were herded out. Tia was still asking questions when June closed the door.

"How's your head?" Lewis asked once it was just them.

She touched a hand to her forehead. The muddiness was still there. Mud in her thoughts and mud behind her eyes.

"Not bad," she said.

But every time she closed her eyes, the image was there, like a cold itch beneath her skin.

When they got to the park, her dad had wrenched the man off Lewis like he weighed nothing, then tossed him to the ground. But he didn't stop there. Dad had grabbed the man and dragged him back to his feet. Then Dad punched him, the blow so violent that the man fell to the grass, crumpling like a rag doll. Effie had squealed, shaking, and crawled toward Lewis. But Dad didn't stop. He hit the man again and again till there was blood on his knuckles.

Sobbing, Effie had crouched on the grass in front of Lewis, blocking his view, not wanting him to see the man in her dad's clothes. Eventually, a howl burst out of the crumpled man, a gurgle of pain and laughter, and Effie had turned to see him looking up at her dad, smiling without enough teeth. Then he spat blood at Dad's feet.

"God will punish you." He laughed.

Then Dad punched him a final time and Effie closed her eyes, too scared to move, too scared to check if the rag-doll man was still alive.

Lewis shuffled an inch closer on the sofa bed and held out a bag of chocolate Pineapple Lumps, offering one to Effie.

"Where'd you get those?" she asked.

He smiled. "Your dad gave them to me when June wasn't looking."

Effie took one. "Thanks," she said. "For jumping on that guy."

"Any time." Lewis gave a ridiculous salute. "Always happy to help a friend in distress."

She raised an eyebrow. "I wasn't in *distress*."

"Well, you sure fooled me."

"Well, you . . ." She put her hands on her hips. "You're the one with broken bones."

"All part of the job."

Effie frowned and took another Pineapple Lump. "What will the police do with him?"

"Dunno." Lewis shrugged. "Apparently he's not from here. Griffiths, the police fellah, said he's from up near Hokitika. Not right in the head, I reckon."

"Who do you think he was talking about?" asked Effie. "About that girl."

"I think he was talking shit."

"But . . ." Something twisted in Effie's stomach. *The otherwise thing*. "The last time we were in Koraha . . ." She paused, worried that the dark bits in her dad might make Lewis like her less. "Last time, you said that thing about my dad. That he hurt that hiker . . ."

"It was just a rumor. Stupid local gossip."

She looked at him, confused. "You said—"

"I was wrong, Effie. People make up stuff all the time round here." His voice was odd, like he was trying out adult words. "Especially about your dad, and your family. But no one knows what they're talking about."

The thing in her stomach stirred. "But," she continued, "my dad, he gets angry sometimes, violent. Like with that man."

"You mean with the man who grabbed you and broke two of my ribs?"

"Yeah, but—"

"Parents do crazy shit when their kids are in trouble. My stepdad once slashed some guy's tires cos his car clipped my bike." Lewis shook his head. "Bloody nice ute too."

"So," said Effie, "you don't think that man was talking about my dad?"

"I think that man was a nutcase."

Her body eased, the blackest parts of her a little lighter. Like maybe she'd been worrying about nothing.

"And hey." Lewis smiled. "School's going to be a breeze after this. We're local heroes now."

Effie smiled back.

"Reckon you'll get the full royal treatment tomorrow," he said. "The kick-arse kids of Koraha. Catchy, don't you think?"

"I think you're an idiot." She rolled her eyes and took the bag of candy.

2025

THE GIRL, BAREFOOT and shivering, walked forward with her arm still outstretched and stopped in front of Effie.

Without a word, Effie removed her jacket and bent down to place it over Anya's shoulders, the raincoat drowning her. The child stood completely still as Effie fastened the top button, staring at her with such intensity that Effie had to force herself not to look away. Then Anya slipped her cold fingers into Effie's, and hand in hand, they walked back across the bridge. Effie knew she was squeezing the child's hand too tight, but she couldn't help it. If she loosened her grip, Effie was afraid she might lose her.

They had only made it ten meters when the lights of a vehicle filled the single-lane bridge. Anya didn't run, but Effie felt her flinch.

The ute stopped a few meters in front of them, and June got out. Effie raised her hand, preventing June from coming any closer, then she turned to Anya. Effie touched her fingers to her mouth and pointed back at the ute. *I need to talk to June.* Anya's expression didn't change, but she pulled her hand free and covered her ears.

"You okay?" asked June.

Effie nodded as she walked forward. "She wants to go back."

"I know." June sighed and a sad smile pulled at the corners of her mouth. "She reminds me of Tia. Your sister was never happy in Koraha. Tia was born of bush and wildness, just like Anya."

"But not me?"

"No." Something unsaid hung in the creases of June's face, but she blinked it away. "You were always meant to leave."

Effie's shoulders softened slightly, releasing a tension she hadn't known was there. Like maybe Tia had needed to stay. Maybe Effie hadn't failed her—hadn't left her sister to die in the bush.

"Here." June held up the keys to her ute. "Let's get the two of you where you need to go."

"What about Lewis?"

"Oh, he'll be mad when he finds out." June's face softened. "But he'll forgive you. Now, come on, there are spare clothes and food in the ute. Which, by the way, was *not* in my driveway this morning."

"Oh god. Sorry, I—"

"Stole it," June offered. "And left the keys in the ignition." She raised an eyebrow. "There's a backpack too, with enough stuff for a few days."

"June, I don't know how to thank you."

"Don't thank me yet." Her eyes darkened. "We don't know what you're going to find out there." She looked over Effie's shoulder. "We've no idea what that poor kid was running from."

Effie turned and looked at Anya, who was still covering her ears, then she held out her hand and the girl walked toward her.

"No," Effie whispered. "We don't."

June parked the ute and Effie jumped out.

She didn't know what she was meant to be feeling. The gurgling sound of the river filled the air, sucking the oxygen from it, and she touched a hand to her chest, her skin suddenly too tight.

After seventeen years, she was going back.

They started to untie the ropes looped around the roof. They'd picked up a raft from a friend of June's, then they'd driven the rest of the way in silence, with the raft whistling on the roof of the car. Anya had stared out the window the entire way, lost in a silent sanctuary of her own. Her body had stiffened when they'd pulled in to get the raft, but Effie had reached across the back seat and placed a hand between them. Not touching. Not invading her space. Just letting the girl know.

A soft breeze blew across from the other side of the river, bringing the smells and memories of the bush with it. The first time it had happened, Effie hadn't done anything. She'd stood silent as his little body was lowered into the dirt. Her insides had screamed, hot with anger and hurt, but Dad had apologized over and over. He told her that it would never happen again, that he hated himself for it. The second time, Effie had run until her legs had folded, then she'd picked herself up, her body bruised and bloody, and she'd kept running, for almost two decades.

Effie's fingers trembled as she undid the knot, and the raft slipped forward. She swore as she lunged to catch it.

"You ready?" asked June.

This time, she wasn't going to stand silent.

"I need to do this."

"I know, love."

Effie glanced back at the ute, at the small vacant face pressed against the window, and took a breath.

What did you see? What did he do to you?

After setting the raft in the water, Effie and Anya got in. The inflatable boat had two seats, but Anya sat on the floor in the middle, her knees tucked to her chest, and watched as Effie paddled away from the shore. June stood on the bank until they were safely on the other side, then she waved and drove off.

It's just us now, kid.

They walked up the steep unmarked terrain without talking, Effie leading the way. Her eyes darted from one tree to the next, following some ingrained map. The sounds and smells of the bush illuminated a dark spot in her memory, and her feet moved by instinct, finding the decades-old markers, the scraps of pink plastic that Dad had hung from trees. It was as though the path had been carved beneath the surface of her skin and the hut was pulling her closer, whispering through the wall of trees. A weak sunlight filtered through the hanging silver ferns, splintering into long misty shafts, and the fronds draped high above their heads, forming a ceiling of hexagons. When Effie glanced up, it was like looking through a green kaleidoscope.

Every now and then, she turned and checked, but the girl was always there, following a few meters behind. The sound of her pushing through branches and snapping twigs was dwarfed by the high-pitched singing and ticking of birds and insects.

When Dad had walked them out, he used to distract them with Māori legends, and he always kept candy in his pockets. He'd hide them, like a Hansel and Gretel trail, under ferns and on tree stumps, and the young ones would forget their tired legs. But Anya hadn't said a word in three hours; she hadn't moaned once. She walked without slowing, pausing only to untangle a scrap of linen that hung from a tree, a stray ribbon of white in a world of green. Effie's chest stung as she glanced back at her. At the child who hadn't complained about her tired legs—the pain nothing to the girl with ligature marks around her ankles.

Anya looked up, her eyes burrowing into Effie, and Effie pointed ahead.

We'll stop up there.

They walked on for another ten minutes, the steep terrain leveling out, and Anya found a second scrap of material. She teased it free from the branch and pocketed it without a word. Old markers for hunters, most likely. Effie pushed the draping ponga aside and stepped over the vines and ferns that carpeted the forest floor. In every direction, the air was thick with trees, making it impossible to see more than a few meters ahead. The spines of kahikatea and tōtara twisted and towered above them, and Effie's chest tightened. She took a deep breath, as though suddenly, in the middle of the bush, there wasn't enough air.

Effie flinched as a small hand slipped into hers, and she turned to look at Anya. For years Effie had been fine. *She'd been fine.* But now her body was thrumming. Here, among the leaves, with the silent kid, the past was taunting her. She squeezed Anya's hand and nodded at the ground.

This spot's good.

Effie stopped and pulled a jacket out of her bag and set it down for Anya to sit on. The child looked at it, then at Effie, and sat down. June had packed them sandwiches and snacks. Anya ate the sandwich first, then she picked up an apple. Her eyes widened as her teeth sunk into the fruit. She ate all of it, apart from three black seeds, which Effie shook her head at.

Don't eat.

Looking back, there had been an exact moment when Anya had changed. It was half an hour into the walk as they crossed through a small clearing, and she had let out a soft whimper, one of relief rather than pain. There had been less anger in her since then, her little body less tense, and she'd started walking closer to Effie. A week ago, the child had appeared from the bush, starving and covered in blood, and yet the closer they got to the hut, the more at ease she seemed. Anya laughed now as she prodded at a fallen tree with a stick. She kicked the end of the log with her heel, and the rotten wood disintegrated under her foot. It was the first time Effie had heard her laugh, and the lightness of it sent a chill down her spine. Effie hadn't laughed for months after leaving the bush.

Anya turned, the residue of laughter caught in her eyes, and Effie looked at her, their green eyes just the same. In Koraha, the girl's feelings had radiated from her: anger, fear, frustration—all the emotions of a caged animal. But here, under the shadow of green, there was something else on her face. The fist in Effie's stomach clenched. It was the lack of sadness in her eyes that unnerved Effie. A lack of pain. She didn't know what Anya had run from, but it had to have been more than the quiet calm her gaze conveyed.

Effie stood and started to pack their things, but she paused with the jacket in her hand, and the rucksack fell against her legs. She couldn't swallow properly. She pressed two fingers into her ribs, pushing hard into bone, trying to stop her body from turning on her. *No.* Effie held out her hands—strange heavy lumps that didn't belong to her—and opened and closed her numb fingers. *Not now.* She hadn't had a panic attack in years. Effie gulped at the air, but her breaths had reverted to short, shallow gasps. The bush pressed in on every part of her body, squeezing the air from her. *Fuck.* Effie closed her eyes, trying to slow the frenzied tide of thoughts that pulsed in her skull, and when she opened them again, Anya was staring at her, almost close enough to touch, but not quite. It was as if she was waiting to see what would happen.

Effie bent forward, resting her hands on her thighs. She had to breathe, to focus on the flow of air through her nose. She forced her eyes open and strained her neck to look up. Anya hadn't moved. She just stood there, watching. Waiting. With nothing in her eyes.

Eventually, the air started to reach Effie's lungs. The sludge in her head began to clear and she stood up. She took a deep breath, her lungs recovering, but the concrete block in her stomach didn't ease. Anya should have been sadder, more affected. *More something.* When

Effie had escaped the bush, she'd felt everything, as though the skin had been peeled from her body and she'd been rolled in hot embers. And as they neared the hut, it felt like she was being skinned all over again.

Effie rubbed her hands over her face and gave Anya a small smile. But the girl just blinked and turned away. Almost as if she was disappointed.

Effie went to lift her rucksack when she spotted something glinting on top of the log where Anya had been playing. She walked over and picked it up. It was a four-inch hunting knife that June had given Effie. Next to it, four words had been carved into the wood.

Don't disrespect the Guardian.

Effie frowned and looked up, the hints of rain dripping through the trees, but the girl was already walking ahead. Anya knew the way now.

They were getting closer.

Just over two hours later, without having stopped once, they reached the Roaring Billy River. Effie sat and tried to unclip her bag, the clasp jammed, but Anya didn't stop.

"Wait!" Effie yelled, but Anya kept running. *"Stop!"*

Effie scrambled to follow her, but by the time she reached the river, Anya was in the water up to her knees. She held her arms out, going deeper with each step. Effie tightened the straps on her rucksack as the swift-flowing water swirled around her ankles. She kept her eyes glued on Anya, who was already at the deepest section in the middle. The current was too strong for her; the kid was too small. And it was deep—the ends of her long red hair were moving in the water. The image of Dad flashed through Effie's mind, and Aiden's little head lolling from side to side in the rucksack.

"Anya, wait!"

The river was too fast. It was too high after the rain. One misstep and Anya would be swept away. Within seconds, the river would pour into her, and she would be more water than child. Effie forced her way through the swirling current, the riverbed visible through the clear water.

"Anya!"

But remarkably, Anya started to rise out of the water, and then she was on the other side. Breathing a sigh of relief, Effie fought her way across and rushed into the trees after her. After ten minutes of bush-bashing, she spotted Anya, soaking and dripping and still. Then Effie saw it. The hut. Right there in front of them.

Anya turned and looked at Effie, her clothes clinging to her concave body, and she pointed at the hut.

Go.

Effie set the rucksack down and signaled for her not to move, then she walked toward the timber deck. The hut was smaller than she remembered. Lesser almost. *Diminished.* But other than its size, it was as if no time had passed. Effie gripped the hunting knife and took a deep breath, then she pushed the door open.

It was the smell that hit her first, like rotting meat and fruit. The smell of death—of something that had once been human. As she stepped inside, holding a hand across her mouth and nose, she saw the body. It was splayed out in the middle of the room, on its back, naked from the waist up, with dried blood crusted across its bare chest.

Effie took a step closer and frowned.

There was something strange about the wound. Unnatural. The two gashes, which had long stopped bleeding, were cut into a mark or a sign. But as she leaned in to get a better look, a scream stole the air from the hut. A terrible, harrowing sound. Effie turned as

Anya rushed through the door. She tore through the hut like a wild thing and threw herself onto the floor.

But not next to the body.

Not next to the lump of human.

The child threw herself to the bare floorboards, crying and whining, and started to claw at them with her fingers.

JULY 2003

EFFIE SAT ON the deck outside the hut, wrapped up in all the clothes she owned. She'd found Mum's old jacket too, and had tucked it around her legs. There was no warmth in the bush in July—the month was cold from start to finish. Less sandflies though. So winter had that going for it, at least.

Four was asleep next to her. He was snuggled up inside a wooden shelter that Dad had made for his naps. Four would only sleep outside during the day, like he was a dog or something, which had annoyed Effie at first. But she'd got used to it. And during the winter, the quiet wasn't so bad. Inside the hut was mad; Tia's stuff was everywhere, and Aiden was so loud.

Four sneezed and swatted at his face with a chubby fist, then he crinkled his eyes, his cheeks like red balloons. Without any of them really noticing, Four had turned one and a half. He ran everywhere now, his legs constantly bruised, and he shouted out the noises of animals. But despite all the running, he still had a big stick-out belly. Insulation for winter, Dad said. Effie, however, was a scrawny frozen twig.

She leaned forward and tucked Four's teddy in next to him. Its right arm had been sewn back on twice, badly, and the one remaining eye gave Effie the creeps. But Four took it everywhere. June said it was probably a health hazard—more germ than bear.

Effie smoothed out Mum's jacket and picked up her tattered copy of *Harry Potter and the Philosopher's Stone*. June had given it to her for her tenth birthday, and it was literally the best thing Effie had ever read. She'd devoured it three and a half times. Apparently there were three more books, and June had promised to keep an eye out for them. June hadn't been back to the hut, not since Four was born, but Dad walked them all out to Koraha once every three months. Then for two weeks, they'd stay with June and go to school. They'd take baths and brush their hair and play at being normal kids. Effie loved those two weeks with Lewis and June and a fridge filled with proper milk. But Tia and Aiden—and probably even Four—always loved going back to the bush, to the stupid cold hut without electricity or Lewis or Mum.

Effie flicked to the page with her marker in it and started reading aloud. The characters felt more real that way. Ron was the best. He had red hair like Effie, always messy, and his voice sounded like Lewis sometimes.

A twig snapped in the distance and she looked up, not breathing for a moment, but there was no one there. Of course there wasn't. Dad would be gone for at least another day. When he left, he was always gone for three days. And when he came back, it was another two days before he was really there. Effie turned back to her book. The young ones knew not to go near Dad when he got home, not until Effie said so.

Dad's bad days had been getting worse. Sitting in silence. Drinking till his body slumped. It always happened just before he left, like an anger bubbled up in him and he had to leave before it burst out. The winter made him worse too.

On the bad days, he and Effie did a sort of side-stepping dance. They lived under the same roof, forced together by the hut, but they didn't really notice each other. They didn't speak or touch. Dad sort of moved around them—like a giant trying not to squish bugs. Effie tidied up and tried to cook, and Tia played with the boys and got them dressed.

But on the good days, Dad hugged them and read them stories and did all the right parent things. On the good days, Effie cried when she fell, ugly dramatic tears, and Dad kissed her—her forehead first, then her grazed knees. She would sneak into bed with him in the mornings, without checking on Four first, and he'd read *The Lord of the Rings*. On the good days, Effie fought with Tia and got annoyed with Aiden, and Dad made them all say sorry.

Most days were good days—days when Dad was Dad—and that made the bad ones feel smaller.

Four stirred in his wooden shelter and Effie giggled. He'd wriggled so much that only his face popped out from the blankets, his lips puckering like a fish's.

"Come on." Effie reached in and gathered him up. "Let's get you some milk."

Four snuggled into her, still half-asleep, and Effie stroked the purple birthmark on his neck. Inside, Effie threw more wood in the fire and heated up some milk, then she and Tia cooked up rice and lentils. The rice still lumped together, not like when June did it, and Tia burned the lentils to the bottom of the pan. But it was edible. The first time Dad had gone, they'd eaten nothing but raw carrots, broccoli and cold baked beans from the tin.

They spent the rest of the day playing in the hut and keeping the fire going. It wasn't until the young ones were all in bed that Effie allowed herself back into Dad's room. She'd made up his bed the day before and picked his clothes up off the floor, so that it would be nice when he got back. Then she'd swept up with a brush and pan. She'd found his journal when she was sweeping, the torn notebook splayed open on the floor. Effie had taken a quick look, not a real one, then she'd snapped it shut. It was bad to snoop.

But now that the rest of the hut was quiet, Effie lifted the notebook again and sat on the bed, staring at the closed cover.

Don't.

She ran her fingers over the worn jacket, adrenaline thrumming beneath her skin, and bit into her lip.

Don't open it.

She sat like that for a minute, gripping the notebook so tightly that the tips of her fingers paled.

You can't open it.

Then she opened it, flattening out the spine, and flicked through the pages. One after the other, cover to cover, then back again. Only the first quarter of the book had been written in, the pages smudged with dirty fingerprints, but it was the same thing on every page. A name. The same name written on each page, followed by a line of numbers—dates, maybe—and a scrawled cross.

Effie touched the writing, her hands shaking. She'd seen that flowery name before.

She traced a finger over the five letters, struggling to think over the punch of her heart.

She'd seen it in the creepy chamois hut.

2025

THE LATE AFTERNOON glow spilled through the windows, creating a pool of white light around the two bodies.

A dead man and a broken child.

Except for Anya's whimpers, softer now, the hut seemed to be holding its breath, waiting in silent expectation. Slowly, Effie moved forward and reached out toward Anya. But she turned and snarled at Effie, her face wet with tears and snot, and Effie pulled her hand back. Without a word, the girl pressed her face to the floor, then stretched her arms out as if trying to hug it.

Effie turned to look at the body, the pungent smell scratching the back of her throat. The man lay on his back with his arms at his sides. His mouth and eyes were wide open, but there was nothing behind them. No life.

"Please." Effie pressed her fingers to her mouth. "Please, no."

Carefully, she knelt down beside him and slid a trembling hand behind his neck. His skin was cold and loose, the outer layer already sloughing from his bones. She lifted his head slightly, then peered under his neck. As she saw it, her body lost all sense of weight and solidness, and a sob escaped her.

"I'm so sorry," she managed.

There at the base of his neck was a small purple splotch. A birthmark.

Four.

With her chest clenched like a fist, she leaned over and pressed her lips to his forehead, kissing the six-year-old boy that she'd left behind. *I'm so sorry.* Her heart ached and her fingers quivered as she closed his eyes—the empty eyes of a fully grown man.

"I'm so sorry, little brother."

Forcing herself to think like a police officer, Effie scanned his body. But there were no signs of harm other than the shallow cuts to his chest, forming a crucifix. Trembling, she pulled her phone from her pocket—still without service—and started taking photos, capturing the lifeless mass of her youngest brother. Vomit burned the back of her throat as she zoomed in, snapping the religious symbol. With each photo, a thought tugged at her—there was no knife, no sign of the weapon that had been used to cut into him. Which meant someone must have taken it. That Four hadn't done it to himself.

"Mum."

Effie turned at the whisper of the girl's voice. Anya was still curled into a ball, her cheek pressed against the floor.

"What did you say?" asked Effie.

She moved closer, but Anya shielded her face with her arm.

"Please," breathed—begged—Effie. "I need you to tell me what happened."

She shook her head.

"I know it's scary," said Effie. "And I want to help you. But it's hard for me to do that if you won't talk to me."

"I'm not allowed to," Anya said eventually, her words muffled by her arm. "He'll punish me."

"Who?" Effie stiffened. "Who will punish you?" She glanced behind her, her skin suddenly cold. "Four? Did Four hurt you?"

"I'm not allowed to talk to you."

Effie looked at the bloodied shell of her brother—at the baby she'd fed and washed and rocked to sleep—then turned to Anya.

"Okay." She paused, trying to think. "What if you just nod and shake your head? Would that be okay?"

Anya looked at her, but she didn't move. She stayed coiled up like a fetus with her eyes glued on Effie. Finally, she nodded.

Effie adjusted her position on the floor so she was sitting next to Anya, shielding her from Four's body.

"Did Four hurt you?"

Anya shook her head.

Oh, thank god.

"And was he dead when you ran away?"

A nod.

"Is this where you live?"

Another nod.

"With Four?"

Anya shook her head.

"With your mum?"

A nod.

Effie closed her eyes. "Is your mum . . . is your mum's name Tia?"

Anya nodded, and a flood of emotions filled Effie's chest, choking her.

She swallowed. "I really am your aunty."

Anya looked at her, then she turned over so her back was to Effie.

"Sorry, I . . ." She stared at the child half-made of her sister.

Effie burned to know where Tia was, to know if she was still alive, but she couldn't ask, not yet. It was too much for the child. And every minute that passed worried her. They needed to get away from the hut. Effie glanced back at Four and took a breath, needing to think like a police officer. To focus on the dried blood and the absence of a knife, and what that meant. On who or what might still be in the trees, watching them.

"Anya," she whispered. "I'm sorry, but we can't stay here. It's not safe."

The muscles stiffened beneath the child's paper-thin skin, holding her to the spot.

"I know I said I would take you home. And we will come back, I promise," said Effie. "But first, we need to get help. We need to find out what happened here and to make it safe for you."

Anya rolled over and stared at her, her green eyes wide and cautious, taking in Effie's every word. She was clever—Effie had witnessed multiple examples of her intelligence; the girl wasn't confused or intellectually stunted. But she was traumatized, and she was naive, and that made her unpredictable. Vulnerable.

"I'm a police officer," said Effie. "Like Lewis. So it's my job to help people and to keep them safe. And right now, to keep you safe, I need to take you back to Koraha. Just for a short while. Then other police officers, like me, can come and find out what happened to Four."

The trees rustled outside, and a branch rattled against the roof.

"Then, if you want, you can come back here."

Anya tilted her head to the side, her big green eyes seeming to look straight through Effie.

"Do you know where your mum is?" Effie asked gently.

She waited. She didn't move. Didn't breathe.

Then the girl shook her head.

Effie swallowed the stab of disappointment, then slowly she held out her hand.

"I promise," she said, knowing she shouldn't. "I promise to help you find her. But now we need to leave."

Without a word, the girl stood and walked past her. Then she opened the door, and Effie followed her out to the deck.

"I need to go back in," said Effie. "Just for a few minutes."

No response.

"Just stay here." She pointed toward a chair with a blanket hung over the arm. "But if you see anything, anything at all, shout for me."

Silently, Anya turned and sat down. She pulled the blanket over her legs. Next to the chair was a box of coloring pencils, crayons and paper. The girl pulled one of the sheets of paper out and started to draw a cross in the top corner, just like the one carved into Four's chest. It occurred to Effie then that everything here belonged to Anya. The chair, the blanket, the crayons—they were all hers. This was her home.

"I won't be long," said Effie as the girl drew two more crosses.

She stepped back into the hut, alone but for Four. Even from the other side of the hut, the smell was suffocating. She coughed and walked farther in, trying to move through the crushing wave of emotions. She had to block it out. This was why she'd come. Why she'd walked into the bush without Lewis.

Effie pulled her phone out to take more photos. The moment it became a crime scene, the hut would be taken from her. It would be wrapped in yellow tape and swabbed and gutted. This was her only chance to find something, anything, to hint at what had happened to her family.

She moved with care, touching as few things as possible. She checked under the sofa, behind the piles of kindling and under the sink, but the knife wasn't there. Someone had taken it. She worked her way around the small hut, the traces of memory lingering in every item. The past was right there, in every creak in the floor and every cold draft of bush air.

Effie walked over to the far end of the room and reached for the curtain that shielded the sleeping nook. It was the same curtain that had hung there for thirty years. As she touched the material, she could almost hear the whispered giggles of children and the sound of small bodies shuffling for space. She paused, like a part of her knew what the tattered screen was hiding. Effie tightened her grip on the curtain. There was something wrong with the hut, something more than just the body. There was an emptiness to it, the type of barrenness that laced the air of a prison cell.

Effie took a breath and pulled the curtain back. And her heart broke.

A set of chains hung from the wall, secured by a bolt, just high enough to detain a child. On the floor was a small bundle of blankets and a pile of books. Effie took a moment to quell the fury in her stomach, then she lifted her phone, capturing every inch.

After a second walk around the main room, careful not to disturb anything, she cracked the front door open and peered at Anya. The girl hadn't moved. Quietly, Effie closed the door and moved on to the bedroom. The bed was made, and the room was neat and tidy. But other than the faint smell of laundry soap, there was no sign of life. No photos on the walls, no pictures drawn by Anya, no hints at Tia's three decades of life. Pulling the sleeves of her jumper down to cover her hand, Effie opened the drawers on the small dressing table Dad had built for her and Tia. But they were both empty. No clothes. No blankets. She frowned as she stood up. The whole thing—the hut, the body, Tia—it was all wrong.

Is this where you live?

A nod.

With your mum?

Another nod.

As Effie looked around, it was as if she were standing in the cell of a monastery, of a life stripped bare. Stripped of her sister.

"Where are you, Tia?" Effie whispered. "Where did you go?"

She moved forward and knelt in front of the bed, then she tried to squeeze underneath it. If there was any part of her sister left, it would be there, in their spot.

A place just for us, Tia, for our secrets.

Effie dug her fingers under the loose floorboard and lifted it up. The small space was filled with paper, familiar pages torn from their old exercise books and drawing pads. Effie pulled them out—leftover pieces of her sister—and shuffled back to sit on the floor. There were about fifteen sheets of paper covered in Tia's looped writing, each starting with the same two words.

Dear Effie.

She bit into her lip. Not crying. Tears wouldn't do her sister any good. Effie flicked through the letters. Most of them contained similar anecdotes, accounts of things that they'd done as children.

Dear Effie

Do you remember that time, when June was still wary of the bush? Gosh, she hated it at first, didn't she? Too dark. Too damp. Too noisy. Too quiet. Too cold. And she tried to give Aiden a bath in the big bucket (he would have been about two) and he escaped. Poor June went berserk. She was convinced he'd be mauled by a savage possum or poisoned by tree nettles. Aiden must have run around the bush, completely naked, for at least an hour before we found him, covered head to toe in dirt. Then when June tried to scold him, he just looked up at her and beamed, his teeth the only mud-free part of him. I can still remember it, that little voice of his, as he held his hands up. "Dirty hands. Aiden has dirty hands." Then he pointed at June. "Dune clean." I think June hugged him so tight that it winded him. She opened two tins of peaches that night and we all slept in her bed.
    It was a good night.

Miss you. X

Effie flicked through the pages, all of them written to her, and all of them signed off with a kiss. There were no dates or markers, but some of the pages looked worn. And three of them were different. Newer. Scrappier. Like maybe Tia's hand had been shaking as she wrote. Effie read them each twice, forcing herself to sit with her sister's words, to accept what they might mean.

Dear Effie
I'm so sorry. I made a mistake. I should have come with you all those years ago. You escaped. You lived.
    X

Dear Effie
I'm scared. I'm worried that I don't know my own child anymore. I love her more than life. But I'm terrified that I'm losing her to him.
    X

Dear Effie
Dad is lost to us.
    X

Effie brushed a finger across her sister's words.
What are you trying to tell me, Tia? What happened to you?
Outside, there was a thump, something hard hitting the ground, and Effie snapped her head around. She'd been in the hut too long. *Stupid. Stupid.* Effie folded the letters, slipped them into her pocket and glanced at her watch. The summer evenings were long in November, but so was the walk out. She wanted to be at least two hours away from the hut—away from her brother's body—before she set up a bivvy shelter for the girl. Then at first light, they'd head back to Koraha.

Effie took one last look at Four, whispered a silent apology, then she stepped outside.

"Anya?"

She glanced at the empty chair, then walked along the deck.

"Anya. We need to go."

Her skin prickled as she walked the entire way around the hut, scanning the edge of the bush. A thick line of trees surrounded the hut, and as Effie looked out at the forest, she felt herself slipping backward, getting smaller and smaller, until she was a kid again, sitting barefoot on the deck waiting for her dad.

But her dad wasn't there.

And neither was Anya.

Effie was about to shout again when she looked up through the distant trees, straight into the eyes of a man. A face, half-hidden in ferns, watching her. He stood completely still, the left side of his body concealed behind a wide rimu. Effie spun around, reaching for something heavy, but when she turned back, he was gone.

Effie ran forward a few steps, her heart racing.

She had seen him. Hadn't she?

She hadn't imagined it. The cold eyes. The flash of red hair.

Blood throbbed in her head and she turned, searching in every direction. But she was alone.

"Fuck."

She swore as she kicked the ground, the thoughts buzzing behind her eyes, and she stumbled back to the hut to get her bag.

Then she saw it. What the girl had drawn.

And Effie froze.

JANUARY 2005

FOUR WALKED BETWEEN Effie and Tia, Effie holding one hand and Tia the other. Since turning three a couple of months ago, Four refused to be carried anywhere. If Effie even tried to lift him, he would scream and do the grass-eating thing that Aiden used to do. The forest floor liked to trick Four's small feet though, tripping him over, but Four just giggled like it was a game.

"You're flying." Tia laughed as they swung Four in the air, lifting his gangly legs over a rotten stump.

"Again," he said. "Do again. I want to fly."

"What's the polite word?" asked Effie.

"Please. Again, please."

Tia smiled and they swung him up. Tia was still small, shorter than other nine-year-olds, but she was strong.

Dad and Aiden walked ahead, their hair and clothes still wet from the river. Dad was being a proper dad, chatting and laughing, and Aiden looked up at him like Dad's bad days never happened. As if the times he left them alone were made up. Effie forgot sometimes too. Like when Dad searched for mushrooms with Four, or when he helped Aiden climb the big tree at the back of the hut. It was harder then—to imagine the blackness in him. But Effie couldn't forget it. Sometimes, though, she had to put a lot of effort into remembering.

"Come on, you three." Dad looked back, grinning. "Hurry up. There's birthday cake to be had."

"Cake," shouted Four.

Twelve felt like an important age. Like Effie could manage anything. She was no longer a little kid. No longer naive and immature. The last year had been good. They still visited Koraha every three months, and Dad hadn't left as often. And when he did, Effie knew how to take care of the young ones. She knew how to fix them dinner, something warm with vegetables, and how to teach Aiden his numbers and words. Effie read to them for fifteen minutes each night, getting them to answer questions about the pictures, just like Mum had taught her. And when Dad came back, he read with the boys and Effie read *Harry Potter* to Tia. Lewis had used his savings from cleaning at the motel to buy her the fifth book. It was the longest and the best so far. Almost eight hundred pages.

"How's my birthday girl?" Dad wrapped an arm around Effie's shoulders and kissed her forehead.

"Hungry."

"Excellent."

She frowned. "Are you sure the cake's edible?"

"Yes." He smiled. "Definitely maybe."

He kept his arm around her as they walked back through the trees. Tia had begged to go for a swim in the river, even though it was Effie's birthday. But Tia had a smile that was hard to say no to, which was usually super annoying. The river had been fun though. The water was the bright turquoise color of summer, and there'd been a white heron that watched them the whole time. Tia and Aiden had swum with Dad while Effie let Four paddle at the edge. Then they'd skimmed stones and had a picnic.

As they neared the hut now, Tia stopped. Then Effie felt it too, that something was different. Tia held out a hand, making them stay, then she looked back at Dad.

"Someone's in the hut."

Dad pulled free of Effie and moved forward. No one knew the way to the hut. Not even June. Dad had sworn them to secrecy.

Not even Lewis, Effie. Promise me.

I promise.

It's important. This is our special place.

Dad lifted Four, who didn't cry—he knew not to—and handed him to Effie.

"Stay here."

The bush hummed as Dad neared the hut, the piercing burst of cicadas vibrating in Effie's chest. Four clung to her, his little arms crushing her neck as a heat prickled her spine. A warning. Dad's body had that look, like every muscle in him was held tight with anger. The look that told Effie to keep her distance. She rubbed Four's back as Dad reached for the door handle.

Effie jumped as the door burst open and a tall boy, a man maybe, filled the frame.

"I thought I heard someone," he said.

The tall man-boy smiled like there was no anger in Dad at all, like he wasn't staring down the barrel of a rifle.

"Hi." He held out a hand. "I'm Asher."

Stupid name.

He was real pale, like the freckled girl at school. Even his hair, which reached his shoulders, was blond, and he had a short beard that circled his lips. Effie disliked him straightaway. Not the pale thing—that was kind of cool, like a Sindar Elf—but the rest of him. It was dangerous, him being there, seeing things that his tiny brain wouldn't understand. Looking at them—at Dad—with his judging outsider eyes and making stupid assumptions.

His eyes.

Effie flinched, momentarily fascinated.

Far out.

The man-boy's eyes were totally different. One of his eyes was bright blue while the other was black. A swirl of ocean and a pit of dirt.

"This is our home," said Dad, without taking his hand.

"Sorry, yes." The stranger with the strange eyes stood aside. "I didn't mean to intrude."

"Why are you here?"

"Oh, right . . ." He smiled as if Dad had said something funny, and shook his head.

He was clearly an idiot.

"Sorry. I got lost. I'm doing this sort of back-to-nature, trying-to-find-myself thing." He smiled again. "Have you ever read *Into the Wild*? Great book."

Dad just stared at him.

"Right, no. Anyway, I got myself a tent and boots and enough dehydrated food to last a month but . . ."

A massive idiot.

"I might have bitten off more than I can chew."

Seriously, it was like he couldn't stop smiling. Maybe he wasn't right in the head.

"Do you want some cake?" Tia bounded forward before Dad or Effie could stop her.

"Oh." The man-boy-idiot looked from Tia to Dad, then back at Tia. "That would be great. I'm pretty starving actually."

"This isn't a café," said Dad.

"But he's hungry," said Tia. "And we've got loads of food. Please, Dad. Please."

Tia smiled that smile, the one Dad could only say yes to.

"One piece."

Tia took one of the stranger's hands and Aiden took the other, and they led him inside. Into their secret place.

"How old are you?" asked Tia.

"Twenty. Well, almost. I'll be twenty soon."

Jesus. Effie rolled her eyes. He didn't even know his own age.

"What's wrong with your eyes?" asked Aiden. "They're weird."

"Sorry." The man half smiled.

"I think it's cool." Aiden grinned.

"Oh." Asher sat on the floor, where Tia had set a cushion out for him. "It's because my left pupil is permanently dilated, which—"

"Dilated?"

"It means big or widened. Which makes my left eye look much darker than the right."

"Are you sick?"

"No." He shook his head. "No. There's nothing wrong with—"

"You're quite pale."

He laughed. "That's from my mum. Her side of the family are from Scandinavia."

"You should go in the sun," said Aiden. "That'll make you less white."

"I don't really tan. I just go red, like a crayfish." Another smile. "I prefer the shade."

Idiot. Effie scoffed. Everyone knew that crayfish were actually dark green.

"I think we should sing 'Happy Birthday' first," said Tia. "It's Effie's birthday. She's twelve."

Effie set a pile of plates on an upturned wooden box, and Asher looked at her for the first time.

"Happy birthday," he said. "I hope you're having a good day."

"I don't care what you hope."

"If I keep my eye open really wide, like this, will it turn black?" asked Aiden.

"No." Asher touched her brother's knee. "It doesn't really work like that."

"Oh," said Aiden, looking disappointed.

"Let's sing," said Tia.

Effie looked up at Dad, who stood in the corner, watching. He didn't like Asher either, Effie could tell.

They sang "Happy Birthday," Tia's voice louder than everyone else's, and ate cake. Then Effie did the dishes. Aiden asked if Asher could sleep on the sofa and Dad said no. Not a hope. Then Tia asked and Asher was allowed to pitch his tent behind the hut.

Tia tapped Effie's arm as they were getting into bed, her skinny body buzzing with sugar and excitement, and she put her mouth right up to Effie's ear.

"I think he's beautiful," she whispered, her words wetting Effie's skin. "Like an elf with magic eyes."

Effie swatted her sister away, then she rolled over.

"That's gross."

―

Asher's stupid little tent was still there three weeks later.

Effie kicked a foot full of dirt against it whenever she walked to the compost toilet, but Asher never mentioned it, not even when he caught her in the act one time. He just held his arm out and offered her a peppermint Snifter like she was a stupid six-year-old. Effie had turned away, pretending not to notice. Aiden and Tia had probably finished the bag later, rotting their teeth. Not that Asher cared.

Dad barely spoke to Asher, and Asher was made to eat and sleep in his tent, but Dad let him stay. Asher was WWOOFing or some bullshit. Dad said that he needed help with the garden and fixing a few things around the hut. And in return, Asher got to eat their food.

It was stupid. Asher and his freaky black eye were stupid.

And it didn't take a genius to work out that he was a lousy gardener. Stuff kept dying and being ruined by possums. Dad had never needed help before; Effie had always done everything. And she never let the vegetables die.

Asher was probably a spy for one of those child-protection government places. One of the parents in Koraha must have dobbed on Dad, said he was an unfit parent or some lie.

Like they knew shit.

2025

EFFIE HELD THE drawing in shaking fingers, the bush breathing around her.

The bush was never fully quiet—there was always the hum of insects and the tweet of birds—but Effie couldn't hear anything beyond the fierce rush of her thoughts.

Dad was out there. Waiting. Watching. Shackled to the hut and the trees.

Effie steeled herself, then she looked at the drawing again, peering into the mind of a child. Seeing what Anya had seen.

She had drawn the inside of the hut. The sofa. The kitchen area. The curtain to the sleeping nook. On the floor, his chest bare and his eyes drawn as two *X*s, was Four. The cross was carved into him with a red pencil, pressed so hard that it had gone through the paper, leaving a hole. Next to the depiction of Four, splayed out with her head resting in a puddle of blood and two *X*s for eyes, was a body labeled "Mum."

Tia.

Effie stiffened as she read the words that were scribbled underneath.

He's taken her. Mum is with God now.

Now she will be properly punished.

Effie swallowed and looked out at the bush.

"What happened, Anya?" Her voice caught. "What happened to you here?"

She bit into the flesh of her cheeks. Blinking the sting from her eyes, Effie turned the paper over and silently mouthed the words on the back.

Leave. Or you will end up like Mum.

"What did he do to you?"

Effie folded the picture and slipped it into her pocket. She didn't run at the trees. She didn't scream Anya's name. The bush had her now. He had her. And, in the maze of trees, they were as good as gone.

Vanished.

Even with dogs and drones and a team of officers, the bush might never give them up. But she would try. Effie lifted her bag onto her back. She would get Lewis and do it right. Then she would strip the bush bare.

"I'll help her, Tia. I promise."

FEBRUARY 2005

EFFIE SLAMMED THE door shut on the outside toilet and stood, staring down at her legs. The blood had seeped through her trousers, and the damp cotton was sticking to her thighs. It was disgusting and filthy and embarrassing.

She was gross.

She was a horrible gross thing.

Effie blinked, her eyes red and swollen from refusing to cry, and she tore off a handful of toilet paper. June said it wouldn't hurt. She said that the first time there would only be a little bit of blood. Effie tried to dab it away, the white paper turning a vibrant red, and her arm started to shake. Something was wrong. Her body didn't know how to do it right. She was bleeding too much, not the little amount that June had said. Effie stuffed the paper into her underwear, sickened by herself. She was going to bleed out in a shitty toilet in the middle of the shitty bush.

Effie ground her hands into her eye sockets. She wouldn't cry. She pushed her hands in harder, bruising her eyeballs, as she pictured the box of pads hidden under the floorboards, far away, in Dad's room.

"You okay?"

Asher's voice drifted through the door, only a few inches away, and Effie wanted the ground to swallow her up.

"Go away," she shouted.

"Are you sure . . ."

A fiery anger pulsed through her. Her thoughts and words and underwear, all of it red.

"Just fuck off."

Effie's heart thumped in her chest as she listened to the softening of Asher's footsteps as he hurried away.

For ten minutes, maybe ten years, Effie didn't move. Then Asher's voice rang out, calling the kids, getting them to chase him.

"You can't catch me," he sang. "I'm the big bad wolf."

"Pow. Pow." Four's voice.

Then Aiden. "You can't run from us, Mr. Wolf. We're coming."

Effie sniffed back tears. Asher was leading them away. Away from the house.

When it went silent, she ran out and sprinted to the hut, to Dad's bedroom. She squeezed under the bed and lifted up the loose floorboard. Then she dashed back to the toilet, her fingers gripped around the prized box of pads.

A couple of days later, Effie woke early to find a small plastic bag next to her head. Inside were ten ginger teabags and a folded piece of paper. Effie took the note out, careful not to wake Tia, then opened it.

I grew up with an older sister.
She said that ginger helped.

Effie threw the bag across the room, and it hit the wall with a soft thud. What sort of creep snuck into someone's bedroom when they were sleeping? She turned over and closed her eyes.

But that afternoon, when everyone was out in the garden, she made herself two cups of tea and gulped them down as fast as she could.

Within a few hours, the cramps had eased.

Dad hadn't smiled all morning.

The darkness had crept into his cheeks and eyes, too heavy to lift. So Effie made Tia take the boys out onto the deck for lunch while Dad ate alone inside.

Effie walked around to the garden, looking for Asher. She couldn't let him see Dad today. She spotted Asher hunched near the vegetable garden, probably overwatering something, and walked over with her arms crossed.

"Are you ever going to leave?" she asked.

He looked up as she approached, showing his blue-eye side. He was hammering nails into a plank of old wood, fixing one of the cages.

"Morning to you too." He smiled.

"You've been here like six weeks." She scuffed at the dirt with her foot. "Isn't there, like, anyone out there who can stand you?"

"You don't like me much, do you?"

"Not much to like."

Asher sucked on his thumb, his finger disappearing into the circle of yellow beard. Cage fixing was a horrible job; the splinters were a bitch. It was probably why Dad got him to do it.

"Was it something that I did?"

Effie shrugged. "I don't care what you do."

"Your siblings seem to think I'm okay."

"Well then." Effie let out an exaggerated puff of air and clapped her hands twice. "Gold star for you. My baby brothers find you more interesting than a tree."

Asher smiled at that. No shock there.

"And Tia?"

"She's nine. And you're nineteen. Bit sick, don't you think?"

"I'm just looking out for her. Playing kid games and searching for fairies."

"Said every pedophile ever."

Asher didn't rise to it, didn't even frown. He just picked up another nail. Dad would have lost it.

Effie sat on a stump, ignoring him, hoping the splinters hurt his fingers.

"Is your dad from that Scandavia place too?" she asked eventually.

"Scandinavia. No." Asher sucked on his other thumb. "He's Kiwi. Olive-skinned, like my sister. I don't look anything like him."

Effie shrugged. "I don't look like my mum either. She's dead though."

"Oh, I'm sorry. That's—"

"Were the kids at school mean to you? Cos, you know, your eyes look sort of weird." Effie blinked as she said it. "Like an alien or something."

A smile crinkled the sides of Asher's eyes—a blue ocean and a dark abyss. "Sometimes, I guess." He grinned. "But some of the girls liked it . . . thought it was exotic."

"Jesus." Effie stuck two fingers down her throat and pretended to be sick. "I think I might vomit."

Asher smiled again and picked up a nail. They sat in silence for the next while as he hammered in the remaining corners. Then he grabbed a piece of the crappy wire netting and a set of pliers. Effie picked up a pair of gloves from behind the stump and chucked them at him.

"Don't want you bleeding on the cage," she said. "Your blood's probably blue or something. Probably poison the chard."

"That explains all the dead broad beans, then."

Effie almost smiled. "Weirdo."

Asher worked and Effie watched.

"My best friend says I shouldn't trust teenage boys," she said. "Says their brains are only made one way."

"And what way's that?"

"Dirty." Effie shrugged. "Full of yuck stuff, he says."

"Your best friend's a boy?"

"Yeah." Effie scowled. "So? Your best friend's probably a possum turd."

"Just seems a bit contradictory of him."

Effie frowned. *Idiot.* "How else would he know what boys are thinking?"

Asher held up his gloved hands. "You got me there."

Effie pulled at the grass and tugged a clump free.

"Do you work for social services?" she asked.

"Me?" His smile was almost a laugh.

Effie didn't smile back.

"Do I look like the poster boy for children's services? Shit, I once made a kid cry just by walking past him in the supermarket." Asher used his fingers to shoot beams from his eyes. "The boy probably thought I was an X-man or something."

Effie let his words sit a moment, refusing to ask what the heck an X-person was. "You're right," she said. "I'd be pretty peeved if you turned up as my social worker."

"One Sunday at church, I sneezed real loud, and a young girl turned and stared at me. She peed herself, right there on the wooden pew. Ruined her best dress."

Effie glowered at him. "You're gross."

"I wasn't the one who peed myself. I just sneezed. There's no law against sneezing."

Effie didn't know what to do with that. *Such a weirdo.*

"You didn't answer my question," she said.

"No," he replied, serious. "I don't work for social services."

"Why are you here, then?" Effie raised an eyebrow. "Cos I reckon the whole back-to-nature thing's total bullshit."

Something changed in Asher's face, like he had an itch under his skin, and he swallowed. Then he set the pliers on the ground.

"My sister," he said. "She went missing when she was fifteen." He looked down, his voice quiet. "I doubt she's alive, but . . ."

Effie's skin tingled, her body suddenly cold, and she pulled her sleeves over her hands. "Are you looking for her?"

"I'll always be looking for her."

"What happened?" Effie frowned. "Why'd she go missing?"

"Someone took her."

"Oh." She didn't know what to say. "I'm sorry."

"Effie!"

Her heart pulsed at the distant yell of her name.

"Effie!"

It was Dad, shouting for her.

"Effie." His voice was heavy. "Are you coming fishing or not?"

"Yes," she shouted as she shot up. "Yes. I'm just—"

Then Dad appeared, emerging from the side of the hut.

"Go get your stuff," he said. "I'm leaving in five minutes."

"Sure."

Then he turned away, leaving a black hole.

Asher looked at her like he wanted to say something—about Dad—but he thought better of it.

"Please," Effie whispered. "Dad . . . he just has bad days sometimes."

Asher stayed silent. Which was worse. He just looked at her—pitying her—with his stupid judging face. His stupid didn't-know-nothing eyes.

It made Effie angry.

"Do you wish your eyes weren't all creepy like that?" she said, irritated.

"God willed it that way."

"You don't actually believe in all that crap?"

"I do."

"Well, your god must be a bit of an arsehole."

Asher didn't say anything, and Effie turned and hurried after her dad.

2025

IT WAS THE middle of the night by the time Effie's fist reached Lewis's door.

She was exhausted and hungry and cold. But she didn't feel any of it. The guy she'd eventually hitched a lift from—just one passing ute in forty minutes—said she looked like shit.

Effie pounded on the wood, leaving a little bit of herself in each knock, until Lewis appeared in front of her, dressed, like he hadn't even tried to sleep.

"What happened?" he asked.

He didn't slam the door in her face, he didn't shout at her, he didn't tell her to piss off. He just moved to the side, letting her into his home.

"Lewis. I fucked up. I really . . ." Effie coughed and clutched the wall. "I'm sorry—"

"Stop." He took her hand, stilling her. "I'm going to look forward to this apology," he said, giving her a smile. "So I don't want you rushing through it now."

Effie smiled back at him, although she couldn't make it reach her eyes.

"Come on," he said, leading her inside.

Effie sat on Lewis's sofa, an untouched plate of toast in front of her, and talked him through what had happened. The girl. The body. Her brother. The drawing. The face in the trees.

"The kid was distraught, Lewis, and she was hugging the floor, really hugging it, like her mother's body was still there." Effie rubbed her face. "I know it sounds crazy, but I think, with the drawing . . ." She groaned. "Shit. I know it's mad, but I think when Anya ran away the first time, there were two bodies. That it wasn't just Four. I think my brother and sister were both killed in that hut, and that someone has moved Tia's body."

Lewis reached out to comfort her, but Effie shook her head. The nearness of him was too much.

"Okay then," he said, "say there were two bodies." He let out a puff of air. "Who could have moved her?"

"I don't know."

"Your dad?"

Effie sighed. "I don't know. I saw something, someone, but I can't be certain." She looked at him. "There's something out there, Lewis. Something in the trees."

He frowned. "What do you mean?"

She glanced at the window. "I'm not sure. For years I lived in that forest. I knew every sound of it. Every whisper in the trees. But it was a different feeling I got this time. It was like . . . like it frightened me."

She ran her hands through her matted hair. "I don't know. Maybe I'm just tired and hungry." She let out a long breath. "I just need to find her."

"We will."

Lewis took her hand this time, locking her fingers with his, and Effie let him.

"Are you ready for what's about to happen?" he said.

She nodded.

"Cos tomorrow's going to be a shitstorm."

Lewis stood and handed her a blanket. "I'm going to make some calls," he said. "And you need to sleep."

"I can help."

"I'm not forcing you into pajamas or even into a proper bed. But you won't be any use to that girl if you don't get some rest." He raised an eyebrow. "You'll scare the shit out of those Christchurch cops looking like that. And if I'm being honest, you kind of smell." Lewis smiled and started to walk away. "The shower's down the hall on the left."

"And your room?" she asked, her heart pounding.

He stopped and turned.

"It's just . . . I could do with some company tonight."

He looked straight at her, at the girl he'd known a lifetime ago, and for a moment Effie forgot how to breathe.

"I know about Charlotte," she said. "June told me."

Lewis didn't move, he didn't look away, and Effie's heart hammered.

"I just don't want to be alone."

"It's the first door on the right," he said. "T-shirts are in the bottom drawer."

Then he walked out with his phone already to his ear, and the ache in Effie's stomach grew.

Lewis was up and gone by the time Effie opened her eyes.

She hadn't heard him come in; she'd fallen asleep to the soft pacing of his footsteps in the hallway. They hadn't spoken—hadn't so much as touched—but the dent and smell of him was still in the covers next to her. Effie stretched a hand out, letting the fading warmth soak into her skin, then she reached for her phone. She unlocked it, read through the hundred messages from Blair, and typed a reply.

I wanted to message you first. No doubt it will be all over the news by tomorrow night. Even in the UK. A runaway bush girl and two bodies. The press is going to have a fucking field day. It's not good, Blair. I messed up. I lost her.

I'm not okay.

Blair's reply was instant.

Do you want me to fly out? I can be on a plane in twelve hours. I could do with a few good movies. Also, I secretly love plane food. Weird. I know. I'm judging myself. X

Effie let out a jolt of laughter. She actually laughed.

No. But thank you.

I'll have my phone on and my passport packed. Super horrid photo, taken when I was hungover. No makeup AT ALL. But I'll do it for you. X

Effie squeezed the phone tight, then stepped from Lewis's bed, ready for the shitstorm.

The next twelve hours were hell. Even with a missing kid and one—maybe two—dead bodies, things took time to mobilize. It didn't help that Christchurch was 550 kilometers away.

Charlotte—his wife—was 550 kilometers away.

Lewis made call after call, and Effie looked through the photos on her phone, over and over, searching for anything. Normally, another sole-charge officer would have been called in from Franz Josef to help secure the scene while they waited on the big guns. But the scene was in the middle of the bush, and the potential murder weapon was missing, so normal was out. Lewis had checked and there was absolutely no precedent for this on the West Coast. Anya, like her name, was an anomaly.

But by 8 p.m., the small police station had been transformed into a bustling incident headquarters. Laptops had been set up on desks, large evidence boards had been pinned to the walls, and the place was littered with half-drunk cups of coffee and leftovers from dinner. Both Effie and Lewis had been interviewed, and she'd handed over the drawing and the notes from Tia. Now they were waiting for instructions. It was no longer Lewis's case; that had been made clear. It was up to Detective Morrow and the real cops now.

"Arseholes," Effie had whispered.

She sat on a plastic chair and stared at the photo of Anya on the wall. Lewis had taken it shortly after she'd turned up, her dress still bloodied and her eyes hollow. There were photos of her ankles too, the skin raw and scarred, and a picture of a badly healed scar along her forearm. From a knife, perhaps. The dress had been sent to the lab in Christchurch, but Effie didn't hold out much hope. The blood would provide DNA, maybe, but that didn't seem particularly useful given that the entire family lived off-grid. *Like ghosts in the trees.* But they had Four's blood, and if they could get Anya's, they might be able to find proof of Tia on the dress, drips of her sister soaked into the fabric.

"We're heading out at 5 a.m.," said Lewis, handing her a coffee. "The weather should have cleared by then."

Effie turned to the window, an onslaught of rain and wind battering the glass, and tried not to think about Anya. Shivering. Wet. Alone. She closed her eyes. Or maybe she wasn't alone. And maybe that was worse.

"We've both got a spot to fly out on the Eagle," Lewis said. "Glorified spectators, I'm told. No touching."

"How considerate of them," she said, her voice cold, "giving a seat to the only person who knows where to go."

"The locals have already mobilized," said Lewis, sitting next to her. "Hanging up on journalists left, right, and center, and blocking emails. It will get out, of course, but we're among good people. The locals are on our side. At the moment, the press is just sniffing. Shooting in the dark."

"And this lot," said Effie, gesturing toward the room of people.

There were eleven of them in total, the whole shebang: Criminal Investigation Branch, the Armed Offenders Squad and the dog team.

"They're doing their jobs," said Lewis. "Morrow's a good detective. Hard. By the book. But she knows what she's doing."

Effie let out a sigh. "I know. I've been watching her." She turned to Lewis. "But even the best detectives can't catch ghosts."

MARCH 2005

"I HATE YOU."

The words broke from her in a whisper, and Effie shoved him hard in the chest, her hands thumping into a mountain. But Dad barely moved. He just stood there in the garden, useless and stinking of sweat and animal shit.

"You missed it." Her voice shook, and she blinked back hot tears. "You missed his birthday."

"Effie—"

Dad reached out but she stepped back from him, her legs trembling.

"You were gone for five days." She clenched her fists. "Not three." She pointed at the steps. "He sat there on that bottom step, waiting for you. He sat there all day, holding on to that stupid slingshot you made, but you didn't come. Cos you're nothing but a stupid, shitty—"

"Effie, I'm—"

"You promised to take him hunting." Then she shouted, "*You promised!*"

Dad looked at her and she hated him, the anger so hot that her cheeks and neck burned.

"I'll take him tomorrow," he said. "Aiden will like—"

"You don't know what Aiden likes." Effie was panting. "You don't know anything about him."

"Effie, that's enough."

"Where do you go anyway?" she spat.

Dad didn't react, he didn't say anything, and Effie wanted to hurt him. She wanted to wound him with something.

"I bet there's some girl," she sputtered, the flood pouring out of her. "Some girl that you're fucking? A—"

He hit her then. His palm collided with her face, and a white pain exploded through her cheekbone. Effie touched her cheek, then she looked up at him—his face wet with tears—and she ran. She ran past him, through the garden and into the bush. Past tree after tree, heart thumping, until she couldn't run anymore. Until the weight in her lungs and legs was too heavy to hold up.

Effie lurched forward, coughing, then she screamed into the ferns, so loud that the bush stilled and the kererū stopped singing. She punched a fist into the earth, cursing him, then she punched it again. She beat her knuckles into the dead leaves, over and over, until her fingers burned. Then she collapsed, defeated, and rolled onto her back. Seconds passed as she stared up at the cover of fronds, then minutes. Eventually, as she lay in the damp leaves, the heat in her started to dilute.

Half an hour later—the wet earth long soaked through her clothes—he found her.

"I brought you a jacket," he said.

Effie closed her eyes. "Piss off."

"And some green tea." He held up a flask.

"I hate green tea."

"Come on." Asher took a step closer. "You'll catch a chill."

She opened her eyes.

He knelt down next to her. "I saw what happened."

"You didn't see anything."

"Your dad . . ." Asher hesitated. "Is he always like that? It's just, sometimes, he seems . . ."

Effie wiped herself off and stood up. "You don't know anything about my dad," she said, glaring at him. "Or me."

Asher followed her as she walked away, trailing her like a pathetic puppy.

"I'm worried about you," he said. "The way he gets, it's not right. He scares me."

"Then leave." Effie turned and looked back at him. "Leave."

"He shouldn't hurt you like that. It's not normal."

She scowled at him. "And what, you are?"

"He needs help."

"And you need to wear sunglasses."

Asher reached out and grabbed her arm, and Effie wanted to punch him. She tried to tug free, but he held her still, staring at her.

"It would be better," he said, quiet and serious, "for him to have a rock hung around his neck and to drown at sea." Asher gripped tight. Too tight. "Better to drown than to harm his children."

Effie pulled her arm free. "Have you gone proper mad?"

"Matthew 18:6," said Asher, his face stern. "God promises to visit terrible consequences upon any man who hurts his children."

"Visit upon?" Effie backed away. "You've definitely gone crazy."

"I'm worried."

"I can take care of myself."

"You're just a kid."

Asher tried to touch her again, and Effie spun around.

"Look," she shouted. "I don't need help from you or your stupid god." She held his gaze. "It's bullshit, all of it."

"You don't know that."

"Ha."

Effie looked into his eyes, into those two deep pools—sky blue and night black—and smiled.

"It's all total crap, Asher."

For a moment, he was quiet, just staring at her. "My eyes weren't always like this," he said eventually. "Different colors."

Effie shrugged. He could have had one green and one purple eye for all she cared.

"They both used to be blue," he continued, like she gave a damn. "Two normal eyes, 'til the day I turned thirteen."

She raised an eyebrow at that. "Pretty shitty birthday present."

"And no return receipt."

Effie rolled her eyes. "So?" she asked, unable to stop herself. "What happened?"

He looked away; his expression different. "My dad," he said. Soft. His voice thinned out. "My dad punched me."

There was a beat of quiet.

Asher gave a sad smile. "Too hard that time, I guess."

Then another.

Effie turned her head away. They weren't the same. She and Asher. Her dad and Asher's dad. Effie blinked, closing her eyes to the glare. To the sun. Not to tears. Not to the sad burn in her stomach and cheekbone. After a few seconds, she turned back.

"I'm sorry," she managed, and she was—sorry. "About your eye."

But Asher's story wasn't her story. His dad wasn't her dad.

"Could . . ." Asher paused. "Could we maybe keep this between us?"

Effie crossed her arms. "Doesn't bother me."

He smiled. No shock there.

"This secret," Effie frowned. "It doesn't make us friends or anything, though." She kicked at a dangling fern. "And the God stuff's still bullshit."

2025

IT WAS THE German shepherds that found the girl. She was curled up like a koru, ropes tied around her ankles and wrists.

"Morrow is coming back to get us," said Lewis, lowering his radio. "Then she'll take us to the girl. Detective Constable Wilson is waiting with her."

Effie glanced over his shoulder toward the hut, her mind incapable of forming words. Unable to still the quiver in her lips and jaw.

"It's not too far," he added.

Lewis put an arm around her, the solidness of him holding her up, and Effie clung on. Behind them, the police swarmed around the property like ants, all of them with a specific task: to bag, photo, swab, draw.

"I should have stayed and looked for her," said Effie. "I should have searched for her until my feet bled."

"Effie. She could have been anywhere. In any direction."

"But she wasn't, was she?" Her throat swelled. "She was only a few hundred meters away."

"Even then, in the dark and with the trees, you could have walked straight past her." He looked at her. "You did the right thing."

"Or I left a scared child to die."

Lewis went to say something—something that she didn't deserve—when Morrow appeared, and Effie pulled away.

"Come on, you two," said Morrow. "You're needed. The nurse practitioner too."

Kyle, who'd been hovering a few meters away, glanced over. Effie walked after Morrow, numbed everywhere but her stomach, and the two men followed.

There'd been a girl on Skye once, in Effie's first month on the rescue team, who'd run off on a family walk. A full callout had followed: helicopters, dogs, locals, police. Rain had lashed down in sheets, and the heather had swollen beneath their feet. They'd walked in lines, their bodies angled against the wind, spaced twenty meters apart, hands tucked under their armpits, eyes to the ground.

If you see anything, raise your hand.

A boot. A glove. A jacket. That's what Keith had been praying for when he barked out orders. A backpack. A hat.

They'd walked for hours, the rain stinging their eyes and their torches illuminating the black hillside. No one had asked to stop. They'd just walked forward, one foot in front of the other, like there was nothing else to do.

It was Effie who'd eventually halted as the line—and the flicker of hope—moved on without her. Then she lifted an arm, her fingers trembling, unable to call out as she looked down.

Raise your hand.

There, among the trees, she'd seen the tangle of dark hair. The back of the child's head. The tiny body, face down in the river.

Connie. Six years old.

"Are you ready?" asked Morrow, jolting Effie back to the present.

"Yes."

"We haven't moved her," she said. "We haven't been able to."

"Is she chained?" asked Effie.

Morrow shook her head. "You'll see."

They walked the remaining hundred meters in silence, bashing through the thick bush, until the crouched figure of Morrow's young colleague, Wilson, came into view, his eyes fixed on a small crate.

Oh god. Effie covered her mouth with her hand. It was Four's shelter, the one he used to nap in. Except where the front had once been open, it was sealed off with a sheet of wire fencing. *A cage.*

Morrow held up a hand, stopping them, then nodded at Effie. "Just you."

Effie stepped up to the wooden shelter. She could still feel the splinters, the tiny shards of memory and trauma buried in her skin.

"Anya?" She knelt in front of the box. "It's Effie."

The girl's coiled fingers gripped the wire door, wrists bound, pulling it shut. Keeping herself in and the world out.

"I'm sorry," said Effie. "I shouldn't have left you."

She crouched down so their eyes were level, just centimeters apart, and Anya snarled at her, her tissue-paper skin so fragile that the anger and wildness threatened to burst out of her. But there was something deeper in the greens of her eyes. She wasn't wild. She was hurting.

"I know that you don't trust me yet," said Effie, "and I have no right to ask that of you. But I promise I just want to keep you safe." She touched a finger to the wire. "I'm not going to hurt you, or make you do anything you don't want to."

Anya studied Effie's mouth, her words.

"But I do need you to come out of there. And I need you to come back to Koraha with me."

Effie moved her hand to the makeshift latch as the girl watched.

"I'm going to open the door now," she said, "so I need you to let go of the wire."

Slowly, Anya uncurled her fingers, her eyes focused on Effie's hands, and Effie pulled the door open. Gently and gradually, she reached for the girl's arms.

"Can I untie you?"

Anya nodded.

Effie released her hands first, the rope sodden and surprisingly loose, then she untied her ankles.

"You're safe now."

Effie was prepared when the girl leaped at her. Anya dove into Effie's body, sobbing, and started hitting her chest, the child's punches weak and fatigued. And Effie let her.

You're safe now. You're safe.

She didn't notice Lewis and Kyle until it was too late. Until Kyle had already forced the needle into the child's arm.

"*No!*" Effie screamed.

She pushed Kyle away, but the damage had been done, the sedative was flowing through the girl's veins. Lewis tried to take Effie's arm, but she elbowed him away and wrapped herself around the girl.

"How could you?" she yelled. "She was just scared!" Effie thumped the ground with her fist. "How is she meant to trust me now?"

"She was attacking you."

"Barely," Effie shot back. "She's exhausted. And I was handling it."

"No." Lewis looked at her, his face hard. "You were letting a child beat you, because you think that's what you deserve."

Effie still hadn't spoken to Lewis by the time the police car dropped them off at June's house.

Anya was asleep in the back seat, balled up under Lewis's jacket. They'd had to stretcher her out to the river, to an open area where the helicopter had managed to land, then they'd been flown out.

Focus on the kid. Morrow's words. *Not the body. That's our problem now.*

Effie opened the car door and lifted Anya out; she was barely the weight of a four-year-old.

"I've put fresh sheets on her bed," said June, appearing in the drive.

"Thank you."

"How long will she be out?"

"Another hour maybe," said Effie. "Kyle said she'll be a bit foggy for a while."

She followed June inside to the girl's room, while Lewis waited in the living room.

"What happened?" asked June, nodding in Lewis's direction.

"Nothing."

"Sure looks like nothing."

Effie tucked the girl in, her body still curled tight, as though even in sleep, she wanted to make herself small and invisible.

"I'll stay with her," said Effie, sitting.

June walked across to the bed and leaned in, kissing Effie on the head.

"I had a nice chat on the phone with that lovely friend of yours."

Effie frowned. "Blair?"

"The very one," said June. "Smart girl. She told me to hug you twice a day, and box you about the ears at least once."

"Bloody Blair."

"Oh." June frowned. "And she said to tell you that Rimu has grown accustomed to Egyptian cotton."

Effie rolled her eyes. "My dog."

"Ah." June's smile widened. "That makes a lot more sense."

She went to leave but stopped, turning briefly in the doorway. "And I agree," said June. "It would never have worked with that Greg fellow."

"Christ."

"Far too short. Not like—"

"Out." Effie pointed at the door. "Now."

"I'm going, I'm going."

Effie placed a pillow on the floor. Then she sat by Anya's bed with her arms resting on the edge of the mattress.

"I'm sorry," she whispered.

After thirty minutes or so, Anya's eyelids fluttered, her mind half in and half out of the world.

"You're back in Koraha," said Effie. "And you're in bed in June's house. You're safe."

Anya stirred, life leaking slowly into her body.

"The nurse sedated you in the bush. He put you to sleep." She swallowed. "I'm sorry, I didn't know he was going to do that. He was just worried you might hurt yourself."

Two green eyes—far older than any other part of her—opened, and Anya stared at Effie, her little body still. The following minutes slipped by in silence—just aunty and niece. Then slowly, Effie reached a hand forward and set it on the bed a few centimeters from the girl's arm.

"I don't want to have to restrain you."

"I won't run away."

Effie blinked.

"I'm not allowed back there now."

The girl curled tighter, shrinking, then she rolled over with her back to Effie.

"I'm not clean." Her voice was barely a whisper. "You dirtied me. Just like Mum."

MARCH 2005

SHE WAS ALONE in the dark. And she was going to die.

Effie tried to move, her legs first, then her arms, but she couldn't. She couldn't, because her body was dying. She was going to die alone in the trees.

Pain shot through her head, like a knife gutting out the bit behind her eye sockets, and she let out a whimper. It was dark, so dark that it swallowed up the bush around her. With no moon to carve out the shapes of the trees, and no torch, she couldn't see anything. Just a wall of black.

Just blackness and the piercing cries of morepork. Effie sniffed and blinked her eyes. She shouldn't have angered him.

She shuffled forward an inch, her bare arms and legs trembling, but her weakened body collapsed to the cold earth.

She shouldn't have said those things.

I bet there's some girl. Some girl that you're fucking.

The muscles in her neck spasmed as she strained to lift her head, a tiredness rooting her body to the ground. The heavy rain had stopped, and the ponga draped in front of her like a curtain. But the ground was wrong. There was no softness to it. No dirt. No dampness. It was hard and flat and rough. Like slats of wood.

Like a box.

Fear beat in Effie's stomach as she strained to remember—to think—but the blade behind her eyes kept slicing up the memories.

His face.

His outstretched arms.

She shouldn't have made him angry.

Effie tried to kick and thrash, screaming at her leaden body. *No. Not heavy.* She was tied up. There was a rope tied around her wrists and ankles. It was tearing into her skin, chewing away at her flesh.

Effie fought until the exhaustion claimed her muscles and forced her to stop. A little voice whispered into her ear that it was her fault. Her cruel words. That she'd done this.

Of course she'd done this.

Her eyes flickered closed. And half-conscious, she saw it. An orange glimmer of light. A sphere.

Then, with her cheek pressed to the floor of the crate, a scream spilled from her. Loud and feral and wild.

And the light vanished.

When she eventually opened her eyes, Dad was carrying her, holding her like a baby. Effie looked up through the haze of pain and sleepiness and caught a glimpse of his face, his eyes and cheeks damp. She pressed herself into the beat of his chest and let him save her.

―

The next morning, as Dad helped her wash—his big hands slow and gentle—he found flecks of tree nettles in Effie's hair.

Little green teeth of poison.

Dad said she must have stumbled through a patch of them when she ran off. The white stinging hairs must have poisoned her. He had paled as he said it, and he'd quickly wiped away tears—but Effie had seen them.

Dad didn't leave her side the whole day. He brought her soup and warm tea and wet flannels, and he let her sleep in his bed.

That evening, Tia found a picture of tree nettles in one of Mum's old nature books, and she laid it out on the bed between Effie and Aiden. Aiden was like a bony hot water bottle, just sharp corners and heat.

"Look," said Tia, her eyes wide. "They're, like, super dangerous. They can give you headaches and make you all confused and blurry. And they can stop your arms and legs from working properly." Tia's mouth hung open. "Woah." She prodded at the page. "It says here that in 1961, some guy even died after he was stung." She turned back to Effie. "You could have died."

Aiden gasped.

"But she didn't," said Dad, squeezing Effie's arm, the skin still red and sore from the nettles. Not rope. "And she's going to be absolutely fine."

Effie looked at the picture. Just some stupid plant.

Asher appeared in the door then, his eyes cold. He flicked his gaze from Effie to her dad, then he walked in and placed a cup of tea on the table next to her. As Tia shoved the book at Dad, saying something about paralysis, Asher leaned in so close that his lips brushed against Effie's hair, and he whispered into her ear.

"He's lying," he said. "I saw him."

Then he stood and walked out. But the chill of his words clung to her as the door closed behind him.

Thud.

Effie pulled Aiden into her. But the heat of him wasn't enough now.

2025

WHEN EFFIE OPENED her eyes, the bedroom was half-hidden in shadow.

Night hadn't fully settled. It was that before time, when the late afternoon light had deepened and lost its strength, and the air was still.

There was a blanket over her, a layer of warmth that hadn't been there before. She rolled over, the hard floor aching in her hips and shoulder blades, and she pushed herself into a seated position. She must have fallen asleep briefly.

Shit.

With a jolt, Effie spun around and thrust her palm onto the girl's bed. But Anya was there. Effie's lungs collapsed with relief. She was there. Awake. Staring back at Effie, her little body drowned in the swell of blankets.

"I'm sorry," said Effie. "I didn't mean to fall asleep."

Anya didn't respond.

"Did you sleep?"

Anya gave a shake of her head, then she held out her arm. Two necklaces hung from her fist, the two swirled halves of a green heart. Instinctively, Effie touched a hand to her chest, but her pounamu was gone. Anya moved her hand and the silver chains swung in the space between them.

"If you place them next to each other," said Effie, "they make a heart."

Anya pushed the two halves together.

"Did your mum give it to you?"

She nodded.

"Before she died?"

The silence hardened and Effie waited, every cell in her body feeling the passing seconds.

Then the child spoke.

"I took it from her body," said Anya, her voice small. "Mum didn't deserve to take it with her."

"Take it where?"

Anya looked down at her hands and rubbed her thumb across the stone heart.

"To hell," she whispered.

The girl didn't flinch. But the words that dripped out of her were small and soft, like they drained her of energy.

Effie swallowed. "Why didn't she deserve it?"

"Mum was bad." Anya sucked her lip. "She broke his rules."

"Whose rules?"

Anya looked at Effie, her eyes wide and pleading, then she shook her head. Tears clouded her green eyes. "I'm not supposed to say."

"It's okay." Effie placed a hand on her arm. "You don't have to tell me."

"You won't make me?"

"I won't make you."

The child frowned.

"I won't make you do anything," said Effie.

Another frown. "What if I want you to leave me alone?"

"Then I'll leave you alone." Effie managed a gentle smile. "Until you're ready for me to come back."

Anya lifted both necklaces and slipped them over her head. "A heart," she said.

"Yes." Effie squeezed her arm. "Our heart. Made from you and me."

Anya curled her fingers around the pendant. "You and me," she repeated.

"You and me. Two parts of a whole."

Anya looked down. "Can I be alone now, please?"

Effie forced the muscles in her neck and body to move—to nod and stand up.

"Of course."

There was nothing to do but walk out. Right now, trust was all that Effie had to offer the girl.

As the door clicked shut behind her, Effie walked along the hall to the living room. The bedroom window had been bolted, and the only way out was through the locked front door. To escape, Anya would have to find the key and walk straight past the living room.

"Hey."

Lewis's voice jolted her, and Effie spun around.

"You're still here?"

He nodded. "June has gone out for a bit."

Effie walked into the room and stopped in front of him. "Did you put a blanket on me?"

Lewis shook his head. "I didn't want to risk disturbing Anya."

It was her then.

Lewis smiled, but not properly. There was a sadness to him, hanging heavy in his eyes and shoulders.

"Are you okay?" she asked.

His smile faded. "I loved them too, you know." He swallowed. "Four and Tia."

"Lewis . . ."

"I've never been quite as tough as you." He wiped his face. "Never been as good at hiding my—"

"I'm sorry." Effie sat next to him.

"Me too." He squeezed her hand. "About your brother and sister."

She moved closer, close enough to feel the warmth of him. Close enough for her heart to remember, for it to hurt. But still, she couldn't make herself move away. She rested her head on his shoulder, and Lewis pulled her into him, the act of kindness a fraction of what she actually wanted.

"I'll watch the door," he said.

"You should sleep."

He smiled. "There isn't a single part of me that could sleep with you this close."

Heat flushed through Effie. "You shouldn't say things like that. You're . . ."

You're married.

She took a breath. "What about Charlotte?"

"Charlotte and I are separated." Lewis paused. "We split up about eight months ago."

"But June said—"

"We tried, for two years we really tried. But we could never . . ." He closed his eyes. "June knew that things had been tough, but I never told her we'd officially ended things."

"I'm so sorry, Lewis." Effie leaned into him. "June said Charlotte was nice."

He managed half a smile. "I moved to Christchurch about two years after you left. I just couldn't stay in Koraha. You were everywhere I looked. Then the earthquakes happened." His body stiffened. "One hundred eighty-five people dead."

Effie swallowed. She'd read the headlines. D*evastating* 6.3 *mag-*

NITUDE EARTHQUAKE ROCKS THE SOUTH. OUR WORST DAY: A CITY TURNED TO RUBBLE. She'd watched the news. The devastation. The deaths. The heartache. All the while thinking Lewis was safe in Koraha.

"You were there," she managed, "when they hit?"

"For the February one, yes. I was on a job in Edgeware, north of the city center." Lewis shook his head. "It was like the whole house suddenly roared and shook around me . . . more violent than anything I'd known, and I had to brace myself." His voice became quiet. "It wasn't like the small earthquakes I'd felt before. It was jarring, like some impossible force was trying to snap the bones of the house in two. I kept looking up at the ceiling, waiting for it to collapse. I'd never heard noise like it." He looked down at his hand in Effie's. "By the time the first shakes stopped, the house was a mess. There were shelves on the floor. Tables and wardrobes smashed. And dust. Dust everywhere."

Effie didn't know what to say.

"I felt I had to stay in Christchurch after that, for a while anyway. To help."

"That's when you met Charlotte?"

He shook his head. "I stayed in Christchurch for about ten months. Then Nan needed a hip replacement, so I came back to help her out, and ended up back home for six years." He teased a strand of Effie's hair through his fingers. "I don't know, maybe it was a post-disaster thing, but I felt that I needed to go back to Christchurch. Like I'd abandoned the city or something. So in early 2018, I returned."

"And," said Effie, "the city?"

"It was unrecognizable," he said. "Completely rebuilt. But after seven years, people were coming back." He smiled then. "And one of them was Charlotte."

Effie forced a small smile in response.

"Charlotte lost her boyfriend in the quakes," he said. "They'd been together since high school. And in a sense, I'd lost you. I guess loss, in its weird way, brought us together." Lewis almost laughed. "Hardly a rock-solid foundation for a marriage."

"No. I guess not."

"And," he continued, "as we healed, we no longer needed each other in the same way."

Healed.

The word stung.

"I moved back to Koraha in 2023—Nan wasn't doing so well. Charlotte stayed in Christchurch. We tried to make it work long-distance, but in reality, we were fighting to save something that hadn't ever really been there. We both knew that." Lewis sighed. "Charlotte moved to Auckland last month, to start afresh."

Effie swallowed. "I'm glad Charlotte was there for you."

He smiled. Then he brushed a hand through her hair.

"The next few days are going to be hard," he said, his voice changed. "They'll want to do interviews. You should rest."

Effie touched the smoothness of his belt, her heart racing, then she placed a hand on his stomach, her fingers separated from him by nothing but a few millimeters of cotton.

"Effie . . ."

She pulled her hand back.

Stupid. Stupid.

She shoved her hands under her arms. What the fuck was she doing? She needed to focus. She needed to think about Anya and Tia and the next forty-eight hours.

She cleared her throat, her body stiffening against his. "Do you think Tia's body was in the hut?" She spoke without looking at him. "That Dad could have moved her?"

"I don't know."

Lewis gave a sigh—a policeman again—and Effie dug her fingers into her arm.

"Or," she continued, "do you think that Tia's been dead for a long time? And that Anya hasn't had a real mum for years?"

"It's possible," he said. "Trauma can do all sorts of things to the mind. And to our memories."

"She's afraid of someone," said Effie. "Someone did something to her."

Lewis hesitated. "You don't think it was Four?"

"No." Effie let her head sink into him again. "I don't."

Lewis's arms tightened around her, protecting her, just like he'd always done.

"If your dad's out there," he said, "we'll find him."

"He can't get away with it again, Lewis."

"He won't." He kissed her head. "You won't let him."

Effie sat at the kitchen table and stared at her phone. Blair, whose face filled the screen, was in her blue work scrubs.

"I just," Effie bent forward, resting her elbows on the table, "I don't know how to be around her, Bee. It's like she's two people in one body and I never know who I'm going to get—the kid who hates me so much that she wants to throw herself off a bridge, or the kid who's sitting in the living room right now doing watercolor paintings with June."

"It's quite calming." Blair yawned. "Shona, the art therapist, gets the patients doing it at work. Could be worth you giving—"

"Blair." Effie snapped. "I'm not about to do a bloody watercolor."

"Right." Blair rubbed her face. "Sorry. I'm running on caffeine and cocaine at the moment." She stopped to take a gulp from a mug with "Born in the NHS" printed across it. "What time is it with you?"

"About three in the afternoon." Effie sighed. "I'm just back from my interview with Morrow."

"Fun had by all, then?"

"Like a day at Disneyland."

"That bad?"

"No," she said. "Not really. Morrow asked all of the right questions. It's just that I don't have anything to tell her. I keep going over it in my head, but I don't know what happened out there."

"Did they grill you about your childhood?"

"Not really." Effie hesitated. "A few questions about Dad and Tia. And Four, of course. But it was a lifetime ago. Tia and Four have been strangers to me for years. When I left, they were just children, Bee."

"So were you." There was a pause before Blair spoke again. "And the kid?" she asked.

"They're coming here to interview her soon," said Effie. "So I guess she'll either sit in silence or try to scratch their eyes out." She sighed. "I don't know. Do you have any advice? Anything from a medical perspective?"

Blair clutched the mug between her hands, staring into it as if the answer might be at the bottom. "Did you ever read *Room*?" she asked. "About the woman who's held captive with her son."

"Blair."

"Just bear with me."

"Yes." Effie rolled her eyes. "I've read it."

"Well, there's this scene where they measure everything in the room, as a sort of fun activity. The walls, and the table, and the chair. Until the mum can't take it anymore. Because she knows it's not just some game. She sees the room for what it is, a prison. But to the boy, who was born there, the room isn't something to be feared or questioned. The room is all that he's ever known. For him, what's scary is outside. The boy understands the rules of the room, and even though he's a prisoner, it's where he feels safe. It's where his life makes sense."

Blair set the mug down and leaned into the screen, just centimeters away, rather than a whole world.

"When the boy escapes," she continued, "everything about the outside world overwhelms him, and he wants to go back. So when his mum tells him that he can't, the boy is distraught." She paused. "It's the same for Anya. Even if she's escaped something terrible, something that *we* know to be wrong, it's going to take time for her to trust this new reality. We also don't know exactly what she's been told about the world. It might be that she's been groomed to distrust outsiders. To fear us."

Blair went quiet, and for a moment, neither of them said anything.

"So," said Effie, "just to be clear . . . after all that, your big takeaway piece of advice for me is time."

"Exactly." A smile pulled at the corners of Blair's mouth. "A good old dollop of time and patience. Your favorites."

"Great."

"I reckon some chocolate wouldn't go amiss either. Most kids can be bought with chocolate."

"Time and chocolate." Effie shook her head. "You really are a rare font of wisdom."

A beeping sounded in the distance and Blair tapped at her phone.

"Right," she said. "That's me. Break's over. Best get back to the trenches."

"Miss you."

"Love you."

Blair blew a kiss into the screen and hung up.

MARCH 2005

THERE WAS NO Asher the next day. Or the day after that.

Without realizing it, Effie found herself on the deck, listening out for the sounds of him—the silly voices he put on for Four, and the crack of twigs when he played chase with Aiden. Effie hated herself for it, and she scuffed at the ground with her foot. She was sick of waiting. For Asher. For dad. Never knowing when some stupid man might show up and decide not to be a twat for half a minute. She kicked at one of her dad's shoes and it rolled off the deck and onto the grass. She wasn't meant to say *twat*. June said it was unladylike. But then, June didn't have to live in the stupid hut with rats crapping in her bed. June didn't know shit. Effie wasn't meant to say *shit* either. But fuck it.

She picked up a twig off the deck and hurled it at the darkening bush.

"Stupid. Stupid."

It was her own stupid fault for waiting for good things to grow from the dirt and the rot. Dark was dark and Dad was Dad.

End. Of. Story.

Besides, she didn't even want Asher to come back. It was good that he was gone. She didn't even know if she liked him. She probably, definitely, didn't. Asher confused things. He put ideas in her head about Dad, ideas that didn't do any good. Dad wasn't the best dad in the world. *Obviously.* But Dad needed her. He wasn't bad. Asher was wrong about him.

"Effie."

She turned at the whisper of Four's voice. He was three now, almost three and a half, his red hair like Effie's and his dark eyes just like Mum's.

"Come here." Effie reached down and scooped him up onto her hip. "Did you brush your teeth?"

"Tia did it."

Effie kissed his head. "Good boy."

"Has Asher gone?"

"I think so."

"I miss him." Four tucked his head under Effie's chin. "Will he come back?"

Four looked at her, needing her to lie to him.

Effie smiled and squeezed his cheek. "You'll get to see Lewis in Koraha next month," she said.

"Will Lewis play with me?"

"Lots. Lewis loves playing with you."

Four smiled. "Lewis holds me upside down sometimes. Like a bat."

"Come on." Effie turned and started to walk toward the door, the shadows chasing the last hints of warmth from the day. "Bedtime."

"But . . ." He looked at her, uncertain. "I still miss Asher."

She squeezed him tight. "That's okay. You can still miss him."

Effie chewed on her lip as she walked into the hut. She still hadn't decided if she was going to miss Asher or not.

"Are you Asher's favorite?" asked Four.

"Sorry?" She frowned, confused. "What do you mean?"

"You got a note."

Effie looked at Four. "What note?"

"In your pillow." Four yawned. "Aiden found it."

She set Four down and hurried to the sleeping nook. The crumpled piece of paper was still there, jammed into her pillowcase. Effie held it out as her eyes scanned the note and her skin warmed.

Effie. I'm sorry. If you ever need anything, write to this address.

On a separate line, Asher had scribbled an address for somewhere in Hokitika. Underneath it were four words.

And I'll come back.

Asher.

Effie balled the paper and all of its stupid promises in her fist, and threw it across the room.

She didn't need anything from him. Not now. Or ever.

2025

THE FOUR OF them sat around the kitchen table, each with a plastic cup of water. Effie had decided against the added complication of hot liquids and hard ceramics.

Anya sat next to Effie with her head down, pulling at her fingers. There was a visible agitation to the girl's legs, the hot hum of fight or flight thrumming through her muscles, but she was there. Lewis hovered in the doorway, just in case.

Morrow nodded at her young colleague, Detective Constable Wilson, then gave Effie an encouraging smile. Effie didn't dislike Morrow, which was something, but there was a formality to the detective that didn't sit well. The woman was all procedure. All rules.

"Are you comfortable, Anya?" asked Morrow.

The girl didn't react. She just stared downward, her attention fully committed to picking the frayed skin from the sides of her nails.

"Anya, your aunty is going to explain the situation to you," Morrow continued, "so that you understand what is about to happen."

Effie slipped a hand across the table. "You don't have to say anything if you don't want to, Anya. Okay? You're not in trouble. The questions the police officer is about to ask you are all about us helping you. Nothing else. You haven't done anything wrong. We just want to try to work out what happened, so we can help."

Anya's eyes flicked toward Effie's hand.

"But," Effie continued, "if you do want to tell us anything, it's really important that you tell us the truth. Do you understand?"

A nod. A small but definite nod.

"Good," said Morrow.

She shuffled on her seat, the chair dwarfed by the detective's big-boned figure. Her uniform pulled tight across her square shoulders, and the buttons at the front of her shirt strained. There was a hardness worn into her face, but her expression was kind.

"Let's start with an easy question, shall we?" Morrow smiled at the top of the girl's bowed head. "How old are you, Anya?"

Nothing.

For a few seconds, it was silent, just the quiet tap of Anya's right foot.

"May I?" asked Effie.

The detective signaled for her to go ahead.

"Anya, would you be willing to answer yes or no to the detective's questions?"

She nodded.

"Are you six?" asked Morrow.

A shake.

"Seven?"

Another shake.

"Eight?"

Anya nodded.

For the next five minutes, the detective asked questions about the bush and the hut, painting a picture of the girl's life. Nothing hard. Nothing about that day. Sometimes Anya answered. Sometimes she didn't.

"And you lived in the hut with your Uncle Four?" asked Morrow.

Anya shook her head.

"So you lived alone?"

Another shake.

"Who did you live with?"

Silence.

"Sorry." Morrow shook her head. "I mean—"

"How about . . ." Effie turned, searching the kitchen bench, then reached over and grabbed a few sheets of paper and a pencil. "Maybe you could draw some of your answers. That way, you don't have to talk to us."

Anya eyed Effie. Thinking. Then she lifted the pencil and started drawing.

The adults sat in silence as the child scratched the pencil back and forth, leaking pain and memory out onto paper. Anya hunched over the table, her face centimeters from the drawing, with her tongue poked out of the corner of her mouth. It was the same picture that she'd drawn for Effie—two bodies with *X*s for eyes. The man had a cross carved into his torso, and the woman was lying in a pool of blood.

Morrow looked over at Effie, then back at Anya. "And the man," she said, pointing at the picture, "that's Four?"

The girl nodded.

"Did Four ever hurt you?"

Anya shook her head.

"Did Four chain you up?"

She nodded, her face calm, and Effie winced.

"Was Four punishing you for something?"

Anya shook her head again.

"But he kept you chained up?"

The child gave another expressionless nod—no anger, no nothing—and Effie had to bite into her tongue.

"And the woman," Morrow continued, as if they were talking about the weather, not about child abuse. Not about the cruel sickness that festered in Effie's family. "The woman is Tia, your mum?"

Another nod.

"Did you live with your mum?"

A nod.

"Was there anyone else who lived in the hut with you?"

She shook her head.

"Did your mum ever hurt you?"

Anya shook her head again and Effie let out a breath.

"And what about Four, did he ever hurt your mum? Did he ever punish her for anything?"

Anya stilled, and the quiet gnawed through Effie's stomach.

"Was your mum scared of Four, Anya?"

The girl didn't move, didn't blink, and Morrow glanced at her colleague, a thousand words caught in a single glimpse.

"When you left the hut," asked Morrow, "was your mum alive?"

Anya shook her head.

"Your mum was dead?"

A nod.

Then the girl's hand slipped into Effie's, and she curled her fingers around Effie's thumb.

Effie caught the detective's eye and frowned at her, pleading, but Morrow kept going. She had to keep going.

"And your mum's body," said Morrow, "it was on the floor next to your uncle's when you left?"

Anya nodded.

"You're sure?"

The girl frowned, then she nodded once, slowly, as though her muscles had jammed and she had to unstick them.

Morrow took a breath, her expression unreadable. "Anya, did someone kill your mum and your uncle?"

Anya nodded.

"And did you see the person who hurt them?"

She nodded again.

"Was it a man?"

Anya held the detective's gaze, her head perfectly still, and for a moment the entire room seemed to pause. Morrow asked the question again, and Anya's fingers uncurled from Effie's thumb, but she didn't respond.

Eventually, Anya dipped her head and returned to her drawing, gripping the pencil so hard that her fingers whitened. No one spoke as she wrote. When she finished, she dropped the pencil without looking up.

Anya had written two sentences, the letters scrawled in thick gray.

Mum broke his rules.

Mum wouldn't say sorry.

Morrow pulled the paper toward her and looked across at Effie.

"Whose rules?" asked Morrow, turning to Anya. "Were they Four's rules?"

Anya looked at the detective, her face and lips unmoving, then she held a finger to her lips.

Morrow looked from Effie to the picture and back again. Anya had added a third person to her drawing—a stick figure in the trees. The figure had long hair and a dress that hung to her ankles. Her eyes were marked with the same two *X*s. And underneath, Anya had written a name.

Hana.

"This person here . . ." Morrow pointed at the figure. "She's called Hana?"

The girl nodded.

"And," asked Morrow, her voice soft, "is Hana dead?"

Another nod.

"Did Hana break the rules?"

Another nod.

"Was Hana a child like you?" asked Morrow.

"Shh," Anya whispered. "No more questions."

JULY 2005

"LEWIS!"

Effie shouted against the wind, but it was pointless. The cold sea air bleached her words of sound, leaving her gaping like a mute fish. She stepped off June's bike and threw it to the sand. The stupid saddle had thumped the feeling from between her legs, bruising her girl bits, and the bones in her butt ached.

"Lewis!"

Effie waved, flailing her arms this time, but he was too far down the beach to notice her. He was just a little red smudge, the only red smudge on the whole beach. There was just miles of white sand and icy gray sea. *Bloody Lewis.* Of all the days to go for a walk down the beach, he had to pick a day that was colder than the Arctic. Effie trudged along the never-ending beach with her hands tucked under her arms, the cold blowing through the broken zip of June's jacket. She removed her sand-filled shoes, swearing as she stepped on a sharp twig.

"Ouch."

She lifted her foot and rubbed at the stinging skin. There was more driftwood than sand, the beach half-made of dregs and dead things. And space, so much open space, like the beach and the sky might never end. In the bush, there was no space.

Effie chucked her shoes next to the carcass of a tree and picked her way through the labyrinth of twisted driftwood.

Lewis hadn't appeared at June's that morning. It was almost the end of the school holidays, and he had been teaching Aiden to kick his ridiculous egg-shaped ball. Lewis turned up outside June's every morning with his rugby ball under his arm. Four joined in too, running after them and shouting, "Punt it," whatever the heck that meant. June made them all eat breakfast—Lewis too—and put on shoes and jackets before they were allowed out. But that morning, Lewis wasn't there, and Effie had cycled around for half an hour before she'd found someone who'd spotted him walking down the Haast-Jackson Bay Road.

Effie blew warm air into her hands, her fingers turned white in the biting salt breeze.

"Lewis!"

Effie splashed through the shallow water toward him. Lewis was standing alone, arms crossed, looking out at nothing. As if the winter air had frozen him there. On the sand behind him was his rugby ball, abandoned, and the approaching waves were threatening to scoop it up. Lewis was in shorts and his red Crusaders T-shirt, his pale skin the same gray-white as the sky.

"Lewis, it's freezing." Effie reached out for him. "Aiden was—"

He flinched and pulled away. "Go away," he said. "Just go home, Effie."

"Lewis?" She stood there, not understanding.

"I don't want you here," he said, without looking at her.

"But—"

"*Go home!*" he shouted. "Go back to June's."

"You'll freeze," said Effie, her words shaky. "You should come back." She reached for his hand. "Please."

But Lewis shoved her away, hard, his new muscles strong and untested, and Effie stumbled back, her twelve-year-old self nothing but air to a fifteen-year-old boy. Her heel caught on a piece of driftwood and she landed with a hard thud. The salt water seeped into her shorts, and her butt bone throbbed.

For a second she just sat there, looking up at him, seeing him differently. The strength and anger in him. *Just like Dad.* Seeing the adult growing beneath his skin.

"Effie." Lewis rushed forward, offering his hand. "I'm so sorry. I didn't mean . . ."

He pulled her up, his eyes swollen from crying, and started brushing the sand from her. The right side of his face was an explosion of purple and blue. There was no white to his right eye, just a pool of blood.

"Your eye," said Effie.

Lewis jerked back, turning his head away. "I didn't want you to see."

"What happened?"

"It was my dad," he said eventually, his voice wobbling. "He came to visit me and Nan last night." Lewis wiped a hand across his mouth. "Hitched here with some hunter."

Effie couldn't look away.

Lewis shifted from one foot to the other. "Dad likes to drink."

"I thought your dad died in a car crash?"

"My stepdad."

She hesitated. "I never thought about you having another dad."

Lewis gave a sad smile.

"Where does he live?"

"Greymouth, I think."

"Why was he . . ."

Lewis shrugged. "Money."

Effie didn't understand. She'd never had money, never really known what it did.

"Apparently," said Lewis, "Nan didn't have enough."

Effie frowned. "Is he still . . ."

"Nah." Lewis shook his head. "He's gone."

She glanced at the ground, her toes peeking out of the sand, and thought about telling Lewis about the anger inside her dad. About the sting of his palm across her face. About living with someone who scared her sometimes. About what Asher had said.

He's lying. I saw him.

Effie dug her fingernails into her hand. Lewis wouldn't understand. He'd just overreact. And besides, her dad wasn't anything like Lewis's dad.

"Griff drove Dad up the road to Fox," said Lewis. "Told him to catch a bus there."

"Constable Griffiths?" she asked. "The old police guy?"

"Yeah. Griff spotted Dad walking down Pauareka Road and followed him to Nan's." Lewis picked up a shell and chucked it into the sea. "Griff's often hanging about Nan's, fixing up the caravan and dropping off deer and pig meat for the freezer. Reckon he's keeping an eye on us."

"Why?"

Lewis looked at her. "Dad left me with Nan when I was seven. Parenting wasn't for him apparently. Him and Nan got in a big fight about it, about him being a piece of shit, and Dad left Nan with two broken ribs." He turned back to the water. "I think Griff and Mum were friends too, before Mum died. Anyway . . . Griff barged in before Dad could make a mess of my left eye too."

"Isn't Griffiths, like, real old?" Effie frowned. "Is your dad strong?"

"Ain't nothing strong about a grown man who hits kids and old women."

Effie stared, not knowing how to respond.

A smile tugged at Lewis's mouth. "Griff says that Dad is nothing but a puffed-up weasel in gum boots." The smile faded then, and he looked at her funny. "But I guess you'd understand that."

"I don't," she said, too quickly.

Lewis looked at her like she was lying, but Effie didn't react, and he kept his mouth shut.

"Right," he said, pulling his T-shirt over his head. "I'm done feeling shite about this crap. Done feeling sorry for myself."

He tugged off his shorts, naked but for his gray boxers, and threw his shorts onto the sand. "You coming?"

Effie gawked at him.

"It's just a bit of water," he said through chattering teeth.

His lips had gone blue, and he was clenching his fists at his sides, jumping.

"You're mad," said Effie.

"Suit yourself."

"You'll probably die."

Lewis gave her a quick salute, then ran at the water, his knees pumping up to his chest.

"I'm not dragging your body back to Koraha," she shouted. "I'm going to leave it here for the birds."

Lewis bopped and jumped in the waves, and Effie watched, unsure where to look. The shape of Lewis, the lankiness that she knew, had changed. His arms and legs were more solid, and his chest was puffed out—his body suddenly more man than boy. Like he'd been blown up. As Effie watched, a warm sensation moved through her, a feeling she didn't have words for.

"The birds will eat your eyes first," she shouted.

"Oh god. Oh god." Lewis bounded back toward her. "It's bloody freezing."

Effie rolled her eyes.

Lewis grabbed his clothes, the material sticking to his wet body—clinging to the strange new mounds and bulges—as he pulled his T-shirt on.

"I don't think I've ever been this cold."

"You're an idiot."

Lewis smiled at her, then he opened his arms. "Fancy a hug?"

"Don't you dare." Effie stumbled back. "Get away from me, you big wet idiot."

"Just a—"

"No!" She laughed and spun around, dodging his outstretched arms, and he chased her across the beach.

They ran, cursing their way through the maze of sharp driftwood. Eventually, they collapsed onto the sand, the cold air peppered with their wheezed laughs and insults.

"I reckon June runs faster than you," Effie panted.

"Yeah, well, June doesn't have to run with a huge pair of frozen balls bashing between her legs."

"Yuck." Effie stuck her tongue out and hit his arm. "You're so gross."

"I've probably got bruises the size of soccer balls."

"You don't know nothing about bruises," Effie spluttered. "Try pedaling that death trap, then you'll . . ." She turned, the right side of Lewis's face shining purple, and wanted to swallow her words back.

"Come on." He pulled them both up. "Aiden's going to be right pissed off with me."

"I forgot to tell you." Effie slapped a palm to her forehead. "Aiden was running around the garden when I left, kicking that stupid ball into the air and trying to catch it—"

"Good lad. No slacking while his coach was off."

"But he tripped," she said. "And fell into that pile of old planks. One of the nails went right into his foot." She grimaced. "He sure made some noise about it. But really, the hole was tiny."

"Shit. I'll be getting blamed for that too."

Effie tutted. "Reckon he'll probably sack you as his coach."

"Never." Lewis smiled. "Your brother reckons he's going to be the next Jonah Lomu."

She raised an eyebrow.

"He was the youngest ever All Black," said Lewis. "Just nineteen."

Effie faked a yawn and Lewis tried, and failed, to push her to the ground.

"Yep." She grinned. "You fight like June too."

Then she stuck her tongue out and sprinted back to the bike. But Lewis caught her after ten meters and took her hand. He slipped his fingers into hers like they'd done it a thousand times, like she was his, and Effie's heart beat wildly.

"Why don't you just stay in Koraha with June?" asked Lewis. "Rather than going back?"

Effie shook her head. "I couldn't leave Tia and the young ones." *Not with Dad.* "And they love the bush."

"And what about me?"

A smile filled his face, his eyes tunneling into her, and Effie's body warmed.

"Hanging out with you every day . . ." She let out a puff of air. "I'd rather throw myself in the sea."

"Liar." Lewis grinned.

They didn't speak after that. They didn't look at each other. They just walked hand in hand along the beach.

Of all the moments of happiness Effie had known, none had felt like this.

JULY 2005

THE NEXT WEEK, back at the hut, Effie woke to the sound of rain and Aiden's wheezing.

Her brother's breathing was getting worse. Louder and more labored. Like a fish gulping for air. He had gone to bed early the day before, feeling a little sore, he'd said. His face had been a bit sunken too, his cheeks sort of scooped out and his skin grayish. But something was real wrong with him that morning.

"Aiden?" Effie placed a hand on his clammy forehead.

Something real bad.

2025

EFFIE PUSHED THE supermarket door open and held it wide.

Anya walked under her arm, moving with the hesitation of a small deer, then she stopped after a few steps. She turned and looked back at Effie. For a moment there was no hate in her face, no flight, just the uncertain expression of an eight-year-old child looking for reassurance.

"It's okay," said Effie. "You can go in."

Anya pointed to the ceiling and squinted.

"They're called strip lights," said Effie. "They're very bright, but they last a long time, so shops often use them."

Anya frowned and shielded her eyes with her hand. "I don't like them," she said.

It wasn't all the time, and it wasn't consistent, but Anya had started talking to Effie. In the past few days since they'd come back from the bush, she had opened up slowly. Nothing about the bush. Nothing—Effie had quickly realized—about the past. But Anya had started to talk about her surroundings, asking questions and commenting on things.

Blair had been great, providing lots of late-night advice and helpful medical jargon.

"Just because she's not talking about it, doesn't mean she isn't thinking about it." Blair had paused, letting Effie process. "It might also be that Anya doesn't fully understand or even remember what happened to her, and that can be extremely overwhelming for a child. Without solid, factual information, Anya is likely speculating. Filling in the empty spaces to try and make sense of things."

Effie frowned. "So she could be lying? Making it up?"

"Not lying intentionally, no. But sometimes, without complete memories of a traumatic event, children will search for the truth. And if necessary, they will create one. But to them, it remains very real."

Effie had gripped the phone tighter at that.

"The other possibility," Blair ventured, "is that she's now responding to her trauma by dissociating—mentally detaching from the past. As a consequence, her brain is altering the way it preserves memory."

"So," Effie asked, "should I question her about it? About this Hana person?"

"For now, just listen and reassure. You need to go at her pace. You don't want to spook her or threaten the trust between you. But yes, at some point you will need to initiate the conversation again."

"Can't wait."

Effie let the shop door close behind her and followed Anya into On the Spot. A handful of customers wandered around, filling carts and reading food labels. Lewis said he'd found Anya near the fridges, covered in milk and dirt.

"Which flavor is the best?" asked Anya.

She stood at the ice-cream freezer, her nose to the glass.

"I don't know. It depends what you like."

Anya looked at her, her brow gathered, like she'd misjudged Effie's intelligence.

"How would I know what I like? I've never had one before."

"Right. Of course. I wasn't . . ."

The expression of skepticism stayed on the girl's face. "June said you were smart."

Effie was taken aback. "I am smart." She grimaced. God, she sounded like a four-year-old.

"Okay," said Anya.

Effie stared at the scrawny creature who had the scrutinizing look of a much older child. It was hard to make sense of her sometimes.

Anya glared at her. "Which one should I get?"

"Well . . ." Effie looked at the freezer, then back at Anya. "How about we get three to try? Then you can see which you like best."

"Really?" Her eyes widened—just an eight-year-old child again.

After picking a mango Fruju, a Magnum and a mint Trumpet, they sat at one of the tables. Anya tested each of them in silence. She licked one after the other, then she set each down on their open wrapper, and licked them again.

"The Magnum," she said. "It's the best."

"Are you sure? You've only had two licks."

"Will the third lick taste different?"

"Well, no."

"You can have those," said Anya, nodding at the Fruju and the Trumpet.

"You don't like them?"

"I do."

"You can have some more if—"

"It's not good to be greedy."

They ate the rest of their ice creams in silence. The Trumpet was surprisingly good.

"Anya," said Effie. "Can I ask you a question?"

"Yes. But I might not answer."

"That's okay."

"Why have you started talking to me?"

She shrugged. "Cos I can."

"But you couldn't before?"

"Nope."

"Why not?"

Anya looked at Effie as she folded her Magnum wrapper into a small square.

"Can we go back to June's now?" she asked. "I don't like people looking at me."

Effie glanced around. She was right. Various sets of eyes and ears were honed on them, angled just enough to be discreet. Just enough to be rude. Effie hadn't even noticed. Some cop she was.

"They're looking at you too," said Anya, fiddling with the foil.

A chill trickled between Effie's shoulders as she caught someone's eye. The elderly woman's brow creased, considering, then she quickly looked away. Of course the small town was putting the pieces together. Of course people were whispering about her. Effie's family had captivated the community for two decades, and they all had the same question.

What happened to the four bush children?

And now, the eldest of them was sitting in the shop eating ice cream. Not feral. Not covered in dirt. She was there, all grown up, sitting opposite a reflection of herself, of the child she'd once been. Red hair. Green eyes. With the bush, and its secrets, buried deep inside her.

Without making a sound, Anya stood up and took Effie's hand, pulling her with her.

"If you don't look at them," she whispered, "they can't hurt you. And if you're quiet enough, you can be invisible. Watch."

Effie looked down at the girl with secrets behind her eyes.

Who's Hana?

Then Anya held a finger to her lips. "Quiet," she mouthed, "like a mouse, Mum said."

Then they walked out together, hand in hand, with Anya's sticky fingers clutched in Effie's. The girl didn't let go until they reached the postbox at the end of June's drive.

And as Anya pulled away, she took a fragile piece of Effie with her.

—

Morrow, Wilson and Lewis were in June's living room when they arrived back. June had made them cups of tea, and there was a plate of Scotch Fingers on the coffee table.

"We need to head over to the station," said Lewis.

Effie looked at Morrow.

"Just you and Lewis," she said. "Not the child."

"Has something happened?" asked Effie. "Did you find something?" She glanced at Lewis. "Is it Dad?"

"Let's talk at the station, shall we?" said Morrow. "We can give you a lift."

Lewis gave her a small supportive smile.

"What about Tia?" said Effie. "Did you find anything—"

"As I said," Morrow interrupted, "it's best if we have this conversation at the station. In private."

Effie's fingers tingled, and she looked down. Anya was there again, holding her hand. She tugged at Effie's arm, signaling for her to kneel down, and Effie sunk to the floor. Then Anya pressed her lips to Effie's ear.

"It's his bush," she whispered. "He wants them to leave."

Then she drew her face away, but her fingers remained coiled around Effie's hand, clinging to her.

"So," said Morrow, "shall we head to the station?"

"Yes. Yes, of course." Effie went to move, but Anya's grip tightened.

"I won't be long," Effie said.

"Then you'll come back?"

"Yes. Of course." A lump caught in Effie's throat. "I'll come back."

AUGUST 2005

"WHAT'S WRONG WITH him?" cried Tia.

"I don't know." Effie touched a hand to Aiden's forehead, his skin wet with sweat. "Aiden," she whispered. "Aiden, can you hear me?"

Nothing. He didn't move. Didn't speak. The small curl of him lay motionless in the sleeping nook.

"I'm scared," said Tia.

Effie wiped her hands on her top, her fingers slimy with her brother's vomit, and wished for Aiden to open his eyes, to be him. She wished it with every part of her.

But then, it happened again.

Tia screamed as some invisible horror took hold of their brother. It thrashed through him, distorting and twisting his limbs, jerking and tugging at him like a puppet pulled on strings. Aiden's arms spasmed and smacked into the mattress, over and over, his bones and skin banging against the floor and the hut wall.

"Make it stop," cried Tia. "Make it stop."

Effie scrambled, grabbing pillows and blankets, anything to soften the force of her brother cracking off the wood. Tears dripped down her cheeks. "I don't know how."

Aiden's body arched, his scrawny frame contorting into a bridge of flesh and bone, and Effie pushed Tia back.

"He's going to snap," cried Tia. "His bones are going to snap."

"Aiden!" Effie shouted as she reached out for him. "Stop it. Please stop it."

Aiden's arm lashed out, fist clenched, and whacked Effie hard across the nose. Pain exploded through her face, and something trickled into her mouth. She wiped it away with the back of her hand, tasting blood, and inched back.

"He's going to kill himself." Tears and snot drenched Tia's words.

Shaking, Effie slipped her hand into Tia's. They stood there, with Tia's fingernails digging into Effie's wrist, and watched Aiden thrash, seeing and feeling it all, not letting their little brother go through it alone.

When Aiden screamed, Effie thought she might throw up. Her brother coughed and wheezed, his face locked in a mask of terror. There was no movement to his jaw. It was as if his mouth was carved from stone, frozen in fear. Aiden screamed again, the sound chilling, and Effie burst into tears.

"Please, Aiden," she whimpered. "Please stop."

Eventually, as before, the invisible horror released what was left of him, and Aiden slumped to the mattress. His head lolled to the side and blood spilled from his mouth as he gurgled and spluttered. Effie rushed to him, scooping it from his mouth with two fingers.

"I don't think he can swallow," she said. "I think—"

"Why's there so much blood?"

"I think he bit his tongue."

Aiden murmured and opened his eyes. "Help me."

Effie climbed over the mattress to lie next to him, and Tia knelt by his side, taking his hand, one hand for each sister.

"We're here," said Effie. "You're going to be okay."

"Dad?" muttered Aiden.

Effie looked at Tia, then back at her brother. Dad and Four had left early to go fishing. They'd left when Aiden was still whole. When Aiden was just a bit pale. Just a bit unwell. They'd gone to get him something nutritious for dinner, to fight off whatever winter bug he'd picked up.

"Dad will be back soon," Effie lied.

She glanced at her watch, an old one of June's, then bit into her cheeks. The last two times, they'd only had three minutes—three minutes before the horror stole him away. And each time, it gave a little bit less of her brother back.

"While we're waiting for Dad," she said, forcing herself to keep talking, to keep the fear from her voice, "I could tell us a story. A rugby story—you'd like that."

Effie squeezed his hand, and she imagined the feel of him squeezing back. She imagined the sound of his voice and the size of his smile.

Please don't die.

Then she supported his head as best she could so that the blood and saliva dribbled out of his lips, and she spoke into his ear.

"There was once a little boy called Aiden. He was only six years old, but he was the best rugby player in the whole country."

Maybe he couldn't hear her. Maybe he couldn't feel her next to him. But she was there. *She was there.* Effie needed her brother to know that she was there.

"His coach said that he'd never seen a boy throw a ball so far or run so fast."

Aiden coughed and gulped for air, his jammed jaw like a fish carved out of stone. But Effie couldn't cry—her tears would scare him. She had to stay strong. She didn't realize she was already sobbing until the drips landed on Aiden's forehead and she wiped them away with her sleeve. His little face was almost unrecognizable, his eyes sunken into two dark holes.

"The All Blacks heard about this magical little boy. So one day, they..."

But before Effie could finish, those cruel invisible fingers lashed out for him again, grabbing hold as he screamed. The merciless hands twisted and contorted his spine like a supplejack vine.

And the All Blacks asked Aiden to play for them.

Effie inched away, safe from her brother's thrashing arms.

And they gave him black shorts and a black T-shirt with his name printed on it.

Aiden's head bowed back and he gagged, his wide lips and his wide eyes gulping for air.

And Aiden smiled that great big smile as he ran onto the pitch.

Effie bit into her lip, breaking the skin.

He was the youngest ever All Black. Even younger than Jonah Lomu.

The next morning, as soon as the sun rose, Dad carried Aiden's body back to Koraha. He wanted a doctor to tell them what had happened. He wanted a doctor to tell them why Aiden, who'd done nothing wrong or bad, had been taken from them.

Like some idiot doctor could ever answer that.

Dad went in front, and the rest of them followed in silence. Four didn't cry as Effie waded through the river up to her waist. He clung to her back, silent, as his bare feet swung in the icy water. He didn't complain when Effie said that he couldn't walk, that he was too slow. Tia didn't moan when it started to rain and the cold soaked through to her bones and gave her heels blisters.

Dad carried Aiden in his arms like a baby, her brother's lifeless legs dangling in the air like two bags of sand.

June arrived at the medical center five minutes after them—she must have driven over as soon as the nurse called her. The doctor took another hour, driven in special, apparently.

June hugged each of them, even the rag doll in Dad's arms, but only Four and Tia cried. Effie's eyes were red-rimmed and sore from refusing any more tears. Tears hadn't stopped Aiden from dying. And they sure as hell wouldn't bring him back.

Dad's eyes were red and swollen too. The grief had buckled his shoulders, shrinking him, and the sadness had scrubbed the color from his face, his skin raw and blotchy. Looking at Dad hurt almost as much as looking at what the invisible horror had left of Aiden.

"I'll watch them," said June, nodding at Dad. "You take Aiden in."

Effie stood in the clinical light, squinting in the white glow, as the doctor touched a hand to Dad's back. Like he could do anything. Like there was any fucking point in them being there. If it wasn't for the strength of Four's grip, his hand clutched around Effie's trembling fingers, she might have marched forward and told the doctor to keep his useless hands off her brother. To piss off.

"Come here, sweethearts." June opened her arms to Tia and Four, and Tia sank into them.

But Four's grip tightened, crushing Effie's fingers, and he shook his head.

"Effie," he mumbled.

She knelt down in front of him and wiped the strands of wet hair from his face. Then she took off his soaking clothes, helped him into a set of pajamas that June had brought, and found him a glass of water.

"We could go back to mine if you'd like," June said.

Effie shook her head. "We're staying here."

June didn't push it.

Effie took two chairs from the waiting room and pushed them together, making a sort of cot, then she walked into the storage room and rummaged around until she found a blanket. Four watched without moving, the confusion and tiredness rooting him to the spot, and Effie folded his jumper into a pillow.

"Do you need to wee?" she asked.

He nodded.

Effie took him through to the bathroom and hovered in the doorway as he relieved himself. Four perched on the toilet seat, legs closed tight as he held the sides. Aiden had peed upright from the moment his skinny legs allowed it. In the bush, against trees, on Mum's vegetables, his wee spraying in the wind. After Four had flushed, Effie got him to wash his hands, then she made him swirl cold water around his teeth.

Four turned and looked up at her with big eyes, spit dripping down his chin.

"Where's Aiden gone?" he asked.

"To somewhere better," said Effie, then she kissed the top of his head. "Come on, it's past your bedtime."

She helped him clamber into the makeshift cot, then she tucked the blanket around him.

"Go to sleep. No more questions."

Effie pulled out a chair and sat next to him, waiting until his eyes closed and his breathing slowed. June was perched on a chair next to Tia, her body tense and wide awake, while Tia slept on her arm. But June's eyes were closed, and she was praying, the useless words making her lips move.

"It's all bullshit, you know," Effie muttered, "the God stuff."

"Oh?" June opened her eyes.

"Praying's a scam."

"A scam?"

"Yeah. A big lie, Dad says. To satisfy those sad people who stare at the sky all day, hoping a miracle might drop out of it."

"And it won't?"

Effie shook her head. "Nothing's going to fall in your eye but rain and bird shit. Praying's a waste of time."

"I wouldn't say that."

"Well." Effie looked at her. "That's cos you're being scammed. But it'll catch you out. One day, something real bad will happen to you, and God won't do nothing. Then you'll wish you'd done something more useful with your time."

"Useful." June looked at her. "Like what?"

"I don't know." Effie scowled. "Painting or some shit."

June considered this. "I do like painting."

"Well, there you go. Problem solved. Paint more. Pray less. Then you won't be let down by the nothing in the sky."

"I think," June let out a small sigh, "that I might stick with the praying. If that's okay with you."

Effie frowned. "Why?"

"Faith, I suppose."

Effie scoffed at that.

"And," June smiled, "I guess, just in case."

"In case what?"

"In case it's not all some scam."

"Suit yourself."

Effie looked away, the itch in her muscles making her legs quiver, then she stood up.

"I'm going to get some fresh air. It smells like bleach and sick in here."

She paused, her fingers curled around the arm of the chair, unable to move away.

"I'll watch them," said June.

"Just no . . ." Effie wavered, "no praying over them."

"Just watching. I promise."

She walked to the door, pulling her jacket around her, then stepped into the clear night. The icy breeze tunneled through her, leaking through every seam in her jacket. Drawing her shoulders to her ears, Effie looked through the dark, and there he was, his hands tucked under his armpits, pacing near the road.

Of course he was there.

Lewis stopped the moment she spotted him, his face paled by the moon, then he strode across the empty carpark. Without speaking, he wrapped his arms around her, holding her steady, and she pressed her face into his chest.

"I'm sorry, Effie. I'm so sorry."

"He was good." She sniffed.

"I know." Lewis pulled her closer. "I know."

2025

AN ELDERLY COUPLE slowed as they walked past the police car, watching Effie as she opened the door and sat in the back seat.

"The locals know who you are," said Morrow from the driver's seat.

"I think they're working it out," Effie replied.

"It wasn't a question." Morrow smiled in the rearview mirror.

Lewis reached across, touching a hand to Effie's thigh.

"That little performance on the bridge," she continued, "the forgotten bush girl saving the bush child—I've heard it from every imaginable angle. Which, I must say, is particularly impressive, given that the entire event was concealed by rain." She gave a soft snort. "One kid thought that you were both going to jump. He reckoned the river was going to take you back to your tree homes. Forest people, he called you."

Effie forced a tight smile.

"I don't imagine it's easy to keep secrets around here," said Morrow.

"Apparently not."

"So." Morrow looked into the mirror. "No one in Koraha knew you'd left the bush?"

"Just Lewis."

"How old were you?"

"Fifteen."

"And forgive me," Morrow gave a small shake of the head, "I've heard a lot of speculation over the past few days. Why was it that you left?"

Effie stiffened, her tone cold. "Is this an interview?"

"No, no. Just making conversation."

Effie turned to the window, to the hills in the distance. "As I told you the other day, I had a fight with my dad."

"Ah, yes."

Effie glanced back at the mirror. "Have there been any signs of him?"

"No," replied Morrow. "No sign of your dad."

The car went quiet and Effie looked away.

"June showed me some pictures of you as a child," said Morrow. "And, I must say, Anya is the spitting image of you. Quite remarkable." She smiled. "There are more than a few conspiracy theories floating around the village. Quite inventive, some of them. Great imaginations, these coast folk."

"People are allowed to talk."

"Well, it might be worth speaking with them. Perhaps telling them where you've been. A number of people thought you'd died, or been reincarnated as a tree."

Effie didn't reply.

"I've wondered myself," said Morrow, "how a fifteen-year-old girl managed to leave the country. Legally, I mean."

Lewis tensed, his fingers tightening around her leg, and Effie stiffened. Maybe she disliked Morrow after all.

The car slowed, pulling up outside the police station, and Effie opened the door before it had come to a complete stop. None of them spoke again until they were seated in the interview room.

"So," Morrow began. "We have theories."

"Theories?" said Effie.

Morrow leaned forward on the table, interlocking her fingers. The softness she'd shown with Anya had gone.

"Possibilities," she said. "Two of them."

Morrow turned her head sideways, looking at Wilson, who gave a single nod, then she turned back to Effie and Lewis. Effie wasn't sure if she'd ever heard the young detective speak.

"One slightly less than ideal. But either way, it's an open-and-shut case."

Effie opened her mouth, but Lewis jumped in.

"CIB have left?" he asked.

"Yep. Gone. Packed up yesterday morning," said Morrow. "Just the two of us left. And we'll be heading back to Christchurch straight after this. We'll continue working from there, but like I said, it's—"

"But—" Effie interrupted.

"There's no point in us staying here," said Wilson. "This . . ." He cocked his head. "This isn't a command center. It's a joke."

Morrow touched her palm to the table and the man hushed.

"We found these," she said, pushing two sheets of paper across the table. "This first photo is of two tutu shoots that we found discarded out the back of the hut."

Effie blinked. "They're poisonous."

"Incredibly toxic, yes." Morrow nodded. "I'm told that tutu shoots have been known to kill full-grown elephants. Within hours, apparently." She shook her head. "Convulsions, loss of consciousness, respiratory distress. Not a nice way to go."

"But even as children we knew not to touch them," said Effie. "Dad made sure we were all aware of the dangers."

"Well," said Morrow, "chemical and pH testing found that the food leftovers on the table, as well as a half-drunk cup of tea, were contaminated. Likely both the vegetables and the drink were boiled in water that contained the tutu shoots." She tapped a finger on the photo. "Meaning that, as the water heated, the poisonous tutin was extracted from the shoots and contaminated the entire meal."

Lewis touched Effie's knee.

"And the postmortem?" asked Effie.

"It confirms poisoning." Morrow paused. "I'm sorry."

Effie rubbed a hand over her mouth, her throat and tongue dry.

"This," said Morrow, moving to the other piece of paper, "we found clutched in Four's fingers."

Effie focused on the creased rectangle of yellow paper, the corners worn by sweat and the crush of her brother's grip. Two words were written on it, the writing smudged and hectic.

I'm sorry.

Effie frowned, then looked up. "You're thinking suicide?"

"Yes."

"But the cross on his chest," said Lewis. "Surely he didn't do that to himself?"

"It's possible," Morrow replied. "But no, we don't think so."

"The girl did it," said Wilson.

"What?" Effie glared at him. "Why on earth would—"

"Anger," he continued. "Hatred."

Morrow silenced her colleague with a glance.

"We found the knife," she said, after clearing her throat. "It had been thrown into the bush, not too far away."

"Prints?" asked Effie.

"Obviously anything concrete will take another few days, maybe a week. And, given the people involved, I doubt there will be any matches. But they were able to tell us one thing. The only prints that were lifted from the knife were small, likely belonging to a child."

For a moment, no one spoke.

"We believe that Four killed himself, most probably out of guilt." Morrow paused. "A growing sense of remorse for what he'd done to the girl."

Effie glanced from one detective to the other. "But Anya said Four never hurt her."

Morrow's colleague scoffed. "He had her chained up. The girl admitted that."

Effie looked at Morrow.

"It's not unusual," said Morrow, "for a child to develop positive feelings toward their captor over time, as a coping mechanism."

Lewis frowned. "You think Anya has Stockholm syndrome?"

Effie shook her head, but she couldn't maneuver her thoughts into words.

"Anya has displayed lots of the signs," said Morrow, looking at Lewis as she spoke. "She was desperate to get back to him, to be back in the familiar world that he'd created for her. And she's consistently exhibited negative feelings toward authority figures. Plus, the girl's demeanor—she's jittery and unpredictable. She's shown that she's unwilling to trust or to open up."

"But the cross." Lewis frowned. "You said that—"

"Anger, maybe." Morrow nodded. "But it could also be that the symbol was a sign of love. That the girl was blessing him."

"Tia," said Effie. "And the picture. What about Tia's body? And Hana?"

Morrow pressed her hands together in front of her face.

"Look," she sighed. "My team were all over that hut for a day and a half."

Effie knew what was coming; she knew, and yet she wasn't ready.

"They didn't find a trace of your sister, or anyone else," said Morrow. "No clothes, no sanitary items, no personal belongings, no pictures. Nothing. We need to wait on DNA, of course, but that could take months. And even then, any female DNA could belong to Anya."

"What about the notes?" asked Effie. "The pages I found under the floorboards?"

I'm terrified that I'm losing her to him.

"Tia wrote those," said Effie. "Tia was there."

You escaped. You lived.

"Yes." There was a softening to Morrow's face. "But they weren't dated. They could have been written years ago."

The reality ached in the center of Effie's chest, stabbing at her like a hot needle. But she wasn't ready for it.

"Effie, we think your sister has been gone for a long time. And that, most likely, the girl has invented her. That, essentially, Anya has been imagining a mother figure. That she's created a parent as a way to survive. It's possible that Anya invented this Hana person too. As a friend or a companion perhaps. Someone to talk to."

Morrow touched her fingers to her lips.

"We've been through the missing persons records, going back years, but there's no mention of anyone called Hana." She looked at Effie. "Do you have any idea who it could be? Growing up, did you come across a Hana in Koraha maybe, or did your dad ever mention her?"

"No." Effie sank back into the chair. She'd asked herself the same question a hundred times. "I never knew a Hana."

"I see." Morrow gave an unsurprised nod.

Effie kept her expression even and focused on the weight of Lewis's hand on her leg.

"The hut was flooded with evidence of the girl and Four," said Morrow. "It was just the two of them living there."

"But," Lewis ventured, "someone else had to have tied Anya up. When your colleagues found her, she was in that crate, secured."

"The knots around her wrists were slack," said Wilson. "And the ones around her ankles were sloppy at best."

"I don't understand," said Lewis.

"She'd tied herself up," Wilson continued. "As punishment."

"For what?"

"For leaving him, perhaps," said Morrow. "Or . . ."

She paused, her expression unreadable, then she slid another piece of paper onto the table. It was the drawing Anya had done—two bodies with two sentences scrawled underneath.

Mum broke his rules. Mum wouldn't say sorry.

Morrow didn't need to say anything. She tapped the pieces of paper with her fingertips—the suicide note, then Anya's picture. The writing was unmistakably similar. The tightness of the *s*. The curl to the *y*.

"The other possibility," said Morrow eventually, "is that Anya poisoned her uncle . . . and wrote the note."

Effie shook her head, but the words fired through her.

Morrow pulled the paper back. "Obviously, there are still a number of things we need to follow up on, and it will be a bit of a wait until we hear from the lab, but we're pretty confident that we've got everything we need."

Effie felt nauseous, the cogs spinning frantically behind her eyes. "But," she said, "I saw someone when I was out there. A man. I felt him watching me."

"Felt or saw?" The question, and judgment, came from Morrow's colleague.

Effie pushed two fingers into the knot between her brows. "Both."

"And you have proof of that?"

"No. But—"

"I think," said Morrow, "that with your history, you are perhaps ascribing more to this case than is actually there."

"We have a traumatized child who was chained up in a hut," said the young detective constable. "Alone. With only her captor for company, and a very damaged and active imagination. Then, miraculously, she escaped. Either because her uncle developed a sudden bout of conscience, or because she killed him."

"I just think," said Lewis, "that with the vastness of the terrain, it's important to consider—"

"Look," Morrow interrupted, "I get that this is hard, on both of you. And that there's a lot of history here. But . . ." Her eyes shifted to Lewis. "You're a sole officer in a small community, dealing with misdemeanors and talking down tourists. Unfortunately, we deal with child abuse cases all of the time. We know what to look for. And we know what we're doing."

Lewis sat back in his chair as if the strength had been sapped from him.

"I'm not meaning to sound like a jerk," said Morrow. "It's just the way it is."

"And," said Wilson, "either way, it should be reasonably straightforward from here. Anya is under ten, so regardless, she can't be held criminally responsible. And suicide isn't a crime. So no headaches there. You should be pleased."

Morrow held her hands out, palms up. "Open and shut," she said.

DECEMBER 2005

EFFIE STARED OUT the classroom window at the tree Aiden used to swing from as the teacher explained how to make tinsel stars for the nativity. Effie was being made to play Mary, which was about as appealing as rubbing stinging nettles over her body.

"Whaea!" little Tom Taylor wailed. "Whaea! I've glued my fingers together."

Effie groaned and sunk her head to the desk. Of the nine kids in the school, she was the oldest by two and a half years—and that was only because Tia was there. Tia was weird at school. Quiet and well-behaved.

"My fingers won't open." Tom Taylor's wail became a sob. "They're stuck."

Effie pushed her forehead into the table and sighed. Maybe she could use the glue gun to stick one of the five-year-olds to the floor. That would be sure to get her sent home. June would go ballistic though.

Tom Taylor yelled as the kids giggled and Whaea tried to calm him. But Tia just sat there. Maybe it was a teacher's pet thing.

During term time, Koraha was rubbish. Lewis was at some

boarding school in Alexandra, like three hours away, and the days dragged. At least on the weekends there was the beach and June's death-trap bike to escape on. But school—without Lewis, and with Tia's weirdly good behavior—was dull as. In an attempt to fend off death-by-boredom, Effie pulled a novel from her bag and leaned over the pages of the book.

After a few pages, the crunch of car tires on gravel pulled Effie's focus and she dragged her eyes to the window.

Outside, the ancient police guy Griffiths pulled up in his police ute. He beeped his horn and eight pairs of feet went scurrying over to the window, followed by eight pairs of grubby hands. Even Whaea walked over and gave him a wave.

Griffiths stepped out and Effie went to look away, her interest waning, when the door on the far side of the ute opened and she dropped her book. Effie stood up, her chair toppling to the floor, and sprinted from the classroom.

"Lewis!"

She ran at him, and he pulled her into a hug with one arm. It wasn't until she drew back that she noticed the crutches.

"What happened?"

"Fractured ankle." He gave a sly smile. "Reckon it won us the game though. Last-minute try. Got landed on pretty hard."

She rolled her eyes.

"Got me a sexy cast too," he said, wiggling it at her. "All ready for your autograph."

"I'm not signing that thing." Effie pulled a face. "I can smell it from here."

Lewis grinned. "Just give it another four weeks."

"Gross." Then she frowned. "Don't you have to be at that fancy school of yours?"

"It's not that fancy. But nah. Griff picked me up a couple of weeks early. Said there was something better waiting for me at home." He glanced away, like maybe he was blushing. "Plus, the end of term's all shows and sports and dancing. I'd be right bored."

Effie wiped her hands down her sides. "Don't you have some silly girlfriend who'll be missing you?"

There were probably herds of them at the big school—girls with short skirts and boobs bulging under their tops. Effie had seen them on the cover of *Seventeen* magazine: all skinny with perfect hair and "moves to make guys go wild." June wouldn't let Effie buy any of the magazines though, so she'd never seen past the cover, never learned what those moves were. It probably involved a lot of butt-jiggling.

"Nah. High school girls are tough work. Stuck-up too."

Effie shrugged like she didn't care, like it wasn't one of the best things Lewis had ever said.

"Why did the police guy bring you back?"

"Griff," said Lewis. "He's been taking me to school since I started. Nan's not too comfortable with driving long distances."

"Oh."

"Come on." He lifted a crutch and pointed ahead. "I said I'd help Whaea out, tutor some of the little ones." His mouth curled upward. "Are you needing any help with your ABCs?"

She glared at him. "I will beat you to death with your own crutches."

Lewis smiled. "Calm down, tiger." Then as they walked off, he moved his arm slightly so his hand brushed against hers and the tips of Effie's fingers touched his.

The next ten days were magic.

As Lewis couldn't walk much, and his foot sweated real bad when they went to the beach, they spent lots of time in June's living room playing cards and flicking through his textbooks. June had let

Effie skive off the baby school on the condition that Lewis taught her some maths and geography. The world was massive, and maps were possibly one of the coolest things ever. Lewis and Effie spent hours studying June's Topo maps and testing each other with grid references. Lewis was a bit useless at it.

Toward the end of the first week, Effie overheard Dad and June talking about what would happen when she turned thirteen soon. June had suggested she could board at the school in Alexandra with Lewis, and Dad hadn't said no. He hadn't quite said yes either, but it definitely wasn't a no. Effie had smiled for so long that her face had started to hurt and Lewis asked if she was trying to hold in a fart. She had wanted to die of embarrassment.

One day before the nativity show—which, apparently, Effie still had to do—she and Lewis were hanging out at the rusty playground. Sea air rusted everything.

Lewis was sitting on the swing and Effie was practicing her lines. She had already hurled the baby Jesus into the bush twice for its insolence. It kept looking at her, judging her with its broken, half-shut eye.

Little shit.

"I think you're meant to love it," Lewis shouted as Effie rummaged through the bush. "You know, be maternal and stuff."

"And you're meant to be helpful, not a mouthy possum turd."

Effie held the baby up by its hard plastic foot.

"I reckon you've hurt its feelings," said Lewis.

Effie frowned. "Do you think I have to hold it? Maybe I could just leave it in its manger thing."

"Social services might do you for neglect."

Effie scowled, then poked a finger into its broken eye, trying to stop the fake eyelid from closing. As she jabbed at it, the distant thud of footsteps made her look up. Not the slow beat of a walk, but the hurried pounding of fear.

"*Effie!*"

The desperate slap of feet grew louder. Closer. Then suddenly Dad was there in front of her, his breath hot on her face, and he grabbed her arm.

"Effie," he panted.

Before she knew what was happening, he began dragging her along behind him.

"Dad! Stop!" Effie tripped and fell, her palms depositing skin on the concrete. "What are you—"

He lifted her back up, like her bones were made of air, and kept going.

"*Dad!*" She kicked out in protest and tried to unpeel his clasped fingers. "*Let go.*"

"We're leaving," he said. "Now."

"Why?"

"Because." His voice was cold. "I said so."

Effie slapped his arm. "Let me go."

"Hey." Lewis trailed behind them. "She doesn't want to go with you."

Dad didn't even blink. He just marched on, lugging Effie with him.

"*Stop!*" Lewis shouted. He hobbled behind, already too far away, his crutches like two paper straws under his arms.

"Dad, you're hurting me."

His grip eased then, but he didn't let her go. "I'm sorry." A single tear leaked down his face. "I'm sorry."

His face. Oh god. She hadn't noticed his face.

"Dad . . . what . . ." Effie swallowed.

The side of his face was sprayed with blood, the liquid gummy like tree sap, and there was an open gash under his left eye. The wound was angry and red, and his eye socket was swollen.

"We can't stay here," he said, and Effie spotted a gap where a tooth had been.

"Where are we going?" she asked.

"Home." His voice steeled. "We never should have left."

Effie sat between Four and Tia, their bodies curled into June's sofa, as the adults whispered in the kitchen.

It was the type of whispering that thickened the air and blotted out all other sounds—that fixed three children to the spot in fear. Her siblings gripped her hands so hard that Effie's fingers numbed, and she knew she could never leave them.

"I hurt him, June." Dad let out a sob. "I hurt him real bad."

There was a moment of quiet—of silent hell—and Effie's stomach clenched.

"I had to," he said.

2025

EFFIE SCREAMED AT the sky, the threat of rain hanging in the air, and she kicked the ground. *"Arghhh."*

She paced across the grass outside the police station and swore. Then she threw a look at Lewis. "My dad is out there, I know he is."

Lewis stood with his hands in his pockets, the salt breeze flapping his jacket.

"Tia is out there!" she shouted.

"Effie—"

"You don't really believe what they're saying, do you?" Her eyes pleaded with him. *"Suicide?"*

He took a step toward her.

"Murder?" The word burned her throat. "She's eight, Lewis. *Eight!* There's no way." Effie pressed her palms against her temples. "They've missed something. I know they have. I know."

"Effie."

"No." She held a hand out, stopping him. "Don't. Don't tell me that—"

"That what?" There was a hardness to his voice.

"That I'm mad. That I'm overreacting. That I should let them do their job."

"They searched the hut from top to bottom, Effie. A whole team."

"You heard Morrow. They knew what they wanted to find. They went in there—"

Lewis reached out and took her hand, their bodies just a foot apart. Breathing the same air.

"There was no evidence of your sister living there," he said. "Or your dad."

"I saw him," she insisted.

"You think you saw someone." His tone was firm. "But CIB had the dogs out, and the drones."

Effie threw her arm out, pointing in the direction of the bush. "Drones and dogs aren't going to find shit out there in two days. It's the bush, Lewis. It's the same world that hid me for fifteen years. *Fifteen years.* The bush swallows you up. It holds tight and doesn't let go."

"That was different. No one was . . ."

Effie stilled, her body heavy, and she stared at him. "Are you saying you didn't look for me?"

"Effie, that was—"

"Did you look for me?"

Lewis was close enough that she could feel the shake in him.

"Effie—"

"*Did you look for me?*" she shouted.

"Yes!" His voice tore through the air. "Yes," he said again, softer. "Of course I looked for you. I searched for you every school break for two years."

He leaned in and placed his hands on either side of her face. His thumb grazed her cheek, the sensation pulsing in every inch of Effie's body. It was like slipping into a memory, into the broken heart of a fifteen-year-old girl.

"That day," he said, "when you turned up on June's doorstep after two years . . . it was the best and worst day of my life."

His eyes burrowed into her, and Effie could almost taste him, he was that close.

"I found you and lost you all at once," he said.

He moved his thumb along her jaw, stopping at the corner of her mouth.

"I've missed you, Effie."

The silence thickened as they stared at each other, broken only by their panted breaths and the whistling of the salt breeze. Effie leaned in and moved her mouth toward his. Like slipping into a memory.

But then Lewis dipped his head, and Effie's fifteen-year-old heart remembered; it felt every crack.

Their foreheads touched, and Lewis let out a breath.

"I can't," he murmured. "Not like this."

His words—the hot, familiar sting of them—made Effie step back, like fingers pulled from a flame.

"You're upset," he said. "And angry. Everything with the girl, and your family." He tried to find her eyes. "I don't want to take advantage."

"No," she stammered, shaking her head. "No. This is about you, *not* me. It's always been you who . . ."

Who said no. Who married someone else.

She clenched her jaw and turned away. The first drops of rain fell from the sky as she started to walk back to the station. But she'd only made it three steps when his hand gripped her arm.

"Effie—"

"What?"

He just stood there, his fingers digging into her skin, as the drizzle grew heavier and water dripped from his brow and cheeks.

"You can't stop me from going back there," she said eventually, her voice raised over the rain. "They're my family. My responsibility."

"No." Lewis released her arm. "I can't. But I'm hoping you'll realize that there's something much more important waiting for you right here."

Effie stood silent.

"The girl needs you," he said.

The girl. *Not him.* Never Lewis.

Effie turned and walked away without looking back. She'd looked back before, and it had nearly broken her.

Effie stirred in her bed, the room flooded by the darkness of the small hours, and pulled at the covers. But something stopped her.

A weight. A child.

Anya was there. In Effie's bed.

Effie stiffened, afraid to move. Afraid to wake the tiny sleeping creature that had burrowed in next to her. Effie lay on her back, soundless and still, as a warmth spread through her body and she waited for sleep to take her. For morning, and the choices that came with it.

When she opened her eyes again, the room was bright, doused in natural light, and the duvet was tucked in around her.

But Anya was gone.

Effie threw the covers off, fully awake, and rushed past the rucksack she'd packed and left at the door—a maybe plan. She made it to the kitchen, her entire body pounding, before the hammering in her heart slowed.

Anya was there, sat at the table.

"Porridge?" Anya asked, pushing a bowl toward her.

"Yes." Effie swallowed, the thrum not quite gone from her skin, and took the seat next to her. "Yes. That would be great."

"I suggested to Anya," said June, stirring a pot on the stove, "that you might take her to the beach today. Then perhaps we could do some painting."

For the next four nights, Effie went to bed by herself, and every morning she woke up alone. But at some point between dusk and dawn, Anya crept in with her. Effie would stir and pull an extra blanket over the two of them, cocooning them together, before drifting back to sleep. Then, when the morning light roused Effie's eyes, Anya would be gone.

Each day after breakfast, they did something outside—the park, or the beach, or trips to the café. Effie had decided against bushwalks. Anya was talking more—nothing about the past, but she was talking, and she was adapting to her new surroundings. TV was still a hard no, as were certain books, and Anya refused to speak to anyone except June and Effie. Blair got the odd wave on WhatsApp. But phones were a tricky subject, like tiny TVs, Anya said.

"You're her new safe place," Blair said. "And right now, she's trying to work out what that means."

The locals were whispering less too. Blair had convinced Effie to give them something. "Just a morsel, to satisfy their cavernous appetites."

"It doesn't have to be entirely accurate." She'd winked. "Loose facts. Let them do the rest."

So June had spread the word—a ten-minute task in a small town—and it was now accepted that Effie had left the bush as an older teenager, wanting to see more of the world, and she'd gone to live with a family friend in Scotland. Effie had lost contact with her family when she left. And Anya—the mirror image of a young Effie—was her niece.

In the afternoons, Effie and June set up a school in June's living room—writing and maths and art projects. Anya was ahead of her age in reading and writing, and she'd clearly had basic instruction in maths.

Their routine continued for the next week, just the beach and books and small steps. There were no mentions of the hut or Four or Tia. And Anya started to settle, the internal itch in her seeming to ease. The locals continued to speculate, imagining wild stories about the voiceless redheaded girl. But quickly their whispers turned to smiles, and smiles turned to hellos, and suddenly, it felt like the town was healing them, protecting their two lost bush children.

Lewis was kept busy fielding calls from reporters and conspiracy theorists. There was nothing new from Morrow, he said, not that Effie was really speaking to him, just the essentials about the girl. The prints on the knife were confirmed as Anya's, and the official cause of death was signed off as poisoning by tutu shoots. Morrow was still waiting on DNA, but she wasn't expecting anything.

Open and shut.

Effie lay in bed, trying not to think about Lewis. About the boy who'd saved her. And the man who flinched at the touch of her. She turned to the curtains, the thin material failing to mask the approaching morning, and she thrust her legs out, needing to stretch.

"Shit." Effie pulled her legs back.

The child sat up, startled. *Kicked.*

"I'm sorry," Anya muttered, her eyes wide and green and apologetic. "I'm sorry." Then she scurried to the foot of the mattress.

"No." Effie placed a hand on the bed next to the girl. "It was my fault. Please. Don't leave. You just gave me a fright."

Anya hesitated, the duvet pulled around her like a wall, and she flicked her gaze from Effie to the door.

"I like that you're here." Effie smiled. "I like that you stayed."

There was a moment of silence before the girl spoke.

"You talk in your sleep," she said.

"No, I don't," Effie retorted. Too forceful.

"It's okay. I don't mind." Anya lowered her eyes and pulled at the duvet.

"Is that why you never stay . . . Why you always leave before I wake up?"

"Is Dinah your friend?" Anya asked after a while.

"Sorry?" Effie stiffened, betrayed by her own fogged mind. "Who?"

"You were shouting for her."

Blood pounded in Effie's stomach. "I don't know."

The name scraped at the back of her head, grazing a memory. It tingled at the nape of her neck—scratch, scratch—carving a word into wood.

Dinah.

"I don't know," Effie said again.

"What's this?" asked Anya, holding up a football.

"A ball."

The child frowned. "It's not round."

Effie contained a smile. "It's a rugby ball."

"Rugby."

"I could show you if you like? On my phone."

The girl shook her head. "Is it yours?" she asked.

"No. It's . . ." Effie looked at it then, really looked at it. Her throat narrowed. "It used to belong to Lewis. He gave it to Aiden. June must have kept it."

"Aiden?"

"My little brother." Effie turned the ball in her hands. "He died. A long time ago."

"How?"

"It was something called tetanus. From a rusted nail that cut into his foot," she said. "I later learned that my dad never had us vaccinated." She forced herself to gulp down the pain and the anger. "I never forgave him for that."

"Vaccinated?" asked Anya.

"It's something that the doctor gives you, a special medicine to protect you from getting ill."

"Am I vaccinated?"

"Not yet."

Distress flashed through the child's face.

"It's okay." Effie touched the girl's arm. "When you're ready, we'll go and see the nurse and he'll sort everything."

The child's shoulders sank, her small body curving inward like a young fern, and she picked at her sleeves.

"Is there a medicine for when it hurts here?"

"Sorry?" Effie frowned.

"Here." Anya touched her chest. "It's always sore. Ever since . . . since leaving Mum and Four, it hurts here. And in my tummy sometimes." She looked up. "Like there's a bruise inside my stomach." Fear stirred behind her eyes. "Am I going to die?"

"No. No." Effie moved over and pulled the girl into her. "You're not going to die." She ran a hand through Anya's hair and kissed her forehead. "You just miss them. Your mum and Four. And sometimes, missing people can be very painful."

"I'm not meant to miss them."

"What do you mean?"

Anya frowned—a wounded expression.

"Mum was a bad person," she said. "Mum never listened. And . . ." She looked up, her face younger than before. "I thought that Four was good. He was kind. Sometimes on rainy days he gave me treats. But the policewoman said that Four wasn't good. She said Four was a bad man and that I shouldn't love him."

"Oh, Anya." Effie squeezed the girl to her chest. "I'm so sorry."

For a moment, they sat like that, curled and pressed together. Effie held her tight, as though it might absorb some of her pain.

"Do you have any pictures of my mum and Four?" asked Anya.

Effie pulled back, her heart thrumming.

"June said you might show me."

Effie turned and stared at the writing desk, a weight pushing on her lungs. "Yes," she said eventually. "I have one. Sort of."

"Can I see?"

Effie slipped from the bed and stepped over to the old desk, unmoved in twenty years. June had left it, just in case Effie wanted to go back there. She tugged the drawer open and lifted out the wad of papers. Letters from Lewis. Drawings and maps that they'd made. Old pictures. And at the bottom was Effie's only family photo, taken just a month before Four was born. A month before Mum died.

Effie touched a shaking finger to each of their faces. Mum and Dad stood in the middle with the sea behind them. Four was safe and invisible in Mum's stomach, his tiny body hidden away from the world, from all of them. There was no evidence of her little brother. No bulge in her mum's top. No swelling to her chest. But he was there, listening and growing and making Mum glow. Ten fingers and ten toes. A cryptic pregnancy, Blair had named it.

A little surprise.

Tia, Aiden and Effie were sitting on the white sand, their feet and legs bare, with wide smiles and wild hair. Aiden was scooping up a fistful of sand, about to eat it, and Tia's mouth was open mid-word.

"That's your mum there," said Effie, pointing at Tia. "A long time ago."

"She looks different." Anya frowned. "Where's Four?"

"In there." Effie smiled. She couldn't not smile. He was her baby brother, the baby she'd fed and loved and rocked to sleep. "Even though there's no bump, there's a—"

Then with a jerk, Anya grabbed the photo and ripped it in two.

"Stop!" Effie tried to hold Anya's hands. "What are you doing?"

"He's there," said Anya, her face white.

"Who?" Effie's hand trembled. "Who's there?"

Effie held the torn pieces together, her mother's face sliced in two.

"Four?" Effie managed. "He's just a fetus. He can't hurt—"

The girl shook her head. "The bad man's there."

"What bad man?"

"In the middle." Anya pointed to the smiling figure in the center of the picture.

Dad.

"You mustn't speak to the bad man," said Anya. "He'll hurt you."

Effie stared at the photo, her body tense, then back at the child. "Anya, did that man do something to you?"

She shook her head. "We can't talk to him." Her eyes widened. "It's not allowed." She shook her head again. "Never ever."

"It's okay. It's okay." Effie placed a hand on her shoulder. "We don't need to talk about him."

"I want June." Anya's eyes were a watery green. "I want June."

"Of course."

Effie drew her hand back and the girl sprinted from the room, leaving Effie with the butchered image of her family.

AUGUST–DECEMBER 2007

EFFIE LAY ON her back, her red hair splayed like roots through the undergrowth as she looked up at the rimu trees. Giants that had been born into darkness, into the dirt, but that had crawled out of the cracks to fill the skies.

She curled her fingers into the damp soil, digging hard and deep enough that the earth clogged under her fingernails and the bush seeped into her. She a part of it, and it a part of her. A girl made of dirt and possum shit, tangled in the roots.

The highest branches moved with the breeze, the long leaves swinging and dancing, while the lower branches had withered and fallen to the forest floor with her, decaying like old bones.

No crawling out. No reaching the skies.

Effie wiped a dirty hand over her top, her newly inflated breasts pulling the material tight, and she whispered into the air.

"I'm scared, Lewis." She pressed the heels of her palms into her eyes and swallowed. "If you tell anyone, I'll deny it, then kick you in the balls. But . . . I'm scared."

She blinked away tears, then bit into her tongue.

Her thirteenth birthday had come and gone. Then her fourteenth. The exact days were hard to tell. But she'd watched the kōwhai trees flower in spring, their drooping branches bursting with color. In autumn, they'd darkened with the cold, and by winter the tūī had deserted them. In August, with the approach of spring, the trees had shed their darkened leaves, and the color returned.

Two springs. Twenty-two months.

Just bush and trees and nothing. No mention of school. No trip to Koraha. No June. No Lewis. Just trees.

Dad lived as a shadow, dark and untouchable. A phantom that haunted the corners of the hut.

"He's keeping us here, Lewis."

Effie sniffed.

"He's forbidden us to leave."

Another full moon passed, shining as bright as the sun, but the light just made the shadows darker.

One moon, then another. Month after month.

Effie stood in the hut—in her prison—gazing out the window. The kahikatea and tōtara stretched their long limbs to the skies, swaying and toying with the wind. The tōtara leaves had already turned yellow with the warming air, but the color taunted her, and Dad's stomping boots and clenched fists pissed on any pleasure the summer might bring.

She sighed and turned from the window. Then she spooned up a serving of lentils and vegetables and placed the bowl in front of Four. She made sure that Tia and Four ate three times a day and that they washed at least twice a week. Four had shot up in the last year, his pants no longer reaching his ankles, and he was always dirty. Dirt stuck to six-year-old boys like sap to tree bark.

"You need to eat the green stuff too," she said.

Dad came to the hut less and less, preferring the company of trees and feral pigs to his children. And when he did, Effie didn't let him eat with them. She left his meals on the deck. He'd starve otherwise. Since Aiden's death, Dad had shriveled away, a skeleton moving beneath skin, his cheeks hollowed out to shallow caves. Effie half expected to find him slumped dead against a tree, his body wet with booze and vomit.

As they bent over their bowls, swallowing down the tasteless goop, Tia talked about summer flowers and fantails and warm river swims. And as their spoons scraped the bottom of their bowls, Dad's footsteps climbed the outside steps. *Thud. Thud. Thud.* Then the door creaked open.

"I have fish," he said, holding his offering up in the doorway. "The boy needs protein."

Effie didn't turn. "I made him lentils," she said.

"It's fresh."

She didn't look at him. She didn't acknowledge him as family, as the man whose blood matched her own.

"He needs—"

"You don't know shit about what he needs." Effie spun around and glared at him, the hut silenced.

He set the bucket on the floor, metal clanging wood, then walked out.

Dad always went hunting after he'd had a bad night. Effie touched a hand to the soft blue of her arm. He always brought them fish or meat after he'd hurt her. After the ugly drink, and empty bottles left discarded on the floor.

—

"Tia. *Tia.*" Effie shook Tia's arm. "Wake up."

Her sister stirred and rolled over. "What?"

"We're leaving."

Tia frowned. "Leaving?"

"Dad's gone again." Adrenaline quickened Effie's words. "On

one of his trips. I've packed enough stuff, and we can use the pink markers to navigate a way out via the river. I've been thinking it over, trying to work out the easiest route, and—"

"Why would we leave?"

Effie moved back, the expression on her sister's face punching the air from her stomach. "I . . ." she stuttered. "Cos . . ."

Tia yawned and pulled herself up, sleep clinging to her face, and Four stretched and murmured in the bundle of blankets next to her.

"Because . . ." Fire tingled in Effie's palms. "Because of Dad."

Tia looked at her. Not nodding. Not understanding.

Effie's heart thumped against her ribs. "Doesn't he scare you?"

"Why would he scare me?" Tia clutched her duvet. "You scare me more than Dad." She mumbled the words into her chest. "Dad's sad and, you know, quiet. But you . . ." Her words shrank further. "You get mad. And sometimes when you shout at Dad, it makes Four cry. Four says you're keeping Dad away from us. As a punishment or something."

"What?" A lump swelled in Effie's throat. "No. No." She shook her head. "This is all wrong. I'm protecting you. I'm trying to keep you safe. Dad's not well." Effie stared at her sister. "It's not safe for us to stay with him. We have to leave."

"Dad loves us."

"*Dad is never here!*" shouted Effie. "We do everything for ourselves. We don't have a dad."

Tia shook her head. "I'm not leaving."

Effie stopped as tears dampened her sister's eyes.

"I hate it out there," said Tia. "With all those people. I hate leaving the bush."

Effie frowned, the world suddenly less solid. "You love visiting Koraha. You love staying with June."

"No." Tia shook her head. "I don't. I only liked it when June came here."

"But I thought—"

"The kids at school are horrible," she said. "They call me bush rat. A stinky little bush rat. And they rub mud in my hair." She wiped a hand across her face. "The girls always laugh at my clothes, and they throw my lunch into the trees, like rat scraps."

The floor shifted and dissolved under Effie's knees, like she was falling through a cloud. Down. Down. Down.

"Tia, I didn't . . ."

"The kids are too scared to tease you. They think you'll bite them with your wolf teeth, or that you'll make gloves from their skin. And Lewis is, like, real big now. Leanne said he tried to kill his own dad."

"Tia, that's not true." Effie paused. Leanne, the tall kid from Tia's class, was a lying bitch. She shook her head. "I'm so sorry, Tia."

"If we leave, those government people with fancy suits will cage us up like possums. Then they'll throw us into one of those foster homes that smell like cats and cigarettes. Foster parents are mean. They beat kids, and they scare them so much that the kids wet the bed. Then the kids have to sleep in it, in the pee, and they have to go to school smelling of wee and cats."

"Tia, I don't think that's true. I bet there are loads of nice foster homes."

She shook her head. "Nope. Leanne knew a kid who got fostered, and they made her sleep in a cardboard box and gave her dog food for dinner. The wet stuff that slops out of cans and looks like sick."

"I think Leanne's lying."

Tia shook her head again. "Leanne pinkie-swore it." Her eyes widened. "I don't want some stupid foster family and their eight stupid cats. I want Dad."

Effie opened and closed her mouth, and glanced over at the packed rucksack. With her insides trembling, she looked back at her sister.

"Mum and Aiden are here too," spluttered Tia, her face hard. "This is our home. If you make us leave, I will hate you forever."

Effie closed her eyes, aching in her stomach and bones, and when she opened them again, Tia's cheeks were damp.

"Please," said Tia. "Please don't make us leave."

2025

THE GRAY OF the sky matched the gray of the sea, the line where the two met hard to distinguish. There was a heat to the afternoon though, a rare tenderness to the salt breeze, and the warmth of the sea air wrapped Effie up.

She stood in shorts and a singlet with her toes buried in the sand as the water lapped at her ankles. It was changing her—the West Coast air and the endless ashen sea.

As she looked out at the water, her phone buzzed in her pocket, stealing her attention from the crashing waves. After a moment, she pulled it out.

Prepare yourself, my friend . . .

Three dots appeared and flashed under Blair's message.

It's all Ewan's doing. Nothing to do with me. The man has issues.

Effie rubbed her forehead, groaning, as her phone pinged and the image came through.

"Jesus, Blair."

Rimu was sitting on Ewan's knee in a checked hoodie, the drawcords tied into a bloody bow. It even had arms for Rimu's front legs. Ewan was wearing a matching one.

> *Ewan got them made. Both with a "calming fleece interior." Ewan says it makes the dog feel hugged. I swear to god.*

Effie buried her face in her palm.

> *Honestly. I TOTALLY LOVE THEM. Ewan's ordering one for me now.*

Effie replied, almost smiling.

> *Well, we always knew you had issues.*

The dots appeared again, dancing as Blair typed, but a figure caught Effie's eye and she turned.
Lewis.
Effie stood still as he walked down the beach, her body rooted to the spot as he closed the gap between them. He kept his gaze set on her, not once looking away, not stopping until they were a few meters apart. Neither of them spoke as the waves rolled in behind them. Then Lewis took a step forward, and Effie's breath caught in her throat.

"How did—" she began.

"Your car. I spotted it from the road." Lewis's face hardened, and he clenched and spread his fingers at his sides. "I . . ." He swore, then kicked at the sand. "I just . . . it's like you're always there, in my head, and I can't—"

"Lewis, we're not going to talk about this now." Effie shook her head. "Look, you're married—sorry, separated. I get it. We don't need—"

"Yes." His raised voice silenced her. "We are going to talk about it. Right now. Because not everything gets to be your decision. You've been like a petulant child since you got back, refusing to listen or to let anyone help you." He threw his hands up. "And god forbid, Effie, that you let anyone get close to you."

"Me?" she snapped. "You're the one who was secretly married. You're the one who pulled away from me."

"It was never a secret." He paused. "And you know that it wasn't, that before . . . I couldn't . . ."

"Couldn't what?" she demanded. "That you couldn't kiss me? Couldn't bear to touch me?"

Lewis shook his head and let out a frustrated groan. "For fuck's sake, Effie."

"I get it," she said. "You want to save me. You think I'm some fragile bush girl in need of rescuing." Her lips trembled. "Well, I'm not. And I don't need your help or your pity."

"Pity?" Lewis balked. "I don't pity you." He threw his arm out in the direction of the water, his voice raised. "You left. You left and you never looked back. You built a whole new life for yourself on the other side of the world, and you didn't give a single thought to the people you left behind."

"That's not what happened."

"You didn't give a shit about the one person who loved you more than . . ." Lewis balled his fingers into a fist, his body shaking, then he turned away.

Effie didn't move or make a sound. She seemed to have forgotten how to form words.

Eventually, Lewis looked back, his eyes damp, and Effie's chest constricted.

"I missed you, Effie."

She shook her head; it was all she could do.

"You didn't call," said Lewis. "In seventeen years, you didn't call."

"I—"

"I thought about you all the time," he said, moving nearer. "I wondered where you might be, or who you might be with. Who was getting to love you." He stepped closer. Too close. "Does that sound like pity to you?"

Effie bit into her lip, her muscles vibrating, and she was fifteen again.

"And now," he said, "you're here."

His face was right there in front of her, the warmth of his breath brushing against her neck and cheek.

She was fifteen and lost and heartbroken. "I thought you didn't want me."

Lewis took her face in his hands and looked into her eyes, then he kissed her. He pulled her close, his mouth forceful, and Effie sank into him, her heart pounding as he lowered her to the sand. Lewis kept kissing her as she tugged at his shirt, pulling it over his head, and she ran a hand down his bare chest.

Effie groaned as he moved his head down to her stomach. He kissed her from her navel up to her neck, the damp warmth of his mouth seeping through the thin fabric of her singlet.

"Lewis," she murmured.

He kissed along her collarbone, taking his time, and Effie clawed into his shoulders. With each touch of his tongue, something surged inside her, and she moved her fingers down to his jeans. She tried to undo the button, but he stopped her.

"Lewis?"

He looked up, a smile eclipsing his face, and lowered himself onto her, her body beating under the weight of him.

"Can I take you home?" he asked.

"Yes."

He kissed her.

"Yes."

He kissed her again. "Thank god." His smile widened. "I might have died if you'd said no."

A few hours later, Effie crept back into June's house. She didn't want Anya to wake in the middle of the night and find she wasn't there. She inched the girl's door open, grimacing as the hinges creaked, and peered inside. But Anya was fast asleep.

"Night, little one," she whispered.

She stepped back, cursing the hinges, and pulled the door closed. The smell of sex clung to her clothes and hair, and her body was too alive with Lewis to consider sleeping. She tiptoed to the kitchen and put the kettle on. June had left a note on the benchtop. *About bloody time.* And she'd signed it off with a kiss and a smiley face.

Effie pocketed the note and took her tea through to the living room. She had only just sat down when Anya appeared in the doorway.

"Anya." She looked up. "I thought you were sleeping."

"June said you were with Lewis."

"I was."

"Are you in trouble?"

"No, no." Effie smiled and shook her head. "I'm fine."

Anya frowned. "He's a policeman."

"Yes." Effie patted the cushion next to her. "But he's also my friend."

Anya walked over and sat on the sofa. "So we like him?"

"Yes. We like him very much."

Anya looked at her. Then she lay down and rested her head on Effie's lap.

"I didn't like the other police people."

"No." Effie pulled a blanket over the child. "I'm not their biggest fan either."

"Is that why you hid Mum's stuff from them?"

"Sorry?" Effie frowned. "What do you mean?"

"Did you not want those police people to have it?"

"Have what?"

"Mum's things." Anya yawned. "Her clothes and books and stuff."

Effie stiffened. "What clothes?"

"The clothes that were in the hut."

"Anya," Effie tried to keep her voice steady, "what do you mean? Who hid them?"

"You did."

Effie took a breath. "When did I hide them?"

Anya turned and pulled the blanket to her chin. "When you took me back to the hut." She rubbed her eyes. "When you made me stay outside and draw."

"Anya, I didn't hide anything."

She yawned again. "Mum was gone, remember? And all her things were gone too." She frowned. "Unless Mum took them." Her frown deepened. "Or he did. He hated Mum's clothes. He said they were ugly."

"Who?" Heat tingled in Effie's chest and neck. "Who said that?"

"The bad man."

"And where is he now?"

Anya shrugged. "Hiding in the trees."

MARCH 2008

THE DRINK WAS in his hair and in his face. It had stolen Dad's eyes and grayed his skin. The drink sloshed through him as he stumbled up the hut steps. He staggered through the door, leaking the morning light into the room, and shuffled forward on shaky legs. Then he stopped in the middle of the hut, swaying, and looked at Effie. She stared back, her teeth clenched and her eyes thinned to tight slits.

"I hate you," she whispered.

She stared at the deep gash across his left eyebrow, feeling nothing but rage. The blood was red and crusted, and his cheek was swollen. There were also four long scratches gouged into his neck, angry and weeping. But Effie didn't care. She wanted to hurl herself at him. To pound into his chest. To claw and scream until the anger gushed out of her.

"Where were you?" she managed.

Dad looked down at his boots. Blood had dried in splotches on his shirt, evidence of where his bottom lip had split open and bled, and his pants were soaked up to his waist. The hut floor darkened around him as the river dripped from his clothes and he started to shiver. To cry. His body shook violently, like something was thrashing inside him, and he pushed his palms into his forehead. Then a sound escaped his lips and he stumbled back.

"Dad?" Effie inched forward.

But he held his hand out and shook his head. He whipped his neck from side to side, shaking and shaking. Too hard. Too fast.

"Dad, stop," Effie begged. "Stop. Please."

His head stilled suddenly and he looked at her, his face sad and unhinged, and a chill flushed through Effie.

"Dad, what happened?"

"She's dead," he whispered.

Her heart stopped. "Who? Who's dead?"

"I should never have left her."

Dad was there, but his mind was somewhere else—adrift.

"I left her . . . and now . . . now she's dead."

"Dad . . ." Effie reached an arm out, but he recoiled. He staggered away and flattened himself against the wall, putting distance between them.

"Leave me," he said. "Leave me alone."

"But—"

"I don't want you here." He turned his face away. "I don't want you to . . ."

"Dad, I don't understand." Effie's lips trembled. "What happened?"

"*Get out,*" he shouted, his eyes wide and fogged with drink. "Get out."

He threw his arm out, pointing at the door. "*Leave,*" he yelled. "Now."

"Dad . . ."

He grabbed a mug and threw it across the room, the ceramic shattering against the wall with a crash. Effie lurched backward, tripping over a basket of firewood and landing on the floor.

"She's dead," he murmured. "Dinah's dead because of me."

Effie scrambled to her feet, her heart pounding against the insides of her ribs—broken—and she ran from the hut. She hurried down the steps, past her siblings in the garden and past the rows of vegetables. She didn't stop until she was deep enough in the trees that the hut was hidden, until the ache in her lungs and the panting of her breath silenced her thoughts.

Puffing, Effie bent forward and rested her hands on her knees. The small clearing—where Mum and Aiden lay—spread out like a dark pool. Trees crowded around it, so dense that only faint rays of sunlight sifted through the canopy. Effie's breathing softened, and the noises of the bush slowly returned.

As she straightened, a sound pierced the haze, like a stone dropping through the surface of a lake. Effie looked around, searching. Then she heard it again. A crack. A twig snapped underfoot.

"Tia?" Effie spun. "Is that you?"

Nothing.

Effie knelt down and touched the small mound of rocks where Mum lay. Then she heard it again, that sharp invisible sound, and she scanned the edges of the clearing.

Something moved, a dark mass in the trees, and Effie's eyes clung to it.

"Tia?" Her stomach tightened as the thing shifted. "Are you there?"

The shape slunk among the ferns, too big to be Tia. Ice trickled down Effie's neck.

"Who's there?"

The shape stopped, then it stepped from the trees, a whiteness emerging from the shadows.

Asher.

Asher, who was the strangest boy she'd ever seen. Asher, who was punched by his dad—*too hard*—but kept smiling anyway. Asher, with one eye like the ocean and one like the dirt. Asher, who'd left them.

"What are you doing here?" she demanded.

There was no kid left in him. No boy. He was older, more angular and solid, his face all man. The beard was gone.

He moved forward, his steps slow, as though she were a fragile deer that might spook.

"Effie, please don't run."

"Why would I run?" She stood tall. "You don't scare me."

"Of course." He shook his head. "Sorry."

"Why are you here?"

He hesitated. "I followed your dad."

Effie frowned at him.

"I've tried to come back a couple of times." Asher looked at her like he was pleading. Like he thought she gave a shit about him or what he did. "But I couldn't find my way back." He stopped and moved closer. "I kept returning to Koraha, waiting to see your dad so I could follow him here."

"I asked you *why* you came back, not how." She scoffed. "You could have ridden here on the back of a pig for all I care."

"I came back," said Asher, "because of your dad."

"What about him?" Effie kicked at the earth. "You don't know shit about my dad."

"You don't . . ." Asher frowned, then he slowed his words. Like she was an idiot who didn't understand English. "You don't know?"

"Know what?" she spat.

"What your dad did to that man."

"What man?"

"In Koraha. The last time you were in town."

"Dad didn't do anything," said Effie. "You're talking shit."

"He killed him, Effie." Concern flooded Asher's face. Then he reached his arm out, like in his deranged world, he thought it might comfort her. "The police have been looking for your dad for two years. He's wanted for murder, Effie."

She stepped back, the calm thumped from her with such force that she found it hard to stand.

"You're lying," she said.

Her legs shook as she pictured him. Dad. The swings. That day. The blood—gummy like tree sap. The black hole—where his tooth was missing.

We can't stay here.

"You're lying," she said again.

"Effie, your dad's dangerous."

I hurt him real bad.

Asher reached out and Effie snapped her arm away.

"It's not safe for you to stay here. You've got to—"

"I don't *got* to do anything you say." Her fingers tingled. "You're nothing to me."

Asher looked at her. A pitying adult expression, like he thought age made him smarter or some shit. But age just turned boys into men. And men were idiots and liars.

"Effie, your dad cracked the man's skull open with a crowbar."

"You're lying."

"He beat him," said Asher. "And left him for dead."

His face contorted into a look of sympathy, and Effie wanted to punch it.

"You don't know what you're—"

The snap of branches silenced them, and they both turned.

Dad was there, standing on the other side of the clearing.

He stepped from the bush and staggered toward them. His right hand was clasped around the shaft of a heavy gardening shovel. It swung at his side, the steel end thumping against his boot as he moved, splitting the silent air. Effie slipped her hand into Asher's, his skin clammy, and started to inch them away. Dad kept walking—the wrong Dad, with the wild, desperate look in his eyes.

"You need to run," Effie whispered. "Run, Asher."

"I'm not leaving you."

"He won't hurt me." She turned her head, pleading, "*Please, Asher.*"

But his fingers tightened around her hand. "I'm not leaving."

Effie tried to shove him, to make him move, but there was not enough strength in her.

"Please," she whispered.

But Dad was on them before the plea left her lips. He grabbed Asher's arm and started dragging him away.

"You deserve to rot in hell," Dad spat.

Effie followed them, tugging at Dad's arm, but he shoved her off—a giant swatting a fly—and she fell to the ground. He turned, a fire burning behind his eyes, and growled at her through gritted teeth.

"Stay," he hissed. "Don't follow us."

"Dad, please," Effie begged, but she didn't—couldn't—stand. The earth had ensnared her, cementing her useless legs to the dirt.

He glared at her. "Stay."

As she lay in the ferns, Dad dragged Asher farther away, and Asher stumbled behind, like he wasn't even trying. Like maybe he just wanted to get Dad away from her. Effie sobbed as they moved farther away. She should run after them. She should throw herself at Dad. She should do something. *Anything.* But fear held her still. Then, with a crack, Dad hit Asher so hard that Asher tripped and slumped to the ground.

"*Asher!*" Effie screamed.

Before he could stand, Dad was over him, pinning him to the ground with his foot. Then he raised the spade above his head.

"*No!*" Effie yelled. "Dad, stop!"

He smashed the spade down, the handle connecting with Asher's stomach, and Asher groaned. Effie let out a scream. Then Dad raised the spade again.

"*Stop!*"

The thud of wood on flesh knocked Effie from her numbness and she lurched forward. But a hand gripped her wrist and she spun around.

"Tia?" Effie stared at her sister. "What are you doing? We need to help him."

Tia shook her head, her eyes teary, and she dug her fingers in.

"Let go," Effie shouted, and tried to tug her arm free. "Dad will kill him!"

But Tia held tight. "Asher shouldn't have come back," she said.

"What?" Effie panted in disbelief. "How can—"

"This is our home," Tia sobbed. "Dad's protecting us."

"Tia, Dad's gone. Something's broken in him." Effie held her gaze. "Dad's dangerous."

Tia shook her head again, tears wetting her face. "We're safe here," she said. "It's the outside world that's dangerous. The outside world that killed Aiden and—"

"That's not true." Effie yanked her hand free. "It's cos of Dad that—"

Asher screamed and Effie tore away. She sprinted across the clearing and threw herself on her dad's back. She tugged at his hair and face, digging her nails into his arms and shoulders, but he didn't lift his eyes from Asher. Asher lay on the ground, a heap splayed among the fallen leaves, unmoving. Blood dripped from his split cheek into the hollow of his gaping mouth, his eyes closed and unresponsive. The only life in him was the soft rise of his chest.

"Dad, stop." Effie clung to his arm. "You'll kill him."

But Dad wasn't there.

He wrenched his arm free, the violent jolt sending Effie to the ground, then he lifted the spade and turned it around in his bloodied hands. The bush inhaled, stunned, as the steel blade cracked off Asher's body.

Then time stopped, and the spade fell to the earth.

And the rise in Asher's chest stilled.

"No," Effie sobbed.

She crawled over to the lifeless white form. Asher's lip had burst, and blood trickled from a gash across his temple. Effie leaned in, the red of him seeping into her clothes as she clutched at his dead body.

"No!" Effie kicked out as two strong hands pulled her away. "*You killed him!*" she screamed.

She punched at her dad's stomach, at his arms and chest, and he released her. He looked at her, tears filling his eyes, and let her hit him.

"You're a monster," she sputtered.

Then she turned and sprinted to her sister.

"We need to go," she said, gripping Tia's hand. "Now."

But Tia didn't move. "I'm not leaving," she said. "Four and I are staying."

"You can't stay here." She pulled at her sister. "Please, Tia, please."

Tia still didn't budge.

"I—" Effie panted, "I'll go and get help. I'll find someone who can—"

"*No!*" Tia shouted.

"I don't . . ." An ache cracked through Effie's body. "What do you—"

"This is our special place. Our secret." Tia stared into her. "If you tell anyone where we are, I'll never forgive you."

"Tia, I can't stay." Tears dripped into her mouth. "I can't live here. Not with him."

"You're wrong about Dad."

Effie swallowed the bile in her throat. "You just watched him kill Asher, how can you—"

"Asher shouldn't have come back."

"Tia, listen to yourself."

Tia just stood there.

"I can't stay here," whispered Effie. "I can't watch while he—"

"Then go." Tia glared at her. "But swear on Mum that you'll never tell anyone where we are."

"Tia—"

"*Swear it*," Tia yelled.

Effie's heart burned.

"I promise."

2025

EFFIE WOKE BEFORE dawn, packed a small rucksack and laced up her walking boots.

Then she scribbled on a piece of paper and left it on the kitchen table next to her pounamu necklace.

I'm sorry, Anya, there's something I have to do. I just need some time. But I'll be back.
I promise.

Then she stepped out into the dark.
Going back. Back to Tia.
To find out what happened to her sister.

1988

ADAM LIFTED HIS hands and splatted them down on the water, sending big splashes out of the bath and over Dinah's dress.

"Adam, stop!" Big sister pulled a funny face, her eyes squished up. "Adam! You're getting the floor wet!"

He gathered bubbles around his tummy, but the bathwater gobbled them up and his belly button peeped through the water. He thumped the water again, and it spilled over the bathroom floor.

"Adam, stop!" Dinah laughed. She leaned over the bath and gripped his hands. "You're making a mess."

Then big sister scooped up bubbles and plopped them on his head.

"There." She smiled. "Now you're an important police officer in his police hat. So you have to behave."

"Just five more minutes, you two." Mummy's voice sneaked in under the bathroom door. "Dad will be home soon."

Adam pushed the open shampoo bottle under the water, making it heavy. Then he squeezed the plastic, and bubbles exploded out of the top.

"Yay." He giggled.

Big sister laughed, then she got a cloth and wiped the bubbles from his face.

"No eyes," Adam squealed. "Not in eyes."

Dinah smiled. "I'm nowhere near your eyes."

Big sister needed to wipe her face too. Her cheek was all grubby, smudged blue and purple.

"Just three minutes."

"Yes, Mum," Dinah called.

MARCH–APRIL 2008

EFFIE CLAMBERED FROM the tin boat and landed on the stones, a small wounded puddle.

The Haast River had churned and tugged under the boat, pulling her astray, but Effie had battled against it, fighting until her arms burned and her palms left skin on the wooden oars.

She spluttered, coughing up bile and phlegm, and wiped the mucus away with her sleeve. Her clothes were damp with dirt and river and Asher's blood. She crawled on hands and knees, reaching out to the water, but her body bowed over, and the stones caught her chin.

Cursing, Effie forced herself up, then she lunged at the river, scooping up handfuls of water and throwing it into her face and down her throat. After hours of stumbling through the bush without food or drink, the skin on her feet was raw and her stomach ached. She'd walked for six hours, too dazed to stop, and the black tinge of nightfall was creeping through the sky.

Effie lay down, allowing herself a short rest, as the shadows lengthened and the sky darkened above her, the moon bright and round.

Slowly, her breath and body came back to her and she stood. It was an easy ten-minute walk through the bush to the road. Then it was twenty-seven kilometers on the hard road to Koraha. In the dark. Alone. Without food or water or warm clothes.

"Stupid idiot."

She should have grabbed her bag. She clenched her fists and kicked at the ground. Then she lifted her face to the moon.

"You up for this?" Effie whispered. "Cos I'm going to need your help."

The moon smiled down, and Effie forced a weak smile back.

"Let's go, then."

The small body that slumped against June's back door, nine hours later, was broken and empty.

Effie had hidden in the verge whenever a car passed, only a handful in total, afraid of strange faces and strange questions, then she'd stumbled on without stopping. As the hours passed, and her feet tore, the cold had eaten through her. First through her clothes, then through her bones.

"June," Effie murmured.

She raised her arm and her fist slumped against the locked screen door.

Nothing.

"June." The word caught in her parched throat, and she blinked away hot tears. "June."

Nothing.

There was a soft *drip-drip-drip* in the dark as water spotted on the stone steps. Then the first raindrop landed on Effie's forehead. She slumped forward against the door, trying not to cry. She was so cold and so tired. Her eyes fluttered closed, and it took forever for her to open them again.

She had to move.

Move, Effie. Do something.

Gritting her teeth, she lifted her head and peered through the gloom. There, just a few meters away, glowing in the moonlight, was a pair of gardening shears. She crawled through the long grass, her feet too sore to hold her weight, then she clambered back to the screen door, dragging the shears behind her. With a huge effort, she lifted the long clippers and cut into the mesh. She cut and cut—the metal blades clanging off the doorframe—until she couldn't hold her arms up anymore.

"Oh god."

Effie turned her head to the voice, to the figure on the other side of the door in sheepskin slippers and a red checked fleece.

"Oh, my sweet girl."

June curled herself around her, blocking the world out, and Effie let herself stop.

Effie didn't see anyone except June and Lewis that week. June said there were too many wagging tongues and prying noses in a small town. Best to lay low.

It wasn't until day three that Effie finally spoke to June, until Tia's voice wasn't so loud in her head.

If you tell anyone where we are, I'll never forgive you.

Sitting opposite June and Lewis at the kitchen table, Effie settled on the half-truth that she'd decided to tell them. Not that lying mattered. Asher was already dead.

"I just needed to get away from Dad," she whispered. "I need to get as far away from here as possible."

From him. From the bush. From the itch to go back.

"Effie." Lewis sat opposite her. "Can you tell us what—"

She shook her head.

Lewis was a policeman now—still supervised, he'd said, but he had a uniform and a badge. So talking to him wasn't an option. The police would cage Dad in a cement box, and the four gray walls would kill him. And Tia would die from it too.

"Effie, I don't understand."

She shook her head again.

Lewis was eighteen now, a man, and looking at him made her palms sweat.

He had cried the morning that Effie showed up, when June had called him and told him to come to the house with food and a first-aid kit. He had squeezed Effie so hard that her ribs hurt, and he'd kept touching her, like he wasn't convinced she was real. Once, when they thought she was sleeping, Effie had caught June hugging Lewis like Mum used to hug Tia.

June and Lewis talked lots over the next week. Effie only participated when they discussed the faraway places that she could escape to.

She had found a globe and spun it halfway around, as far away as she could get, and she'd pressed her finger to a mass of land on the other side. Europe. A continent about twenty thousand kilometers away.

Apparently, years ago, June had stolen Effie's birth certificate from a metal box under the hut. *Just in case.* Which meant that Effie could get a black piece of card with her name and photo printed on it. A necessity, June said, although she didn't explain why. Some government nonsense. And June had a cousin in Scotland who kept being mentioned. Katy or Kate or something.

All the talking was tiring, and Effie's thoughts were bruised and foggy. Even at night, behind the darkness of her eyelids, she pictured Asher. His eyes. The gurgle from his lips. The stillness of his chest. Certain details of his face were harder to cling to. Some things were already rubbing out. Effie just wanted to escape. To get far enough away that Asher's dead face couldn't follow her.

The rise in Lewis's voice stole Effie from her thoughts, and she looked up from the table. He was pacing the room in his uniform, and June was watching him. There was some legal issue that they were fighting about, some complication that Lewis had brought up before. But Effie tried not to listen. She didn't know why she should care about pissing off a few cops in Christchurch.

"We would be party to kidnapping, June. He's still her legal guardian," said Lewis. "You get that, right? She's only fifteen, meaning her consent is immaterial."

June shrugged. "Who would find out anyway? The police?" She winked at him. "Are you planning on telling on us?"

"No." Lewis scowled. "Of course not."

"And it's in the girl's interests. Juries look favorably on those things."

"Juries, yes. But . . ."

"But what?"

Lewis shook his head. "Nothing."

"Lewis?"

He avoided June's eyes. "The police tend to come down hard on their own."

The expression on June's face changed—like someone had died—and she looked from Effie to Lewis. Something was happening between them, something that Effie didn't understand. Words that didn't make sense.

June paused. "I wasn't thinking. You're right. It's too risky."

"No. That's not what I'm saying. I just . . ." Lewis hesitated, looking sad rather than angry, which didn't make sense either.

"If you think it's the right thing," he said, "then I'm happy to take the risk. I just want you to be sure. For her. Not me."

June touched his hand, patting him slightly.

Lewis looked hurt.

And Effie felt like a child.

"I'm leaving tomorrow," whispered Effie.

She sat on her bed and picked at her thumb.

"Yes." Lewis gave a small smile.

Idiot. Of course he knew she was leaving. Lewis had booked the bloody ticket. It had been all they'd talked and not talked about for three weeks.

"Will you miss me?" she asked.

Lewis walked over from his spot in the corner and sat on the bed next to her. He put his hand on her knee, and Effie moved closer. Then he reached his arm out and pulled her into his chest. Effie leaned into the warmth of him, his heart beating in her ear, and closed her eyes. Lewis rested his chin on her head, their bodies curled together.

For a couple of minutes, neither of them spoke, and Effie wanted the moment to last forever. But it couldn't. All the clothes that June had collected were already washed and packed for the flight, and Effie was in nothing but an oversized T-shirt and a pair of boy's shorts.

Lewis touched his hand to her waist, his fingers finding skin, and her body tensed. Gently, he placed his other hand on her thigh, and the tingling sensation moved through her body.

"Lewis . . ." Effie inhaled, and he looked away.

"Can't you stay?" he asked. "I promise I'll never let him hurt you."

Effie shook her head. "I don't trust myself. I'm terrified that one day I'll wake up and want to go back." She looked down at her hands. "If I stay here, I'll never escape him."

Lewis pressed his lips to her head. "But I only just got you back."

"I know."

Effie bit into her tongue, her body burning in a strange and exciting way, wanting things that she barely understood. Things that she'd only read about in books. She closed her eyes, like they did on TV, and moved in to kiss him. But when she was close enough to feel his breath, close enough to feel the thump of his heart, Lewis pressed a hand to her shoulder, stopping her.

"Effie, I . . ." He shook his head. "I'm so sorry."

She opened her eyes, the pain like a knife to her heart, and stared at him.

"We can't, Effie."

She frowned. "I don't understand. Don't you want to kiss me?"

"Of course I do." He shook his head again. "But we can't. Not yet."

"But I'm leaving"

Lewis shuffled back, like touching her made him feel sick.

"*Why won't you kiss me?*" she shouted.

"I . . ."

"*Why?*" Effie shouted again. "Tell me."

"Effie, I want to kiss you more than anything." He ran his hands through his hair. "Christ, it's all I think about. It's—"

"Then what's wrong?"

"You're fifteen, Effie." He stopped and looked at her. "And I'm an eighteen-year-old cop."

"So?"

"So, we . . . we just can't."

"It's just a stupid kiss."

Lewis tensed and his jaw clenched.

Effie hesitated. "Do you want to do more than kiss?"

"Of course I do. Of course, I—"

"You can do whatever you want to me."

"Effie, don't say that."

"I'm not a kid anymore," she said. "And I'm leaving tomorrow." She swallowed. "I want you to do it. I want to do it with you."

Lewis turned away from her. "We just can't, Effie," he whispered. "I'm so sorry."

"Then go," she said.

"What?" He looked at her, his eyes wet.

"Go," she said. "I don't want you here."

The next day, as June and Effie packed up the car, she kept looking back down June's drive.

But there was no car.

No Lewis.

As they drove from Koraha, Effie craned her neck to look out the rear window.

But there was no Lewis.

No boy running after her.

And by the time they reached Christchurch, Effie's body ached so much that it hurt to breathe. And when June touched a hand to Effie's thigh, tears spilled down her face.

2025

EFFIE STOOD IN front of the hut, the evening light pulling long shadows from the surrounding trees, and let her backpack fall to the ground.

She felt it—a tingle down her neck and spine—before she saw anything. The sense that something was wrong. The presence of someone else.

"*Hello,*" she shouted.

But there was nothing. Just air and birds and the soft rustle of branches. Just a line of trees, watching in quiet anticipation.

She shouted again.

Then, at the side of the hut, a figure appeared. A man. Tall and strong across the shoulders. His head and face were hidden, his hood up despite the lack of rain, and he had his back to her. Effie stepped forward, but he disappeared behind the building.

"Wait."

She hurried after him, but when she turned the corner, he was gone.

"Shit."

She looked from left to right, desperately searching for any sign of life. She cursed herself, wishing she'd thought to bring a weapon, and lifted a heavy stick from the grass. Her heart raced as she walked around the hut, the sound of her footsteps cracking like whips in the silence.

Then he was there. A mass stood still. Twenty meters away.

The man's features were concealed behind a camouflage balaclava—a hunter's mask—with nothing exposed but the two dark hollows of his eyes. There was a knife swinging from his right hand.

Run, Effie. Run.

Heat seized her muscles—not fear, but anger—and she forced herself to move. Not away. But toward him. The figure watched as she neared, an obscured shadow, and Effie held his gaze. Her legs numbed and her stomach burned, but she stepped across the covering of leaves, moving closer to him.

There was a rush of movement. Something behind her. Then pain. An intense consuming pain that flooded her head, raking through the bones of her skull.

Effie tried to scream. But there was no sound in her.

She tried to move. But her body was lost.

Then the pain stopped.

When she woke, it was to darkness.

Effie groaned and stretched out her arms, trying to place her limbs in the liquid black. She was on her back, lying on something solid and man-made, with her legs out straight. Traces of warm fabric covered her skin, meaning she was still dressed, but her feet were bare.

Bending her arms, Effie tried to lift her head, but the pain sloshed like vomit behind her eyes, and she blinked away specks of white. Then she lay back, her head lolling on her neck, and the dark spun around her. Around and around, making her want to throw up.

She covered her mouth with her palm, swallowing back bile, and sucked in air through her nose. Mercifully, the sharp pain had eased.

But it had been replaced by a constant pulsing, a hot throbbing in her skull and at the roots of her hair.

Effie reached her arm above her head, trailing her fingers through the endless black. There was nothing. No edges. No shapes. Just the far-off noise of the bush. As she listened, the minutes slipped by and the fog in her head thinned. Eventually, she pressed her hands into the hard surface and pushed herself up. The insides of her head swirled, leaking dots into her vision, but slowly the swell settled.

"Small movements," whispered Effie. "Just one step at a time."

She went to stand, but something pulled on her leg. Something hard and cold bit into the skin around her ankle. Effie frowned as she slid her hand down her legs, trying to locate the new pain. Then her fingers brushed against the links of metal.

"Oh god."

Effie tugged at the length of steel, violently and desperately, but it was futile. She was chained up.

She slumped back, her tongue suddenly too large and too dry for her mouth, and nausea washed through her. A sob escaped her, the contents of her stomach threatening to follow, and she tasted salt on her lips. But she didn't scream out.

Screaming was pointless.

Instead, she curled up in the dark, unable to make out the shape of her fingers or the links of the cold chain, and a wave of fear washed down her back like ice.

1989

DINAH JUMPED UP and down in the sea, waving her arms.

"Come on, Adam."

Big sister splashed in the little waves, her clothes getting wet. Dad would be mad. Cameron was there too. Dinah's best friend.

"Come on, mate," Cameron shouted.

Adam giggled and ran down the beach. "You have to find me," he squealed.

His legs zoomed beneath him, flying him away as Dinah and Cameron turned into tiny dots. Adam hurried behind a grassy sand dune, where Dinah and Cameron would never look. Then he scrunched his eyes shut, waiting and invisible, as a hundred million hours passed. Eventually, he poked his head up to take a quick peek and spotted Cameron. Cameron was a teenager. Fourteen. Even bigger than Dinah.

"We're coming," Cameron yelled.

An excited squeal slipped from Adam's lips, and he pushed it back with his hand.

"Come out," sang Dinah. "Come out, come out, wherever you are."

Adam closed his eyes, doing his best hiding ever, and flattened himself against the sand.

One, two, three . . . He squeezed his fists tight . . . *eight, nine, ten, twelve* . . .

Adam popped his head up, getting bored. Dinah was running across the sand with her arms out like an airplane.

"Dinah!" Adam crawled over the grass, his knees and hands sinking into the sand. "Dinah, wait for me."

Big sister stopped in the water, the bottom of her skirt dark and wet, then she scooped up a handful of sea and splashed it toward the beach.

"Come get me!"

Then, from nowhere, two hands picked him up, and fingers tickled his tummy.

"Stop!" Adam giggled. "Stop it."

He squirmed and laughed and snorted until Cameron put him down.

"Come on," he said, taking Adam's hand. "Let's get her."

Then they ran at the water. But Cameron was too fast, his legs were too long, and Adam tripped and stumbled to the ground, his mouth filling with sand.

"Shit." Cameron knelt next to him. "Sorry, buddy."

He dusted the sand from Adam's face, then ruffled his hair.

"What are you silly boys up to?"

Dinah collapsed onto the sand next to them, lying with her arms out like a Christmas angel, and Adam snuggled into her. Dinah wrapped her arms around him and kissed his head—not like at home.

"Can we go swimming?"

"I think we need to get back," she said. "Dad will want lunch soon."

"Can we go tomorrow?"

"Maybe. We'll see how Dad is doing."

"He'll just be reading his silly book."

"We'll see." Dinah squeezed his hand a bit hard. "Okay?"

"Okay."

2025

TIME WAS DIVIDED into two. Complete dark and almost dark.

During the day, light peeked in through the cracks and small gaps, and Effie could make out the outlines of her fingers and legs. During the day, the air turned a shade lighter than ink, and the items in the room took shape.

A bed. A chair. A small desk. A solid metal chain.

Effie reached down and touched her ankle, where the skin had been rubbed raw, and tried to move into a more comfortable position. Two days had passed. Twice a line of light had entered through the small boarded-up window, spilling across the floor in a white ribbon, and Effie had watched it shrink and disappear.

She forced a piece of bread through her teeth, the dough moving around in her dry mouth, then she took a sip of water. The packages—food and water and a bucket for relieving herself—were snuck in during the night. There was no face or voice that went with them. At night, when the bedroom door opened, no light came in with it. The room on the other side was just as dark.

Effie grimaced at the pain between her eyes. The headaches and the dizziness were constant. Whoever had thumped her had done a bloody good job of it. The last thing Effie remembered was wading across the Roaring Billy, then waking up in the hut. In her parents' old bedroom.

"Fuck." Effie swore and punched the bed, the sudden movement making her nauseous. "Fuck."

When the spinning eased, she crawled forward until the length of chain pulled tight against the solid bed frame, and she threw the stale bread the remaining meter to the door. It hit the wood with a soft thump.

"*What do you want with me?*" she shouted.

Nothing.

"*Let me go, you cowardly shit.*"

Nothing.

Effie focused on the bottom of the door where there was a strip of light, a small gap in the darkness. It was still daytime somewhere out there. She lifted the plate and threw it at the wall. The loud clang split the quiet, vibrating in her chest and fingers. Then she turned, searching the shadows. Looking for something. For anything. On her right, she spotted the silhouette of a row of books. She lifted one after the other and hurled them at the door.

Thud. Thud. Thud.

As Effie reached for the fourth book, a shadow—perhaps two feet—moved across the strip of light.

"Stop." The female voice was quiet—frightened. "Please. He'll punish you."

"Who?" Effie clambered toward the voice. "Who will punish me?"

There was a scraping of wood, of shuffled furniture, then the feet disappeared.

"*No,*" Effie yelled. "Wait. Come back."

She tried to lunge forward, but the chain dug into her skin and the force flattened her to the floor. When she looked up again, the light had gone from under the door, blocked by something.

"Come back," Effie pleaded. "Please come back."
But there was no reply.

The cold woke her, trailing its fingers along her skin.

Effie shifted on the bed, the chain long enough that she could lie on her right side comfortably, and she reached out, feeling for the extra blanket. She combed the bed with her fingers, searching for wool, but instead finding solid wood.

A box.

Shivering, Effie pulled herself up and held the box in her palm. She traced over the lid and around the edges, then popped it open. There was a small strip of paper inside, and what felt like a well-used matchbox. But there was just one match. One chance at light. Unable to quell the shake in her fingers, she took the match out slowly, carefully, and held it in her right hand. Then, with a shallow inhale of air, she dragged it across the rough strip.

Nothing happened. No fire.

Effie held her breath, gripped the match tighter and tried again. *Please. Please.*

Then, with a flick, a small flame pierced through the dark. Quickly, Effie lifted the piece of paper and held it to the light. The flame flickered in her trembling fingers and she had to force her hands to be still. There were just four words, scribbled in purple crayon.

You need to pray.

Effie read it three times, her eyes darting back and forth, looking for something other than those four words.

Then, as quickly as it had been breached, the darkness returned.

1990

MUM WAS INSIDE the wooden box.

She hadn't fought when they closed the lid on her. No waving fists. No kicking legs. She just lay there. Maybe she'd been too tired. Or maybe she hadn't wanted to damage her nails. Mum always had nice painted nails.

"I want to go home," Adam whispered.

"I know."

"I don't like it here."

Dinah squeezed his hand. "We can't leave yet. We have to stay a bit longer."

Adam looked at his feet. At his new shiny black shoes. Then at Dad. Dad pulled his hand away when Adam reached for it, and Adam shoved his hand into his pocket. Maybe his fingers were cold. The church was always freezing. Daniel sat on Dad's other side. Daniel was two years younger than Dinah, but he told everyone that he was the oldest. Dad and Daniel weren't holding hands either.

The priest was talking. His lips were full and soft like a donut, and bits of spittle sprayed out from the little black donut hole when he spoke. Adam shifted, his bum going to sleep on the hard wood, and he kicked at the pew in front of him. Dinah touched his leg when he did that, and Adam stopped.

"I'm so sorry that this is happening to you," she whispered. Her eyes were red and puffy and wet. "That you're losing her."

Adam frowned. Confused. Dinah was losing Mum too.

Eventually the priest told them to bow their heads, and Adam did it perfectly. He knew how to pray. He could do that bit. He pushed his palms together super tight, then dipped his head low. Mum would be proud of his praying.

A woman on the other side of the aisle smiled at him and wiggled her fingers—interrupting his good praying—and Adam pretended to look at his shoes. The woman came to the house sometimes, to bother Mum, but Dad always shooed her away. The woman smiled again, her eyes wet and sad, and Adam scrunched his eyes shut.

When the priest finally finished, Adam glanced up too fast and stars flooded the church. He blinked lots, until the stars faded, then peered across at Dinah. But she didn't raise her head. She didn't even open her eyes. Dinah didn't look up until his bum was fully asleep and it was time to leave.

As they walked from the church, Dinah gripped his hand, and Adam pressed his head against her arm. Dinah liked it when he did that.

It was raining outside. Yucky cold blobs. Adam frowned as he looked down. The muddy ground was going to ruin his new shoes. He clung to his sister, pulling warmth from her as they moved toward the car. Sad people moved slow. Even in the rain. Like big black slugs. *Squelch. Squelch.* Dad and Daniel were at the front, leading the slug train.

Adam wiped the water from his eyes and looked around.

Grass. Gray rain. Gray church. Gray skies. Trees.

Cameron.

Adam blinked. Cameron was there, standing behind a tree at the edge of the grassy area. With no jacket or nothing. He'd be cold. Adam looked at Dinah, but she didn't look at Cameron. Not a single peek. But she smiled, super small and quick, and Cameron stayed at the tree. He was still there when they drove off in Dad's big ute.

Adam peered out the window.

Cameron was probably real wet. Probably real bored of all that standing.

Stop. Stop.

Adam rolled over in bed, his body shaking, and buried his face into the pillow.

Go away. Go away.

But Mum wouldn't go away. She was behind his eyelids. Dead. Rotting in the soil. With worms and bugs gobbling at her skin.

"*Stop*," he shouted. "Go away."

Adam opened his eyes and slapped at his face. But the mum thing was still there. The mum made of bones and worms. Adam curled into a ball and started to cry, his body cold and scooped out.

"Dinah," he sobbed. "Dinah."

But Dinah didn't come. She didn't curl under the covers with him.

"Dinah."

Dinah always came.

Adam lifted his head, his eyes soggy and hot, and peered through the dark. But Dinah's bed was empty.

"*Dinah*," he yelled.

Snot and tears dripped down his cheeks.

"*Dinah!*"

Then the bedroom door flung open and the hall light poured in.

"I'm here, Adam. I'm here." The bed sank with big sister's body, and she stroked her fingers through his hair. "You're okay," she whispered. "You're okay."

"Where were you?" he sobbed.

"Dad says I can't sleep in here anymore."

Adam frowned. "Why?"

"He says it's not right for us to share now. That I need to learn my place."

"What place?" he sniffed.

Dinah just stroked his hair. Maybe she didn't know where the place was either.

"But I like sharing a room with you," said Adam.

Dinah smiled. "Me too."

"I feel wet," he said, starting to cry again. "I got scared. I thought that . . ."

Dinah kissed his head. "It's okay."

Big sister pulled back the wet duvet and threw it onto the floor, making a mountain with the sheets. Then she lifted his pajama top over his head.

"Let's get you cleaned up."

Adam sniffed. "Can you sleep here tonight?"

Dinah peeled the damp pants from his legs and squeezed his hand.

"Our little secret." She smiled.

2025

THAT MORNING A kerosene lamp, only a quarter full, and a book had been waiting for her when she woke up. A bloody Bible of all things. Effie had sworn and kicked it under the bed.

Over the past twenty-four hours, Effie had tried shouting out and throwing things at the door, but the voice never returned. She'd searched every inch of the room that she could reach, cursing when the chain pulled taut and the padlock dug into her ankle bone. She'd spent hours in the dark, mapping the shapes and edges of her prison, searching for a source of light or something she could use as a weapon. Anything that might help her. But her efforts had resulted in little more than a child's crayon and an old rusted fork.

She stood in front of the boarded window, using the lamp for light, and tried to prize the boards loose with her fingers. If she could just force one away slightly, a few millimeters, perhaps she could find something to lever it open. She dug into the wood, her arms shaking, but the tips of her fingers tore and bled, and the rusted nails held tight.

"Fuck."

Effie slumped back, defeated. She turned off the lamp and sat in the dark, breathless and bleeding, as the minutes passed and the fist in her stomach clenched tighter. *Too tight.* Effie groaned and leaned forward, curling into a ball, but the pain deepened, getting worse. As she rocked, heat crept through her, burning in her muscles.

"Something's wrong," she murmured. But her words bled out into the black air with nothing to catch them, with no one to make them real. "I don't feel well."

Effie held her stomach and shouted, her voice thick with anger, "*I know you can hear me.*"

Then she lurched forward and spewed over the floor. Twice she convulsed and emptied—the second attempt more bile and saliva than anything of substance. Eventually, the cramps eased. Effie wiped the back of her hand across her mouth. Groaning, she lit the lamp and glanced around the room, half knowing what she was looking for.

There.

"You cowardly fucker," she murmured, the words foul-smelling on her tongue.

The cup of tea. He'd put something in her fucking tea.

Effie grabbed the bed, using it to pull herself up. Holding her stomach, she stumbled around the sour puddle of vomit and lifted the empty cup from the desk. She ran her finger around the inside, the smooth ceramic dusted with something gritty, then she hurled it at the wall.

"Stupid." She swore. "Stupid."

As she turned, she noticed a corner of white paper poking out from under the saucer. Her stomach tensed again, and she grabbed the paper. The writing was different from the previous note, the tight block capitals neater and more uniform.

READ THE BIBLE. IT WASN'T A REQUEST.

Effie scrunched the note in her hand and threw it into the vomit.

"Screw you."

Exhausted, she curled up on the bed. And at some point, sleep took her.

When she woke up, there was no food. No water. Nothing to clean herself with.

There was no food the next day either. Just a small jug of water.

On the third day, dehydrated and filthy, Effie reached under the bed and grabbed the Bible. As she held the small book, tears trickled down her cheeks, and the thick drips of salt congealed on her parched tongue. She hated that she needed him. That without him, she would starve, that her stomach and head and bones would ache with it, and she would die. Trembling, she opened the cover and flicked to the first of the bookmarked pages. Each contained a strip of paper and an underlined passage.

1 Corinthians 11:3—The head of every man is Christ, the head of a wife is her husband.

Effie flicked to the next one. Then the next.

1 Timothy 2:12—I do not permit a woman to teach or exercise authority over a man; rather, she is to remain quiet.

Shaking, and not willing to read any more, she tossed the book aside. Her thoughts churned, hot and thick and confused, and a tightness spread through her chest.

"Hello."

A voice echoed in the void between Effie's ears, lost in the mess of her thoughts.

"Hello."

The voice again—female. Soft and far away. Real. Perhaps.

"Are you there?"

The voice dragged Effie from the tar in her head, and she blinked the darkened room back into view. Then she pulled her shattered self toward the door.

"Hello," she panted. "Yes, hello. I'm here."
"Did you read it?"
"Yes." Effie's heart thumped. "Yes."
She waited. But there was no reply.
"Hello." She strained against the chain. "Are you still there?"
There was a shuffling of feet. Then silence.
"Please," Effie begged. "Please. I just want to talk."
But the woman had gone, and Effie was alone again.
Rotting in the dark.

In the morning, there was food. It must have been slipped through the door when Effie was asleep. Food and water and basic cleaning supplies.

1991

ADAM BALLED HIS fists, his body hot and angry, as he stomped across the park.

"What are you doing?" he demanded.

Dinah spun around, so fast that the roundabout wobbled.

"Nothing," she said.

"You were holding hands," Adam shouted, the red-hot pulsing in his tummy.

"We were just chatting, bro," said Cameron.

Adam shook his head. "You're lying. I saw you."

Cameron held his hands up in surrender—almost as big as Dad now—then he shuffled around the roundabout, moving away from Dinah.

"You're not allowed to touch my sister." Adam put his hands on his hips. "She's mine. Not yours." He pointed at Cameron. "Dinah looks after me. Not you."

"Adam," Dinah snapped.

"You're always talking." He looked from Dinah to Cameron. "Always doing naughty things."

"Naughty?" Cameron frowned.

"That bad stuff." Adam spat out saliva with his words.

Cameron looked at Dinah.

"Dinah's not meant to be friends with you." Adam tapped his head. "You have evil outside thoughts. Dad will get mad. Then he'll shut—"

"Adam, quiet!" Dinah glared at him. She looked back at Cameron. "He's just being dramatic."

Dinah was lying. *Liar. Liar.* Lying was a sin.

"*Am not,*" Adam yelled.

He glued his feet to the ground. Not moving. Not taking his eyes off Cameron.

"Maybe I should tell Dad," said Adam, his arms shaking.

Dinah stared at him, and the sad look on her face hurt his tummy—even sorer than when Dad belted him for swearing. Adam slapped a hand to his mouth, wanting to swallow his words back, to wipe the sad away from Dinah's face.

"I'm sorry," he muttered.

Adam took a step toward Dinah, but she flinched, and the sore in his tummy hurt even worse.

"I won't tell Dad," he pleaded. "I won't. I promise."

Dinah looked at him, her face different. Ages passed and she just looked at him.

"I'm sorry," she whispered. "I'm sorry that I couldn't keep you from him."

"From who?"

Dinah gave a small sad smile. "From Dad."

Dinah went quiet, and Adam stood with his arms hanging at his sides. He wanted to say something—something good—but he didn't know what that was.

Dad loved them. Dad was the best.

2025

SHE HAD TO ESCAPE.

Effie sat on the floor and stared at the chain around her ankle. She needed to get back to Anya.

I'll be back. I promise.

No one would be looking for her—she hadn't even said where she was going. Effie was a grown woman. An adult who'd left of her own volition. Who'd left them. Effie swallowed.

It was daytime—a fine veil of light covered the room. Effie reached a hand down her leg. The area around her ankle felt odd, deadened by the constant rub of metal. But still, what she was about to do was going to hurt.

Effie tested the range of motion in her foot, pointing her toes, then pulling them back, sending a twinge of pins and needles through her calf and heel.

It was going to hurt a lot.

Effie scrunched her eyes tight and puffed out her cheeks. "Come on. You can do this."

She changed position, the steel links rattling on the hard floor. Her restraint wasn't a solid cuff but rather a length of chain that had been looped around her lower leg, then secured with a large padlock, like a lasso.

"Okay..."

Effie straightened her foot, tucking her heel in, then she pushed down on the metal, her arms vibrating with the effort.

"Move."

Slowly the chain edged down. But when she let go, it slipped back up.

"Fuck."

Her ankle throbbed, the skin red and broken.

"Come on," she panted. "Just move."

Effie drove the chain downward. The hard knobs of her ankle pulsed with pain, but she kept pushing. "Please," she grunted.

She let out a scream of agony and looked down. A jagged piece of steel had caught the thin surface of her skin, peeling her like an orange.

Blood leaked from the fresh wound, but Effie kept going. She thrust the weight of her body into it, but the chain held tight, clinging to her like a metal leech. She screamed again, the echo of pain mixed with frustration.

Then there was a thud on the door.

"Stop," the woman begged. "Please, whatever you're doing, stop."

Effie's arm fell limp and she collapsed forward.

"Please." The voice was soft and scared. "Please. You have to stop. You have to repent. Or he'll kill you."

Defeated, Effie slumped to the floor, her hands and legs wet with sweat and blood, too tired to find words. And besides, what was there to say anyway?

Maybe the woman wasn't even there.

Maybe she never had been.

As the fight leaked from her body, she closed her eyes, broken.

1992

DAD HAD TO do it. It was the only way to make Dinah clean and good again.

Adam reached out a skinny arm and knocked on her door. Dinah was lucky to have Dad. Adam loved Dinah too much. He wouldn't be able to do the things that Dad had to. And because Adam was weak, God wouldn't love Dinah anymore.

"Dinah," he whispered. "You can come out now."

Three days shut away wasn't too bad. Sometimes Dinah was locked away for more than a week. No talking. No visits. No playing. No leaving her room. Sometimes it took a long time for Dinah to say sorry.

"Dinah?" Adam pushed the door open and walked inside.

She was sitting on her bed, looking out the window. There was nothing to see but trees and sky and thick bush. But she kept staring at the glass. Daniel's old bush hut was out there—a few branches and wooden planks that he'd turned into a den—although it was too deep in the trees to see.

"I missed you," said Dinah.

Adam stepped toward her. "What did you do?" he asked.

She turned. A dark purple bruise—not nice to look at—covered one side of her jaw.

"Dad caught me watching TV through the neighbor's window."

Adam frowned. "But you're not allowed to watch TV."

Dinah just smiled at that, her lips stretched thin and straight.

Dad said that Dinah didn't know how to behave, that she allowed the outside world to poison her thoughts. Dad said that Dinah made God angry.

Adam hopped onto the small bed. The bed was the only thing in Dinah's room. No toys. No books. No spare clothes. Nothing to distract her from saying sorry. Adam bit into his tongue, a little afraid of the purple-blue smudge, but Dinah shuffled over and pulled him in for a hug.

"Aren't you scared of him?" asked Adam.

"Of Dad?"

"No." Adam shook his head and pulled away. "Of God."

"Why would I be afraid of God?"

"Cos he's mad at you."

"God isn't mad at me."

"Dad says that God wants to punish you for being bad . . . for not doing the right girl things." Adam frowned. Maybe Dinah didn't understand. Maybe if he helped her, then she could be good again. "When girls are bad," he said slowly, "God won't let them go to heaven."

"And what do good girls do?"

"Well, they always look after their family . . ." Adam paused to think. "And they don't do anything sinful, like talking and eating with outside people, or watching TV, or wearing pants."

"And why can't I wear pants?"

Adam frowned. "It just . . . it just makes God real angry."

"I see."

"And when God's angry, he's real scary and he stops loving you."

"God isn't someone to fear, Adam." Dinah smiled. "God loves me no matter what. And he loves you too." She touched his cheek. "God's love is so big and so strong that he has enough love for everyone. For every single person in the whole world, even people who sin. God made us who we are, and he loves us. He doesn't need us to be perfect." She reached out and took Adam's hand. "Because he is perfect."

"No." Adam snatched his hand back, shaking his head fiercely. "Dad said that—"

"Dad doesn't know anything about God or God's love. Dad just wants to control us and keep us afraid."

Adam inched away. Dinah was making it worse; she was making God madder.

"Dad twists things and makes things up," she said, "and then he says it comes from God. But it's all a lie."

"Stop saying that," Adam begged. "He'll punish you."

"Dad might punish me, yes. But not God."

Dinah's voice sounded different, louder and bigger, and Adam didn't like it.

"Dad is not a good man, Adam."

"Don't say that!" he cried.

"Do you really think that a good man would lock his daughter up for days?"

"Stop talking. Stop!"

He covered his ears, but Dinah tugged his hands away.

"Do you really think it's okay that Dad has stopped me from going to school and that he shuts me up in this room with nothing to do and barely anything to eat?"

"Stop it. *Stop it.*"

"God doesn't talk to Dad," Dinah snapped.

"You're lying. Liar. Liar." Adam was shaking. "God does talk to Dad. Dad is protecting you."

"From what?"

"From the wicked world."

Dinah snorted. "Cameron is going to come and get me," she said, "and we're going to leave this prison. We're going to run away and be free and happy and never come back."

"No!" Adam shouted. "You're not allowed to leave."

Dinah flinched, her eyes wide and sad and hurt, but Adam didn't care.

"*You're my Dinah*," he yelled. "If you ever try and leave, I'll tell Dad, and he'll lock you up forever and—"

She slapped him then.

Fire exploded through Adam's cheek, and he started to cry. The bones in his face hurt. His eyeball hurt. His teeth hurt.

"Adam," Dinah said, her strong voice gone. Tears trailed down her face as she reached for him. "I'm sorry, Adam. I'm so sorry. I didn't mean to hurt you."

She curled her arms around him, and Adam let her. He didn't want to fight. He needed her. She was warm and smelled like summer.

"Please don't leave me," he sniffed.

"I won't." She stroked his hair and kissed his head. "Of course I won't leave you."

"And you'll be good?" Adam wiped a hand across his dripping nose. "Please."

"Yes," she whispered. "I'll be good."

2025

"MORNING, EFFIE."

The voice was male. His words floated under the door, the thin line of light broken by the shadow of two feet.

"I trust that you slept well after your little attempt?"

Effie looked up from her crouched position on the floor and balled her fists.

"Effie," he said again, "I asked you a question."

His voice was old, but it wasn't him. It wasn't Dad. Effie moved forward on hands and knees, her ankle swollen and throbbing.

"It's rude to ignore a man when he's talking to you, Effie."

She inched closer to the door. If silence was all she could hurt him with, she'd willingly chew off her own tongue and spit it out. Then the bastard could choke on it.

"Effie." His voice was raised. "I asked you a question."

His heavy breathing leaked through the wood. But she didn't speak.

"Answer me!" he demanded.

He drove his fist into the door, and the crack vibrated in Effie's chest. She bit into her cheeks and held her body completely still.

"Disobedient little whore," he spat. "I've half a mind to come in there and smash in that little bitch face of yours."

The door handle rattled but it didn't open. Effie frowned. Why hadn't he come in? Why hadn't he hurt her? Why, since she'd been there, hadn't she seen anyone?

He thumped the door again.

"You're welcome to come in," she said, the words beating hot in her stomach.

Then the thumping stopped. There was a pulse of silence before he snorted.

"You're not permitted to socialize with us." He grunted again. "You're a poison."

"Who's us?"

"*Quiet!*" he snarled. "You are not to ask questions."

"I thought you wanted me to talk."

A furious bang silenced her as he struck the door. "You will talk when I want you to."

Anger pounded beneath Effie's skin and she pressed her fingers into her forehead. Anya was there, behind her eyes, pleading with her. *Come back, Effie. Please, come back.* Effie wanted to yell at him—to retaliate. She wanted to rile him to the point of self-destruction. Until her words needled beneath his skin, and his fingers clasped around her throat. But instead, she did nothing. She stayed quiet. For Anya.

"Are you repentant?" he asked eventually.

"I don't understand," she said, keeping her voice even. "I don't know what I'm meant to be repentant of."

He snorted. "Clearly you need more time."

Sweat prickled at the base of her neck.

"Or perhaps," he continued, "those born of sin are beyond saving."

"Who are you? What am I to you—"

His fist pounded on the door. "*No questions!*" he yelled. "You are to be silent unless spoken to."

Then there was shuffling on the other side of the wall, and the man spoke to someone as a faraway door creaked open.

"She's only to get one meal today," he said. "And nothing for bathing."

The shadowed feet moved from the door.

"Answer me," he shouted.

"Yes." The reply was whispered and small.

"And you are not to talk to her."

There was another pulse of quiet.

"Speak up," he shouted. "I hate it when you mumble."

"No talking," said the voice.

"Good," he said. "You're a good girl now, aren't you, Tia?"

"Yes."

Tia.

The sound and shape of her sister's name slammed into Effie's chest and she lurched forward.

Tia.

Aching and exhausted, Effie lifted her head and stared at the door.

"You're alive," she whispered.

1992

ADAM STOPPED IN the trees, his new slingshot hanging from his fingers, and turned his head.

The bush hummed with cicada song. *Buzz. Click. Buzz. Click.* And the sharp whining vibrated in his chest. *Thrum. Thrum.*

Adam bent over and rummaged through the dead leaves, finding his marble. Then he straightened up and aimed his slingshot, like Daniel had taught him, and went to shoot again. But something stopped him—a thickness to the air, like there was something living in it.

More than just bugs.

He pocketed his favorite marble and set off through the trees. The branches got closer together every few steps, and the air got heavier. The bush darkened, gobbling him up. Then, a little way ahead, he saw it.

Daniel's bush hut.

Adam crept up and hid behind a tree. He wasn't allowed to go to the hut without Daniel. Daniel would whack him, and Adam's arm would throb for a week. Holding his breath, Adam peered through the branches. His eyes widened as he absorbed the strange unknown thing. A thing that he shouldn't be seeing.

Bad. Bad.

A bad-feeling thing.

But Adam couldn't look away. His eyes were glued to it. As he stood there, his skin thrumming with cicada song, the bad thing stuck to his memory. It snuck in, uninvited, and tread muddy footprints through his head.

There was a figure. But not Daniel. The figure was kneeling with his back to Adam. A man. The man crouched forward on all fours, knees dug into the dirt, just inside the three-walled hut. His T-shirt was wet between his shoulders, and it clung to his back like cling film.

Adam strained his neck, trying to see better. It was an odd image, hard to understand. The figure was struggling with something. His arms leaned forward, and he was pushing his hands into the earth. He thumped at the ground, then he raised his back up, like he was doing press-ups, and he made a weird growling noise. Then his shoulders pulled up to his ears and his body started shaking.

Adam blinked at the strangeness of it. Daniel would be angry. Daniel hated people in his hut. Then the figure shifted slightly to the side, panting, and Adam saw her.

Dinah.

Fear swirled in Adam's stomach, his heart racing, but still he didn't move. He didn't do anything. Dinah was squished flat under the man's body. *Under Cameron.* And her legs were sticking out from each side of his waist. *Cameron's waist.* His sister's legs floated in midair, trembling, as Cameron grunted.

Adam wanted to look away. To scream. Yet he stood frozen, quiet but for the buzz of cicadas and the thump in his chest. Quiet but for the weird yelps that came out of his sister and stabbed into his tummy.

Not a single muscle in Adam's body would work. Sick trickled down the back of his tongue, and Adam wished, prayed, that he could disappear.

2025

EFFIE GOT AS close to the door as the chain would allow. Then she waited.

The faint hue of evening light had gone, and the air had darkened with the encroaching night—thick and impenetrable. And it was cold. The chill locked her joints as she waited, hunched on the floor. The weight of her limbs and the scent of her unwashed skin were real. But in the dark, her body was without lines or shape. She was just sound and smell in a void of shadow.

Eventually, there was a soft scraping on the other side of the door—a chair dragged along the floor, or a box perhaps—then the click of metal. The door eased open. She stood there, silhouetted by a soft glow, with a bowl held in her hands.

"Tia?" Effie whispered.

A squeal escaped the woman's lips, and the bowl hit the floor with a clang.

"Wait . . ." Effie reached out an arm.

But the shadowed figure scurried from the room—a frightened mouse—and bolted the door.

"I'm sorry," Effie panted. "Please. I didn't mean to frighten you."

Effie waited, the anticipation threatening to rip her open, but there was no reply.

"Please, I just want to talk."

Still nothing. No sound. But Effie could feel her there, hear her swallowing and breathing.

"Has he hurt you?" asked Effie.

There was a further beat of silence, then Tia spoke. "You were meant to be asleep."

"I needed to see you."

"Contact isn't allowed. No looking. No touching. I'm just to listen."

"To listen?"

"And slip food in at night." She paused, the air tarred by a thick quiet. "How do you know my name?"

Effie's heart stopped.

Then she breathed, "It's really you?"

There was a shuffling, a chair scraped and floorboards creaked. The sound of her sister moving—leaving.

"*Wait.*" Effie searched for words, anything to keep Tia there. "Are you in the dark too?"

"Yes. No." She seemed rattled. "There's a small candle attached to the stove."

A shiver ran between Effie's shoulder blades, an icy realization taking form. "Tia, have you ever seen me?"

"It's not allowed."

Effie leaned forward. "Do you know who I am?"

"It's not for me to know."

Oh god. "Tia, it's me. It's Effie."

It went quiet—a hushed eternity—then her sister's voice filled the darkness. "Effie?"

"Yes," she said. "Yes, it's me."

"No," Tia sobbed, the sound small and helpless. "No. You shouldn't have come back."

"Tia . . ."

"This place will kill you," she stuttered. "No one ever leaves here . . . he's made sure of that." She paused. "This is the vanishing place."

Effie pulled against her restraints. "That's not true. Anya got out—your daughter got out."

There was a loud thud as Tia slumped on the other side of the door. Effie could feel her, the presence of her sister's body, as Tia pressed against the wood.

"Anya?" Tia panted. "You've seen her? You've seen Anya?"

"Yes. Anya's safe. She's in Koraha. She's with June and Lewis."

"Oh god." Tia exhaled. "She's okay?"

"Yes." Effie smiled through tears. "Your little girl's okay."

Tia broke then. She dissolved into sobs and half-uttered words. "He told me he had Anya," she said. "He said if I ever disappointed him again, he would kill her. That's why . . . why I couldn't . . ."

Tia stopped and there was a fumbling sound as she stood up. Then there was the clunk of a key turning in the lock and the handle shook.

"I'm sorry," whispered Tia, her slight figure appearing in the doorway. "I only have a key for the door. I don't have—"

"You're alive. You're really alive."

Tia sat on the floor next to Effie and reached out and traced the sides of Effie's face with her fingers. Effie pulled her sister into her. Tia was nothing but bones, her ribs jutting out like the rungs of a ladder, her hair falling down to her tailbone.

"I've missed you," said Tia.

Effie clung to her little sister. "Who's done this to you?" she spluttered. "Was it Dad?"

Tia pulled away and shook her head. "Dad's dead, Effie."

"What?"

"He disappeared, just after you." Tia sat hunched over and tucked her knees into her chest. "What Dad did . . . it broke him, and he left. He left us. Just two kids, alone in the bush with a body."

Guilt stabbed Effie's chest, and she pressed into it with her fist.

"When Dad eventually returned," Tia continued, "the others were already here, and I'd . . . I'd already started to hate him." She wiped her eyes. "They shot at Dad when he turned up, and threatened to kill him if he ever came back." Her voice softened. "But he did come back. Every year, on my birthday, he came back and left something for me by the river. But I never took it. I never spoke to him. And then it was too late." Tia swallowed. "We were both wrong about him. Dad tried to save me from this, but I didn't listen."

"I don't understand, Tia. What happened here?"

"For so long, I thought I was in love. I thought I was doing the right thing. Then one day, I woke up and I realized I was a prisoner. And that it was all too late."

"What was too late?" asked Effie. "Who's done this to you?"

"To us," whispered Tia. "There were eight of us."

"Here?"

"There's another hut farther up," she said. "A couple of kilometers, maybe. For the men. And for Dinah."

Effie inhaled, the core of her suddenly cold. "Dinah?"

"His daughter."

"Whose daughter?"

"His name is Peter," said Tia. "The Guardian." She hesitated. "But there's something else, Effie. Something that you—"

She stopped abruptly, the sudden quiet robbing the air from Effie's chest.

"Tia?"

"He's here." Tia's eyes snapped toward the door. "He's back."

"It's okay, we can—"

"Oh god. He's going to know." Tia started to shake. "He's going to know I broke his rules."

"Tia, listen to—"

"Oh god, he's going to kill us." Her voice had faded to nothing. She started to cry. "I can't . . . not again . . ."

"Tia? Tia?" Effie reached out. "You need to stand up now and walk out. Then you need to lock the door behind you. Can you do that?"

"The door?" she spluttered.

"Yes. You need to go—now."

"Yes, I . . ." Another sob. "I can . . ."

"You're okay." Effie squeezed her wrist. "You're going to—"

The pounding of heavy footsteps sounded, mounting steps.

"Oh god." Fear pulsed through Tia's voice. "It's too late. He's going to find me in here."

Then there was the squeak of wooden floorboards—he was on the deck.

"Go." Effie pushed at the air with her hands. *"Go."*

Tia stumbled over to the bedroom door, and a breath of light moved through the room as she pushed the door wide. Then, with a thump, it closed again.

Please be okay.

Effie hugged her arms around her body, doing her best to stay quiet, and waited for the murmur of voices.

1992

"WHAT'S WRONG WITH your belly?"

"Adam," Dinah jumped, pulling the towel around her naked body. "You frightened me."

"It looks ugly."

"You should knock." She grabbed for a cardigan.

"Dad says I don't need to knock."

She curled her arms around her fat body, trying to cover the gross lump—something that hadn't been there before.

"Why's it all swollen?"

"I'm pregnant," said Dinah. "I'm having a baby."

Adam frowned. "How did it get in there?"

"Cameron." She smiled a stupid smile. "It's Cameron's baby."

Adam grimaced. Thinking about Cameron stretching his sister's skin to fit a baby in her made him feel a bit sick. "How?"

"Love, I guess."

"But babies come from God."

"That's just one of Dad's lies. It's not true, Adam." Dinah frowned. "I thought you knew that."

"Dad wouldn't lie."

Dinah looked at him, her eyes sad. "I'm so sorry," she said. "I'm sorry I didn't do more for you."

"You do lots."

She shook her head. "Dad has too much control over you, Adam. He hides you away from the world, only letting you think what he wants you to think."

"That's not true."

"You should be in a normal school, not taught by Dad and his followers. You should be learning about science and geography. Not being told that God puts babies in people. There's a whole world beyond the walls of this house, Adam."

"But it's dangerous out there. We're safe in this house."

"We're not safe, Adam. We're trapped."

"I don't like what the baby is doing to you. Put it back," he demanded. "I don't want it."

"It doesn't work like that."

Dinah's lips curved into an odd smile, and part of Adam wanted to hit her.

"When did Cameron put it there?"

"I'm not entirely sure." She rubbed a hand over the disgusting bump. "I started feeling sick about five months ago."

"Does Dad know?"

"No." She snapped her head up and looked at him, her eyes big and scared. "Dad can't ever know."

"But you're fat."

Dinah snorted. "Dad wouldn't even notice if I shaved my head," she said. "Not if the chores got done and he got his three meals a day. Dad barely looks at me these days."

"But girls aren't allowed short hair." Adam looked at her. Dinah would look scary with a bald head. He'd forbid her from cutting her hair.

"Plus," said Dinah, ignoring him, "Cameron says my belly is tiny compared to what his aunty was like. Apparently, she had to buy new clothes."

"What are you going to do with it?" asked Adam. "The baby."

"Keep it and love it and—"

"Dad won't let you. He'll make you—"

"I turned sixteen last month," said Dinah. "Dad can't make me do anything anymore."

Adam frowned. There hadn't been any presents or cake. Maybe once you were sixteen, you didn't get cake.

"Cameron and I are going to leave before the baby comes. Cameron's sorting everything. We're going to live—"

"I don't want you to leave."

"You can come." She took his hand and pulled him up onto the bed next to her. "Come with us."

"No." Adam shook his head. "No."

Dad wouldn't like that. Dinah was ruining everything. Adam shook his head again. He wanted Dinah to put the baby back. He wanted her to stop talking about Cameron. To stop talking about leaving. To stop touching the baby that had crawled inside her.

Dinah grabbed his hand and thrust it under her cardigan and Adam screamed, like the baby might reach out and bite him. But Dinah held tight.

"It's kicking," she said. "Can you feel it?"

Adam tried to pull away. He didn't want to be anywhere near it.

"It's okay, Adam," said Dinah. "He can't hurt you. He loves you already. You're his uncle."

Adam stilled, a small part of him interested—he'd never felt a baby before. Then Dinah's tummy swelled and moved under his hand, prodding and poking at his palm.

"He's saying hello," said Dinah. "Hello, Uncle Adam."

Adam touched his other hand to Dinah's belly, searching for the little creature.

"Not too hard." Dinah smiled.

Then it kicked again, and Adam grinned so big it hurt his cheeks. "Hello, baby." He giggled.

Dinah stroked Adam's hair. "He likes you."

2025

TIA'S MUFFLED SCREAMS—guttural and terrified—leaked under the door.

Effie scrambled forward but the chain held tight, striking against her damaged ankle.

"*Let her go,*" she screamed. "Let her go!"

Effie yanked so violently that the stabs of pain, of steel grinding on bruised bone, winded her.

"Stop," she panted. "Please."

But Tia's cries didn't stop. Her moans penetrated the walls. Then there was a shriek, followed by a soft thud. And for a moment it went silent. Effie clenched her teeth, her eyes filling with tears, and she strained her ears.

"Tia?"

Then just as quickly as it had gone silent, the sounds returned. It wasn't the same desperate shouting—there was no energy left in her sister's pleas—but a persistent thumping and scraping.

A dragging.

Each thump pulsed in Effie's chest, and she forced herself not to cover her ears. She forced herself to listen to every sound. It was all that Effie could do for her sister. Finally, the front door slammed shut, the bang vibrating through the shadows, and the hut fell silent.

For a moment, Effie didn't move. She couldn't move. Then eventually, she stretched her fingers out toward the door and whispered into the dark.

"Tia. Are you there?"

But there was no answer.

Tia was gone.

Effie had failed her.

Again.

1993

"ADAM! ADAM!"

He ran up the stairs, following the sound of his sister's screams.

"Adam!" she yelled again.

Dinah's voice was too loud and too frightening. Adam didn't want to get too near to it. He didn't want to see what was behind her door. Something horrible and not allowed. But he kept running.

"Adam, I need you to unlock the door."

"I'm not supposed to," he panted.

"Please. Please," she begged. "Something's wrong. Something's wrong with the baby."

A horrible sound erupted from his sister—a squeal of fear and pain, like when Dad kicked the neighbor's dog—and Adam covered his ears.

"Stop it. *Stop it*," he said.

But Dinah got louder. She kept groaning and screaming and crying.

"Stop making those noises," he shouted. "You're scaring me."

"It hurts," she sobbed. "I think I'm dying. I think the baby's dying."

Adam pressed up against the door.

"Please . . . please, Adam."

He wasn't allowed to open the door. Dad and Daniel had gone fishing, and Adam was in charge. But he didn't want Dinah to die. Dad would be angry if he let Dinah die.

Dinah spluttered and howled, and Adam started to shake. He dug into his pockets for the key, then he prodded it at the keyhole. He couldn't keep his hands still with all the groaning. But eventually, the key turned and Adam fell into the room.

Dinah was on the floor, balled up, and her skirt was wet, like she'd peed herself.

"Thank you, Adam," she panted. "Thank you."

Adam didn't like looking at her when she was like that, all wet and gross.

"Something's wrong," she moaned. "I need you to get Cameron. I think the baby's coming . . . but it's . . . it's too early. The baby's going to die." She screamed again and clutched at her fat belly. "It's too early."

Dinah rocked, wet and disgusting and sweaty, then she groaned.

"Stop doing that," Adam snapped.

"It hurts too much. I need you to get Cameron."

Fear froze Adam's legs and muscles.

"Please," Dinah screamed.

He couldn't move.

She pushed herself up, planting her hands in a disgusting puddle of something, then she took a big breath.

"Please," she said again. Less scary. More like Dinah. "I need your help, Adam. Can you do that for me?"

He nodded.

Then he sprinted from the room.

The waiting room in the medical center smelled like soap and plasters.

Adam gripped the squeaky white cup that the nurse had given him. The liquid inside was purple, Ribena maybe, but he hadn't touched it. He'd wanted to ask the nurse what it was, but she had run off. There was only one nurse and one doctor in the clean-smelling building, and both of them were in the room with his sister. Cameron was in there too.

Not a place for kids.

The waiting room was empty, apart from a reception lady with loose skin and hair on her face. Adam had looked at her once, but he wasn't going to make that mistake again. The doctor's door was closed, but Adam could still hear his sister moaning. He curled his legs to his chest and squeezed his shins. Dinah had never screamed like that before. It was a bad sound, and Adam wanted it to stop.

What if Dinah died? What if Dad locked Adam up as punishment?

He held his hands over his ears, dropping the cup and spilling the purple liquid across the floor, but the animal sounds still snuck through. He hummed and rocked back and forth. Dinah wasn't meant to make those noises.

Stop it. Stop it. Stop it.

He bit into his tongue, the blades of his teeth sinking into the squishy flesh.

He had to do something.

"You can come in now, Adam." The nurse was smiling. "Mum and baby are well."

"The baby got out?" he said.

"Yes." She took his hand. "The baby got out."

Adam hesitated. "Is there a big hole in Dinah?" He shook his head. "I don't want to see the hole."

"No hole. Your sister looks just like your sister. She just needs to rest for a while."

"Okay," he muttered.

He followed the nurse in. Dinah was sitting in the bed, and Cameron was next to her. They were both grinning, lips stretched wide, staring at a tiny creature.

"Come on, Uncle Adam." Dinah looked up and smiled at him. "Come say hello."

Adam shuffled over to the bed and peered into the bundle of blankets. The thing wrapped up inside was super small and ugly.

"We'll leave you in peace," said the doctor as he walked toward the door. "Congratulations."

The thing didn't look right. It was purple and covered in white goop. Like an alien. And its eyes were all smooshed up.

"What's wrong with its head?" Adam frowned. "It's all squashed."

"Nothing, mate." Cameron patted Adam's back. "It's just a baby."

"Babies are kind of ugly."

Dinah squeezed Adam's hand. "You can touch her," she said.

He shook his head. No way was he touching it. He kept shaking his head as he reached out and pushed his finger against the baby's tiny palm. The baby moved as Adam's white skin touched purple, and a warmth filled him up. Then the baby twitched its little hand, squeezing his finger, and Adam smiled.

Maybe it wasn't super ugly.

"She loves you already," said Dinah.

Then Adam remembered, and he felt sick.

"Adam . . ." Cameron held his arm. "Are you okay, buddy?"

"I . . . I . . ." Adam looked from the baby to Dinah. Then he scratched at his arms, his skin itchy and tight. "You were screaming and yelling and I . . . I thought they were hurting you," he stammered. "I thought that you were dying. I got scared."

"I'm fine," said Dinah. "I'm fine. I promise."

Adam felt ill in his tummy. *Bad Adam.* Like his insides wanted to spill out. "Dinah..." He scuffed the squeaky floor. "I did something..."

She frowned and Adam looked away. "Adam?" she said, sounding frightened. "What did you do?"

"I thought they were going to kill you," he said. "I just wanted to help."

Dinah stared at him.

He burst into tears. "I asked the lady with the hairy face... I asked her to phone Dad."

"No!" Dinah cried out, a feral sound, and her body started to heave. *"No. No. No."*

"I'm sorry. I'm sorry." Tears streamed down Adam's face.

"*I hate you,*" she screamed.

Adam stumbled back, his stomach and chest pulsing hot. "I'm sorry. I—"

"Get out," yelled Dinah. *"Get out!"*

But Adam couldn't move.

Dinah shoved the baby at Cameron. "Please, you have to take her. You have to get out of here."

"Dinah..." Cameron was shaking.

"Please," she begged. "You have to get away from here. My mum's friend... remember, at the funeral, she promised if ever I needed help or—"

"Dinah, I can't."

"Please." Her voice was clogged with tears. "Please, you have to get her away from him."

Adam stared at the tiny baby, unable to look away, and his heart hurt.

2025

A DAY HAD passed and there had been nothing of Tia.

Nothing of Peter.

Effie sat in the gloom with her back to the wall, the mounds of her legs visible in the half light, and turned the corroded fork over in her fingers. The steel handle was covered in blotches of orange rust, and the four thin tines were bent.

Useless.

Effie hurled it across the room. The fork thumped against the table, knocking something off, and a clanging reverberated through the room—then the hut fell silent again.

The quiet was louder than before—more suffocating. Speaking to Tia and hearing her voice had ignited something in Effie. And now the return to silence was crippling. Knowing that her sister was alive—that Effie needed to survive for Tia and Anya—had changed something. And for a brief moment, she had seen hope beyond the dark.

She bit into her lip and rested her head back. No one would be looking for her. She hadn't been taken or forced. Effie had left of her own free will, into a bush that the police had already searched—dogs, helicopters, drones—and found nothing but her dead brother's body.

Effie had asked for space. *I just need some time.* She wasn't missing or in danger, as far as anyone knew.

"I'm scared, Lewis."

Her throat tightened and she slunk to the floor, the chain hanging limp over her legs. Minutes crept by, then hours, and Effie slipped in and out of a daze, never quite sleeping but never fully awake. She should move. She should eat some of the remaining food scraps. But then, what was the point? Effie turned onto her side and closed her eyes, more lost than she'd ever been.

Eventually, a soft buzzing stirred her—a bug or an insect—and Effie rubbed at her face. She pulled herself up, her crushed ankle tingling as the nerves fired, and she swatted at the air.

Then she saw it.

One of the boards that was nailed across the window wasn't flush. There was a slim gap, just a few millimeters. A space for air and light and something pointy. Effie sat up and crawled forward, sweeping her hands across the floor.

"Yes."

She held up the tarnished fork and crawled back to the window. The rust flaked off in her fingers as she angled the metal prongs into the gap.

"Come on."

Effie pushed the pointed steel into the small space and wiggled at it, widening the gap a millimeter at a time.

"Come on."

If she could find a way out, then she would tackle the chain again. One small step at a time. There was a creak as the wood shifted and the fork wedged in deeper. A smile crept across Effie's face. It was working. She jammed and tugged and grunted, the skin on her palm rubbed raw, until eventually, the end of the wooden slat came away.

She'd done it.

Effie pushed her hand through the thin gap, touching glass. But something was wrong. It wasn't bright enough. *No. No.* There were more planks. The window was boarded up on the outside too. *No.* Her heart screamed as she peered through the glass at the second barrier of wood.

"No." Effie punched the wall.

The grief rose in her stomach like a fog, and Effie slid to her knees. As she sunk downward, a voice pierced the mist.

"It's futile, Effie." It came from outside the hut. Low and male. "God's the only one who can save you now."

Effie dragged herself back up.

"What have you done to her?" she shouted.

She thumped at the planks, spitting out hot saliva with her words. *"Peter!"*

The muscles in her jaw tensed, her heart racing.

"Answer me!"

1993

ADAM WRAPPED HIS arms around his head and pushed his back against the living room wall. It was bad.

Bad. Bad.

Dad crashed and swore his way around the house. Anger bloated under his skin, making his cheeks and eyes red, then it burst out. The air cracked as Dad hurled a stool at the wall, and Daniel flinched in the corner.

Daniel never flinched. Daniel never got scared.

Adam squeezed his eyes shut, then pushed his arms against his ears. He didn't like it. He wanted Dad to stop shouting—to stop yelling bad words.

"How old's the prick?" demanded Dad.

Daniel mumbled something.

"Speak up, boy."

"Nineteen," said Daniel. "Cameron's nineteen."

There was a pause, and Adam opened his eyes. But Dad's face was all wrong.

"She was fifteen." Dad smirked. "Just fifteen when he put that bastard thing in her."

He laughed, a terrifying hollow sound, and Adam thought he might spew.

"That boy's going to rot in jail." The horrible smile grew on Dad's face. "Fucking pedophile," he spat. "The pigs'll get him, you'll see, and they'll mess that boy up inside. With any luck, they'll beat the fucking life out of him."

He pointed a shaking finger at Daniel.

"Hell's waiting for him," he leered. "For him and his devil spawn."

Daniel straightened up. "What about Dinah?"

Dad's expression changed, his teeth vanished and his face turned to stone. Then he walked over to Daniel and placed a hand on his shoulders.

"The wickedness of the outside world has polluted your sister's mind. She's been lured and corrupted by opponents of God's truth." He moved closer to Daniel. "Cameron's words dripped into her like poison, leading her toward hell. And when your sister was at her most naive, Cameron filled her with the devil."

Daniel nodded.

"We must protect her from this immoral world." Dad spat as he spoke, his face shiny with sweat. "We must show her a life of purity . . . a life free of sin."

Daniel nodded again.

"Only by separating ourselves from the evils of the outside world can we save your sister."

Daniel's head kept nodding. Up and down.

"Tomorrow," Dad continued, "we'll start anew. Away from here. Somewhere new. Away from the temptations of outsiders."

Adam pressed a hand against his mouth, keeping the frightened sounds in. *Stay. Stay.* He didn't make a noise, didn't move a muscle. He made himself small and invisible, so that Dad wouldn't remember he was there.

"Go." Dad pointed toward the hall. "Your sister needs you to be strong for her now."

He kissed Daniel's head, then Daniel walked out.

Adam gripped his shins, his heart racing, as the room silenced around him. The slap of Daniel's footsteps softened as he moved farther away, then they stopped, and a bolt slid open with a clang.

Dinah's room.

Adam bit into his tongue at the first scream and dug his palms into his ears. He closed his eyes, his cheeks wet with tears, and when he opened them again, Dad was staring at him.

"You failed her." Dad pointed at the door. "Listen," he yelled. "*Listen!* Those screams are because of you. Because of your disobedience and your weakness."

Adam sniffed, his stomach too sore to breathe.

"I expected better of you, boy."

2025

EFFIE WOKE TO the sound of her sister's voice.

Her sister who never stopped talking. Her sister who had an answer for everything. And suddenly, Effie was twelve years old again, tucked up in the sleeping nook, wishing that Tia would be quiet for just two minutes.

"Tia, it's not even light outside," Effie groaned. "I'm trying to sleep."

"There's no light anymore."

"The sun will be up soon." Effie turned over.

"It won't make a difference," whispered Tia.

"What are you talking about?"

Effie dug the heels of her hands into her eyes, grinding out the final grains of sleep, and the moment changed, becoming solid—and Effie was back, chained to her mother's bed. Body first, bruised and hollow, then her mind.

"Tia?" Effie moved forward, reality hardening beneath her palms as she crawled toward the door. "Tia? Is that you?"

"Yes."

"Oh god." Effie let out a lungful of air. "I thought . . . Did he hurt you?"

"He's taken away the key and the matches." Her voice was small and cracked. "As punishment. I can't open your door."

"That's okay." Effie took a breath. "Are you okay?"

"We're both shut up now. We must confess to our sins or—"

"Tia, are you hurt?"

There was a shuffling.

"My ribs . . . it's sore to breathe."

"Can you try and—"

"You can't beat them," Tia interrupted. "He'll never let you go." She started to sob. "Daniel's wife, Hana, she tried to escape once, to leave this place, but he dragged her back and locked her away. Then, one day . . . Hana was just gone. Vanished. And we never saw her again."

Hana. Effie clutched a hand to her stomach. Hana was real.

"Who's Daniel?" she asked. "I don't understand."

"I wanted to be braver." Tia's voice trembled. "I wanted to run away. To leave. But Anya loved him. He twisted and polluted her little mind until she wouldn't . . . until she wouldn't listen to me. To her own mother." A tortured moan leaked from Tia. "When they tied her up to stop me from leaving, Anya let them. She let them chain her up, like a caged animal, because she thought my behavior needed punishing. That my disobedience was sinful."

Tears flowed freely through Tia's words, and the pain in her voice dislodged something in Effie's chest.

"I should have done more," said Tia. "I should have left before Anya was born." There was a pause. "Dad was right all along."

Effie exhaled. "Tia, what happened? What happened to Dad?"

For a moment, the cold air was quiet, stagnant.

"I was twelve years old when you and Dad left. It was just me and Four, and I didn't—"

"Tia, I'm so sorry."

"Then Peter and his family came. And for a long time, I was

happy. I wanted it, this secluded life in the trees. I wanted what Peter was offering—a family. Faith. A life away from the world. After everyone I'd lost, Peter made me feel safe." Tia paused. "But every birthday, Dad hid something for me by the river—a secret, a sign that he was there . . . that I could go to him. But I ignored him. I was so angry with him. I hated him for leaving."

The words landed as a punch in Effie's stomach.

"Then Anya was born, and things . . . things changed. Peter's rules got stricter, less rational, and he started to punish any defiant behavior. His son Daniel was even worse. Daniel is . . ." Tia took a breath. "He's cruel."

There was a thick beat of silence.

"It was Daniel who found Dad's body," she said. "Floating face down in the river, when Anya was still a baby."

Effie stiffened, fighting the instinct to cry.

"But Dad didn't drown," said Tia. "They spotted him coming to see me, I'm sure of it, and they killed him. Dad was stronger than that river. He didn't drown. He was murdered." She paused. "It's strange, I don't remember much from that time. Perhaps I've blocked it out, but I remember the way Dinah screamed. She cried for weeks after Daniel found Dad's body."

Dinah. The name scratched at the insides of Effie's skull.

"I think," Tia continued, "that perhaps Dinah knew, and she was scared—scared of what her own family was capable of."

"But . . ." Effie frowned, a half-formed moment coming back to her. "You said Dad died when Anya was a baby . . . but . . ." The image crept into her thoughts—ripped in two. "Anya knew who he was. I showed her a picture of Dad, and she recognized him. She was afraid of him." Effie hesitated. "Anya said that he would hurt her."

The bad man.

There was a soft tapping on the door—fingers perhaps—and when Tia finally replied, her words felt labored. "Peter used to tell

Anya ghost stories about Dad, about the dead man who haunted the woods. Peter found an old photo of Dad in the hut, and he used it to frighten Anya. To manipulate her."

Effie closed her eyes, her heart leaden, and she swallowed. "How many people are there?" she asked. "Out here?"

"There's only five of us left now."

"Left?"

"Daniel's wife, Four and Anya—they're all gone, one way or another."

"Tia," said Effie, "did Daniel kill Four?"

"No."

"Then what happened to him? Did Four really take his own life—"

"It was me."

"What was?"

"It was my fault." A small strangled sound escaped from Tia's throat. "I'm the reason our brother's dead."

"I don't understand."

"I kept pushing him . . ." she said, her words hard and blunt. "Pushing and pushing, making him do things."

"What things?"

"I just wanted what was best for Anya. I wanted her to be free of this place. For her to live a normal life. So eventually, I convinced Four to help me, to teach Anya that there was more to the world, and that the outside wasn't a place of sin. Four talked to her about Koraha and school, and small details from his childhood—June's baking, the park, kicking a rugby ball. He even found our old schoolbooks from when Mum taught us, and novels that Peter had hidden away."

"Why didn't you run, Tia? Why didn't you leave and get help?"

"I couldn't leave," she whispered. "They had my daughter, Effie. They had her chained to a wall. And Peter made it very clear that if I ever left, I'd never see Anya again. That by the time I brought the police back, she'd be gone."

Effie had no words. Her sister had lived through hell. There were no words for that.

"Four spent months marking the way back to the river with scraps of material. He hung them from trees and wrapped them around branches. I talked Anya through it again and again, about the markers and the old tinnie hidden in the rushes. I drew her picture after picture, pointing out the narrowed sections in the river, and showing her how to launch the tinnie. You remember—across the shallow water, where the Haast River is only sixty meters wide. Everything Dad taught us as kids. Often Anya held her hands to her ears and screamed until I stopped talking, and a few times she threatened to tell Peter. But I kept trying, just in case."

"Why didn't Four leave?"

Effie stared at the door. It was impossible, of course it was, but she felt the sad smile that settled on her sister's mouth.

"Four hadn't been in the outside world since he was six years old," said Tia. "The bush, and this, it's all he's . . . he'd . . . ever known. Crossing that river was never an option for him." She paused. "Four believed that if he left Peter, he'd go straight to hell."

"But he wanted Anya to leave?"

"Four wanted Anya to have a choice." Tia drew a breath. "Because I asked it of him. And it cost Four his life. Peter found out what Four was doing—the whispers about school and the outside world, the books—and he . . ."

Her words thinned to a quiet whimper.

"I gave Four that meal. I set that plate in front of him." Tia's tears filled the quiet. "I had no idea what Peter had done."

"They poisoned him? Just for talking?"

"You don't understand. Peter demands, without exception, that we hold ourselves separate from the outside world. He says we would be better to eat possum bait than to be poisoned by the sinful words of outsiders. And Peter's word—the Guardian's word—is law."

"Guardian?"

"The Guardian of truth. Of God's message." Tia's voice dropped to a whisper. "Peter claims to speak for God. He says that separating ourselves from the corrupt world is the only way to stave off evil and save ourselves."

A wave of heat pulsed through Effie's brain. The scene, the empty hut, Morrow's words. *My team were all over that hut for a day and a half. They didn't find a trace of your sister.* It didn't add up.

"But the police went through the hut," she said. "There was no evidence of Peter or you. There was nothing to indicate that anyone else had been there." Effie hesitated, trying to make sense of it. "And the prints on the knife, they were small . . . Anya said that when she left you, that you were dead."

Tia didn't answer.

"I don't understand." Effie frowned. There were so many holes, so many things that didn't make sense. "If Anya loved Peter, why would she run away? Why would she—"

"She was scared."

Effie pushed her fingers into her temples. "It doesn't make—"

"People only see what Peter wants them to see," said Tia. "Peter controls everything. He is everything. And Anya loved him fiercely. She would never have left him. They would have died in the trees together." Tia paused. "But then, Anya loved Four too."

Effie pulled against her restraints, willing herself an inch closer.

"The last thing Four did," said Tia, "before he took his final breath, was to unchain her. To set her free."

Effie waited for more, but Tia fell silent. A second. A minute.

"Anya cut a cross into Four's chest," Tia said eventually, "so that God would know to take him."

Effie closed her eyes and pictured Anya in Koraha, waiting for her.

"There's something else you should know," Tia went on. "Peter, he's . . . Peter is Asher's dad. Except he's not Asher. His real name is Adam. Adam lied to us . . . about his name and who he was."

Effie stared at the door, at the spot where her sister sat on the other side, then she reached her hand out.

"Adam didn't die that day, Effie." Tia took a breath. "Adam never left."

A cold understanding pulsed through Effie's chest. "Is Asher—Adam, I mean—is he . . . ?"

"Yes," said Tia. "Adam is Anya's dad."

Effie covered her mouth with her hand, knowing what her sister was going to say next.

"Adam brought Peter here. Adam did all of this."

1994

ADAM REMOVED THE untouched plate of food from his sister's room.

Dinah sat on her bed, staring at the wall. Her mouth hung open slightly, and strands of greasy hair stuck to her face. She didn't look at him. She didn't move her head. Maybe she hadn't noticed him slip in. Adam could be quiet as a mouse when he needed to be.

Dad had boarded up Dinah's window in the new house, but Adam had stuck up pictures of the beach and the forest for her. There was a pretty one of a fantail too. Dinah liked birds.

"I've brought you some tea," said Adam. "Peppermint."

But she just stared at the wall. His sister had cried and screamed for months after the baby. The house had echoed with it, even when Adam was sure that she was sleeping. And if ever Adam went near her, she tried to attack him. One time, she'd scratched a deep chunk out of his cheek, and the scab had taken weeks to heal.

"You like peppermint," he said.

She was chained up now though. Dad had attached the chain to Dinah's bed after she'd tried to escape the third time. Dad said if they didn't tie her up, she might try to hurt herself. That she might try to kill herself. And Adam definitely didn't want that. He never ever wanted Dinah to die. He loved her.

"I put sugar in it." He pushed the mug forward. "To give you energy."

The chain kept Dinah safe in her room, safe from the outside world. Dad had removed anything that might corrupt her thoughts, and Adam made sure that she always had food and warm tea. It was Adam's job to look after Dinah now. He'd let Cameron poison his sister's mind and put the devil in her tummy. But Adam would fix all of it.

"I'll bring you a cloth and some soap later," he said gently. "It's important to keep clean, Dinah."

Adam would fix his sister. And then God would love her again.

2025

"HELLO, EFFIE."

She didn't move from the bed as the figure appeared in the open doorway. A pale ghost, one eye as blue as the ocean and the other black as night.

Lying, cowardly shit.

"Where's Tia?" she demanded.

But Adam just grinned. "It's nice to see you, Effie."

She let out a sharp laugh. "It would be nicer if I had a gun to put a hole in your deceitful head."

Adam's smile widened. "I trust that Tia has filled you in on our arrangement here."

"Your deranged and narcissistic little cult?" Effie matched his smile. "Yes, I believe I have the gist of it."

"Enlighten me."

"A woman. Enlighten you? That seems somewhat off-brand, wouldn't you say, Asher? Sorry, *Adam*." Effie smirked. "Me being corrupted by my evil vagina and all."

Adam flinched, but his smile didn't falter.

"What's it like?" asked Effie. "Playing God? Does he talk to you directly? Or does God prefer to leave clues? Chauvinistic tidbits carved into trees, perhaps."

"I wouldn't mock if I was you."

"What would you do?" Effie looked at him. "If you were me, I mean? Repent. Sin. Marry. Make babies. Masturbate so furiously you'd need to lash yourself a hundred times for it? What is it that us women do exactly?"

"Quiet."

"Oh, I'm sorry." Effie smiled. "Is this not appropriate ladylike conversation? Am I making you uncomfortable?" She paused. "You do look a little ill, now that I think about it."

"Shut your mouth."

"A little insane around the eyes."

"Quiet. Or I'll come over there and shut your mouth for you."

"Apologies." Effie held her hands up. "I forgot. What is it that you preach again . . . that women should be seen and not heard? That I am to remain quiet and submit to God? Or is it to you?"

There was a pause as their eyes met.

"I tried to help you once, a long time ago. To give you the quiet in which to hear God." The corner of Adam's mouth twitched. "You might remember it? A night in a little crate."

A cold moved through Effie's body, but she forced her lips to smile. Adam was a worthless piece of shit. And he could go to hell.

"Unfortunately, your dad heard your whining." Adam shook his head. "And I had to untie you before he found you. Before you found God."

"Sorry I ruined your plans."

"No matter." He smiled. "We have time now. You'll repent soon enough."

Adam moved farther into the room. "You're in a special place. Away from temptation and sin. Here, you will be cleansed."

"Right." Effie stared into his dark eye. "And what if I don't want to be cleansed?"

"You'll come around eventually."

"I doubt that."

Adam grinned. "I like your tattoo by the way. Very touching."

Effie slapped a hand to her wrist, covering the small *A*. "It's for Aiden."

He raised an eyebrow. "And the second *A*?"

"There's just one."

Adam chuckled. "You seem very chipper for someone in your situation."

"I'm not planning to stay."

"Is that right?"

"Lewis won't wait forever," said Effie. "He will look for me. And he will find me."

A cruelness spread like roots through his face, but Effie forced herself to keep looking at him. He was thinner than she remembered, and his hair was cut close to his skull.

"I doubt that very much," he said.

Effie's stomach flipped, and for a moment she couldn't find the words that she'd practiced. As she stared into his eyes, a numbness swelled in her throat and tongue.

"You don't know anything," she managed.

"Oh, I think I know a few things."

Then, slowly, Adam moved aside.

No.

A beat of fear, like nothing she'd felt before, pounded through every inch of her.

"Someone wanted to say a quick hello," he said.

"No," Effie murmured, the word barely a whisper.

Anya.

The child stood there, her small hand clutching Adam's.

"I always knew she'd come back to me." He picked Anya up, and she wrapped her arms around his neck. "Daddy missed you, didn't he?"

Then he kissed her on the forehead, and Effie saw it. *Love*. The unconditional bond between a father and a daughter. And the earth fell away from under her.

"Where's Lewis?" she asked.

"Pining, I imagine," said Adam. "For the childhood sweetheart who broke his heart. Who, for all he knows, is back in Scotland."

"I left a note."

"For Anya, yes." He smiled. "But she got rid of that, didn't you, sweetie?"

"Anya." Tears stung Effie's eyes. "Why would—"

"Quiet," Adam barked. "You are not to talk to her."

"Lewis will come for her," said Effie. "He'll keep looking for her."

"Wrong again."

Effie went to say something, but Adam's smile—white teeth set into a white face—stole her words.

"I'm afraid," he said, "that your perfect Lewis isn't quite so perfect after all." He touched his daughter's cheek. "He had Anya moved into emergency foster care after you left."

"I don't believe you."

"I guess it was too much for him. You deserting him again." Adam tilted his head, observing his child. "And with her looking so much like you."

"June would never—"

"June's an old woman."

"That's—"

"Six kids in one home," Adam interrupted. He set Anya down. "Nasty place." He pulled up the girl's sleeve, revealing a line of crusted circular burns. "The dad was a smoker."

"No." Effie let out a sob, her body shaking as the strength emptied from her. *"No."*

"But my girl's back home now."

Anya clung to her father's leg as he moved back to the door.

"So." He smiled at Effie. "I trust you will be on your best behavior." He stroked his daughter's red hair. "Your sister was quick to atone when Anya returned to us."

"No." The word came out as little more than a whisper.

"Come, sweetheart."

Anya took her father's hand, and the door shut behind them.

2025

EFFIE SCRUNCHED HER eyes shut, the sunlight bright and painful.

Squinting, she held a hand across her forehead, blocking out the glare, then she looked down at her body. Her feet were bare, the skin on her soles tender, and her right ankle was purple and blistered where the chain had been.

"If you run, I'll shoot you." Daniel tapped the muzzle of a rifle against her thigh, signaling for her to move on, then he shoved her with his free hand. "You got that?"

Effie nodded. It was the first time since leaving Koraha that she'd been outside.

"Fifteen minutes of exercise," he said.

She stumbled forward, her legs like heavy stumps, then she lifted her face to the sky. The sun warmed her skin, and for a brief moment, she knew nothing but the breeze and the bell-like song of korimako.

"Move." Daniel hit the gun against Effie's leg again. "Go on."

She walked in a body that wasn't hers, and itched at her arms, her skin tight and hot.

"You'd better be less trouble than that sister of yours," Daniel grunted.

Effie wanted to hit him. She wanted to land her fist right in the center of his face. But she didn't. She did nothing.

"After Anya ran off, your bitch sister thought that the kid would bring the cops back, and that the fuckers would rescue her." He snorted. "Took me fucking hours to clean that place out. To make it look like Four offed himself."

Effie stopped. "It was you? You cleaned the hut?" Her head spun. "You removed Tia's stuff?"

"Shut it."

"Why? Why not just get rid of Four's body too?"

"You reckon I'm thick or something?" Daniel laughed. "If the little shit had brought the pigs back and there'd been no body, them bastards would've started poking their noses around. Asking unwanted questions. Nah . . ." He shook his head. "Better to give those pricks an easy answer."

"Was it you or Peter who put the poison—"

"I said shut it, woman." Daniel whacked her leg with the gun, then barked at her to keep walking.

"Fuck, Tia went proper mental when she realized what we'd done to her brother." Daniel sneered. "Thought I killed her, I punched the bitch that hard when she came at me. She whacked her head real fucking good on that table. Made a right bloody mess. Scared the kid shitless too." He lifted his shirt, revealing a thin scar. "The kid went nuts. Fucking stabbed me. I would have rung her scrawny neck if she hadn't legged it."

Effie frowned. "You're the reason Anya left?"

"I told you to shut your face."

She turned away, too tired to do anything else, and stared at the ground, at the familiar shapes of ferns and fallen leaves. But the bush was no longer hers. The place she'd once known had gone.

It was the sound of the girl's voice that eventually lifted her gaze.

She stood in the vegetable garden hunched over a bunch of green leaves, a basket at her feet.

There was a woman with her. *Not Tia*. Tia was kept somewhere else. The older woman moved slowly around the vegetables. Not talking. Not looking up. It was only when Anya touched a hand to her arm that the woman gave her the smallest smile.

"Here," said Anya. "These will be good for dinner." She threw the greens in her basket. "And these." Anya held up two carrots. "You should cook these, Dinah."

The woman reached out a shaky arm.

"Right," Daniel barked. "That's enough."

He shoved Effie forward.

"Back to your cage."

2025

ADAM HELD THE door open and Anya ducked under his arm.

Effie gasped at the sight of the girl.

No.

They'd taken her hair.

"Breakfast," said Adam.

Her beautiful long red hair.

Anya set a small bowl on the floor and backed away, quick and flustered, without looking at Effie.

"It's okay," said Adam. "She can't reach you, sweetheart. She's chained up."

Anya's hair wasn't completely gone; they'd left her a pinkie's length—uneven tufts that jutted out from her scalp. Effie imagined the child sitting frozen as Adam hacked at her hair, tearing away chunks with blunt scissors.

"It's oats," said Adam. "With water."

Then father and daughter walked out, holding hands.

—

Anya wouldn't talk to her. In the past two days, she'd spoken but a few words to Effie, and only when Peter or Adam was present.

But it was just the two of them now, just Effie and the girl.

Anya came in twice a day with food—in place of Tia—and left it near the door. There was a cross marked on the floor, just close enough that Effie could strain against the chain and almost reach it, but far enough away that Anya was kept safe—from her.

"Anya . . ." Effie inched forward, the chain and padlock clunking on the floor as she moved, and stretched a hand toward her. "I'm sorry. I shouldn't have left you. I shouldn't—"

"Quiet," Anya snapped. The child would barely even look at her. "We're not to talk."

"I'm sorry," said Effie softly. "About your hair."

"Quiet."

"I'm sure it will grow back in—"

"I needed to be punished." Anya looked straight at her. "To be cleaned."

"Anya, that's not—"

She glared at her, and Effie went quiet.

"Is your mum okay?"

"Stop talking," said Anya.

She set down a bowl of lentils and a piece of bread.

"Please, Anya, I just need to know that my sister—"

"*Quiet!*" she yelled.

But Anya looked at her, her eyes wide, and mouthed a single word. *Alive.* Then she looked away, like it had never happened.

Effie pressed a hand to the thrum in her stomach and whispered back a quick *thank you*.

Anya set a cup on the ground by the bowl, then she lifted a blue jug and started to pour water into it.

"What can I do?" asked Effie. "What can I do to make it up to you?"

Anya stopped. She dipped her chin, whispering into her chest.

"Pray," she murmured.

Effie sat still as the girl lifted the jug and tipped it over the cup again.

"Shit," Anya cursed as the plastic jug slipped from her fingers and landed on the ground with a thud, spilling water across the floor. She crawled past the cross mark and stretched out, trying to catch the flow of water with her fingers.

Effie placed a hand on the girl's arm. "Please, I just—"

Anya screamed, loud and guttural. "She's got me! She's got me!"

Effie jumped away from her.

"She tried to grab me," Anya yelled. Her eyes were wild, honed on Effie. "She was trying to—"

The door slammed open and Adam appeared. "It's okay," he said. "It's okay."

Anya threw herself at him, clinging to his arm.

Adam stroked the tufts of her red hair, then he peeled the girl from his body and pushed her behind him. Effie tried to scramble farther away, but her back met with the wall and she winced. Adam eyed her as he stepped across the room, his face expressionless, and Effie's pulse raced. Then slowly, he bent down and slapped her hard across the face.

"Never touch my daughter."

He stood and walked back to the door, kicking over the bowl of lentils as he passed. He turned back at the last moment, his voice dark.

"You've earned yourself another twenty-four hours of alone time to reflect."

Effie flinched as the key clicked in the door, her heart aching.

2025

THE THOUGHT OF trying to stand brought a new heaviness to Effie's limbs.

She sat on the floor, unmoved since Adam had left with the girl, and stared at the door. For a while, feet moved and chairs scraped on the other side of the wall. Voices filtered through—a child's laugh and a male chuckle—but eventually, the front door slammed shut and the hut went quiet.

And Effie was alone.

Thirst crept through her, coating her tongue and mouth. Groaning, she stretched out and reached for the overturned jug.

The chain clattered along the floor as she inched herself forward. She just needed a sip. Just a few remaining drips, anything to purge the thirst from the insides of her cheeks. Effie held the jug to her lips and tipped it upside down. Trickles of water dripped onto her face and neck, and she opened her mouth, licking at the plastic.

"Ouch."

Effie flinched as something hard hit her front tooth. She looked down to where a small item had fallen to the floor.

A key.

Effie inhaled as the realization hit her. *Anya.* Anya had left the key in the jug. Effie's fingers trembled as she grabbed for it, then she pulled the padlock around her ankle. The key shook as she tried to fit it into the small hole.

Breathe, Effie.

Her hands steadier, the key glided in and the padlock clicked open.

"Oh god." Effie pressed a hand across her mouth. "Thank you," she sobbed. "Thank you, Anya." She let out a breath of laughter. "Thank you. You wonderful, brilliant little girl."

Anya had given Effie a key and twenty-four hours. *To reflect.* To pull herself together and get them both out.

2025

EFFIE SAT ON the bed—unchained—staring at the door.

Ready.

She'd eaten the chunk of bread as well as some of the spilled lentils from the floor, and she'd salvaged a tablespoon of water from the cup. Her feet and ankle were wrapped in scraps of fabric from the sheets, and she'd pulled on the few items of clothing she had. It was still summer, but at night, the bush was cold, and her drained body shivered at its edges. Not her stomach though—it was filled with fire.

Sometime after dark, someone had returned to the hut. There had been a shuffling of furniture and a flicker of light under the door, but nothing else. No food. No grunted insults or thumps on the door. But they would come. In the morning, the door would open, and they would come. And Effie would be ready. Minutes ticked away, then hours, and Effie closed her eyes. Resting. But not sleeping.

Her eyes flicked open at the first soft knock.

Tap. Tap.

Effie dug her nails into her palms as the door inched open, candlelight leaking in, and the girl appeared.

"Anya."

The girl held a finger to her lips and shook her head violently, fear creeping into her eyes. Then she gestured for Effie to go with her.

Effie nodded and followed in silence. When she reached the door, the girl took her hand, and Effie felt the touch of skin deep in her stomach. She had to force herself not to crush the bones in the child's fingers.

Without a sound, they stepped from the bedroom and into the guts of the small dark hut. Then Effie gasped—too loudly—and Anya flashed her a frightened look.

Shh, she mouthed.

Daniel was there, his sleeping body lolling across the couch, his right arm hanging down, fingers brushing the floor. Anya pointed at the door, her palm damp in Effie's, then she guided Effie across the room. The girl's steps were so light, so impossibly quiet, that Effie feared it was a dream.

Then there was a groan, and Effie glanced across at Daniel, fear flooding her chest. Just one sound and the sleeping figure would transform into something dangerous. Anya tugged at her arm, and together they forged a path to the door. One step at a time. Quiet as mice. The door creaked as Effie pushed it open, and her heart stopped. Daniel was going to wake up. His fingers were going to grip her arm. And they would never leave.

No one ever leaves here. This is the vanishing place.

But then, miraculously, they were out in the cool night air. Anya released Effie's hand and scurried along the deck, her small body eaten by the darkness, and Effie held her breath. But seconds later, Anya returned with two head-torches.

"Run," she whispered.

For meter after meter, neither of them spoke. They just ran, hand in hand—two white dots in the dark—deeper into the trees. Eventually, the sounds of the bush—the call of morepork and the scrape of climbing possums—drowned out the thump in Effie's veins and she stopped. She bent over and gulped at the night air.

"Thank you," she panted. "Thank you."

Anya tugged at Effie, digging her small fingers into her arm.

"Come on," she puffed. "We need to find Mum. She's at the other hut, but Lewis is getting her."

"Lewis?" Effie couldn't move.

"At Peter's hut, where he keeps Mum. It's farther away." Anya's voice was hurried and shaky. "Come on. We need to meet Lewis and Mum at—"

"Anya." Effie held the girl's hand. "Stop. Stop. I don't understand. Adam said you were in foster care."

"I lied."

"But . . ." Effie frowned and shook her head. "The burns on your arm?"

The smallest smile tugged at the corners of Anya's mouth. "I burned myself on June's shitty oven. On the stupid wire shelf. Then Lewis suggested the smoker thing. He said it would be convincing."

"Lewis is here?"

"We came to get you."

"The police?"

Anya looked down, her torch illuminating her feet. "Nah." She kicked at the dead leaves. "Just me and Lewis."

"Jesus. Why on earth would . . ." Effie hesitated, realization stopping her, and she looked at the girl.

"Lewis didn't know," said Effie. "He didn't know about any of this, did he? Peter, and all of them."

Anya shook her head.

"Why didn't you tell—"

"I didn't think he'd believe me," she said. "Or I thought maybe he'd tell that big police lady and she'd make me stay behind in Koraha."

"Shit." Effie let out a long breath. "Right."

"Lewis has been sleeping in a bivvy thing somewhere close, and watching."

Effie gave the girl an encouraging smile. "You've done great, Anya. Really great."

"I thought, you know, that Lewis would phone his police friends when we got here. When he saw that..." She stopped. "Then they'd bring the big helicopters and the dogs and stuff. But there's no phone signal out here. Lewis was real mad at me. He said if we don't die, that I'm grounded for life." Anya glanced up. "But Lewis wouldn't go back to Koraha. He said he wouldn't leave you again."

Effie took her hand. "Come on. Let's go find them."

"We need to get to the clearing. Lewis said to meet there."

They walked for fifteen minutes, just two specks of light, nothing stirring but the leaves beneath their feet. The fabric wrapped around Effie's feet had soaked through, and the soles of her feet throbbed, but the pain was numbed by the beat of adrenaline. By the thought of Lewis.

"We're close," said Anya. She pointed to a marked tree. "See?"

A crack exploded through the still air, and the tree next to them shook. Splinters of bark swept past Effie's face, and she threw herself in front of the child, shielding her. Then she looked up, the light of her head-torch sending a beam of white through the trees. A figure appeared in the shaft of light. A dark mass. There—then gone. A trick of the light—of her mind.

"What is it?" whispered Anya.

"I don't—"

A second crack tore a hole in the night, the sound throbbing in Effie's skull, and she stumbled back. But in the dark, there was nothing. Her chest heaved so loudly that she could barely hear her own thoughts.

"*Effie!*" Anya screamed.

"It's okay." Effie swung her head from left to right. Then she saw him.

Daniel stood ten meters away, his legs braced wide, the fingers of his right hand curled around the handle of a gun. For a second, none of them moved. They just stared at each other. Then Daniel's face broke into a cold smile and he started to walk forward. As he raised his gun, aiming at them, Effie pushed the girl behind her.

"No!" A scream fractured the quiet. And suddenly, Tia was there. She threw herself at Daniel, wild and loud and vicious, and he dropped the gun. She lunged at him, curling her arms and legs around his body and clawing at his face. But Daniel threw Tia off like she was nothing. Anya tried to run forward but Effie clutched the girl's clothes, holding her tight as she writhed and squirmed. Effie turned, using her body to block the child's view, then she reached out and switched their head-torches off, plunging them into darkness.

Only the white circles of Daniel's and Tia's torches remained, one glowing dot unmoving on the ground and the other towering high. The sounds that accompanied the black made Effie want to cry.

The thud of feet kicked into flesh. The animallike groans of pain.

"*Mum*," Anya screamed.

Then a voice, a stillness, came out of nowhere.

"We need to keep moving," he whispered.

"Lewis?"

"Yes."

The warmth of his breath brushed against Effie's cheek as the outline of his face appeared from the shadows.

"You need to get Anya away from here," he said.

"We can't leave Tia."

"Cover the girl. Make sure she can't see."

Then Lewis turned on his head-torch, illuminating the image of Daniel and Tia. There was blood smeared across Daniel's face and his clothes were covered in dirt, but he was smiling. Tia was curled on the ground, unmoving but not dead, her arms held up to protect her head and face. Lewis took a step forward, pointing a gun at Daniel.

"Police," said Lewis. "I need you to step back."

Daniel raised his arms, then started to inch back from the mound at his feet.

"You can have the bitch," he said. "She's not worth it."

Effie stood behind Lewis, Anya clutched at her side. "I'm going to go and help your mum," she said. "Okay?"

Anya nodded and Effie released her. She walked in the light from Lewis's torch, watching Daniel the whole way, until she reached her sister's side. Daniel stood a few meters away, hands still raised, held by the threat of Lewis's gun.

"Tia," she whispered. "It's me."

Her sister turned her head, then lowered her arms.

"It's time to get up," said Effie softly. "Then we're going to leave." She stroked her sister's cheek. "All of us. You and me and Anya. We're getting out of here."

A smile parted Tia's lips, her teeth lined with blood, and she placed a shaking hand in Effie's.

"You came back." She coughed.

"Yes. I came back." Effie brushed the hair from Tia's swollen face. "Tia, I'm so—"

A gunshot splintered the black air, stealing Effie's words and vibrating through her ears. She spun her head around, spotting the darkened figure in the trees. He stood with his arms raised and a gun held to his face.

Peter? Or Adam?

Effie scanned the scene, trying to make sense of it. But it was too dark. There were too many unknowns.

Lewis, outnumbered now, had turned toward the new threat.

And Daniel was gone.

Before Effie had time to react, her stomach exploded with pain—the force of a foot—and she crumpled to the ground. The trees and ferns spun around her and she vomited into the dirt. The pain in her abdomen rooted her to the ground, her body emptied of breath, and there was nothing but white behind her eyelids.

A bright white light, flooding her vision.

Then somewhere, far away, there were voices. A violent splintering of air.

Crack.

Then another. Two gunshots.

Effie stumbled forward on hands and knees until she was stopped by something soft and warm.

A body.

Hacking up saliva, Effie rubbed at her eyes, blinking the white flashes from her vision. Then she sat up. But when she pulled her hands away, she froze.

Tia lay there, eyes closed and lips open. Unresponsive.

"No."

At some point, two figures crouched down next to her in the leaves—the girl and Lewis—but she couldn't think or see past her sister's body.

"Tia." Effie sobbed and sank to the ground, her words barely a whisper. "You can't leave me."

"They're gone," said Lewis. "Peter and Daniel. They're gone."

This can't be the end.

"Peter's dead. I shot him."

This is meant to be the beginning.

He touched a hand to Effie's shoulder. "Daniel ran off after he shot . . ."

Anya was crying.

"I'm so sorry." Lewis again. "But we have to go, Effie. It's not safe to stay here."

She held a hand out and cupped her sister's face. Effie had only just found her again. Tia would open her eyes. She would blink, and her eyes would open.

"Effie," Lewis said. "We can't stay. We can try and carry her."

But her sister's eyes didn't open; they didn't so much as flicker.

And with a single gunshot, there was only one of them left, one of Mum's four bush children.

NEW ZEALAND
THREE MONTHS LATER

BLAIR'S LAUGHTER FILLED June's small kitchen, big and bright, and Effie stood in the hallway letting it wash through her. Blair and Ewan had insisted on a New Zealand holiday, to drink sauvignon blanc and do the whole *Lord of the Rings* thing. And to make sure that Lewis wasn't a complete eejit. Blair's words.

"You cheated," June exclaimed. "I demand a rematch."

"How?" There was a burst of laughter from Blair. "How could I have cheated?"

Anya giggled.

"I don't know," said June. "You must have additional saliva stores or something."

"Ew." Anya snorted.

Effie smiled to herself, then stepped into the kitchen.

"What on earth are you lot up to?"

"The Weet-Bix challenge." Anya beamed, her lips coated in wheat dust. "It's a race to eat two."

"Dry," said June. "Barbaric, if you ask me."

Blair winked at Anya. "Sounds like someone's a sore loser."

"I am not!"

Anya was smiling from ear to ear. And as Effie looked at her, she had to bite down on her lip to stop the prickle of tears. At the little girl, who was still smiling despite it all.

"Morning, team." Lewis's voice carried through from the front door. "I come bearing coffee and brownies." His face appeared in the doorway. "Anyone here like brownies?"

"Me." Anya hurried from her chair and crashed into his legs. *"Me."*

"You sure?" Lewis frowned and lifted the box above his head.

"Yes. Yes."

Blair walked up to him. "I suggest you hand those over, mister, before anyone gets hurt."

Lewis gulped and held them out.

"Wise choice, my friend."

Blair smiled at Anya, then took her hand. "If anyone needs us, we'll be in the living room stuffing our faces. And if Ewan gets back from his run, you never saw us." She winked. "What do you reckon, June, fancy a brownie challenge?"

"I'll tell you where you can shove your brownie challenge."

The three of them walked out giggling, and Lewis slipped his hand into Effie's. Like it belonged there. Like he'd been holding her hand every day for twenty years. Then he kissed the side of her face.

"How's she doing?" he asked, nodding in Anya's direction.

"Today's a good day," said Effie with a small smile.

Anya was healing—processing and trusting—but they weren't all good days. There was still a darkness there, still days when she barely spoke. And perhaps there always would be.

"One day at a time, right?" she said.

Lewis squeezed Effie's hand, then took a seat at the small kitchen table. "I spoke with Detective Morrow again this morning." He sipped his coffee. "She doubts that Daniel will ever see the light of day."

"The Crown wants consecutive life sentences?"

"I believe so."

"And Adam?"

Lewis shook his head. "Still nothing," he said. "There was a possible sighting from hunters out near Mataketake Hut, but nothing came of it. Given the landscape, the vastness of it, I'm afraid the police aren't hopeful."

Effie picked up her coffee and held it between her hands. Adam was long gone, she was sure of it.

Lewis slipped a hand into his pocket and pulled out an envelope, placing it on the table.

"This was in the postbox," he said. "It's for you."

Effie frowned and sat down next to him. "Me?"

She turned it over in her hands before opening it. A letter fell out along with an old almost-familiar photograph. For the next five minutes, she didn't speak.

Effie,

I don't really know how to write this.

I guess I should just start with the important stuff.

Firstly, I'm sorry I was gone for so long. Too long. But I thought that's what your sister wanted. Adam told me Tia hated me, and that she didn't want anything to do with me. So I left.

I didn't know about Tia's child—about my granddaughter—not until I saw her on the news. She's beautiful. She looks just like you, Effie.

Adam lied to me all of those years ago. He lied about so many things. I know that now. Too late. And I'll never forgive myself. I'm not asking for your sympathy. I will never ask that of you. I just want you to know that I thought I was doing right by Tia.

But I've done wrong too. I've kept things from you.

There's something you need to know. Something that we'd always planned to tell you, when you were older, but then your mum died bringing Four into the world and I could never find the words.

I loved your mum, Effie, very much, you must know that. She saved me—us—at a time when I thought everything was lost. But the truth is, I didn't meet your mum until you were seven months old. She was still your mum, and always will be. She loved you more than anything, Effie. But she didn't give birth to you.

Your birth mum's name is Dinah.

Effie closed her eyes, the paper shaking in her hand as her dad's voice pressed upon her, the weight of his words making it hard to breathe.

Exhaling, she continued.

I—we—lost Dinah on the day you were born. Not dead lost, just separated. Dinah and I were separated against our will because of her father's beliefs, and it nearly broke me. But you kept me going. You and your mum. Then, of course, your siblings came along.

But there was always a part of me that couldn't let Dinah go. And because of that, I spent the rest of my life looking for her. I know it was wrong of me to leave you kids alone for days in the bush, but I couldn't stop looking. I couldn't stop searching for her.

I got close a couple of times. I found one house just days after the family had moved on. And I got into fights with people who knew things but wouldn't talk. The guy from the park, the one who broke Lewis's ribs, had been one of your grandfather's early followers. I recognized him from Hokitika. But by then, the family was long gone, and the guy knew nothing.

Once, Dinah managed to get a note to me. Just seven words: "He has me shut up. Help me." It tore me apart. Then for years I thought she was dead. When Adam (Asher then) turned up at the hut, I didn't recognize him. His eyes, they weren't like that when he was younger. It wasn't until he'd left us that I worked it out. Then, when he came back, something in me snapped. I thought Dinah was dead because of him. I thought I'd lost her. But it was you who found her in the end, Effie. It was you who brought her back to me.

Dinah is here with me now. She's watching me from a chair by the window. The day the police released her name, and your sister's, I got on a bus, and I don't think I fully breathed again until Dinah took my hand.

She's been through a lot, as you know, and her mind and body are tired. But she's here, alive, with me. And one day, if or when you're ready, we would like to tell you our full story. Your story.

Over the years, I've imagined a thousand lives for you. All of them happy. I needed that. I needed you to be happy.

I'm sorry I wasn't a better dad. I've got more sorries in me than I can count, Effie. But I want to try. I want to try and do better. To deserve you.

Love, Dad

P.S. There's one other person who can give you answers—if you want them. Ask June about Lily.

When Effie lowered the letter, there was no air left in her.

She lifted the photograph—a boy laughing as a girl kissed his cheek—and turned it over. *To the boy who tried to save my life.* Under the faded sentence, her dad had scribbled a short note.

Dinah found this at the hut. Us as kids. She wanted you to have it.

"What is it?" asked Lewis.

Effie stared at her dad's words, the photo shaking in her fingers, unable to look away.

"Effie?" Lewis placed his hand on hers.

She wiped her face. She didn't know when she had started crying. *Oh, Dad.* Then she looked at Lewis. "My dad . . . he . . ."

But she wasn't ready. It was too big.

Lewis frowned. "Are you okay?"

Dinah. Peter. Adam.

She was related to all of them.

"I think I need a minute with her," said Effie.

Lewis released her hand and smiled. "She's on the deck."

Then Effie got up from the table, clutching her dad's words to her chest, not quite ready to share him with Lewis. There was someone else who needed Dad first.

NEW ZEALAND

EFFIE PUSHED THE front door open and stepped out onto the deck. There wasn't a cloud in the sky. It was just a blanket of endless space, so blue it almost looked purple. Tears misted her eyes, but she walked toward the swinging porch chair with a smile on her face.

She was sitting in the shade with her back to Effie, her eyes locked on the horizon.

"It's beautiful, isn't it?" said Tia. "This country of ours."

She turned, her movements still slow, still painful, but every time Effie looked into her sister's eyes, she saw the flicker of light. Of life. Every day, a little bit of her came back.

"Come." Tia patted the spot next to her. "Sit. It was too noisy in there for me."

The bullet from Daniel's gun had ripped through Tia's stomach, diaphragm, and left lung, and she'd spent two weeks in hospital. But it was the beating—the force of Daniel's fists and feet—that had caused her to lose consciousness that night. After two follow-ups, she'd finally been discharged; the appointments with the therapist, however, were ongoing.

"It's easier to breathe out here," said Tia.

Her sister's brain would need a lot longer than two weeks to heal. The doctors said to take it slow, one day at a time. Tia was no longer living in survival mode, but as Blair explained, the shift from the survival part of her brain to the processing part of her brain was not a quick or easy one.

Effie sat next to her sister, taking her hand, and for a while they sat in comfortable silence.

"I've been reading *Harry Potter* with Anya," Tia said eventually. "The boy with white-blond hair . . ."

"Malfoy?"

"Yes." Tia gave a half smile. "He reminds me of Adam."

"Oh god, I didn't even . . ." Effie squeezed Tia's fingers. "I can get her another book. Something that—"

"No, no." Tia patted Effie's hand. "It's nice. I enjoy reading it with her. I can feel her warming to me again."

"Anya loves you, Tia."

"I know she does, deep down." Tia smiled softly. "But she's still clouded by what Adam taught her."

Effie looked at the pain and fear visible on her sister's face. The trauma was etched into her skin, no matter how often she smiled.

"Sometimes," said Tia, "I think that maybe I deserve it. That I should have done more for her. That there was—"

"Stop, Tia. Stop."

She smiled again and leaned into Effie. And for a moment, they stayed like that. Two children who'd run together through the trees and washed their hair in the river. Who'd lost each other for so long.

"So," Tia said, "are you going to tell me what that poor piece of paper ever did to you?"

Effie glanced down at the letter crumpled in her hand. She turned to Tia as the tears fell. "It's Dad. He—"

"Dad?" Tia frowned.

"He's alive, Tia. Dad's alive."

Tia's body stilled—as if she'd stopped breathing. When she finally spoke, her voice was barely a whisper.

"Dad's not dead?"

"No." Effie dabbed at her eyes. "Dad's not dead."

Tia pressed a hand to her chest, her words spoken between shallow breaths. "He can meet his granddaughter. Dad can meet Anya."

"Yes." Effie couldn't keep her eyes dry. "When you're ready, he can meet his granddaughter."

"Effie . . ." Tears stole her sister's words.

"I know." Effie pulled her into a hug. "I know."

NEW ZEALAND

LEWIS MOVED CLOSER on the sofa, his fingers lifting her top, then he touched her face. Effie leaned into him, her eyes and heart open, and brushed her lips against his. The kiss spread through her body, and she shivered.

"You okay?" Lewis pulled back, their eyes locked.

"Yes."

He held her there, their bodies breathing in time, as June walked through the living room door.

"Right, you two lovebirds"—she waved her arms—"enough of that."

Lewis smiled as he pulled away. "Sorry." Then he kissed Effie on the head. "I was actually just heading out. Couple of things to sort at home."

As he stepped from the room, June turned to leave, but Effie stood and took her hand, squeezing it.

"Effie?" June frowned. "Is everything all right?"

Without answering, Effie pulled her into a hug, sinking her face into June's hair, and they stayed like that. Still and quiet. Until June stroked Effie's cheek.

"What's wrong?"

Effie shook her head. "It's Dad," she said eventually, the words harder than she expected. "In his letter, he mentioned someone called Lily."

June stepped back but kept hold of Effie's hand.

"I think we should sit."

Effie nodded and moved them to the sofa, June holding her gaze. "You're sure?"

"Yes," said Effie. "I'm sure."

June smiled softly as she sat down. "Lily was my best friend, and she was also your grandmother. Lily was Dinah's mum."

Effie inhaled, the words punching her, but she stayed quiet.

"When Lily died, your grandfather, Peter, refused to let me anywhere near the house." June's grip tightened. "I tried, at the funeral, to talk to him, to offer help, but Peter's mind was already gone. He hid them away, Dinah and her brothers, and I . . . I didn't do enough. I failed Lily. I failed her children." June's voice trembled. "I failed Dinah."

"June—"

She shook her head. "Years later, when Cameron appeared on my doorstep with you in his arms, only two days old, I knew I would do anything to protect you."

Effie opened her mouth, a whirl of questions hanging in the vacant space, but nothing came out.

"From that first moment, I loved you," said June. "And on the days that your dad was too broken, I held you and bathed you and sang you to sleep." She smiled then. "Your mum was in my step class in the village, and gosh, did she adore you. It was your mum who eventually asked your dad out." June paused, and the warmth drained from her face. "But when you were just one, we discovered that your grandfather was looking for you. That's when your parents decided to leave for the bush.

"We all agreed to keep the truth of your birth a secret," June continued, "until your dad found Dinah. We didn't want to say anything to confuse or hurt you." Tears formed in her eyes. "I'm sorry if that was the wrong thing."

Effie squeezed June's hand.

"Your mum loved you like her own. Because you were hers, in every way that mattered," said June. "But Lily and Dinah are also a part of you. The pounamu necklaces . . ."

Effie touched a hand to the stone at her chest.

"One was Lily's, and the other was meant for Dinah on her eighteenth birthday. Lily gave them to me before she died."

"But why . . ." Effie said eventually, looking at June. "Why did Dad stop bringing us to Koraha?"

June let out a long breath. "He couldn't risk it."

"Risk what? I don't understand."

June shook her head.

"Please, just tell me."

June touched a hand to Effie's leg. "The last time you came to town, Peter was here. He'd found you." Her face hardened. "Your grandfather marched onto my land, threatening to take you away and to have your dad locked up. Cameron begged Peter to tell him where Dinah was, but Peter just laughed, and something in your dad snapped." June paused. "Your dad nearly killed Peter that day; he just about beat him to death with a crowbar."

Effie flinched.

"It was one of your dad's biggest regrets," said June, "that he didn't kill him. Rather than leaving Peter there, barely alive, Cameron phoned the police. And that call saved Peter's life. I don't think your dad ever forgave himself for that, for saving the man who abused his family." June touched Effie's cheek. "Cameron hated it, that he had to hide you away in the bush. He said he would be robbing you of your life, and it ate him up."

Effie let the tears fall, and a quiet settled between them. Eventually, June stood up.

"I think we need a strong drink," she said. "Go check on our girl. Then I'll answer your questions."

Effie took a breath. Then she walked through to Anya's room to kiss her good night.

"You're still awake?" said Effie as she inched the door open.

Anya peered over the top of her duvet. "I was reading."

She grinned, sheepish, and pulled *Harry Potter* out from under the covers.

"Come on." Effie reached for the book. "You need to get some sleep. Blair and Ewan have all sorts of fun things planned for tomorrow."

Anya stiffened slightly, and Effie patted her arm.

"It's all right," she said. "We don't have to go if you don't want to. We'll just do what you feel comfortable with, okay?"

Anya nodded. "Will there be ice cream?"

"I've definitely heard rumors about ice cream."

"Blair lets me have two scoops."

"Oh, does she now?"

Anya giggled, then snuggled in. She rested her head on Effie's leg, her arm clutched around a worn teddy. Effie set the book on the bedside table, misjudging the edge, and the book fell to the floor. A slip of paper escaped from the pages and fluttered to the carpet.

"Oh, sorry." Effie grabbed for it. "Was that your marker?"

"Yeah," Anya murmured. "But it's okay. I know where I am."

Effie picked up the paper—a child's drawing of a hut in the trees—then slipped it back into the book.

"Anya, I'm so happy you're here."

"Me too." Anya rubbed at her face. "Are you going to stay?"

Effie stroked the girl's forehead. "For as long as you and Tia need me."

Anya yawned and stretched out.

"Although I might take Lewis on a holiday to Scotland, if that's okay?"

"To see Rimu?"

"Yes." Effie smiled. "To see Rimu."

Anya yawned again, then her eyes closed, her head growing heavy on Effie's lap. After a few minutes, Effie slipped out from under her, adjusted her pillow and stood up.

The bedroom curtains moved with the cool breeze. It was going to be a cold cloudless night. Effie stepped across the room and pulled back the curtain. The handle catch had been released, and the old single-pane window swung out like an arm into the black night. Effie shivered and reached out to close it, the room probably filled with bugs now. But as she pulled the window inward, a different sort of cold seized her body. There, jammed in the hinges, was a folded piece of paper.

Effie glanced back at Anya, who was fast asleep, then tugged the paper from the window. As she unfolded it, her heart pounded against her ribs.

"Oh god."

She leaned out the window, her pulse racing, and looked out at the trees.

Nothing. Just blackness.

She yanked her head back in and slammed the window shut. Then she locked the handle in place.

She gripped the paper, keeping her eyes fixed on the sleeping child, and the scribbled words carved through her.

Anya, I have to leave now, baby girl, to go far away from here. I'm sorry I failed you. I won't fail the next one.

Effie touched the final two words with her fingertips, then whispered them out loud.

"Love, Dad."

ACKNOWLEDGMENTS

Without Kate Stephenson, this book would not exist. I'm so grateful to Kate for believing in me and for taking a chance on a few thousand words and a lost bush girl.

I would like to thank my agent, Stephanie Glencross, and the team at David Higham Associates. Stephanie has been on this journey with me since long before I started this book. She has guided me through the highs and lows of writing with such genuine kindness and consideration.

When I signed with Moa Press, and then Berkley and Viper, something magical happened. Suddenly, rather than being alone with my thoughts, I had a whole team of incredible people behind me, working tirelessly to strengthen my novel.

A huge thank-you to my editors and proofreaders, Kate Stephenson, Dianne Blacklock, and Theresa Crewdson, whose insights and guidance improved my story immeasurably. Also, to Lee Moir for her enthusiasm, warmth, and dedication.

Likewise, the whole team at Moa Press and Hachette have been so welcoming and brilliant. Thank you to Melanee Winder, Dom Visini, Tania Mackenzie-Cooke, Sacha Beguely, Katrina Duncan, and Emma Dorph.